# The American Note-books

# The American Note-books

by

Nathaniel Hawthorne

CAMBRIDGE
SCHOLARS
PUBLISHING
classic texts

The American Note-books, by Nathaniel Hawthorne

This book in its current typographical format first published 2008 by

Cambridge Scholars Publishing

12 Back Chapman Street, Newcastle upon Tyne, NE6 2XX, UK

British Library Cataloguing in Publication Data
A catalogue record for this book is available from the British Library



ISBN (10): 1-4438-0323-5, ISBN (13): 978-1-4438-0323-6

# CONTENTS

# PASSAGES FROM HAWTHORNE'S AMERICAN NOTE-BOOKS

Salem, June 15, 1835.—A walk down to the Juniper. The shore of the coves strewn with bunches of sea-weed, driven in by recent winds. Eel-grass, rolled and bundled up, and entangled with it,—large marine vegetables, of an olive-color, with round, slender, snake-like stalks, four or five feet long, and nearly two feet broad: these are the herbage of the deep sea. Shoals of fishes, at a little distance from the shore, discernible by their fins out of water. Among the heaps of sea-weed there were sometimes small pieces of painted wood, bark, and other driftage. On the shore, with pebbles of granite, there were round or oval pieces of brick, which the waves had rolled about till they resembled a natural mineral. Huge stones tossed about, in every variety of confusion, some shagged all over with sea-weed, others only partly covered, others bare. The old ten-gun battery, at the outer angle of the Juniper, very verdant, and besprinkled with white-weed, clover, and buttercups. The juniper-trees are very aged and decayed and moss-grown. The grass about the hospital is rank, being trodden, probably, by nobody but myself. There is a representation of a vessel under sail, cut with a penknife, on the corner of the house.

Returning by the almshouse, I stopped a good while to look at the pigs,—a great herd,—who seemed to be just finishing their suppers. They certainly are types of unmitigated sensuality,—some standing in the trough, in the midst of their own and others' victuals,—some thrusting their noses deep into the food,—some rubbing their backs against a post,—some huddled together between sleeping and waking, breathing hard,—all wallowing about; a great boar swaggering round, and a big sow waddling along with her huge paunch. Notwithstanding the unspeakable defilement with which these strange sensualists spice all their food, they seem to have a quick and delicate sense of smell. What ridiculous-looking animals! Swift himself could not have imagined anything nastier than what they practise by the mere impulse of natural genius. Yet the Shakers keep their pigs very clean, and with great advantage. The legion of devils in the herd of swine,—what a scene it must have been!

Sunday evening, going by the jail, the setting sun kindled up the windows most cheerfully; as if there were a bright, comfortable light within its darksome stone wall.

June 18th.—A walk in North Salem in the decline of yesterday afternoon,—beautiful weather, bright, sunny, with a western or northwestern wind just cool enough, and a slight superfluity of heat. The verdure, both of trees and grass, is now in its prime, the leaves elastic, all life. The grass-fields are plenteously bestrewn with white-weed, large spaces looking as white as a sheet of snow, at a distance, yet with an indescribably warmer tinge than snow,—living white, intermixed with living green. The hills and hollows beyond the Cold Spring copiously shaded, principally with oaks of good growth, and some walnut-trees, with the rich sun brightening in. the midst of the open spaces, and mellowing and fading into the shade,—and single trees, with their cool spot of shade, in the waste of sun: quite a picture of beauty, gently picturesque. The surface of the land is so varied, with woodland mingled, that the eye cannot reach far away, except now and then in vistas perhaps across the river, showing houses, or a church and surrounding village, in Upper Beverly. In one of the sunny bits of pasture, walled irregularly in with oak-shade, I saw a gray mare feeding, and, as I drew near, a colt sprang up from amid the grass,—a very small colt. He looked me in the face, and I tried to startle him, so as to make him gallop; but he stretched his long legs, one after another, walked quietly to his mother, and began to suck,—just wetting his lips, not being very hungry. Then he rubbed his head, alternately, with each hind leg. He was a graceful little beast.

I bathed in the cove, overhung with maples and walnuts, the water cool and thrilling. At a distance it sparkled bright and blue in the breeze and sun. There were jelly-fish swimming about, and several left to melt away on the shore. On the shore, sprouting amongst the sand and gravel, I found samphire, growing somewhat like asparagus. It is an excellent salad at this season, salt, yet with an herb-like vivacity, and very tender. I strolled slowly through the pastures, watching my long shadow making grave, fantastic gestures in the sun. It is a pretty sight to see the sunshine brightening the entrance of a road which shortly becomes deeply overshadowed by trees on both sides.

At the Cold Spring, three little girls, from six to nine, were seated on the stones in which the fountain is set, and paddling in the water. It was a pretty picture, and would have been prettier, if they had shown bare little legs, instead of pantalets. Very large trees overhung them, and the sun was so nearly gone down that a pleasant gloom made the spot sombre, in contrast with these light and laughing little figures. On perceiving me, they rose up, tittering among themselves. It seemed that there was a sort of playful malice in those who first saw me; for they allowed the other to keep on paddling, without warning her of my approach. I passed along, and heard them come chattering behind.

June 22d.—I rode to Boston in the afternoon with Mr. Proctor. It was a coolish day, with clouds and intermitting sunshine, and a pretty fresh breeze. We stopped about an hour at the Maverick House, in the sprouting branch of the city, at East Boston,—a stylish house, with doors painted in imitation of oak; a large bar; bells ringing; the bar-keeper calls out, when a bell rings, "Number —"; then a waiter replies, "Number — answered"; and scampers up stairs. A ticket is given by the hostler, on taking the horse and chaise, which is returned to the bar-keeper when the chaise is wanted. The landlord was fashionably dressed, with the whitest of linen, neatly plaited, and as courteous as a Lord Chamberlain. Visitors from Boston thronging the house,—some standing at the bar, watching the process of preparing tumblers of punch,—others sitting at the windows of different parlors,—some with faces .flushed, putting cigars. The bill of fare for the day was stuck tip beside the bar. Opposite this principal hotel there was another, called "The Mechanics," which seemed to be equally thronged. I suspect that the company were about on a par in each; for at the Maverick House, though well dressed, they seemed to be merely Sunday gentlemen,—mostly young fellows,—clerks in dry-goods stores being the aristocracy of them. One, very fashionable in appearance, with a handsome cane, happened to stop by me and lift up his foot, and I noticed that the sole of his boot (which was exquisitely polished) was all worn out. I apprehend that some such minor deficiencies might have been detected in the general showiness of most of them. There were girls, too, but not pretty ones, nor, on the whole, such good imitations of gentility as the young men. There were as many people as are usually collected at a muster, or on similar occasions, lounging about, without any apparent enjoyment; but the observation of this may serve me to make a sketch of the mode of spending the Sabbath by the majority of unmarried, young, middling-class people, near a great town. Most of the people had smart canes and bosom-pins.

Crossing the ferry into Boston, we went to the City Tavern, where the bar-room presented a Sabbath scene of repose,—stage-folk lounging in chairs half asleep, smoking cigars, generally with clean linen and other niceties of apparel, to mark the day. The doors and blinds of an oyster and refreshme.nt shop across the street were closed, but I saw people enter it. There were two owls in a back court, visible through a window of the bar-room,—speckled gray, with dark-blue eyes,—the queerest-looking birds that exist,—so solemn and wise,—dozing away the day, much like the rest of the people, only that they looked wiser than any others. Their hooked beaks looked like hooked noses. A dull scene this. A stranger, here and there, poring over a newspaper. Many of the stage-folk sitting in chairs on the pavement, in front of the door.

We went to the top of the hill which formed part of Gardiner Greene's estate, and which is now in the process of levelling, and pretty much taken away, except the highest point, and a narrow path to ascend to it. It gives an admirable view of the city, being almost as high as the steeples and the dome of the State House, and overlooking the whole mass of brick buildings and slated roofs, with glimpses of streets far below. It was really a pity to take it down. I noticed the stump of a very large elm, recently felled. No house in the city could have reared its roof so high as the roots of that tree, if indeed the church-spires did so.

On our drive home we passed through Charlestown. Stages in abundance were passing the road, burdened with passengers inside and out; also chaises and barouches, horsemen and footmen. We are a community of Sabbath-breakers!

August 31st.—A drive to Nahant yesterday afternoon. Stopped at Rice's, and afterwards walked down to the steamboat wharf to see the passengers land. It is strange how few good faces there are in the world, comparatively to the ugly ones. Scarcely a single comely one in all this collection. Then to the hotel. Barouches at the doors, and gentlemen and ladies going to drive, and gentlemen smoking round the piazza. The bar-keeper had one of Benton's mint-drops for a bosom-brooch! It made a very handsome one. I crossed the beach for home about sunset. The tide was so far down as just to give me a passage on the hard sand, between the sea and the loose gravel. The sea was calm and smooth, with only the surf-waves whitening along the beach. Several ladies and gentlemen on horseback were cantering and galloping before and behind me.

A hint of a story,—some incident which should bring on a general war; and the chief actor in the incident to have something corresponding to the mischief he had caused.

September 7th.—A drive to Ipswich with B—. At the tavern was an old, fat, country major, and another old fellow, laughing and playing off jokes on each other,—one tying a ribbon upon the other's hat. One had been a trumpeter to the major's troop. Walking about town, we knocked, for a whim, at the door of a dark old house, and inquired if Miss Hannah Lord lived there. A woman of about thirty came to the door, with rather a confused smile, and a disorder about the bosom of her dress, as if she had been disturbed while nursing her child. She answered us with great kindness.

Entering the burial-ground, where some masons were building a tomb, we found a good many old monuments, and several covered with slabs of red freestone or slate, and with arms sculptured on the slab, or an inlaid circle of slate. On one slate gravestone, of the Rev. Nathl. Rogers, there was a portrait of that worthy, about a third of the size of life, carved in relief, with his cloak, band, and wig, in excellent preservation, all the buttons of his waistcoat being cut with great minuteness,—the minister's nose being on a level with his cheeks. It was an upright gravestone. Returning home, I held a colloquy with a young girl about the right road. She had come out to feed a pig, and was a little suspicious that we were making fun of her, yet answered us with a shy laugh and good-nature,—the pig all the time squealing for his dinner.

Displayed along the walls, and suspended from the pillars of the original King's Chapel, were coats of arms of the king, the successive governors, and other distinguished men. In the pulpit there was an hourglass on a large and elaborate brass stand. The organ was surmounted by a gilt crown in the centre, supported by a gilt mitre on each side. The governor's pew had Corinthian pillars, and crimson damask tapestry. In 1727 it was lined with china, probably tiles.

Saint Augustin, at mass, charged all that were accursed to go out of the church. "Then a dead body arose, and went out of the church into the churchyard, with a white cloth on its head, and stood there till mass was over. It was a former lord of the manor, whom a curate had cursed because he refused to pay his tithes. A justice also commanded the dead curate to arise, and gave him a rod; and the dead lord, kneeling, received penance thereby." He then ordered the lord to go again to his grave, which he did, and fell immediately to ashes. Saint Augustin offered to pray for the curate, that he might remain on earth to confirm men in their belief; but the curate refused, because he was in the place of rest.

A sketch to be given of a modern reformer,—a type of the extreme doctrines on the subject of slaves, cold water, and other such topics. He goes about the streets haranguing most eloquently, and is on the point of making many converts, when his labors are suddenly interrupted by the appearance of the keeper of a mad-house, whence he has escaped- Much may be made of this idea.

A change from a gay young girl to an old woman; the melancholy events, the effects of which have clustered around her character, and gradually imbued it with their influence, till she becomes a lover of sick-chambers, taking pleasure in receiving dying breaths and in laying out the dead; also having her mind full of funeral reminiscences, and possessing more acquaintances beneath the burial turf than above it.

A well-concerted train of events to be thrown into confusion by some misplaced circumstance, unsuspected till the catastrophe, yet exerting its influence from beginning to end.

On the common, at dusk, after a salute from two field-pieces, the smoke lay long and heavily on the ground, without much spreading beyond the original space over which it had gushed from the guns. It was about the height of a man. The evening clear, but with an autumnal chill.

The world is so sad and solemn, that things meant in jest are liable, by an overpowering influence, to become dreadful earnest,—gayly dressed fantasies turning to ghostly and black-clad images of themselves.

A story, the hero of which is to be represented as naturally capable of deep and strong passion, and looking forward to the time when he shall feel passionate love, which is to be the great event of his existence. But it so chances that he never falls in love, and although he gives up the expectation of so doing, and marries calmly, yet it is somewhat sadly, with sentiments merely of esteem for his bride. The lady might be one who had loved him early in life, but whom then, in his expectation of passionate love, he had scorned.

The scene of a story or sketch to be laid within the light of a street-lantern; the time, when the lamp is near going out; and the catastrophe to be simultaneous with the last flickering gleam.

The peculiar weariness and depression of spirits which is felt after a day wasted in turning over a magazine or other light miscellany, different from the state of the mind after severe study; because there has been no excitement, no difficulties to be overcome, but the spirits have evaporated insensibly.

To represent the process by which sober truth gradually strips off all the beautiful draperies with which imagination has enveloped a beloved object, till from an angel she turns out to be a merely ordinary woman. This to be done without caricature, perhaps with a quiet humor interfused, but the prevailing impression to be a sad one. The story might consist of the various alterations in the feelings of the absent lover, caused by successive events that display the true character of his mistress; and the catastrophe should take place at their meeting, when he finds himself equally disappointed in her person; or the whole spirit of the thing may here be reproduced.

Last evening, from the opposite shore of the North River, a view of the town mirrored in the water, which was as smooth as glass, with no perceptible tide or agitation, except a trifling swell and reflux on the sand, although the shadow of the moon danced in it. The picture of the town perfect in the water,—towers of churches, houses, with here and there a light gleaming near the shore above, and more faintly glimmering under water,—all perfect, but somewhat more hazy and indistinct than the reality. There were many clouds flitting about the sky; and the picture of each could be traced in the water,—the ghost of what was itself unsubstantial. The rattling of wheels heard long and far through the town. Voices of people talking on the other side of the river, the tones being so distinguishable in all their variations that it seemed as if what was there said might be understood; but it was not so.

Two persons might be bitter enemies through life, and mutually cause the ruin of one another, and of all that were dear to them. Finally, meeting at the funeral of a grandchild, the offspring of a son and daughter married without their consent,—and who, as well as the child, had been the victims of their hatred,—they might discover that the supposed ground of the quarrel was altogether a mistake, and then be wofully reconciled.

Two persons, by mutual agreement, to make their wills in each other's favor, then to wait impatiently for one another's death, and both to be informed of the desired event at the same time. Both, in most joyous sorrow, hasten to be present at the funeral, meet, and find themselves both hoaxed.

The story of a man, cold and hard-hearted, and acknowledging no brotherhood with mankind. At his death they might try to dig him a grave, but, at a little space beneath the ground, strike upon a rock, as if the earth refused to receive the unnatural son into her bosom. Then they would put him into an old sepulchre, where the coffins and corpses were all turned to dust, and so he would be alone. Then the body would petrify; and he having died in some characteristic act and expression, he would seem, through endless ages of death, to repel society as in life, and no one would be buried in that tomb forever.

Cannon transformed to church-bells.

A person, even before middle age, may become musty and faded among the people with whom he has grown up from childhood; but, by migrating to a new place, he appears fresh with the effect of youth, which may be communicated from the impressions of others to his own feelings.

In an old house, a mysterious knocking might be heard on the wall, where had formerly been a doorway, now bricked up.

It might be stated, as the closing circumstance of a tale, that the body of one of the characters had been petrified, and still existed in that state.

A young man to win the love of a girl, without any serious intentions, and to find that in that love, which might have been the greatest blessing of his life, he had conjured up a spirit of mischief which pursued him throughout his whole career,—and this without any revengeful purposes on the part of the deserted girl. Two lovers, or other persons, on the most private business, to appoint a meeting in what they supposed to be a place of the utmost solitude, and to find it thronged with people.

October 17th.—Some of the oaks are now a deep brown red; others are changed to a light green, which, at a little distance, especially in the sunshine, looks like the green of early spring. In some trees, different masses of the foliage show each of these hues. Some of the walnut-trees have a yet more delicate green- Others are of a bright sunny yellow.

Mr. — was married to Miss — last Wednesday. Yesterday Mr. Brazer, preaching on the comet, observed that not one, probably, of all who heard him, would witness its reappearance. Mrs. — shed tears. Poor soul! she would be contented to dwell in earthly love to all eternity!

Some treasure or other thing to be buried, and a tree planted directly over the spot, so as to embrace it with its roots. '

A tree, tall and venerable, to be said by tradition to have been the staff of some famous man, who happened to thrust it into the ground, where it took root.

A fellow without money, having a hundred and seventy miles to go, fastened a chain and padlock to his legs, and lay down to sleep in a field. He was apprehended, and carried gratis to a jail in the town whither he desired to go.

An old volume in a large library,—every one to be afraid to unclasp and open it, because it was said to be a book of magic.

A ghost seen by moonlight; when the moon was out, it would shine and melt through the airy substance of the ghost, as through a cloud.

Prideaux, Bishop of Worcester, during the. sway of the Parliament, was forced to support himself and his family by selling his household goods. A friend asked him, "How doth your lordship?" "Never better in my life," said the Bishop, "only I have too great a stomach; for I have eaten that little plate which the sequestrators left me. I have eaten a great library of excellent books. I have eaten a great deal of linen, much of my brass, some of my pewter, and now I am come to eat iron; and what will come next I know not."

A scold and a blockhead,—brimstone and wood,— a good match.

To make one's own reflection in a mirror the subject of a story.

In a dream to wander to some place where may be heard the complaints of all the miserable on earth.

Some common quality or circumstance that should bring together people the most unlike in all other respects, and make a brotherhood and sisterhood of them,—the rich and the proud finding themselves in the same category with the mean and the despised.

A person to consider himself as the prime mover of certain remarkable events, but to discover that his actions have not contributed in the least thereto. Another person to be the cause, without suspecting it.

October 25th.—A person or family long desires some particular good. At last it comes in such profusion as to be the great pest of their lives.

A man, perhaps with a persuasion that he shall make his fortune by some singular means, and with an eager longing so to do, while digging or boring for water, to strike upon a salt-spring.

To have one event operate in several places,—as, for example, if a man's head were to be cut off in one town, men's heads to drop off in several towns.

Follow out the fantasy of a man taking his life by instalments, instead of at one payment,—say ten years of life alternately with ten years of suspended animation.

Sentiments in a foreign language, which merely convey the sentiment without retaining to the reader any graces of style or harmony of sound, have somewhat of the charm of thoughts in one's own mind that have not yet been put into words. No possible words that we might adapt to them could realize the unshaped beauty that they appear to possess. This is the reason that translations are never satisfactory,—and less so, I should think, to one who cannot than to one who can pronounce the language.

A person to be writing a tale, and to find that it shapes itself against his intentions; that the characters act otherwise than he thought; that unforeseen events occur; and a catastrophe comes which he strives in vain to avert; It might shadow forth his own fate,—he having made himself one of the personages.

It is a singular thing, that, at the distance, say, of five feet, the work of the greatest dunce looks just as well as that of the greatest genius,—that little space being all the distance between genius and stupidity.

Mrs. Sigourney says, after Coleridge, that "poetry has been its own exceeding great reward." For the writing, perhaps; but would it be so for the reading?

Four precepts: To break off customs; to shake off spirits ill-disposed; to meditate on youth; to do nothing against one's genius.

Salem, August 31, 1836.—A walk, yesterday, down to the shore, near the hospital. Standing on the old grassy battery, that forms a semicircle, and looking seaward. The sun not a great way above the horizon, yet so far as to give a very golden brightness, when it shone out. Clouds in the vicinity of the sun, and nearly all the rest of the sky covered with clouds in masses, not a gray uniformity of cloud. A fresh breeze blowing from land seaward. If it had been blowing from the sea, it would have raised it in heavy billows, and caused it to dash high against the rocks. But; now its surface was not all commoved with billows; there was only roughness enough to take off the gleam, and give it the aspect of iron after cooling. The clouds above added to the black appearance. A few sea-birds were flitting over the water, only visible at moments, when they turned their white bosoms towards me, —as if they were then first created. The sunshine had a singular effect. The clouds would interpose in such a manner that some objects were shaded from it, while others were strongly illuminated. Some of the islands lay in the shade, dark and gloomy, while others were bright and favored spots. The white light-house was sometimes very cheerfully marked. There was a schooner about a mile from the shore, at anchor, laden apparently with lumber. The sea all about her had the black, iron aspect which I have described; but the vessel herself was alight. Hull, masts, and spars were all gilded, and the rigging was made of golden threads. A small white streak of foam breaking around the bows, which were towards the wind. The shadowiness of the clouds overhead made the effect of the sunlight strange, where it fell.

September.—The elm-trees have golden branches intermingled with their green already, and so they had on the first of the month.

To picture the predicament of worldly people, if admitted to paradise.

As the architecture of a country always follows the earliest structures, American architecture should be a refinement of the log-house. The Egyptian is so of the cavern and mound; the Chinese, of the tent; the Gothic, of overarching trees; the Greek, of a cabin.

"Though we speak nonsense, God will pick out the meaning of it,"—an extempore prayer by a New England divine.

In old times it must have been much less customary than now to drink pure water. Walker emphatically mentions, among the sufferings of a clergyman's wife and family in the Great Rebellion, that they were forced to drink water, with crab-apples stamped in it to relish it.

Mr. Kirby, author of a work on the History, Habits, and Instincts of Animals, questions whether there may not be an abyss of waters within the globe, communicating with the ocean, and whether the huge animals of the Saurian tribe—great reptiles, supposed to be exclusively antediluvian, and now extinct—may not be inhabitants of it. He quotes a passage from Revelation, where the creatures under the earth are spoken of as distinct from those of the sea, and speaks of a Saurian fossil that has been found deep in the subterranean regions. He thinks, or suggests, that these may be the dragons of Scripture.

The elephant is not particularly sagacious in the wild state, but becomes so when tamed. The fox directly the contrary, and likewise the wolf.

A modern Jewish adage,—"Let a man clothe himself beneath his ability, his children according to his ability, and his wife above his ability."

It is said of the eagle, that, in however long a flight, he is never seen to clap his wings to his sides. He seems to govern his movements by the inclination of his wings and tail to the wind, as a ship is propelled by the action of the wind on her sails.

In old country-houses in England, instead of glass for windows, they used wicker, or fine strips of oak disposed checkerwise. Horn was also used. The windows of princes and great noblemen were of crystal; those of Studley Castle, Holinshed says, of beryl. There were seldom chimneys; and they cooked their meats by a fire made against an iron back in the great hall. Houses, often of gentry, were built of a heavy timber frame, filled up with lath and plaster. People slept on rough mats or straw pallets, with a round log for a pillow; seldom better beds than a mattress, with a sack of chaff for a pillow.

October 25th.—A walk yesterday through Dark Lane, and home through the village of Danvers. Landscape now wholly autumnal. Saw an elderly man laden with two dry, yellow, rustling bundles of Indian corn-stalks,—a good personification of Autumn. Another man hoeing up potatoes. Rows of white cabbages lay ripening. Fields of dry Indian corn. The grass has still considerable greenness. Wild rose-bushes devoid of leaves, with their deep, bright red seed-vessels. Meeting-house in Danvers seen at a distance, with the sun shining through the windows of its belfry. Barberry-bushes,—the leaves now of a brown red, still juicy and healthy; very few berries remaining, mostly frost-bitten and wilted. All among the yet green grass, dry stalks of weeds. The down of thistles occasionally seen flying through the sunny air.

In this dismal chamber FAME was won. (Salem, Union Street.)

Those who are very difficult in choosing wives seem as if they would take none of Nature's ready-made works, but want a woman manufactured particularly to their order.

A council of the passengers in a street: called by somebody to decide upon some points important to him.

Every individual has a place to fill in the world, and is important, in some respects, whether he chooses to be so or not.

A Thanksgiving dinner. All the miserable on earth are to be invited,—as the drunkard, the bereaved parent, the ruined merchant, the broken-hearted lover, the poor widow, the old man and woman who have outlived their generation, the disappointed author, the wounded, sick, and broken soldier, the diseased person, the infidel, the man with an evil conscience, little orphan children or children of neglectful parents, shall be admitted to the table, and many others. The giver of the feast goes out to deliver his invitations. Some of the guests he meets in the streets, some he knocks for at the doors of their houses. The description must be rapid. But who must be the giver of the feast, and what his claims to preside? A man who has never found out what he is fit for, who has unsettled aims or objects in life, and whose mind gnaws him, making him the sufferer of many kinds of misery. He should meet some pious, old, sorrowful person, with more outward calamities than any other, and invite him, with a reflection that piety would make all that miserable company truly thankful.

*Merry,* in "merry England," does not mean mirthful; but is corrupted from an old Teutonic word signifying famous or renowned.

In an old London newspaper, 1678, there is an advertisement, among other goods at auction, of a black girl, about fifteen years old, to be sold.

We sometimes congratulate ourselves at the moment of waking from a troubled dream: it may be so the moment after death.

The race of mankind to be swept away, leaving all their cities and works. Then another human pair to be placed in the world, with native intelligence like Adam and Eve, but knowing nothing of their predecessors or of their own nature and destiny. They, perhaps, to be described as working out this knowledge by their sympathy with what they saw, and by their own feelings.

Memorials of the family of Hawthorne in the church of the village of Dundry, Somersetshire, England. The church is ancient and small, and has a prodigiously high tower of more modern date, being erected in the time of Edward IV. It serves as a landmark for an amazing extent of country.

A singular fact, that, when man is a brute, he is the most sensual and loathsome of all brutes.

A snake taken into a man's stomach and nourished there from fifteen years to thirty-five, tormenting him most horribly. A type of envy or some other evil passion.

A sketch illustrating the imperfect compensations which time makes for its devastations on the person,—giving a wreath of laurel while it causes baldness, honors for infirmities, wealth for a broken constitution,—and at last, when a man has everything that seems desirable, death seizes him. To contrast the man who has thus reached the summit of ambition with the ambitious youth.

Walking along the track of the railroad. I observed a place where the workmen had bored a hole through the solid rock, in order to blast it: but, striking a spring of water beneath the rock, it gushed up through the hole. It looked as if the water were contained within the rock.

A Fancy Ball, in which the prominent American writers should appear, dressed in character.

A lament for life's wasted sunshine.

A new classification of society to be instituted. Instead of rich and poor, high and low, they are to be classed,—First, by their sorrows: for instance, whenever there are any, whether in fair mansion or hovel, who are mourning the loss of relations and friends, and who wear black, whether the cloth be coarse or superfine, they are to make one class. Secondly, all who have the same maladies, whether they lie under damask canopies or on straw pallets or in the wards of hospitals, they are to form one class. Thirdly, all who are guilty of the same sins, whether the world knows them or not; whether they languish in prison, looking forward to the gallows, or walk honored among men, they also form a class. Then proceed to generalize and classify the whole world together, as none can claim utter exemption from either sorrow, sin, or disease: and if they could, yet Death, like a great parent, comes and sweeps them all through one darksome portal,—all his children.

Fortune to come like a pedlar with his goods,—as wreaths of laurel, diamonds, crowns: selling them, but asking for them the sacrifice of health, of integrity, perhaps of life in the battle-field, and of the real pleasures of existence. Who would buy, if the price were to be paid down?

The dying exclamation of the Emperor Augustus, "Has it not been well acted?" An essay on the misery of being always under a mask. A veil may be needful, but never a mask. Instances of people who wear masks in all classes of society, and never take them off even in the most familiar moments, though sometimes they may chance to slip aside.

The various guises under which Ruin makes his approaches to his victims: to the merchant, in the guise of a merchant offering speculations; to the young heir, a jolly companion; to the maiden, a sighing, sentimentalist lover.

What were the contents of the burden of Christian in the "Pilgrim's Progress"? He must have been taken for a pedlar travelling with his pack.

To think, as the sun goes down, what events have happened in the course of the day,—events of ordinary occurrence: as, the clocks have struck, the dead have been buried.

Curious to imagine what murmurings and discontent would be excited, if any of the great so-called calamities of human beings were to be abolished,—as, for instance, death.

Trifles to one are matters of life and death to another. As, for instance, a farmer desires a brisk breeze to winnow his grain; and mariners, to blow them out of the reach of pirates.

A recluse, like myself, or a prisoner, to measure time by the progress of sunshine through his chamber.

Would it not be wiser for people to rejoice at all that they now sorrow for, and *vice versa*? To put on bridal garments at funerals, and mourning at weddings? For their friends to condole with them when they attained riches and honor, as only so much care added?

If in a village it were a custom to hang a funeral garland or other token of death on a house where some one had died, and there to let it remain till a death occurred elsewhere, and then to hang that same garland over the other house, it would have, methinks, a strong effect.

No fountain so small but that Heaven may be imaged in its bosom.

Fame! Some very humble persons in a town may be said to possess it,—as, the penny-post, the town-crier, the constable,—and they are known to everybody; while many richer, more intellectual, worthier persons are unknown by the majority of their fellow-citizens. Something analogous in the world at large.

The ideas of people in general are not raised higher than the roofs of the houses. All their interests extend over the earth's surface in a layer of that thickness. The meeting-house steeple reaches out of their sphere.

Nobody will use other people's experience, nor have any of his own till it is too late to use it.

Two lovers to plan the building of a pleasure-house on a certain spot of ground, but various seeming accidents prevent it. Once they find a group of miserable children there; once it is the scene where crime is plotted; at last the dead body of one of the lovers or of a dear friend is found there; and, instead of a pleasure-house, they build a marble tomb. The moral,—that there is no place on earth fit for the site of a pleasure-house, because there is no spot that may not have been saddened by human grief, stained by crime, or hallowed by death. It might be three friends who plan it, instead of two lovers; and the dearest one dies.

Comfort for childless people. A married couple with ten children have been the means of bringing about ten funerals.

A blind man on a dark night carried a torch, in order that people might see him, and not run against him, and direct him how to avoid dangers.

To picture a child's (one of four or five years old) reminiscences at sunset of a long summer's day,—his first awakening, his studies, his sports, his little fits of passion, perhaps a whipping, etc.

The blind man's walk.

To picture a virtuous family, the different members examples of virtuous dispositions in their way; then introduce a vicious person, and trace out the relations that arise between him and them, and the manner in which all are affected.

A man to flatter himself with the idea that he would not be guilty of some certain wickedness,—as, for instance, to yield to the personal temptations of the Devil—yet to find, ultimately, that he was at that very time committing that same wickedness.

What would a man do, if he were compelled to live always in the sultry heat of society, and could never bathe himself in cool solitude?

A girl's lover to be slain and buried in her flower-garden, and the earth levelled over him. That particular spot, which she happens to plant with some peculiar variety of flowers, produces them of admirable splendor, beauty, and perfume; and she delights, with an indescribable impulse, to wear them in her bosom, and scent her chamber with them. Thus the classic fantasy would be realized, of dead people transformed to flowers.

Objects seen by a magic-lantern reversed. A street, or other location, might be presented, where there would be opportunity to bring forward all objects of worldly interest, and thus much pleasant satire might be the result.

The Abyssinians, after dressing their hair, sleep with their heads in a forked stick, in order not to discompose it.

At the battle of Edge HilL October 23, 1642, Captain John Smith, a soldier of note, Captain Lieutenant to Lord James Stuart's horse, with only a groom, attacked a Parliament officer, three cuirassiers, and three arquebusiers, and rescued the royal standard, which they had taken and were guarding. Was this the Virginian Smith?

Stephen Gowans supposed that the bodies of Adam and Eve were clothed in robes of light, which vanished after their sin.

Lord Chancellor Clare, towards the close of his life, went to a village church, where he might not be known, to partake of the Sacrament.

A missionary to the heathen in a great city, to describe his labors in the manner of a foreign mission.

In the tenth century, mechanism of organs so clumsy, that one in Westminster Abbey, with four hundred pipes, required twenty-six bellows and seventy stout men. First organ ever known in Europe received by King Pepin, from the Emperor Constantine, in 757. Water boiling was kept in a reservoir under the- pipes; and, the keys being struck, the valves opened, and steam rushed through with noise. The secret of working them thus is now lost. Then came bellows organs, first used by Louis le Débonnaire.

After the siege of Antwerp, the children played marbles in the streets with grape and cannon shot.

A shell, in falling, buries itself in the earth, and, when it explodes, a large pit is made by the earth being blown about in all directions,—large enough, sometimes, to hold three or four cart-loads of earth. The holes are circular.

A French artillery-man being buried in his military cloak on the ramparts, a shell exploded, and unburied him.

In the Netherlands, to form hedges, young trees are interwoven into a sort of lattice-work; and, in time, they grow together at the point of junction, so that the fence is all of one piece.

To show the effect of gratified revenge. As an instance, merely, suppose a woman sues her lover for breach of promise, and gets the money by instalments, through a long series of years. At last, when the miserable victim were utterly trodden down, the triumpher would have become a very devil of evil passions,—they having overgrown his whole nature; so that a far greater evil would have come upon himself than on his victim.

Anciently, when long-buried bodies were found undecayed in the grave, a species of sanctity was attributed to them.

Some chimneys of ancient halls used to be swept by having a culverin fired up them.

At Leith, in 1711, a glass bottle was blown of the capacity of two English bushels.

The buff and blue of the Union were adopted by .Fox and the Whig party in England. The Prince of Wales wore them.

In 1621, a Mr. Copinger left a certain charity, an almhouse, of which four poor persons were to partake, after the death of his eldest son and his wife. It was a tenement and yard. The parson, headboroughs, and his five other sons were to appoint the persons. At the time specified, however, all but one of his sons were dead; and he was in such poor circumstances that he obtained the benefit of the charity for himself, as one of the four.

A town clerk arranges the publishments that are given in, according to his own judgment.

To make a story from Robert Raikes seeing dirty children at play, in the streets of London, and inquiring of a woman about them. She tells him that on Sundays, when they were not employed, they were a great deal worse, making the streets like hell: playing at church, etc. He was therefore induced to employ women at a shilling to teach them on Sundays, and thus Sunday-schools were established.

To represent the different departments of the United States government by village functionaries. The War Department by watchmen, the law by constables, the merchants by a variety store, etc.

At the accession of Bloody Mary, a man, coming into a house, sounded three times with his mouth, as with a trumpet, and then made proclamation to the family. A bonfire was built, and little children were made to carry wood to it, that they might remember the circumstance in old age. Meat and drink were provided at the bonfires.

To describe a boyish combat with snowballs, and the victorious leader to have a, statue of snow erected to him. A satire on ambition and fame to be made out of this idea. It might be a child's story.

Our body to be possessed by two different spirits; so that half of the visage shall express one mood, and the other half another.

An old English sea-captain desires to have a fast-sailing ship, to keep a good table, and to sail between the tropics without making land.

A rich man left by will his mansion and estate to a poor couple. They remove into it, and find there a darksome servant, whom they are forbidden by will to turn away. He becomes a torment to them; and, in the finale, he turns out to be the former master of the estate.

Two persons to be expecting some occurrence, and watching for the two principal actors in it, and to find that the occurrence is even then passing, and that they themselves are the two actors.

There is evil in every human heart, which may remain latent, perhaps, through the whole of life; but circumstances may rouse it to activity. To imagine such circumstances. A woman, tempted to be false to her husband, apparently through mere whim,—or a young man to feel an instinctive thirst for blood, and to commit murder. This appetite may be traced in the popularity of criminal trials. The appetite might be observed first in a child, and then traced upwards, manifesting itself in crimes suited to every stage of life.

The good deeds in an evil life,—the generous, noble, and excellent actions done by people habitually wicked,—to ask what is to become of them.

A satirical article might be made out of the idea of an imaginary museum, containing such articles as Aaron's rod, the petticoat of General Hawion, the pistol with which Benton shot Jackson,—and then a diorama, consisting of political or other scenes, or done in wax-work. The idea to be wrought out and extended. Perhaps it might be the museum of a deceased old man.

An article might be made respecting various kinds of ruin,—ruin as regards property,—ruin of health,—ruin of habits, as drunkenness and all kinds of debauchery,—ruin of character, while prosperous in other respects,—ruin of the soul. Ruin, perhaps, might be personified as a demon, seizing its victims by various holds.

An article on fire, on smoke. Diseases of the mind and soul,—even more common than bodily diseases.

Tarleton, of the Revolution, is said to have been one of the two handsomest men in Europe,—the Prince of Wales, afterwards George IV., being the other. Some authorities, however, have represented him as ungainly in person and rough in manners. Tarleton was originally bred for the law, but quitted law for the army early in life. He was son to a mayor of Liverpool, born in 1754, of ancient family. He wrote his own memoirs after returning from America. Afterwards in Parliament. Never afterwards distinguished in arms. Created baronet in 1818, and died childless in 1833. Thought he was not sufficiently honored among more modern heroes. Lost part of his right hand in battle of Guilford Court House. A man of pleasure in England.

It would be a good idea for a painter to paint a picture of a great actor, representing him in several different characters of one scene,—Iago and Othello, for instance.

Maine, July 5, 1837.—Here I am, settled since night before last with B—, and living very singularly. He leads a bachelor's life in his paternal mansion, only a small part of which is occupied by a family who serve him. He provides his own breakfast and supper, and occasionally his dinner; though this is oftener, I believe, taken at a hotel, or an eating-house, or with some of his relatives. I am his guest, and my presence makes no alteration in his way of life. Our fare, thus far, has consisted of bread, butter, and cheese, crackers, herrings, boiled eggs, coffee, milk, and claret wine. He has another inmate, in the person of a queer little Frenchman, who has his breakfast, tea, and lodging here, and finds his dinner elsewhere.

Monsieur S— does not appear to be more than twenty-one years old,—a diminutive figure, with eyes askew, and otherwise of an ungainly physiognomy; he is ill-dressed also, in a coarse blue coat, thin cotton pantaloons, and unbrushed boots; altogether with as little of French coxcombry as can well be imagined, though with something of the monkey aspect inseparable from a little Frenchman. He is, nevertheless, an intelligent and well-informed man, apparently of extensive reading in his own language,—a philosopher, B— tells me, and an infidel. His insignificant personal appearance stands in the way of his success, and prevents him from receiving the respect which is really due to his talents and acquirements, wherefore he is bitterly dissatisfied with the country and its in- habitants, and often expresses his feelings to B— (who has gained his confidence to a certain degree) in very strong terms.

Tims here are three characters, each with something out of the common way, living together somewhat like monks. B—, our host, combines more high and admirable qualities, of that sort which make up a gentleman, than any other that I have met with. Polished, yet natural, frank, open, and straightforward, yet with a delicate feeling for the sensitiveness of his companions; of excellent temper and warm heart; well acquainted with the world, with a keen faculty of observation, which he has had many opportunities of exorcising, and never varying from a code of honor and principle which is really nice and rigid in its way. There is a sort of philosophy developing itself in him which will not impossibly cause him to settle down in this or some other equally singular course of life. He seems almost to have made up his mind never to be married, which I wonder at; for he has strong affections, and is fond both of women and children.

The little Frenchman impresses me very strongly, too,—so lonely as he is here, struggling against the world, with bitter feelings in his breast, and yet talking with the vivacity and gayety of his nation; making this his home from darkness to daylight, and enjoying here what little domestic comfort and confidence there is for him; and then going about the live-long day, teaching French to blockheads who sneer at him, and returning at about ten o'clock in the evening (for I was wrong in saying he supped here,—he eats no supper) to his solitary room and bed. Before retiring, he goes to B—'s bedside, and, if he finds him awake, stands talking French, expressing his dislike of the Americans.—"*Je hais, je hais le Yankees!*"—

thus giving vent to the stifled bitterness of the whole day. In the morning I hear him getting up early, at sunrise or before, humming to himself, scuttling about his chamber with his thick boots, and at last taking his departure for a solitary ramble till breakfast. Then he comes in, cheerful and vivacious enough, eats pretty heartily, and is off again, singing French *chansons* as he goes down the gravel-walk. The poor fellow has nobody to sympathize with him but B—, and thus a singular connection is established between two utterly different characters.

Then here is myself, who am likewise a queer character in my way, and have come to spend a week or two with my friend of half a lifetime,—the longest space, probably, that we are ever destined to spend together; for Fate seems preparing changes for both of us. My circumstances, at least, cannot long continue as they are and have been: and B—, too, stands between high prosperity and utter ruin.

I think I should soon become strongly attached to our way of life, so independent and untroubled by the forms and restrictions of society. The house is very pleasantly situated,—half a mile distant from where the town begins to be thickly settled, and on a swell of land, with the road running at a distance of fifty yards, and a grassy tract and a gravel-walk between. Beyond the road rolls the Kennebec, here two or three hundred yards wide. Putting my head out of the window, I can see it flowing steadily along straightway between wooded banks; but arriving nearly opposite the house, there is a large and level sand island in the middle of tint stream; and just below the island the current is further interrupted by the works of the mill-dam, which is perhaps half finished, yet still in so rude a state that it looks as much like the ruins of a dam destroyed by the spring freshets as like the foundations of a dam yet to be. Irishmen and Canadians toil at work on it, and the echoes of their hammering and of the voices come across the river and up to the window. Then there is a sound of the wind among the trees round the house; and, when that is silent, the calm, full, distant voice of the river becomes audible. Looking downward thither, I see the rush of the current, and mark the different eddies, with here and there white specks or streaks of foam; and often a log comes floating on, glistening in the sun, as it rolls over among the eddies, having voyaged, for aught I know, hundreds of miles from the wild upper sources of the river, passing down, down, between lines of forest, and sometimes rough clearing, till here it floats by cultivated banks, and will soon pass by the village. Sometimes a long raft of boards comes along, requiring the nicest skill in navigating it through the narrow passage left by the mill-dam. Chaises and wagons occasionally go over the road, the riders all giving a passing glance at the dam, or perhaps alighting to examine it more fully, and at last departing with ominous shakes of the head as to the result of the enterprise. My position is so far retired from the river and mill-dam, that, though the latter is really rather a scene, yet a sort of quiet seems to be diffused over the whole. Two or three times a day this quiet is broken by the sudden thunder from a quarry, where the workmen are blasting rocks; and a peal of thunder sounds strangely in such a green, sunny, and quiet landscape, with the blue sky brightening the river.

I have not seen much of the people. There have been, however, several incidents which amused me, though scarcely worth telling. A passionate tavern-keeper, quick as a flash of gunpowder, a nervous man, and showing in his demeanor, it seems, a consciousness of his infirmity of temper. I was a witness of a scuffle of his with a drunken guest. The tavern-keeper, after they were separated, raved like a madman, and in a tone of voice having a drolly pathetic or lamentable sound mingled with its rage, as if he were lifting up his voice to weep. Then he jumped into a chaise which was standing by, whipped up the horse, and drove off rapidly, as if to give his fury vent in that way.

On the morning of the Fourth of July, two printer's apprentice-lads, nearly grown, dressed in jackets and very tight pantaloons of check, tight as their skins, so that they looked like harlequins or circus-clowns, yet appeared to think themselves in perfect propriety, with a very calm and quiet assurance of the admiration of the town. A common fellow, a carpenter, who, on the strength of political partisanship, asked B—'s assistance in cutting out great letters from play-bills in order to print "Martin Van Buren Forever" on a flag; but B— refused. B— seems to be considerably of a favorite with the lower orders, especially with the Irishmen and French Canadians,—the latter accosting him in the street, and asking his assistance as an interpreter in making their bargains for work.

I meant to dine at the hotel with B— to-day; but having reutrned t the house, leaving him to do some business in the village, I found myself unwilling to move when the dinner-hour approached, and therefore dined very well on bread, cheese, and eggs. Nothing of much interest takes place. We live very comfortably in our bachelor establishment on a cold shoulder of mutton, with ham and smoked beef and boiled eggs; and as to drinkables, we had both claret and brown sherry on the dinner-table to-day. Last evening we had a long literary and philosophical conversation with Monsieur S—. He is rather remarkably well-informed for a man of his age, and seems to have very just notions on ethics, etc., though damnably perverted as to religion. It is strange to hear philosophy of any sort from such a boyish figure. "We philosophers," he is fond of saying, to distinguish himself and his brethren from the Christians. One of his oddities is, that, while steadfastly maintaining an opinion that he is a very small and slow eater, and that we, in common with other Yankees, eat immensely and fast, he actually eats both faster and longer than we do, and devours, as B— avers, more victuals than both of us together.

Saturday, July 8th.—Yesterday afternoon, a stroll with B— up a large brook, he fishing for trout, and I looking on. The brook runs through a valley, on one side bordered by a high and precipitous bank; on the other there is an interval, and then the bank rises upward and upward into a high hill, with gorges and ravines separating one summit from another, and here and there are bare places, where the rain-streams have washed away the grass. The brook is bestrewn with stones, some bare, some partially moss-grown, and sometimes so huge as—once at least—to occupy almost the whole breadth of the current. Amongst these the stream brawls, only that this word does not express its good-natured voice, and "murmur" is too quiet. It sings along, sometimes smooth, with the pebbles visible beneath, sometimes rushing dark and swift, eddying and whitening past some rock, or underneath the hither or the farther bank; and at these places B-cast his line, and sometimes drew out a trout, small, not more than five or six inches long. The farther we went up the brook, the wilder it grew. The opposite bank was covered with pines and hemlocks, ascending high upwards, black and solemn. One knew that there must be almost a precipice behind, yet we could not see it. At the foot you could spy, a little way within the darksome shade, the roots and branches of the trees; but soon all sight was obstructed amidst the trunks. On the hither side, at first the bank was bare, then fringed with alder-bushes, bending and dipping into the stream, which, farther on, flowed through the midst of a forest of maple, beech, and other trees, its course growing wilder and wilder as we proceeded. For a considerable distance there was a causeway, built long ago of logs, to drag lumber upon; it was now decayed and rotten, a red decay, sometimes sunken down in the midst, here and there a knotty trunk stretching across, apparently sound. The sun being now low towards the west, a pleasant gloom and brightness were diffused through the forest, spots of brightness scattered upon the branches, or thrown down in gold upon the last year's leaves among the trees. At last we came to where a dam had been built across the brook many years ago, and was now gone to ruin, so as to make the spot look more solitary and wilder than if man had never left vestiges of his toil there. It was a framework of logs, with a covering of plank sufficient to obstruct the onward flow of the brook; but it found its way past the side, and came foaming and struggling along among scattered rocks. Above the dam there was a broad and deep pool, one side of which was bordered by a precipitous wall of rocks, as smooth as if hewn out and squared, and piled one upon another, above which rose the forest. On the other side there was still a gently shelving bank, and the shore was covered with tall trees, among which I particularly remarked a stately pine, wholly devoid of bark, rising white in aged and majestic ruin, thrusting out its barkless arms. It must have stood there in death many years, its own ghost. Above the dam the brook flowed through the forest, a glistening and babbling water-path, illuminated by the sun, which sent its rays almost straight along its course. It was as lovely and wild and peaceful as it could possibly have been a hundred years ago; and the traces of labors of men long departed added a deeper peace to it. I bathed in the pool, and then pursued my way down beside the brook, growing dark with a pleasant gloom, as the sun sank and the water became more shadowy. B— says that there was formerly a tradition that the Indians used to go up this brook, and return, after a brief absence, with large masses of lead, which they sold at the trading-stations in Augusta; whence there has always been an idea that there is a lead-mine hereabouts. Great toadstools were under the trees, and some small ones as yellow and almost the size of a half-broiled yolk of an egg. Strawberries were scattered along the brookside.

Dined at the hotel or Mansion House to-day. Men were playing checkers in the parlor. The Marshal of Maine, a corpulent, jolly fellow, famed for humor. A passenger left by the stage, hiring an express onward. A bottle of champagne was quaffed at the bar.

July 9th.—Went with B— to pay a visit to the shanties of the Irish and Canadians. He says that they sell and exchange these small houses among themselves continually. They may be built in three or four days, and are valued at four or five dollars. When the turf that is piled against the walls of some of them becomes covered with grass, it makes quite a picturesque object. It was almost dusk—just candle-lighting time—when we visited them. A young Frenchwoman, with a baby in her arms, came to the door of one of them, smiling, and looking pretty and happy. Her husband, a dark, black-haired, lively little fellow, caressed the child, laughing and singing to it; and there was a red-bearded Irishman, who likewise fondled the little brat. Then we could hear them within the hut, gabbling merrily, and could see them moving about briskly in the candle-light, through the window and open door. An old Irishwoman sat in the door of another hut, under the influence of an extra dose of rum,—she being an old lady of somewhat dissipated habits. She called to B—, and began to talk to him about her resolution not to give up her house: for it is his design to get her out of it. She is a true virago, and, though somewhat restrained by respect for him, she evinced a sturdy design to remain here through the winter, or at least for a considerable time longer. He persisting, she took her stand in the doorway of the hut, and stretched out her fist in a very Amazonian attitude. "Nobody," quoth she, "shall drive me out of this house, till my praties are out of the ground." Then would she wheedle and laugh and blarney, beginning in a rage, and ending as if she had been in jest. Meanwhile her husband stood by very quiet, occasionally trying to still her; but it is to be presumed, that, after our departure, they came to blows, it being a custom with the Irish husbands and wives to settle their disputes with blows; and it is said the woman often proves the better man. The different families also have battles, and occasionally the Irish fight with the Canadians. The latter, however, are much the more peaceable, never quarrelling among themselves, and seldom with their neighbors. They are frugal, and often go back to Canada with considerable sums of money. B— has gained much influence both with the Irish and the French,—with the latter, by dint of speaking to them in their own language. He is the umpire in their disputes, and their adviser, and they look up to him as a protector and patron-friend. I have been struck to see with what careful integrity and wisdom he manages matters among them, hitherto having known him only as a free and gay young man. He appears perfectly to understand their general character, of which he gives no very flattering description. In these huts, less than twenty feet square, he tells me that upwards of twenty people have sometimes been lodged.

A description of a young lady who had formerly been insane, and now felt the approach of a new fit of madness. She had been out to ride, had exerted herself much, and had been very vivacious. On her return, she sat down in a thoughtful and despondent attitude, looking very sad, but one of the loveliest objects that ever were seen. The family spoke to her, but she made no answer, nor took the least notice; but still sat like a statue in her chair,—a statue of melancholy and beauty. At last they led her away to her chamber.

We went to meeting this forenoon. I saw nothing remarkable, unless a little girl in the next pew to us, three or four years old, who fell asleep, with her head in the lap of her maid, and looked very pretty: a picture of sleeping innocence.

*July 11th, Tuesday.*—A drive with B— to Hallowell, yesterday, where we dined, and afterwards to Gardiner. The most curious object in this latter place was the elegant new mansion of —. It stands on the site of his former dwelling, which was destroyed by fire. The new building was estimated to cost about thirty thousand dollars; but twice as much has already been expended, and a great deal more will be required to complete it. It is certainly a splendid structure; the material, granite from the vicinity. At the angles it has small, circular towers; the portal is lofty and imposing. Relatively to the general style of domestic architecture in our country, it well deserves the name of castle or palace. Its situation, too, is fine, far retired from the public road, and attainable by a winding carriage-drive; standing amid fertile fields, and with large trees in the vicinity. There is also a beautiful view from the mansion, adown the Kennebec.

Beneath some of the large trees we saw the remains of circular seats, whereupon the family used to sit before the former house was burned down. There was no one now in the vicinity of the place, save a man and a yoke of oxen; and what he was about, I did not ascertain. Mr. — at present resides in a small dwelling, little more than a cottage, beside the main road, not far from the gateway which gives access to his palace.

At Gardiner, on the wharf, I witnessed the starting of the steamboat New England for Boston. There was quite a collection of people, looking on or taking leave of passengers,—the steam puffing,—stages arriving, full-freighted with ladies and gentlemen. A man was one moment too late; but running along the gunwale of a mud-scow, and jumping into a skiff, he was put on board by a black fellow. The dark cabin, wherein, descending from the sunshiny deck, it was difficult to discern the furniture, looking-glasses, and mahogany wainscoting. I met two old college acquaintances,—O—, who was going to Boston, and B—, with whom we afterwards drank a glass of wine at the hotel. B—, Mons. S—, and myself continue to live in the same style as heretofore. We appear mutually to be very well pleased with each other. Mons. S— displays many comical qualities, and manages to insure us several hearty laughs every morning and evening, those being the seasons when we meet. I am going to take lessons from him in the pronunciation of French. Of female society I see nothing. The only petticoat that comes within our premises appertains to Nancy, the pretty, dark-eyed maid-servant of the man who lives in the other part of the house.

On the road from Hallowell to Augusta we saw little booths, in two places, erected on the roadside, where boys offered beer, apples, etc., for sale. We passed an Irishwoman with a child in her arms, and a heavy bundle, and afterwards, an Irishman with a light bundle, sitting by the highway. They were husband and wife; and B— says that an Irishman and his wife, on their journeys, do not usually walk side by side, but that the man gives the woman the heaviest burden to carry, and walks on lightly ahead!

A thought comes into my mind: Which sort of house excites the most contemptuous feelings in the beholder,—such a house as Mr. —'s, all circumstances considered, or the board-built and turf-buttressed hovels of these wild Irish, scattered about as if they had sprung up like mushrooms, in the dells and gorges, and along the banks of the river? Mushrooms, by the way, spring up where the roots of an old tree are hidden under the ground.

Thursday, July 13th.—Two small Canadian boys came to our house yesterday, with strawberries to sell. It sounds strangely to hear children bargaining in French on the borders of Yankee-land. Among other languages spoken hereabouts must be reckoned the wild Irish. Some of the laborers on the mill-dam can speak nothing else. The intermixture of foreigners sometimes gives rise to quarrels between them and the natives. As we were going to the village yesterday afternoon, we witnessed the beginning of a quarrel between a Canadian and a Yankee,—the latter accusing the former of striking his oxen. B— thrust himself between and parted them; but they afterwards renewed their fray, and the Canadian, I believe, thrashed the Yankee soundly—for which he had to pay twelve dollars. Yet he was but a little fellow.

Coming to the Mansion House about supper-time, we found somewhat of a concourse of people, the Governor and Council being in session on the subject of the disputed territory. The British have lately imprisoned a man who was sent to take the census; and the Mainiacs are much excited on the subject. They wish the Governor to order out the militia at once, and take possession of the territory with the strong hand. There was a British army-captain at the Mansion House; and an idea was thrown out that it would be as well to seize upon him as a hostage. I would, for the joke's sake, that it had been done. Personages at the tavern: the Governor, somewhat stared after as he walked through the bar-room; Councillors seated about, sitting on benches near the bar, or on the stoop along the front of the house: the Adjutant-General of the Stale; two young Blue-Noses. from Canada or the Provinces; a gentleman "thumbing his hat" for liquor, or perhaps playing off the trick of the "honest landlord" on some stranger. The decanters and wine-bottles on the move, and the beer and soda founts pouring out continual streams, with a whiz. Stage drivers, etc., asked to drink with the aristocracy, and my host treating and being treated. Rubicund faces; breaths odorous of brandy and water. Occasionally the pop of a champagne cork.

Returned home, and took a lesson in French of Mons. S—. I like him very much, and have seldom met with a more honest., simple, and apparently so well-principled a man; which good qualities I impute to his being, by the father's side, of German blood. He looks more like a German—or, as he says, like a Swiss—than a Frenchman, having very light hair and a light complexion, and not a French expression. He is a vivacious little fellow, and wonderfully excitable to mirth; and it. is truly a sight to see him laugh;—every feature partakes of his movement, and oven his whole body shares in it, as he rises and dances about the room. He has great variety of conversation, commensurate with his experiences in life, and sometimes will talk Spanish, *ore rotunda*—sometimes imitate the Catholic priests, chanting Latin songs for the dead, in deep, gruff, awful tones, producing really a very strong impression,—then he will break out into a light, French song, perhaps of love, perhaps of war, acting it out, as if on the stage of a theatre: all this intermingled with continual fun, excited, by the incidents of the passing moment. He has Frenchified all our names, calling B— Monsieur Du Pont, myself M. de L'Aubépine, and himself M. le Berger, and all, Knights of the Round-Table. And we live in great harmony and brotherhood, as queer a life as anybody leads, and as queer a set as may be found anywhere. In his more serious intervals, he talks philosophy and deism, and preaches obedience to the law of reason and morality; which law he says (and I believe him) he has so well observed, that, notwithstanding his residence in dissolute countries, he has never yet been sinful. He wishes me, eight or nine weeks hence, to accompany him on foot to Quebec, and then to Niagara and New York. I should like it well, if my circumstances and other considerations would permit. What pleases much in Mons. S— is the simple and childlike enjoyment he finds in trifles, and the joy with which he speaks of going back to his own country, away from the dull Yankees, who here misunderstand and despise him. Yet I have never heard him speak harshly of them. I rather think that B— and I will be remembered by him with more pleasure than anybody else in the country; for we have sympathized with him, and treated him kindly, and like a gentleman and an equal; and he comes to us at night as to home and friends.

I went down to the river to-day to see B— fish for salmon with a fly,—a hopeless business; for he says that only one instance has been known in the United States of salmon being taken otherwise than with a net. A few chubs were all the fruit of his piscatory efforts. But while looking at the rushing and rippling stream, I saw a great fish, some six feet long and thick in proportion, suddenly emerge at whole length, turn a somerset, and then vanish again beneath the water. It was of a glistening, yellowish brown, with its fins all spread, and looking very strange and startling, darting out so lifelike from the black water, throwing itself fully into the bright sunshine, and then lost to sight and to pursuit. I saw also a long, flat-bottomed boat go up the river, with a brisk wind, and against a strong stream. Its sails were of curious construction: a long mast, with two sails below, one on each side of the boat, and a broader one surmounting them. The sails were colored brown, and appeared like leather or skins, but were really cloth. At a distance, the vessel looked like, or at least I compared it to, a monstrous water-insect skimming along the river. If the sails had been crimson or yellow, the resemblance would have been much closer. There was a pretty spacious raised cabin in the after part of the boat. It moved along lightly, and disappeared between the woody banks. These boats have the two parallel sails attached to the same yard, and some have two sails, one surmounting the other. They trade to Waterville and thereabouts,—names, as "Paul Pry," on their sails.

Saturday, July 15th.—Went with B— yesterday to visit several Irish shanties, endeavoring to find out who had stolen some rails of a fence. At the first door at which we kndeked (a shanty with an earthen mound heaped against the wall, two or three feet thick), the inmates were not up, though it was past eight o'clock. At last a middle-aged woman showed herself, half dressed, and completing her toilet. Threats were made of tearing down her house; for she is a lady of very indifferent morals, and sells rum. Few of these people are connected with the mill-dam,—or, at least, many are not so, hut have intruded themselves into the vacant huts which were occupied by the mill-dam people last year. In two or three places hereabouts there is quite a village of these dwellings, with a clay and board chimney, or oftener an old barrel, smoked and charred with the fire. Some of their roofs are covered with sods, and appear almost subterranean. One of the little hamlets stands on both sides of a deep dell, wooded and bush-grown, with a vista, as it were, into the heart of a wood in one direction, and to the broad, sunny river in the other: there was a little rivulet, crossed by a plank, at the bottom of the dell. At two doors we saw very pretty and modest-looking young women,—one with a child in her arms. Indeed, they all have innumerable little children; and they are invariably in good health, though always dirty of face. They come to the door while their mothers are talking with the visitors, standing straight up on their bare legs, with their little plump bodies protruding, in one hand a small tin saucepan, and in the other an iron spoon, with unwashed mouths, looking as independent as any child or grown person in the land. They stare unabashed, but make no answer when spoken to. "I've no call to your fence, Misser B—." It seems strange that a man should have the right, unarmed with any legal instrument, of tearing down the dwelling-houses of a score of families, and driving the inmates forth without a shelter. Yet B— undoubtedly has this right; and it is not a little striking to see how quietly these people contemplate the probability of his exercising it,—resolving, indeed, to burrow in their holes as long as may be, yet caring about as little for an ejectment as those who could find a tenement anywhere, and less. Yet the women, amid all the trials of their situation, appear to have kept up the distinction between virtue and vice; those who can claim the former will not associate with the latter. When the women travel with young children, they carry the baby slung at their backs, and sleeping quietly. The dresses of the new-comers are old-fashioned, making them look aged before their time.

Monsieur S-shaving himself yesterday morning. He was in excellent spirits, and could not keep his tongue or body still more than long enough to make two or three consecutive strokes at his beard. Then he would turn, flourishing his razor and grimacing joyously, enacting droll antics, breaking out into scraps and verses of drinking-songs, "*A boire! à boire!*"—then laughing heartily, and crying, "*Vive la gaîté!*"—then resuming his task, looking into the glass with grave face, on which, however, a grin would soon break out anew, and all his pranks would be repeated with variations. He turned this foolery to philosophy, by observing that mirth contributed to goodness of heart, and to make us love our fellow-creatures. Conversing with him in the evening, he affirmed, with evident belief in the truth of what he said, that he would have no objection, except that it would be a very foolish thing, to expose his whole heart, his whole inner man, to the view of the world. Not that there would not be much evil discovered there; but, as he was conscious of being in a state of mental and moral improvement, working out his progress onward, he would not shrink from such a scrutiny. This talk was introduced by his mentioning the "Minister's Black Veil," which he said he had seen translated into French, as an exercise, by a Miss Appleton of Bangor.

Saw by the river-side, late in the afternoon, one of the above-described boats going into the stream with the water rippling at the prow, from the strength of the current and of the boat's motion. By and by comes down a raft, perhaps twenty yards long, guided by two men, one at each end,—the raft itself of boards sawed at Waterville, and laden with square bundles of shingles and round bundles of clapboards. "Friend," says one man, "how is the tide now?"—this being important to the onward progress. They make fast to a tree, in order to wait for the tide to rise a little higher. It would be pleasant enough to float down the Kennebec on one of these rafts, letting the river conduct you onward at its own pace, leisurely displaying to you all the wild or ordered beauties along its banks, and perhaps running you aground in some peculiarly picturesque spot, for your longer enjoyment of it. Another object, perhaps, is a solitary man paddling himself down the river in a small canoe, the light, lonely touch of his paddle in the water making the silence seem deeper. Every few minutes a sturgeon leaps forth, sometimes behind you, so that you merely hear the splash, and, turning hastily around, see nothing but the disturbed water. Sometimes he darts straight on end out of a quiet black spot on which your eyes happen to be fixed, and, when even his tail is clear of the surface, he falls down on his side and disappears.

On the river-bank, an Irishwoman washing some clothes, surrounded by her children, whose babbling sounds pleasantly along the edge of the shore; and she also answers in a sweet, kindly, and cheerful voice, though an immoral woman, and without the certainty of bread or shelter from day to day. An Irishman sitting angling on the brink with an alder pole and a clothes-line. At frequent intervals, the scene is suddenly broken by a loud report like thunder, rolling along the banks, echoing and reverberating afar. It is a blast of rocks. Along the margin, sometimes sticks of timber made fast, either separately or several together; stones of some size;, varying the pebbles and sand; a clayey spot, where a shallow brook runs into the river, not with a deep outlet, but finding its way across the bank in two or three single runlets. Looking upward into the deep glen whence it issues, you see its shady current. Elsewhere, a high acclivity, with the beach between it and the river, the ridge broken and caved away, so that the earth looks fresh and yellow, and is penetrated by the nests of birds. An old, shining tree-trunk, half in and half out of the water. An island of gravel, long and narrow, in the centre of the river. Chips, blocks of wood, slabs, and other scraps of lumber, strewed along the beach: logs drifting down. The high hank covered with various trees and shrubbery, and, in one place, two or three Irish shanties.

Thursday, July 20th.—A drive yesterday afternoon to a pond in the vicinity of Augusta, about nine miles off. to fish for white perch. Remarkables: the steering of the boat through the crooked, labyrinthine brook, into the open pond,—the man who acted as pilot,—his talking with B— about politics, the bank, the iron money of "a king who came to reign, in Greece, over a city called Sparta,"—his advice to B— to come amongst the laborers on the mill-dam, because it stimulated them "to see a man grinning among them." The man took hearty tugs at a bottle of good Scotch whiskey, and became pretty merry. The fish caught were the yellow perch, which are not esteemed for eating; the white perch, a beautiful, silvery, round-backed fish, which bites eagerly, runs about with the line while being pulled up, makes good sport for the angler, and an admirable dish; a great chub; and three horned pouts, which swallow the hook into their lowest entrails. Several dozen fish were taken in an hour or two, and then we returned to the shop where we had left our horse and wagon, the pilot very eccentric behind us. It was a small, dingy shop, dimly lighted by a single inch of candle, faintly disclosing various boxes, barrels standing on end, articles hanging from the ceiling; the proprietor at the counter, whereupon appear gin and brandy, respectively contained in a tin pint-measure and an earthenware jog, with two or three tumblers beside them, out of which nearly all the party drank; some coming up to the counter frankly, others lingering in the background, waiting to be pressed, two paying for their own liquor and withdrawing. B— treated them twice round. The pilot, after drinking his brandy, gave a history of our expedition, and how many and how large fish we caught. B— making acquaintances and renewing them, and gaining great credit for liberality and free-heartedness,—two or three boys looking on and listening to the talk,—the shopkeeper smiling behind his counter, with the tarnished tin scales beside him,—the inch of candle burning down almost to extinction. So we got into our wagon, with the fish, and drove to Robinson's tavern, almost five miles off, where we supped and passed the night. In the bar-room was a fat old countryman on a journey, and a quack doctor of the vicinity, and an Englishman with a peculiar accent. Seeing B—'s jointed and brass-mounted fishing-pole, he took it for a theodolite, and supposed that we had been on a surveying expedition. At supper, which consisted of bread, butter, cheese, cake, doughnuts and gooseberry-pie, we were waited upon by a tall, very tall woman, young and maiden-looking, yet with a strongly outlined and determined face. Afterwards we found her to be the wife of mine host. She poured out our tea, came in when we rang the table-bell to refill our cups, and again retired. While at supper, the fat old traveller was ushered through the room into a contiguous bedroom. My own chamber, apparently the best in the house, had its walls ornamented with a small, gilt-framed, foot-square looking-glass, with a hair-brush hanging beneath it; a record of the deaths of the family written on a black tomb, in an engraving, where a father, mother, and child were represented in a graveyard, weeping over said tomb; the mourners dressed in black, country-cut clothes; the engraving executed in Vermont. There was also a wood engraving of the Declaration of Independence, with facsimiles of the autographs; a portrait of the Empress Josephine, and another of Spring. In the two closets of this chamber were mine hostess's cloak, best bonnet, and go-to-meeting apparel. There was a good bed, in which I slept tolerably well, and, rising betimes, ate breakfast, consisting of some of our own fish, and then started for Augusta. The fat old traveller had gone off with the harness of our wagon, which the hostler had put on to his horse by mistake. The tavern-keeper gave us his own harness, and started in pursuit of the old man, who was probably aware of the exchange, and well satisfied with it.

Our drive to Augusta, six or seven miles, was very pleasant, a heavy rain having fallen during the night, and laid the oppressive dust of the day before. The road lay parallel with the Kennebec, of which we occasionally had near glimpses. The country swells back from the river in hills and ridges, without any interval of level ground; and there were frequent woods, filling up the valleys or crowning the summits. The land is good, the farms look neat, and the houses comfortable. The latter are generally but of one story, but with large barns; and it was a good sign, that, while we saw no houses unfinished nor out of repair, one man at least had found it expedient to make an addition to his dwelling. At the distance of more than two miles, we had a view of white Augusta, with its steeples, and the State-House, at the farther end of the town. Observable matters along the road were the stage,—all the dust of yesterday brushed off, and no new dust contracted,—full of passengers, inside and out; among them some gentlemanly people and pretty girls, all looking fresh and unsullied, rosy, cheerful, and curious as to the face of the country, the faces of passing travellers, and the incidents of their journey; not yet damped, in the morning sunshine, by long miles of jolting over rough and hilly roads,—to compare this with their appearance at midday, and as they drive into Bangor at dusk;—two women dashing along in a wagon, and with a child, rattling pretty speedily down hill;—people looking at us from the open doors and windows;—the children staring from the wayside;—the mowers stopping, for a moment, the sway of their scythes;—the matron of a family, indistinctly seen at some distance within the house, her head and shoulders appearing through the window, drawing her handkerchief over her bosom, which had been uncovered to give the baby its breakfast,—the said baby, or its immediate predecessor, sitting at the door, turning round to creep away on all fours;—a man building a flat-bottomed boat by the roadside: he talked with B— about the Boundary question, and swore fervently in favor of driving the British "into hell's kitchen " by main force.

Colonel B—, the engineer of the mill-dam, is now here, after about a fortnight's absence. He is a plain country squire, with a good figure, but with rather a heavy brow; a rough complexion; a gait stiff, and a general rigidity of manner, something like that of a schoolmaster. He originated in a country town, and is a self-educated man. As he walked down the gravel-path to-day, after dinner, he took up a scythe, which one of the mowers had left on the sward, and began to mow, with quite a scientific swing. On the coming of the mower, he laid it down, perhaps a little ashamed of his amusement. I was interested in this; to see a man, after twenty-five years of scientific occupation, thus trying whether his arms retained their strength and skill for the labors of his youth,—mindful of the day when he wore striped trousers, and toiled in his shirt-sleeves,—and now tasting again, for pastime, this drudgery beneath a fervid sun. He stood awhile, looking at the workmen, and then went to oversee the laborers at the mill-dam.

Monday, July 24th.—I bathed in the river on Thursday evening, and in the brook at the old dam on Saturday and Sunday,—the former time at noon. The aspect of the solitude at noon was peculiarly impressive, there being a cloudless sunshine, no wind, no rustling of the forest-leaves, no waving of the boughs, no noise but the brawling and babbling of the stream, making its way among the stones, and pouring in a little cataract round one side of the mouldering dam. Looking up the brook, there was a long vista,—now ripples, now smooth and glassy spaces, now large rocks, almost blocking up the channel; while the trees stood upon either side, mostly straight, but here and there a branch thrusting itself out irregularly, and one tree, a pine, leaning over,—not bending,—but leaning at an angle over the brook, rough and ragged; birches, alders; the tallest of all the trees an old, dead, leafless pine, rising white and lonely, though closely surrounded by others. Along the brook, now the grass and herbage extended close to the water; now a small, sandy beach. The wall of rock before described looking as if it had been hewn, but with irregular strokes of the workman, doing his job by rough and ponderous strength, —now chancing to hew it away smoothly and cleanly, now carelessly smiting, and making gaps, or piling on the slabs of rock, so as to leave vacant spaces. In the interstices grow brake and broad-leaved forest-grass. The trees that spring from the top of this wall have their roots pressing close to. the rock, so that there is no soil between; they cling powerfully, and grasp the crag tightly with their knotty fingers. The trees on both sides are so thick, that the sight and the thoughts are almost immediately lost among confused stems, branches, and clustering green leaves,—a narrow strip of bright blue sky above, the sunshine falling lustrously down, and making the pathway of the brook luminous below. Entering among the thickets, I find the soil strewn with old leaves of preceding seasons, through which may be seen a black or dark mould; the roots of trees stretch frequently across the path; often a moss-grown brown log lies athwart, and when you set your foot down, it sinks into the decaying substance,—into the heart of oak or pine. The leafy boughs and twigs of the underbrush enlace themselves before you, so that you must stoop your head to pass under, or thrust yourself through amain, while they sweep against your face, and perhaps knock off your hat. There are rocks mossy and slippery; sometimes you stagger, with a great rustling of branches, against a clump of bushes, and into the midst of it. From end to end of all this tangled' shade goes a pathway scarcely worn, for the leaves are not trodden through, yet plain enough to the eye, winding gently to avoid tree-trunks and rocks and little hillocks. In the more open ground, the aspect of a tall, fire-blackened stump, standing alone, high up on a swell of land, that rises gradually from one side of the brook, like a monument. Yesterday, I passed a group of children in this solitary valley,—two boys, I think, and two girls. One of the little girls seemed to have suffered some wrong from her companions, for she was weeping and complaining violently. Another time, I came suddenly on a small Canadian boy, who was in a hollow place, among the ruined logs of an old causeway, picking raspberries,—lonely among bushes and gorges, far up the wild valley,—and the lonelier seemed the little boy for the bright sunshine, that showed no one else in a wide space of view except him and me.

Remarkable items: the observation of Mons. S— when B— was saying something against the character of the French people,—"You ought not to form an unfavorable judgment of a great nation from mean fellows like me, strolling about in a foreign country." I thought it very noble thus to protest against anything discreditable in himself personally being used against the honor of his country. He is a very singular person, with an originality in all his notions;—not that nobody has ever had such before, but that lie has thought them out for himself. He told me yesterday that one of his sisters was a waiting-maid in the Rocher de Caucale. He is about the sincerest man I ever knew, never pretending to feelings that are not in him,—never flattering. His feelings do not seem to be warm, though they are kindly. He is so single-minded that he cannot understand badinage, but takes it all as if meant in earnest,—a German trait. He values himself greatly on being a Frenchman, though all his most valuable qualities come from Germany. His temperament is cool and pure, and he is greatly delighted with any attentions from the ladies. A short time since, a lady gave him a bouquet of roses and pinks; he capered and danced and sang, put it in water, and carried it to his own chamber; but he brought it out for us to see and admire two or three times a day, bestowing on it all the epithets of admiration in the French language,—"*Superbe! magniflque!*" When some of the flowers began to fade, he made the rest, with others, into a new nosegay, and consulted us whether it would be fit to give to another lady. Contrast this French foppery with his solemn moods, when we sat in the twilight, or after B— is abed, talking of Christianity and Deism, of ways of life, of marriage, of benevolence,—in short, of all deep matters of this world and the next. An evening or two since, he began singing all manner of English songs,—such as Mrs. Hemans's "Landing of the Pilgrims," "Auld Lang Syne," and some of Moore's,—the singing pretty fair, but in the oddest tone and accent. Occasionally he breaks out with scraps from French tragedies, which he spouts with corresponding action. He generally gets close to me in these displays of musical and histrionic talent. Once he offered to magnetize me in the manner of Monsieur P—.

Wednesday, July 26th.—Dined at Barker's yesterday. Before dinner, sat with several other persons in the stoop of the tavern. There were B—, J. A. Chandler, Clerk of the Court, a man of middle age or beyond, two or three stage people, and, near by, a negro, whom they call "the Doctor," a crafty-looking fellow, one of whose occupations is nameless. In presence of this goodly company, a man of a depressed, neglected air, a soft, simple-looking fellow, with an anxious expression, in a laborer's dress, approached and inquired for Mr. Barker. Mine host being gone to Portland, the stranger was directed to the barkeeper, who stood at the door. The man asked where he should find one Mary Ann Russell,—a question which excited general and hardly suppressed mirth; for the said Mary Ann is one of a knot of women who were routed on Sunday evening by Barker and a constable. The man was told that the black fellow would give him all the information he wanted. The black fellow asked,—

"Do you want to see her?"

Others of the by-standers or by-sitters put various questions as to the nature of the man's business with Mary Ann. One asked,—

"Is she your daughter?"

"Why, a little nearer than that, I calkilate," said the poor devil.

Here the mirth was increased, it being evident that the woman was his wife. The man seemed too simple and obtuse to comprehend the ridicule of his situation, or to be rendered very miserable by it. Nevertheless, he made some touching points.

"A man generally places some little dependence on his wife," said he, "whether she's good or not."

He meant, probably, that he rests some affection on her. He told us that she had behaved well, till committed to jail for striking a child; and I believe he was absent from home at the time, and had not seen her since. And now he was in search of her, intending, doubtless, to do his best to get her out of her troubles, and then to take her back to his home. Some advised him not to look after her; others recommended him to pay "the Doctor" aforesaid for guiding him to her; which finally "the Doctor" did, in consideration of a treat; and the fellow went off, having heard little but gibes and not one word of sympathy! I would like to have witnessed his meeting with his wife.

There was a moral picturesqueness in the contrasts of the scene,—a man moved as deeply as his nature would admit, in the midst of hardened, gibing spectators, heartless towards him. It is worth thinking over and studying out. He seemed rather hurt and pricked by the jests thrown at him, yet bore it patiently, and sometimes almost joined in the laugh, being of an easy, unenergetie temper.

Hints for characters: Nancy, a pretty, black-eyed, intelligent servant-girl, living in Captain H—'s family. She comes daily to make the beds in our part of the house, and exchanges a good-morning with me, in a pleasant voice, and with a. glance and smile,—somewhat shy, because we are not acquainted, yet capably of being made conversable. She washes once a week, and may be seen standing over her tub, with her handkerchief somewhat displaced from her white neck, because it is hot. Often she stands with her bare arms in the water, talking with Mrs H—, or looks through the window, perhaps, at B—, or somebody else crossing the yard,—rather thoughtfully, but soon smiling or laughing. Then goeth she for a pail of water. In the afternoon, very probably, she dresses herself in silks, looking not only pretty, but lady-like, and strolls round the house, not unconscious that some gentleman may be staring at her from behind the green blinds. After supper, she walks to the village. Morning and evening, she goes a-milking. And thus passes her life, cheerfully, usefully, virtuously, with hopes, doubtless, of a husband and children. —Mrs. H— is a particularly plump, soft-fleshed, fair-complexioned, comely woman enough, with rather a simple countenance, not nearly so pleasant as Nancy's. Her walk has something of the roll or waddle of a fat woman, though it were too much to call her fat. She seems to be a sociable body, probably laughter-loving. Captain H— himself has commanded a steamboat, and has a certain knowledge, of life.

Query, in relation to the man's missing wife, how much desire and resolution of doing her duty by her husband can a wife retain, while injuring him in what is deemed the most essential point?

Observation. The effect of morning sunshine on the wet grass, on sloping and swelling land, between the spectator and the sun at some distance, as across a lawn. It diffused a dim brilliancy over the whole surface of the field. The mists, slow-rising farther off, part resting on the earth, the remainder of the column already ascending so high that you doubt whether to call it a fog or a cloud.

Friday, July 28th.—Saw my classmate and formerly intimate friend, —, for the first time since we graduated. He has met with good success in life, in spite of circumstance, having struggled upward against bitter opposition, by the force of his own abilities, to be a member of Congress, after having been for some time the leader of his party in the State Legislature. We met like old friends, and conversed almost as freely as we used to do in college days, twelve years ago and more. He is a singular person, shrewd, crafty, insinuating, with wonderful tact, seizing on each man by his manageable point, and using him for his own purpose, often without the man's suspecting that he is made a tool of; and yet, artificial as his character would seem to be, his conversation, at least to myself, was full of natural feeling, the expression of which can hardly be mistaken, and his revelations with regard to himself had really a great deal of frankness. He spoke of his ambition, of the obstacles which he had encountered, of the means by which he had overcome them, imputing great efficacy to his personal intercourse with people, and his study of their characters; then of his course as a member of the Legislature and Speaker, and his style of speaking and its effects; of the dishonorable things which had been imputed to him, and in what manner he had repelled the charges. In short, he would seem to have opened himself very freely as to his public life. Then, as to his private affairs, he spoke of his marriage, of his wife, his children, and told me, with tears in his eyes, of the death of a dear little girl, and how it affected him, and how impossible it had been for him to believe that she was really to die. A man of the most open nature might well have been more reserved to a friend, after twelve years' separation, than-was to me. Nevertheless, he is really a crafty man, concealing, like a murder-secret, anything that it is not good for him to have known. He by no means feigns the good-feeling that he professes, nor is there anything affected in the frankness of his conversation; and it is this that makes him so very fascinating. There is such a quantity of truth and kindliness and warm affections, that a man's heart opens to him, in spite of himself. He deceives, by truth. And not only is he crafty, but, when occasion demands, bold and fierce as a tiger, determined, and even straightforward and undisguised in his measures,—a daring fellow as well as a sly one. Yet, notwithstanding his consummate art, the general estimate of his character seems to be pretty just. Hardly anybody, probably, thinks him better than he is, and many think him worse. Nevertheless, if no overwhelming discovery of rascality be made, he will always possess influence; though I should hardly think that he would take any prominent part in Congress. As to any rascality, I rather believe that he has thought out for himself a much higher system of morality than any natural integrity would have prompted him to adopt; that he has seen the thorough advantage of morality and honesty; and the sentiment of these qualities has now got into his mind and spirit, and pretty well impregnated them, I believe him to be about as honest as the great run of the world, with something even approaching to high-mindedness. His person in some degree accords with his character,—thin and with a thin face, sharp features, sallow, a projecting brow not very high, deep-set eyes, an insinuating smile and look, when he meets you, and is about to address you. I should think that he would do away with this peculiar expression, for it reveals more of himself than can be detected in any other way, in personal intercourse with him. Upon the whole, I have quite a good liking for him, and mean to go to — to see him.

Observation. A steam-engine across the river, which almost continually during the day, and sometimes all night, may be heard puffing and panting, as if it uttered groans for being compelled to labor in the heat and sunshine, and when the world is asleep also.

Monday, July 31st.—Nothing remarkable to record. A child asleep in a young lady's arms,—a little baby, two or three months old. Whenever anything partially disturbed the child, as, for instance, when the young lady or a by-stander patted its cheek or rubbed its chin, the child would smile; then all its dreams seemed to be of pleasure and happiness. At first the smile was so faint, that I doubted whether it were really a smile or no; but, on further efforts, it brightened forth very decidedly. This, without opening its eyes.—A constable, a homely, good-natured, business-looking man, with a warrant against an Irishman's wife for throwing a brick-bat at a fellow. He gave good advice to the Irishman about the best method of coming easiest through the affair. Finally settled,—the justice agreeing to relinquish his fees, on condition that the Irishman would pay for the mending of his old boots!

I went with Monsieur S— yesterday to pick raspberries. He fell through an old log bridge thrown over a hollow; looking back, only his head and shoulders appeared through the rotten logs and among the bushes.—A shower coming on, the rapid running of a little barefooted boy, coming up unheard, and dashing swiftly past us, and showing the soles of his naked feet as he ran adown the path, and up the opposite rise.

Tuesday, August 1st.—There having been a heavy rain yesterday, a nest of chimney-swallows was washed down the chimney into the fireplace of one of the front rooms. My attention was drawn to them by a most obstreperous twittering; and looking behind the fire-board, there were three young birds, clinging with their feet against one of the jambs, looking at me, open-mouthed, and all clamoring together, so as quite to fill the room with the short, eager, frightened sound. The old birds, by certain signs upon the floor of the room, appeared to have fallen victims to the appetite of the eat. La belle Nancy provided a basket filled with cotton-wool, into which the poor little devils were put; and I tried to feed them with soaked bread, of which, however, they did not eat with much relish. Tom, the Irish boy, gave it as his opinion that they were not old enough to be weaned. I hung the basket out of the window, in the sunshine, and upon looking in, an hour or two after, found that two of the birds had escaped. The other I tried to feed, and sometimes, when a morsel of bread was thrust into its open mouth, it would swallow it. But it appeared to suffer very much, vociferating loudly when disturbed, and panting, in a sluggish agony, with eyes closed, or half opened, when let alone. It distressed me a good deal; and I felt relieved, though somewhat shocked, when B— put an end to its misery by squeezing its head and throwing it out of the window. They were of a slate-color, and might, I suppose, have been able to shift for themselves.—The other day a little yellow bird flew into one of the empty rooms, of which there are half a dozen on the lower floor, and could not find his way out again, flying at the glass of the windows, instead of at the door, thumping his head against the panes or against the ceiling. I drove him into the entry and chased him from end to end, endeavoring to make him fly through one of the open doors. He would fly at the circular light over the door, clinging to the casement, sometimes alighting on one of the two glass lamps, or on the cords that suspended them, uttering an affrighted and melancholy cry whenever I came near and flapped my handkerchief, and appearing quite tired and sinking into despair. At last he happened to fly low enough to pass through the door, and immediately vanished into the gladsome sunshine.—Ludicrous situation of a man, drawing his chaise down a sloping bank, to wash in the river. The chaise got the better of him, and, rushing downward as if it were possessed, compelled him to run at full speed, and drove him up to his chin into the water. A singular instance, that a chaise may run away with a man without a horse!

Saturday August 12th.—Left Augusta a week ago this morning for-. Nothing particular in our drive across the country. Fellow-passenger, a Boston dry-goods dealer, travelling to collect bills. At many of the country shops he would get out, and show his unwelcome visage. In the tavern, prints from Scripture, varnished and on rollers,—such as the Judgment of Christ; also a droll set of colored engravings of the story of the Prodigal Son, the figures being clad in modern costume,—or, at least, that of not more than half a century ago. The father, a grave, clerical person, with a white wig and black broadcloth suit; the son, with a cocked hat and laced clothes, drinking wine out of a glass, and caressing a woman in fashionable dress. At — a nice, comfortable boarding-house tavern, without a bar or any sort of wines or spirits. An old lady from Boston, with her three daughters, one of whom was teaching music, and the other two schoolmistresses. A frank, free, mirthful daughter of the landlady, about twenty-four years old, between whom and myself there immediately sprang up a flirtation, which made us both feel rather melancholy when we parted on Tuesday morning. Music in the evening, with a song by a rather pretty, fantastic little mischief of a brunette, about eighteen years old, who has married within a year, and spent the last summer in a trip to the Springs and elsewhere. Her manner of walking is by jerks, with a quiver, as if she were made of calves-feet jelly. I talk with everybody: to Mrs. T— good sense,—to Mary, good sense, with a mixture of fun,—to Mrs. G—, sentiment, romance, and nonsense.

Walked with — to see General Knox's old mansion,—a large, rusty-looking edifice of wood, with some grandeur in the architecture, standing on the banks of the river, close by the site of an old burial-ground, and near where an ancient fort had been erected for defence against the French and Indians. General Knox once owned a square of thirty miles in this part of the country, and he wished to settle it in with a tenantry, after the fashion of English gentlemen. He would permit no edifice to be erected within a certain distance of his mansion. His patent covered, of course, the whole present town of Waldoborough, and divers other flourishing commercial and country villages, and would have been of incalculable value could it have remained unbroken to the present time. But the General lived in grand style, and received throngs of visitors from foreign parts, and was obliged to part with large tracts of his possessions, till now there is little left but the ruinous mansion and the ground immediately around it. His tomb stands near the house, a spacious receptacle, an iron door at the end of a turf-covered mound, and surmounted by an obelisk of marble. There are inscriptions to the memory of several of his family: for he had many children, all of whom are now dead, except one daughter, a widow of fifty, recently married to Hon. John H—. There is a stone fence round the monument. On the outside of this are the gravestones, and large, flat tombstones of the ancient burial ground. the tombstones being of red freestone, with vacant spaces, formerly inlaid with slate, on which were the inscriptions, and perhaps coats of arms. One of these spaces was in the shape of a heart. The people were very wrathful that the General should have laid out his grounds over this old burial-place; and he dared never throw down the gravestones, though his wife, a haughty English lady, often teased him to do so. But when the old general was dead, Lady Knox (as they called her) caused them to be prostrated, as they now lie. She was a woman of violent passions, and so proud an aristocrat, that, as long she lived, she would never enter any house in the town except her own. When a married daughter was ill, she used to in her carriage to the door and send up to inquire how she did. The General was personally very popular; but his wife ruled him. The house and its vicinity, and the whole tract covered by Knox's patent, may be taken as an illustration of what must be the result of American schemes of aristocracy. It is not forty years since this house was built, and Knox was in his glory; but now the house is all in decay, while within a stone's throw of it there is a street of smart white edifices of one and two stories, occupied chiefly by thriving mechanics, which as been laid out where Knox meant to have forests and parks. On the banks of the river, where he intended to have only one wharf for his own West Indian vessels and yacht, there are two wharves, with stores and a lime-kiln. Little appertains to the mansion except the tomb and the old burial-ground, and the old fort.

The descendants are all poor, and the inheritance was merely sufficient to make a dissipated and drunken fellow of the only one of the old General's sons who survived to middle age. The man's habits were as bas as possible as long as he had any money; but when quite ruined, he reformed. The daughter, the only survivor among Knox's children (herself childless), is a mild, amiable woman, therein totally different from her mother. Knox, when he first visited his estate, arriving in a vessel, was waited upon by a deputation of the squatters, who had resolved to resist them to the death. He received them with genial courtesy, mad them dine with him aboard the vessel, and sent them back to their constituents in great love and admiration of him. He used to have a vessel running to Philadelphia, I think, and bringing him all sorts of delicacies. His way of raising money was to give a mortgage on his estate of a hundred thousand dollars at a time, and receive that nominal amount in goods, which he would immediately sell at auction for perhaps thirty thousand. He died by a chicken-bone. Near the house are the remains of a covered way, by which the French once attempted to gain admittance into the fort; but the work caved in and buried a good many of them, and the rest gave up the siege. There was recently an old inhabitant living who remembered when the people used to reside in the fort.

Owl's Head,—a watering-place, terminating a point of land, six or seven miles from Thomaston. A long island shuts out the prospect of the sea. Hither coasters and fishing-smacks run in when storm is anticipated. Two fat landlords, both young men, with something of a contrast in their dispositions: one of them being a brisk, lively, active, jesting, fat man; the other more heavy and inert, making jests sluggishly, if at all. Aboard the steamboat, Professor Stuart of Andover, sitting on a sofa in the saloon, generally in conversation with some person, resolving their doubts on one point or another, speaking in a very audible voice; and strangers standing or sitting around to hear him, as if he were an ancient apostle or philosopher. He is a bulky man, with a large, massive face, particularly calm in its expression, and mild enough to be pleasing. When not otherwise occupied, he reads, without much notice of what is going on around him. He speaks without effort, yet thoughtfully.

We got lost in a fog the morning after leaving Owl's Head. Fired a brass cannon, rang bell, blew steam, like a whale snorting. After one of the reports of the cannon, we heard a horn blown at no great distance, the sound coming soon after the report. Doubtful whether it came from the shore or a vessel. Continued our ringing and snorting; and by and by something was seen to mingle with the fog that obscured everything beyond fifty yards from us. At first it seemed only like a denser wreath of fog; it darkened still more, till it took the aspect of sails; then the hull of a small schooner came beating down towards us, the wind laying her over towards us, so that her gunwale was almost in the water, and we could see the whole of her sloping deck.

"Schooner ahoy!" say we. "Hallo" Have you seen Boston Light this morning/"

"Yes; it bears north-northwest, two miles distant."

"Very much obliged to you," cries our captain.

So the schooner vanishes into the mist behind. We get up our steam, and soon enter the harbor, meeting vessels of every rig; and the fog, clearing away, shows a cloudy sky. Aboard, an old one-eyed sailor, who had lost one of his feet, and had walked on the stump from Eastport to Bangor, thereby making a shocking ulcer.

Penobscot Bay is full of islands, close to which the steamboat is continually passing. Some are large, with portions of forest and portions of cleared land; some are mere rocks, with a little green or none, and inhabited by sea-birds, which fly and flap about hoarsely. Their eggs may be gathered by the bushel, and are good to eat. Other islands have one house and barn on them, this sole family being lords and rulers of all the land which the sea girds. The owner of such an island must have a peculiar sense of propriety and lordship; he must feel more like his own master and his own man than other people can. Other islands, perhaps high, precipitous, black bluffs, are crowned with a white light-house, whence, as evening comes one, twinkles a star across the melancholy deep,—seen by vessels coming on the coast, seen from, the mainland, seen from island to island. Darkness descending, and, looking down at the broad wake left by the wheels of the steamboat, we may see sparkles of sea-fire glittering through the gloom.

Salem, August 22d.—A walk yesterday afternoon down to the Juniper and Winter Island. Singular effect of partial sunshine, the sky being broadly and heavily clouded, and land and sea, in consequence, being generally overspread with a sombre gloom. But the sunshine, somehow or other, found its way between the interstices of the clouds, and illuminated some of the distant objects very vividly. The white sails of a ship caught it, and gleamed brilliant as sunny snow, the hull being scarcely visible, and the sea around dark; other smaller vessels too, so that they looked like heavenly-winged things, just alighting on a dismal world. Shifting their sails, perhaps, or going on another tack, they almost disappear at once in the obscure distance. Islands are seen in summer sunshine and green glory; their rocks also sunny and their beaches white; while other islands, for no apparent reason, are in deep shade, and share the gloom of the rest of the world. Sometimes part of an island is illuminated and part dark. When the sunshine falls on a very distant island, nearer ones being in shade, it seems greatly to extend the bounds of visible space, and put the horizon to a farther distance. The sea roughly rushing against the shore, and dashing against the rocks, and grating back over the sands. A boat a little way from the shore, tossing and swinging at anchor. Beach birds flitting from place to place.

The family seat of the Hawthornes is Wigcastle, Wigton, Wiltshire. The present head of the family, now residing there, is Hugh Hawthorne. William Hawthorne, who came over in 1635–36, was a younger brother of the family.

A young man and girl meet together, each in search of a person to be known by some particular sign. They watch and wait a great while for that person to pass. At last some casual circumstance discloses that each is the one that the other is waiting for. Moral,—that what we need for our happiness is often close at hand, if we knew but how to seek for it.

The journal of a human heart for a single day in ordinary circumstances. The lights and shadows that flit across it; its internal vicissitudes.

Distrust to be thus exemplified: Various good and desirable things to be presented to a young man, and offered to his acceptance,—as a friend, a wife, a fortune; but he to refuse them all, suspecting that it is merely a delusion. Yet all to be real, and he to be told so, when too late.

A man tries to be happy in love; he cannot sincerely give his heart, and the affair seems all a dream. In domestic life, the same; in politics, a seeming patriot; but still he is sincere, and all seems like a theatre.

An old man, on a summer day, sits on a hill-top, or on the observatory of his house, and sees the sun's light pass from one object to another connected with the events of his past life,—as the school-house, the place where his wife lived in her maidenhood,—its setting beams falling on the churchyard.

An idle man's pleasures and occupations and thoughts during a day spent by the sea-shore: among them, that of sitting on the top of a cliff, and throwing stones at his own shadow, far below.

A blind man to set forth on a walk through ways unknown to him, and to trust to the guidance of anybody who will take the trouble; the different characters who would undertake it: some mischievous, some well-meaning, but incapable; perhaps one blind man undertakes to lead another. At last, possibly, he rejects all guidance, and blunders on by himself.

In the cabinet of the Essex Historical Society, old portraits.—Governor Leverett; a dark mustachioed face, the figure two thirds length, clothed in a sort of frock-coat, buttoned, and a broad sword-belt girded round the waist, and fastened with a large steel buckle; the hilt of the sword steel,—altogether very striking. Sir William Pepperell, in English regimentals, coat, waistcoat, and breeches, all of red broad-cloth, richly gold-embroidered; he holds a general's truncheon in his right hand, and extends the left towards the batteries erected against Louisbourg, in the country near which he is standing. Endicott, Pyncheon, and others, in scarlet robes, bands, etc. Half a dozen or more family portraits of the Olivers, some in plain dresses, brown, crimson, or claret; others with gorgeous gold-embroidered waistcoats, descending almost to. the knees, so as to form the most conspicuous article of dress. Ladies, with lace ruffles, the painting of which, in one of the pictures, cost five guineas. Peter Oliver, who was crazy, used to fight with these family pictures in the old Mansion House; and the face and breast of one lady bear cuts and stabs inflicted by him. Miniatures in oil, with the paint peeling off, of stern, old, yellow faces. Oliver Cromwell, apparently an old picture, half length, or one third, in an oval frame, probably painted for some New England partisan. Some pictures that had been partly obliterated by scrubbing with sand. The dresses, embroidery, laces of the Oliver family are generally better done than the faces. Governor Leverett's gloves,—the glove part of coarse leather, but round the wrist a deep, three or four inch border of spangles and silver embroidery. Old drinking-glasses, with tall stalks. A black glass bottle, stamped with the name of Philip

English, with a broad bottom. The baby-linen, etc., of Governor Bradford of Plymouth County. Old manuscript sermons, some written in short-hand, others in a hand that seems learnt from print.

Nothing gives a stronger idea of old worm-eaten aristocracy—of a family being crazy with age, and of its being time that it was extinct—than these black, dusty, faded, antique-dressed portraits, such as those of the Oliver family; the identical old white wig of an ancient minister producing somewhat the impression that his very scalp, or some other portion of his personal self, would do.

The excruciating agonies which Nature inflicts on men (who break her laws) to be represented as the work of human tormentors; as the gout, by screwing the toes. Thus we might find that worse than the tortures of the Spanish Inquisition are daily suffered without exciting notice.

Suppose a married couple fondly attached to one another, and to think that they lived solely for one another; then it to be found out that they were divorced, or that they might separate if they chose. What would be its effect?

Monday, August 27th.—Went to Boston last Wednesday. Remarkables:—An author at the American Stationers' Company, slapping his hand on his manuscript, and crying, "I'm going to publish."—An excursion aboard a steamboat to Thompson's Island, to visit the Manual Labor School for boys. Aboard the steamboat several poets and various other authors; a Commodore,—Colton, a small, dark brown, sickly man, with a good deal of roughness in his address; Mr. Waterston, talking poetry and philosophy. Examination and exhibition of the boys, little tanned agriculturists. After examination, a stroll round the island, examining the products, as wheat in sheaves on the stubble-field; oats, somewhat blighted and spoiled; great pumpkins elsewhere; pastures; mowing ground;—all cultivated by the boys. Their residence, a great brick building, painted green, and standing on the summit of a rising ground, exposed to the winds of the bay. Vessels flitting past; great ships, with intricacy of rigging and various sails; schooners, sloops, with their one or two broad sheets of canvas: going on different tacks, so that the spectator might think that there was a different wind for each vessel, or that they scudded across the sea spontaneously, whither their own wills led them. The farm boys remain insulated, looking at the passing show, within sight of the city, yet having nothing to do with it; beholding their fellow-creatures skimming by them in winged machines, and steamboats snorting and puffing through the waves. Methinks an island would be the most desirable of all landed property, for it seems like a little world by itself; and the water may answer instead of the atmosphere that surrounds planets. The boys swinging, two together, standing up, and almost causing the ropes and their bodies to stretch out horizontally. On our departure, they ranged themselves on the rails of the fence, and, being dressed in blue, looked not unlike a flock of pigeons.

On Friday, a visit to the Navy Yard at Charlestown, in company with the Naval Officer of Boston, and Cilley. Dined aboard the revenue-cutter Hamilton. A pretty cabin, finished off with bird's-eye maple and mahogany; two looking-glasses. Two officers in blue frocks, with a stripe of lace on each shoulder. Dinner, chowder, fried fish, corned beef,—claret, afterwards champagne. The waiter tells the Captain of the cutter that Captain Percival (Commander of the Navy Yard) is sitting on the deck of the anchor hoy (which lies inside of the cutter), smoking his cigar.

The captain sends him a glass of champagne, and inquires of the waiter what Percival says of it. "He said, sir, 'What does he send me this damned stuff for?' but drinks, nevertheless." The Captain characterizes Percival as the roughest old devil that ever was in his manners, but a kind, good-hearted man at bottom. By and by comes in the steward. "Captain Percival is coming aboard of you, sir." "Well, ask him to walk down into the cabin"; and shortly down comes old Captain Percival, a white-haired, thin-visaged, weather-worn old gentleman, in a blue, Quaker-cut coat, with tarnished lace and brass buttons, a pair of drab pantaloons, and brown waistcoat. There was an eccentric expression in his face, which seemed partly wilful, partly natural. He has not risen to his present rank in the regular line of the profession; but entered the navy as a sailing-master, and has all the roughness of that class of officers. Nevertheless, he knows how to behave and to talk like a gentleman. Sitting down, and taking in hand a glass of champagne, he began a lecture on economy, and how well it was that Uncle Sam had a broad back, being compelled to bear so many burdens as were laid on it,—alluding to the table covered with wine-bottles. Then he spoke of the fitting up of the cabin with expensive woods,—of the brooch in Captain Scott's bosom. Then he proceeded to discourse of politics, taking the opposite side to Cilley, and arguing with much pertinacity. He seems to have moulded and shaped himself to his own whims, till a sort of rough affectation has become thoroughly imbued throughout a kindly nature. He is full of antique prejudices against the modern fashions of the younger officers, their mustaches and such fripperies, and prophesies little better than disgrace in case of another war; owning that the boys would fight for their country, and die for her, but denying that there are any officers now like Hull and Stewart, whose exploits, nevertheless, he greatly depreciated, saying that the Boxer and Enterprise fought the only equal battle which we won during the war; and that, in that action, an officer had proposed to haul down the Stars and Stripes, and a common sailor threatened to cut him to pieces if he should do so. He spoke of Bainhridge as a sot and a poltroon, who wanted to run from the Macedonian, pretending to take her for a line-of-battle ship: of Commodore. Elliot as a liar; but praised Commodore Downes in the highest terms. Percival seems to be the very pattern of old integrity; taking as much care of Uncle Sam's interests as if all the money expended were to come out of his own pocket. This quality was displayed in his resistance to the demand of a new patent capstan for the revenue-cutter, which, however, Scott, is resolved in such a sailor-like way to get, that he will probably succeed. Percival spoke to me of how his business in the yard absorbed him, especially the fitting of the Columbus, Seventy-four, of which ship he discoursed with great enthusiasm. He seems to have no ambition beyond his present duties, perhaps never had any; at any rate, he now passes his life with a sort of gruff contentedness, grumbling and growling, yet in good humor enough. He is conscious of his peculiarities: for when I asked him whether it would be well to make a naval officer Secretary of the Navy, he said, "God forbid, for that an old sailor was always full of prejudices and stubborn whim-whams," instancing himself; whereto I agreed. We went round the Navy Yard with Percival and Commodore Downes, the latter a sailor and a gentleman too, with rather more of the ocean than the drawing-room about him, but courteous, frank, and good-natured. We looked at rope-walks, rigging-lofts, ships in the stocks; and saw the sailors of the station laughing and sporting with great mirth and cheerfulness, which the Commodore said was much increased at sea. We returned to the wharf at Boston in the cutter's boat. Captain Scott, of the cutter, told me a singular story of what occurred during the action between the Constitution and Macedonian,—he being powder-monkey aboard the former ship. A cannon-shot came through the ship's side, and a man's head was struck off, probably by a splinter, for it was done without bruising the head or body, as clean as by a razor. Well, the man was walking pretty briskly at the time of the accident; and Scott seriously affirmed that he kept walking onward at the same pace, with two jets of blood gushing from his headless trunk, till, after going about twenty feet without a head, he sunk down at once, with his legs under him.

[In corroboration of the truth of this, see Lord Bacon. Century IV. of his "Sylva Sylvarum," or Natural History, in Ten Centuries, paragraph 400.]

On Saturday, I called to see E. H—, having previously appointed a meeting for the purpose of inquiring about our name. He is an old bachelor, and truly forlorn. The pride of ancestry seems to be his great hobby. He had a good many old papers in his desk at the Custom House, which he produced and dissertated upon. and afterwards went with me to his sister's, and showed me an old book, with a record of the children of the first emigrant (who came over two hundred years ago), in his own handwriting. E—'s manners are gentlemanly, and he seems to be very well informed. At a little distance, I think, one would take him to be not much over thirty; but nearer at hand one finds him to look rather venerable,—perhaps fifty or more. He is nervous, and his hands shook while he was looking over the papers, as if he had been startled by my visit; and when we came to the crossings of streets, he darted across, cautioning me, as if both were in great danger to be run over. Nevertheless, being very quick-tempered, he would face the Devil if at all irritated. He gave a most forlorn description of his life; how, when he came to Salem, there was nobody except Mr. — whom he cared about seeing; how his position prevented him from accepting of civilities, because he had no home where he could return them; in short, he seemed about as miserable a being as is to be found anywhere,—lonely, and with sensitiveness to feel his loneliness, and capacities, now withered, to have enjoyed the sweets of life. I suppose he is comfortable enough when busied in his duties at the Custom House; for when I spoke to him at my entrance, he was too much absorbed to hear me at first. As we walked, he kept telling stories of the family, which seemed to have comprised many oddities, eccentric men and women, recluses and other kinds,—one of old Philip English (a Jersey man, the name originally L'Anglais), who had been persecuted by John Hawthorne, of witch-time memory, and a violent quarrel ensued. When Philip lay on his death-bed, he consented to forgive his persecutor; "But if I get well," said he, "I'll be damned if I forgive him!" This Philip left daughters, one of whom married, I believe, the son of the persecuting John, and thus all the legitimate blood of English is in our family. E— passed from the matters of birth, pedigree, and ancestral pride to give vent to the most arrant democracy and locofocoism that I ever happened to hear, saying that nobody ought to possess wealth longer than his own life, and that then it should return to the people, etc. He says S. I— has a great fund of traditions about the family, which she learned from her mother or grandmother (I forget which), one of them being a Hawthorne. The old lady was a very proud woman, and, as E— says, "proud of being proud," and so is S. I—.

October 7th.—A walk in Northfields in the afternoon. Bright sunshine and autumnal warmth, giving a sensation quite unlike the same degree of warmth in summer. Oaks,—some brown, some reddish, some still green; walnuts, yellow,—fallen leaves and acorns lying beneath; the footsteps crumple them in walking. In sunny spots beneath the trees, where green grass is overstrewn by the dry, fallen foliage, as I passed, I disturbed multitudes of grasshoppers basking in the warm sunshine; and they began to hop, hop, hop, pattering on the dry leaves like big and heavy drops of a thunder-shower. They were invisible till they hopped. Boys gathering walnuts. Passed an orchard, where two men were gathering the apples. A wagon, with barrels, stood among the trees; the men's coats flung on the fence; the apples lay in heaps, and each of the men was up in a separate tree. They conversed together in loud voices, which the air caused to ring still louder, jeering each other, boasting of their own feats in shaking down the apples. One got into the very top of his tree, and gave a long and mighty shake, and the big apples came down thump, thump, bushels hitting on the ground at once. "There! did you ever hear anything like that?" cried he. This sunny scene was pretty. A horse feeding apart, belonging to the wagon. The barberry-bushes have some red fruit on them, but they are frost-bitten. The rose-bushes have their scarlet hips.

Distant clumps of trees, now that the variegated foliage adorns them, have a phantasmagorian, an apparition-like appearance. They seem to be of some kindred to the crimson and gold cloud-islands. It would not be strange to see phantoms peeping forth from their recesses. When the sun was almost below the horizon, his rays, gilding the upper branches of a yellow walnut-tree, had an airy and beautiful effect,—the gentle contrast between the tint of the yellow in the shade and its ethereal gold in the fading sunshine. The woods that crown distant uplands were seen to great advantage in these last rays, for the sunshine perfectly marked out and distinguished every shade of color, varnishing them as it were; while the country round, both hill and plain, being in gloomy shadow, the woods looked the brighter for it.

The tide, being high, had flowed almost into the Cold Spring, so its small current hardly issued forth from the basin. As I approached, two little eels, about as long as my finger, and slender in proportion, wriggled out of the basin. They had come from the salt water. An Indian-corn field, as yet unharvested,—huge, golden pumpkins scattered among the hills of corn,—a noble-looking fruit. After the sun was down, the sky was deeply dyed with a broad sweep of gold, high towards the zenith; not flaming brightly, but of a somewhat dusky gold. A piece of water, extending towards the west, between high banks, caught the reflection, and appeared like a sheet of brighter and more glistening gold than the sky which made it bright.

Dandelions and blue flowers are still growing in sunny places. Saw in a barn a prodigious treasure of onions in their silvery coats, exhaling a penetrating perfume.

How exceeding bright looks the sunshine, casually reflected from a looking-glass into a gloomy region of the chamber, distinctly marking out the figures and colors of the paper-hangings, which are scarcely seen elsewhere. It is like the light of mind thrown on an obscure subject.

Man's finest workmanship, the closer you observe it, the more imperfections it shows; as in a piece of polished steel a microscope will discover a rough surface. Whereas, what may look coarse and rough in Nature's workmanship will show an infinitely minute perfection, the closer you look into it. The. reason of the minute superiority of Nature's work over man's is, that the former works from the innermost germ, while the latter works merely superficially.

Standing in the cross-road that leads by the Mineral Spring, and looking towards an opposite shore of the lake, an ascending bank, with a dense border of trees, green, yellow, red, russet, all bright colors, brightened by the mild brilliancy of the .descending sun; it was strange to recognize the sober old friends of spring and summer in this new dress. By the by, a pretty riddle or fable might be made out of the changes in apparel of the familiar trees round a house adapted for children. But in the lake, beneath the aforesaid border of trees,—the water being not rippled, but its grassy surface somewhat moved and shaken by the remote agitation of a breeze that was breathing on the outer lake,—this being in a sort of bay,—in the slightly agitated mirror, the variegated trees were reflected dreamily and indistinctly; a broad belt of bright and diversified colors shining in the water beneath. Sometimes the image of a tree might be almost traced; then nothing but this sweep of broken rainbow. It was like the recollection of the real scene in an observer's mind,—a confused radiance.

A whirlwind, whirling the dried leaves round in a circle, not very violently.

To well consider the characters of a family of persons in a certain condition,—in poverty, for instance,—and endeavor to judge how an altered condition would affect the character of each.

The aromatic odor of peat-smoke in the sunny autumnal air is very pleasant.

Salem, October 14th.—A walk through Beverly to Browne's Hill, and home by the iron-factory. A bright, cool afternoon. The trees, in a large part of the space through which I passed, appeared to be in their fullest glory, bright red, yellow, some of a tender green, appearing at a distance as if bedecked with new foliage, though this emerald tint was likewise the effect of frost. In some places, large tracts of ground were covered as with a scarlet cloth,—the underbrush being thus colored. The general character of these autumnal colors is not gaudy, scarcely gay; there is something too deep and rich in it: it is gorgeous and magnificent, but with a sobriety diffused. The pastures at the foot of Browne's Hill were plentifully covered with barberry-bushes, the leaves of which were reddish, and they were hung with a prodigious quantity of berries. From the summit of the hill, looking down a tract of woodland at a considerable distance, so that the interstices between the trees could not be seen, their tops presented an unbroken level, and seemed somewhat like a richly variegated carpet. The prospect from the hill is wide and interesting; but methinks it is pleasanter in the more immediate vicinity of the hill than miles away. It is agreeable to look down at the square patches of cornfield, or of potato-ground, or of cabbages still green, or of beets looking red,—all a man's farm, in short,—each portion of which he considers separately so important, while you take in the whole at a glance. Then to cast your eye over so many different establishments at once and rapidly compare them,—here a house of gentility, with shady old yellow-leaved elms hanging around it; there a new little white dwelling; there an old farm-house; to see the barns and sheds and all the out-houses clustered together; to comprehend the oneness and exclusiveness and what constitutes the peculiarity of each of so many establishments, and to have in your mind a multitude of them, each of which is the most important part of the world to those who live in it,—this really enlarges the mind, and you come down the hill somewhat wiser than you go up. Pleasant to look over an orchard far below, and see the trees, each casting its own shadow; the white spires of meetinghouses; a sheet of water, partly seen among swelling lands. This Browne's Hill is a long ridge, lying in the midst of a large, level plain; it looks at a distance somewhat like a whale, with its head and tail under water, but its immense back protruding, with steep sides, and a gradual curve along its length. When you have climbed it on one side, and gaze from the summit at the other, you feel as if you had made a discovery,—the landscape being quite different on the two sides. The cellar of the house which formerly crowned the hill, and used to be named Browne's Folly, still remains, two grass-grown and shallow hollows, on the highest part of the ridge. The house consisted of two wings, each perhaps sixty feet in length, united by a middle part, in which was the entrance-hall, and which looked lengthwise along the hill. The foundation of a spacious porch may be traced on either side of the central portion; some of the stones still remain; but even where they are gone, the line of the porch is still traceable by the greener verdure. In the cellar, or rather in the two cellars, grow one or two barberry-bushes, with frost-bitten fruit: there is also yarrow with its white flower, and yellow dandelions. The cellars are still deep enough to shelter a person, all but his head at least, from the wand on the summit of the hill; but they are all grass-grown. A line of trees seems to have been planted along the ridge of the hill. The edifice must have made quite a magnificent appearance.

Characteristics during the walk:—Apple-trees with only here and there an apple on the boughs, among the thinned leaves, the relics of a gathering:. In others you observe a rustling, and see the boughs shaking and hear the apples thumping down, without seeing the person who does it. Apples scattered by the wayside, some with pieces bitten out, others entire, which you pick up and taste, and rind them harsh, crabbed cider-apples, though they have a pretty, waxen appearance. In sunny spots of woodland, boys in search of nuts, looking picturesque among the scarlet and golden foliage. There is something in this sunny autumnal atmosphere that gives a peculiar effect to laughter and joyous voices,—it makes them infinitely more elastic and gladsome than at other seasons. Heaps of dry leaves tossed together by the wind, as if for a couch and lounging-place for the weary traveller, while the sun is warming it for him. Golden pumpkins and squashes, heaped in the angle of a house till they reach the lower windows. Ox-teams, laden with a rustling load of Indian corn, in the stalk and ear. When an inlet of the sea runs far up into the country, you stare to see a large schooner appear amid the rural landscape; she is unloading a cargo of wood, moist with rain or salt water that has dashed over it. Perhaps you hear the sound of an axe in the woodland; occasionally, the report of a fowling-piece. The travellers in the early part of the afternoon look warm and comfortable as if taking a, summer drive; but as eve draws nearer, you meet them well wrapped in topcoats or cloaks, or rough, great surtouts, and red-nosed withal, seeming to take no great comfort, but pressing homeward. The characteristic conversation among teamsters and country squires, where the ascent of a hill causes the chaise to go at the same pace as an ox-team,—perhaps discussing the qualities of a yoke of oxen. The cold, blue aspects of sheets of water. Some of the country shops with the doors closed: others still open as in summer. I meet a wood-sawyer, with his horse and saw on his shoulders, returning from work.

As night draws on, you begin to see the gleaming of fires on the ceilings in the houses which you pass. The comfortless appearance of houses at bleak and bare spots,—you wonder how there can be any enjoyment in them. I meet a girl in a chintz gown, with a small shawl on her shoulders, white stockings, and summer morocco shoes,—it looks observable. Turkeys, queer, solemn objects, in black attire, grazing about, and trying to peck the fallen apples, which slip away from their bills.

October 16th.—Spent the whole afternoon in a ramble to the sea-shore, near Phillips's Beach. A beautiful, warm, sunny afternoon, the very pleasant-est day, probably, that there has been in the whole course of the year. People at work, harvesting, without their coats. Cocks, with their squad of hens, in the grass-fields, hunting grasshoppers, chasing them eagerly with outspread wings, appearing to take much interest in the sport, apart from the profit. Other hens picking up the ears of Indian corn. Grasshoppers, flies, and flying insects of all sorts are more abundant in these warm autumnal days than I have seen them at any other time. Yellow butterflies flutter about in the sunshine, singly, by pairs, or more, and are wafted on the gentle gales. The crickets begin to sing early in the afternoon, and sometimes a locust may be heard. In some warm spots, a pleasant buzz of many insects.

Crossed the fields near Brookhouse's villa, and came upon a long beach,—at least a mile long, I should think,—terminated by craggy rocks at either end, and backed by a high broken bank, the grassy summit of which, year by year, is continually breaking away, and precipitated to the bottom. At the foot of the bank, in some parts, is a vast number of pebbles and paving-stones, rolled up thither by the sea long ago. The beach is of a brown sand, with hardly any pebbles intermixed upon it. When the tide is part way down, there is a margin of several yards from the water's edge, along the whole mile length of the beach, which glistens like a mirror, and reflects objects, and shines bright in the sunshine, the sand being wet to that distance from the water. Above this margin the sand is not wet, and grows less and less damp the farther towards the bank you keep. In some places your footstep is perfectly implanted, showing the whole shape, and the square toe, and every nail in the heel of your boot. Elsewhere, the impression is imperfect, and even when you stamp, you cannot imprint the whole. As you tread, a dry spot flashes around your step, and grows moist as you lift your foot again. Pleasant to pass along this extensive walk, watching the surf-wave;—how sometimes it seems to make a feint of breaking, but dies away ineffectually, merely kissing the strand; then, after many such abortive efforts, it gathers itself, and forms a high wall, and rolls onward, heightening and heightening without foam at the summit of the green line, and at last throws itself fiercely on the beach, with a loud roar, the spray flying above. As you walk along, you are preceded by a flock of twenty or thirty beach birds, which are seeking, I suppose, for food on the margin of the surf, yet seem to be merely sporting, chasing the sea as it retires, and running up before the impending wave. Sometimes they let it bear them off their feet, and float lightly on its breaking summit; sometimes they flutter and seem to rest on the feathery spray. They are little birds with gray backs and snow-white breasts; their images may be seen in the wet sand almost or quite as distinctly as the reality. Their legs are long. As you draw near, they take a flight of a score of yards or more, and then recommence their dalliance with the surf-wave. You may behold their multitudinous little tracks all along your way. Before you reach the end of the beach, you become quite attached to these little sea-birds, and take much interest in their occupations. After passing in one direction, it is pleasant then to retrace your footsteps. Your tracks being all traceable, you may recall the whole mood and occupation of your mind during your first passage. Here you turned somewhat aside to pick up a shell that you saw nearer the water's edge. Here you examined a long sea-weed, and trailed its length after you for a considerable distance. Here the effect of the wide sea struck you suddenly. Here you fronted the ocean, looking at a sail, distant in the sunny blue. Here you looked at some plant on the bank. Here some vagary of mind seems to have bewildered you; for your tracks go round and round, and interchange each other without visible reason. Here you picked up pebbles and skipped them upon the water. Here you wrote names and drew faces with a razor sea-shell in the sand.

After leaving the beach, clambered over crags, all shattered and tossed about everyhow; in some parts curiously worn and hollowed out, almost into caverns. The rock, shagged with sea-weed,—in some places, a thick carpet of sea-weed laid over the pebbles, into which your foot would sink. Deep tanks among these rocks, which the sea replenishes at high tide, and then leaves the bottom all covered with various sorts of sea-plants, as if it were some sea-monster's private garden. I saw a crab in one of them; five-fingers too. From the edge of the rocks, you may look off into deep, deep water, even at low tide. Among the rocks, I found a great bird, whether a wild-goose, a loon, or an albatross, I scarcely know. It was in such a position that I almost fancied it might be asleep, and therefore drew near softly, lest it should take flight; but it was dead, and stirred not when I touched it. Sometimes a dead fish was cast up. A ledge of rocks, with a beacon upon it, looking like a monument erected to those who have perished by shipwreck. The smoked, extempore fire-place, where a party cooked their fish. About midway on the beach, a fresh-water brooklet flows towards the sea. Where it leaves the land, it is quite a rippling little current; but, in flowing across the sand, it grows shallower and more shallow, and at last is quite lost, and dies in the effort to carry its little tribute to the main.

An article to be made of telling the stories of the tiles of an old-fashioned chimney-piece to a child.

A person conscious that he was soon to die, the humor in which he would pay his last visit to familiar persons and things.

A description of the various classes of hotels and taverns, and the prominent personages in each. There should be some story connected with it,—as of a person commencing with boarding at a great hotel, and gradually, as his means grew less, descending in life, till he got below ground into a cellar.

A person to be in the possession of something as perfect as mortal man has a right to demand; he tries to make it better, and ruins it entirely.

A person to spend all his life and splendid talents in trying to achieve something naturally impossible,—as to make a conquest over Nature.

Meditations about the main gas-pipe of a great city,—if the supply were to be stopped, what would happen? How many different scenes it sheds light on? It might be made emblematical of something.

December 6th.—A fairy tale about chasing Echo to her hiding-place. Echo is the voice of a reflection in a mirror.

A house to be built over a natural spring of inflammable gas, and to be constantly illuminated therewith. What moral could be drawn from this? It is carburetted hydrogen gas, and is cooled from a soft shale or slate, which is sometimes bituminous, and contains more or less carbonate of lime. It appears in the vicinity of Lockport and Niagara Falls, and elsewhere in New York. I believe it indicates coal. At Fredonia, the whole village is lighted by it. Elsewhere, a farm-house was lighted by it, and no other fuel used in the coldest weather.

Gnomes, or other mischievous little fiends, to be represented as burrowing in the hollow teeth of some person who has subjected himself to their power. It should be a child's story. This should be one of many modes of petty torment. They should be contrasted with beneficent fairies, who minister to the pleasures of the good.

A man will undergo great toil and hardship for ends that must be many years distant,—as wealth or fame,—but none for an end that may be close at hand,—as the joys of heaven.

Insincerity in a man's own heart must make all his enjoyments, all that concerns him, unreal; so that his whole life must seem like a merely dramatic representation. And this would be the case, even though he were surrounded by true-hearted relatives and friends.

A company of men, none of whom have anything worth hoping for on earth, yet who do not look forward to anything beyond earth!

Sorrow to be personified, and its effect on a family represented by the way in which the members of the family regard this dark-clad and sad-browed inmate.

A story to show how we are all wronged and wrongers, and avenge one another.

To personify winds of various characters.

A man living a wicked life in one place, and simultaneously a virtuous and religious one in another.

An ornament to be worn about the person of a lady,—as a jewelled heart. After many years, it happens to be broken or unscrewed, and a poisonous odor comes out.

Lieutenant F. W— of the navy was an inveterate duellist and an unerring shot. He had taken offence at Lieutenant F—, and endeavored to draw him into a duel, following him to the Mediterranean for that purpose, and harassing him intolerably. At last, both parties being in Massachusetts, F— determined to fight, and applied to Lieutenant A— to be his second. A— examined into the merits of the quarrel, and came to the conclusion that F— had not given F. W— justifiable cause for driving him to a duel, and that he ought not to be shot. He instructed F— in the use of the pistol, and, before the meeting, warned him, by all means, to get the first fire; for that, if F. W— fired first, he, F—, was infallibly a dead man, as his antagonist could shoot to a hair's-breadth. The parties met; and F—, firing immediately on the word's being given, shot F. W-through the heart. F. W—, with a most savage expression of countenance, fired, after the bullet had gone through his heart, and when the blood had entirely left his face, and shot away one of F—'s side-locks. His face probably looked as if he were already in the infernal regions; but afterwards it assumed an angelic calmness and repose.

A company of persons to drink a certain medicinal preparation, which would prove a poison, or the contrary, according to their different characters.

Many persons, without a consciousness of so doing, to contribute to some one end; as to a beggar's feast, made up of broken victuals from many tables; or a patch carpet, woven of shreds from innumerable garments.

Some very famous jewel or other thing, much talked of all over the world. Some person to meet with it, and get possession of it in some unexpected manner, amid homely circumstances.

To poison a person or a party of persons with the sacramental wine.

A cloud in the shape of an old woman kneeling, with arms extended towards the moon.

On being transported to strange scenes, we feel as if all were unreal. This is but the perception of the true unreality of earthly things, made evident by the want of congruity between ourselves and them. By and by we become mutually adapted, and the perception is lost.

An old looking-glass. Somebody finds out the secret of making all the images that have been reflected in it pass back again across its surface.

Our Indian races having reared no monuments, like the Greeks, Romans, and Egyptians, when they have disappeared from the earth their history will appear a fable, and they misty phantoms.

A woman to sympathize with all emotions, but to have none of her own.

A portrait of a person in New England to be recognized as of the same person represented by a portrait in Old England. Having distinguished himself there, he had suddenly vanished, and had never been heard of till he was thus discovered to be identical with a distinguished man in New England.

Men of cold passions have quick eyes.

A virtuous but giddy girl to attempt to play a trick on a man. He sees what she is about, and contrives matters so that she throws herself completely into his power, and is ruined,—all in jest.

A letter, written a century or more ago, but which has never yet been unsealed.

A partially insane man to believe himself the Provincial Governor or other great official of Massachusetts. The scene might be the Province House.

A dreadful secret to be communicated to several people of various characters,—grave or gay. and they all to become insane, according to their characters, by the influence of the secret.

Stories to be told of a certain person's appearance in public, of his having been seen in various situations, and of his making visits in private circles; but finally, on looking for this person, to come upon his old grave and mossy tombstone.

The influence of a peculiar mind, in close communion with another, to drive the latter to insanity.

To look at a beautiful girl, and picture all the lovers, in different situations, whose hearts are centred upon her.

May 11, 1838.—At Boston last week. Items:—A young man, with a small mustache, dyed brown, reddish from its original light color. He walks with an affected gait, his arms crooked outwards, treading much on his toes. His conversation is about, the theatre, where he has a season ticket,—about, an amateur who lately appeared there, and about, actresses, with other theatrical scandal.—In the smoking-room, two checker and backgammon boards: the landlord a great player, seemingly a stupid man, but, with considerable shrewdness and knowledge of the world.—F—, the comedian, a, stout, heavy-looking Englishman, of grave deportment, with no signs of wit or humor, yet, aiming at both in conversation, in order to support his character. Very steady and regular in his life, and parsimonious in his disposition,—worth $50,000, made by his profession.—A clergyman, elderly, with a white neck-cloth, very unbecoming, an unworldly manner, unacquaintance with the customs of the house, and learning them in a childlike way. A ruffle to his shirt, crimped.—A gentleman, young, handsome, and sea-flushed, belonging to Oswego, New York, but just, arrived in port, from the Mediterranean: he inquires of me about the troubles in Canada, which were first beginning to make a noise when he left the country,—whether they are all over. I tell him all is finished, except the hanging of the prisoners. Then we talk over the matter, and I tell him the fates of the principal men,—some banished to New South Wales, one hanged, others in prison, others, conspicuous at first, now almost forgotten.—Apartments of private families in the hotel,—what sort of domesticity there may be in them; eating in public, with no board of their own. The gas that lights the rest of the house lights them also, in the chandelier from the ceiling.—A shabby-looking man, quiet, with spectacles, at first wearing an old, coarse brown frock, then appearing in a suit of elderly black, saying nothing unless spoken to, but talking intelligently when addressed. He is an editor, and I suppose printer, of a country paper. Among the guests, he holds intercourse with gentlemen of much more respectable appearance than himself, from the same part of the country.—Bill of fare; wines printed on the back, but nobody calls for a bottle. Chairs turned down for expected guests. Three-pronged steel forks. Cold supper from nine to eleven p.m. Great, round, mahogany table, in the sitting-room, covered with papers. In the morning, before and soon after breakfast, gentlemen reading the morning papers, while others wait for their chance, or try to pick out something from the papers of yesterday or longer ago. In the forenoon, the Southern papers are brought in, and thrown damp and folded on the table. The eagerness with which those who happen to be in the room start up and make prize of them. Play-bills, printed on yellow paper, laid upon the table. Towards evening comes the "Transcript."

June 15th.—The red light which the sunsets at this season diffuse; there being showery afternoons, but the sun setting bright amid clouds, and diffusing its radiance over those that are scattered in masses all over the sky. It gives a rich tinge to all objects, even to those of sombre hues, yet without changing the hues. The complexions of people are exceedingly enriched by it; they look warm, and kindled with a mild fire. The whole scenery and personages acquire, methinks, a passionate character. A love-scene should be laid on such an evening. The trees and the grass have now the brightest possible green, there having been so many showers alternating with such powerful sunshine. There are roses and tulips and honeysuckles, with their sweet perfume; in short, the splendor of a more gorgeous climate than ours might be brought into the picture.

The situation of a man in the midst of a crowd, yet as completely in the power of another, life and all, as if they two were in the deepest solitude.

Tremont, Boston, June 16th.—Tremendously hot weather to-day. Went on board the Cyane to see Bridge, the purser. Took boat from the end of Long Wharf, with two boatmen who had just landed a man. Row round to the starboard side of the sloop, where we pass up the steps, and are received by Bridge, who introduces us to one of the lieutenants,—Hazard. Sailors and midshipmen scattered about,—the middies having a foul anchor, that is, an anchor with a cable twisted round it, embroidered on the collars of their jackets. The officers generally wear blue jackets, with lace on the shoulders, white pantaloons, and cloth caps. Introduced into the cabin,—a handsome room, finished with mahogany, comprehending the width of the vessel; a sideboard with liquors, and above it a looking-glass; behind the cabin, an inner room, in which is seated a lady, waiting for the captain to come on board; on each side of this inner cabin, a large and convenient state-room with bed,—the doors opening into the cabin. This cabin is on a level with the quarter-deck, and is covered by the poop-deck. Going down below stairs, you come to the ward-room, a pretty large room, round which are the state-rooms of the lieutenants, the purser, surgeon, etc. A stationary table. The ship's main-mast comes down through the middle of the room, and Bridge's chair, at dinner, is planted against it. Wine and brandy produced; and Bridge calls to the Doctor to drink with him, who answers affirmatively from his state-room, and shortly after opens the door and makes his appearance. Other officers emerge from the side of the vessel, or disappear into it, in the same way. Forward of the wardroom, adjoining it, and on the same level, is the midshipmen's room, on the larboard side of the vessel, not partitioned off, so as to be shut up. On a shelf a few books; one midshipman politely invites us to walk in; another sits writing. Going farther forward, on the same level, we come to the crew's department, part of which is occupied by the cooking-establishment, where all sorts of cooking is going on for the officers and men. Through the whole of this space, ward-room and all, there is barely room to stand upright, without the hat on. The rules of the quarterdeck (which extends aft from the main-mast) are, that the midshipmen shall not presume to walk on the starboard side of it, nor the men to come upon it at all, unless to speak to an officer. The poop-deck is still more sacred,—the lieutenants being confined to the larboard side, and the captain alone having a right to the starboard. A marine was pacing the poop-deck, being the only guard that I saw stationed in the vessel,—the more stringent regulations being relaxed while she is preparing for sea. While standing on the quarter-deck, a great piping at the gangway, and the second cutter conies alongside, bringing the consul and some other gentleman to visit the vessel. After a while, we are rowed ashore with them, in the same boat. Its crew are new hands, and therefore require much instruction from the cockswain. We are seated under an awning. The guns of the Cyane are medium thirty-two pounders; some of them have percussion locks.

At the Tremont, I had Bridge to dine with me: iced champagne, claret in glass pitchers. Nothing very remarkable among the guests. A wine-merchant, French apparently, though he had arrived the day before in a bark from Copenhagen: a somewhat corpulent gentleman, without so good manners as an American would have in the same line of life, but good-natured, sociable, and civil, complaining of the heat. He had rings on his fingers of great weight of metal, and one of them had a seal for letters; brooches at the bosom, three in a row, up and down; also a gold watch-guard, with a seal appended. Talks of the comparative price of living, of clothes, etc., here and in Europe. Tells of the prices of wines by the cask and pipe. Champagne, he says, is drunk of better quality here than where it grows.—A vendor of patent medicines, Doctor Jaques, makes acquaintance with me, and shows me his recommendatory letters in favor of himself and drugs, signed by a long list of people. He prefers, he says, booksellers to druggists as his agents, and inquired of me about them in this town. He seems to be an honest man enough, with an intelligent face, and sensible in his talk, but not a gentleman, wearing a somewhat shabby brown coat and mixed pantaloons, being ill-shaven, and apparently not well acquainted with the customs of a fashionable hotel. A simplicity about him that is likable, though, I believe, he comes from Philadelphia. —Naval officers, strolling about town, bargaining for swords and belts, and other military articles; with the tailor, to have naval buttons put on their shore-going coats, and for their pantaloons, suited to the climate of the Mediterranean. It is the almost invariable habit of officers, when going ashore or staying on shore, to divest themselves of all military or naval insignia, and appear as private citizens. At the Tremont, young gentlemen with long earlocks,—straw hats, light, or dark-mixed. —The theatre being closed, the play-bills of many nights ago are posted up against its walls.

July 4th.—A very hot, bright, sunny day; town much thronged; booths on the Common, selling gingerbread, sugar-plums, and confectionery, spruce beer, lemonade. Spirits forbidden, but probably sold stealthily. On the top of one of the booths a monkey, with a tail two or three feet long. He is fastened by a cord, which, getting tangled with the flag over the booth, he takes hold and tries to free it. He is the object of much attention from the crowd, and played with by the boys, who toss up gingerbread to him, while he nibbles and throws it down again. He reciprocates notice, of some kind or other, with all who notice him. There is a sort of gravity about him. A boy pulls his long tail, whereat he gives a slight squeak, and for the future elevates it as much as possible. Looking at the same booth by and by, I find that the poor monkey has been obliged to betake himself to the top of one of the wooden joists that stick up high above. There are boys going about with molasses candy, almost melted down in the sun. Shows: A mammoth rat; a collection of pirates, murderers, and the like, in wax. Constables in considerable number, parading about with their staves, sometimes conversing with each other, producing an effect by their presence, without having to interfere actively. One or two old salts, rather the worse for liquor: in general the people are very temperate. At evening the effect of things rather more picturesque; some of the booth-keepers knocking down the temporary structures, and putting the materials in wagons to carry away: other booths lighted up, and the lights gleaming through rents in the sail-cloth tops. The customers are rather riotous, calling loudly and whimsically for what they want; a young fellow and a girl coming arm in arm; two girls approaching the booth, and getting into conversation with the folks thereabout. Perchance a knock-down between two half-sober fellows in the crowd: a knockdown without a heavy blow, the receiver being scarcely able to keep his footing at any rate. Shoutings and hallooings, laughter, oaths,—generally a good-natured tumult; and the constables use no severity, but interfere, if at all, in a friendly sort of way. I talk with one about the way in which the day has passed, and he bears testimony to the orderliness of the crowd, but suspects one booth of selling liquor, and relates one scuffle. There is a talkative and witty seller of gingerbread holding forth to the people from his cart, making himself quite a noted character by his readiness of remark and humor, and disposing of all his wares. Late in the evening, during the fire-works, people are consulting how they are to get home,—many having long miles to walk: a father, with wife and children, saying it will be twelve o'clock before they reach home, the children being already tired to death. The moon beautifully dark-bright, not giving so white a light as sometimes. The girls all look beautiful and fairy-like in it, not exactly distinct, nor yet dim. The different characters of female countenances during the day,—mirthful and mischievous, slyly humorous, stupid, looking genteel generally, but when they speak often betraying plebeianism by the tones of their voices. Two girls are very tired,—one a pale, thin, languid-looking creature; the other plump, rosy, rather overburdened with her own little body. Gingerbread figures, in the shape of Jim Crow and other popularities.

In the old burial ground, Charter Street, a slate gravestone, carved round the borders, to the memory of "Colonel John Hathorne, Esq.," who died in 1717. This was the witch-judge. The stone is sunk deep into the earth, and leans forward, and the grass grows very long around it; and, on account of the moss, it was rather difficult to make out the date. Other Hathornes lie buried in a range with him on either side. In a corner of the burial-ground, close under Dr. P—'s garden fence, are the most ancient stones remaining in the graveyard; moss-grown, deeply sunken. One to "Dr. John Swinnerton, Physician," in 1688; another to his wife. There, too, is the grave of Nathaniel Mather, the younger brother of Cotton, and mentioned in the Magnalia as a hard student, and of great promise. "An aged man at nineteen years," saith the gravestone. It affected me deeply, when I had cleared away the grass from the half-buried stone, and read the name. An apple-tree or two hang over these old graves, and throw down the blighted fruit on Nathaniel Mather's grave,—he blighted too. It gives strange ideas, to think how convenient to Dr. P—'s family this burial-ground is,—the monuments standing almost within arm's reach of the side windows of the parlor,—and there being a little gate from the back yard through which we step forth upon those old graves aforesaid. And the tomb of the P. family is right in front, and close to the gate. It is now filled, the last being the refugee Tory, Colonel P—, and his wife. M. P— has trained flowers over this tomb, on account of her friendly relations with Colonel P—.

It is not, I think, the most ancient families that have tombs,—their ancestry for two or three generations having been reposited in the earth before such a luxury as a tomb was thought of. Men who founded families, and grew rich, a century or so ago, were probably the first.

There is a tomb of the Lyndes, with a slab of slate affixed to the brick masonry on one side, and carved with a coat of arms.

July 10th.—A fishing excursion, last Saturday afternoon, eight or ten miles out in the harbor. A fine wind out, which died away towards evening, and finally became quite calm. We cooked our fish on a rock named "Satan," about forty feet long and twenty broad, irregular in its shape, and of uneven surface, with pools of water here and there, left by the tide,—dark brown rock, or whitish; there was the excrement of sea-fowl scattered on it, and a few feathers. The water was deep around the rock, and swelling up and downward, waving the sea-weed. We built two fires, which, as the dusk deepened, cast a red gleam over the rock and the waves, and made the sea, on the side away from the sunset, look dismal; but by and by up came the moon, red as a house afire, and, as it rose, it grew silvery bright, and threw a line of silver across the calm sea. Beneath the moon and the horizon, the commencement of its track of brightness, there was a cone of blackness, ear of very black blue. It was after nine before we finished our supper, which we ate by firelight and moonshine, and then went aboard our decked boat again,—no safe achievement in our ticklish little dory. To those remaining in the boat, we had looked very picturesque around our fires, and on the rock above them,—our statues being apparently increased to the, size of the. sons of Anak. The tide, now coming up, gradually dashed over the fires we had left, and so the rock again became a desert. The wind had now entirely died away, leaving the sea smooth as glass, except a quiet swell, and we could only float along, as the tide bore us, almost imperceptibly. It was as beautiful a night as ever shone,—calm, warm, bright, the moon being at full. On one side of us was Marblehead light-house, on the other, Baker's Island; and both, by the influence of the moonlight, had a silvery hue, unlike their ruddy beacon tinge in dark nights. They threw long reflections across the sea, like the moon. There we floated slowly with the tide till about midnight, and then, the tide turning, we fastened our vessel to a pole, which marked a rock, so as to prevent being: carried back by the reflux. Some of the passengers turned in below; some stretched themselves on deck; some walked about, smoking cigars. I kept the deck all night. Once there was a little cat's-paw of a breeze, whereupon we untied ourselves from the pole; but it almost immediately died away, and we were compelled to make fast again. At about two o"clock, up rose the morning-star, a round, red, fiery ball, very comparable to the moon at its rising, and, getting upward, it shone marvellously bright, and threw its long reflection into the sea, like the moon and the two lighthouses. It was Venus, and the brightest star I ever beheld; it was in the northeast. The moon made but a very small circuit in the sky, though it shone all night. The aurora borealis shot upwards to the zenith, and between two and three o'clock the first streak of dawn appeared, stretching far along the edge of the eastern horizon,—a faint streak of light; then it gradually broadened and deepened, and became a rich saffron tint, with violet above, and then an ethereal and transparent blue. The saffron became intermixed with splendor, kindling and kindling, Baker's Island lights being in the centre of the brightness, so that they were extinguished by it, or at lea-I grew invisible. On the other side of the boat, the Marblehead light-house still threw out its silvery gleam, and the moon shone brightly too, and its light looked very singularly, mingling with the growing daylight. It was not like the moonshine, brightening as the evening twilight deepens; for now it threw its radiance over the landscape, the green and other tints of which were displayed by the daylight, whereas at evening all those tints are obscured. It looked like a milder sunshine,—a dreamy sunshine,—the sunshine of a world not quite so real and material as this. All night we had heard the Marblehead clocks telling the hour. Anon, up came the sun, without any bustle, but quietly, his antecedent splendors having gilded the sea for some time before. It had been cold towards morning, but now grew warm, and gradually burning hot in the sun. A breeze sprang up, but our first use of it was to get aground on Coney Island about five o'clock, where we lay till nine or thereabout, and then floated slowly up to the wharf. The roar of distant surf, the rolling of porpoises, the passing of shoals of fish, a steamboat smoking along at a distance, were the scene on my watch. I fished during the night, and, feeling something on the line, I drew up with great eagerness and vigor. It was two of those broad-leaved sea-weeds, with stems like snakes, both rooted on a stone,—all which came up together. Often these sea-weeds root themselves on mussels. In the morning, our pilot killed a flounder with the boat-hook, the poor fish thinking himself secure on the bottom.

Ladurlad, in "The Curse of Kehama," on visiting a certain celestial region, the fire in his heart and brain died away for a season, but was rekindled again on returning to earth. So may it be with me in my projected three months' seclusion from old associations.

Punishment of a miser,—to pay the drafts of his heir in his tomb.

July 13th.—A show of wax-figures, consisting almost wholly of murderers and their victims,—Gibbs and Hansley, the pirates, and the Dutch girl whom Gibbs murdered. Gibbs and Hansley were admirably done, as natural as life; and many people who had known Gibbs would not, according to the showman, be convinced that this wax-figure was not his skin stuffed. The two pirates were represented with halters round their necks, just ready to be turned off; and the sheriff stood behind them, with his watch, waiting for the moment. The clothes, halter, and Gibbs's hair were authentic. E. K. Avery and Cornell,—the former a figure in black, leaning on the back of a chair, in the attitude of a clergyman about to pray; an ugly devil, said to be a good likeness. Ellen Jewett and R. P. Robinson, she dressed richly, in extreme fashion, and very pretty; he awkward and stiff, it being difficult to stuff a figure to look like a gentleman. The showman seemed very proud of Ellen Jewett, and spoke of her somewhat as if this wax-figure were a real creation. Strong and Mrs. Whipple, who together murdered the husband of the latter. Lastly the Siamese twins. The showman is careful to call his exhibition the "Statuary." He walks to and fro before the figures, talking of the history of the persons, the moral lessons to be drawn therefrom, and especially of the excellence of the wax-work. He has for sale printed histories of the personages. He is a friendly, easy-mannered sort of a half-genteel character, whose talk has been moulded by the persons who most frequent such a show; an air of superiority of information, a moral instructor, with a great deal of real knowledge of the world. He invites his departing guests to call again and bring their friends, desiring to know whether they are pleased; telling that he had a thousand people on the 4th of July, and that they were all perfectly satisfied. He talks with the female visitors, remarking on Ellen Jewett's person and dress to them, he having "spared no expense in dressing her; and all the ladies say that a dress never set better, and he thinks he never knew a handsomer female." He goes to and fro, snuffing the candles, and now and then holding one to the face of a favorite figure. Ever and anon, hearing steps upon the stair-case, he goes to admit a new visitor. The visitors,—a half-bumpkin, half country-squire-like man, who has something of a knowing air, and yet looks and listens with a good deal of simplicity and faith, smiling between whiles; a mechanic of the town; several decent-looking girls and women, who eye Ellen herself with more interest than the other figures,—women having much curiosity about such ladies; a gentlemanly sort of person, who looks somewhat ashamed of himself for being there, and glances at me knowingly, as if to intimate that he was conscious of being out of place; a boy or two, and myself, who examine wax faces and faces of flesh with equal interest. A political or other satire might be made by describing a show of wax-figures of the, prominent public men; and by the remarks of the showman and the spectators, their characters and public standing might be expressed. And the incidentof Judge Tyler as related by E— might be introduced.

A series of strange, mysterious, dreadful events to occur, wholly destructive of a person's happiness. He to impute them to various persons and causes, but ultimately finds that he is himself the sole agent. Moral, that our welfare depends on ourselves.

The strange incident in the court of Charles IX. of France: he and five other maskers being attired in coats of linen covered with pitch and bestuck with flax to represent hairy savages. They entered the hall dancing, the five being fastened together, and the king in front. By accident the five were set on fire with a torch. Two were burned to death on the spot, two afterwards died; one fled to the buttery, and jumped into a vessel of water. It might be represented as the fate of a squad of dissolute men.

A perception, for a moment, of one's eventual and moral self, as if it were another person,—the observant faculty being separated, and looking intently at the qualities of the character. There is a surprise when this happens,—this getting out of one's self,—and then the observer sees how queer a fellow he is.

July 11th.—Left home [Salem] on the 23d instant. To Boston by stage, and took the afternoon cars for Worcester. A little boy returning from the city, several miles, with a basket of empty custard-cups, the contents of which he had probably sold at the depot. Stopped at the Temperance House. An old gentleman, Mr. Phillips, of Boston, got into conversation with me, and inquired very freely as to my character, tastes, habits, and circumstances,—-a freedom sanctioned by his age, his kindly and beneficent spirit, and the wisdom of his advice. It is strange how little impertinence depends on what is actually said, but rather on the manner and motives of saying it. "I want to do you good," said he with warmth, after becoming, apparently, moved by my communications. "Well, sir," replied I, "I wish you could, for both our sakes; for I have no doubt it would be a great satisfaction to you." He asked the most direct questions of another young man; for instance, "Are you married?" having before ascertained that point with regard to myself. He told me by all means to *act,* in whatever way; observing that he himself would have no objection to be a servant, if no other mode of action presented itself.

The landlord of the tavern, a decent, active, grave, attentive personage, giving me several cards of his house to distribute on my departure. A judge, a stout, hearty country squire, looking elderly; a hale and rugged man, in a black coat, and thin, light pantaloons.

Started for Northampton at half past nine in the morning. A respectable sort of man and his son on their way to Niagara,—grocers, I believe, and calculating how to perform the tour, subtracting as few days as possible from the shop. Somewhat inexperienced travellers, and comparing everything advantageously or otherwise with Boston customs; and considering themselves a long way from home, while yet short of a hundred miles from it. Two ladies, rather good-looking. I rode outside nearly all day, and was very sociable with the driver and another outside passenger. Towards night, took up an essence-vendor for a short distance. He was returning home, after having been out on a tour two or three weeks, and nearly exhausted his stock. He was not exclusively an essence-pedlar, having a large tin box, which had been filled with dry goods, combs, jewelry, etc., now mostly sold out. His essences were of aniseseed, cloves, red-cedar, wormwood, together with opodeldoc, and an oil for the hair. These matters are concocted at Ashfield, and the pedlars are sent about with vast quantities. Cologne-water is among the essences manufactured, though the bottles have foreign labels on them. The pedlar was good-natured and communicative, and spoke very frankly about his trade, which he seemed to like better than farming, though his experience of it is yet brief. He spoke of the trials of temper to which pedlars are subjected, but said that it was necessary to be forbearing, because the same road must be travelled again and again. The pedlars find satisfaction for all contumelies in making good bargains out of their customers. This man was a pedlar in quite a small way, making but a narrow circuit, and carrying no more than an open basket full of essences; but some go out with wagon-loads. He himself contemplated a trip westward, in which case he would send on quantities of his wares ahead to different stations. He seemed to enjoy the intercourse and seeing of the world. He pointed out a rough place in the road, where his stock of essences had formerly been broken by a jolt of the stage. What a waste of sweet smells on the desert air! The essence-labels stated the efficacy of the stuffs for various complaints of children and grown people. The driver was an acquaintance of the pedlar, and so gave him his drive for nothing, though the pedlar pretended to wish to force some silver into his hand; and afterwards he got down to water the horses, while the driver was busied with Other matters. This driver was a little, dark ragamuffin, apparently of irascible temper, speaking with great disapprobation of his way-bill not being *timed* accurately, but so as to make it appear as if he were longer upon the road than he was. As he spoke, the blood darkened in his cheek, and his eye looked ominous and angry, as if he were enraged with the person to whom he was speaking; yet he had not real grit, for he had never said a word of his grievances to those concerned. "I mean to tell them of it by and by. I won't bear it more than three or four times more," said he.

Left Northampton the next morning, between one and two o'clock. Three other passengers, whose faces were not visible for some hours; so we went on through unknown space, saying nothing, glancing forth sometimes to see the gleam of the lanterns on wayside objects.

How very desolate looks a forest when seen in this way,—as if, should you venture one step within its wild, tangled, many-stemmed, and dark-shadowed verge, you would inevitably be lost forever. Sometimes we passed a house, or rumbled through a village, stopping perhaps to arouse some drowsy postmaster, who appeared at the door in shirt and pantaloons, yawning, received the mail, returned it again, and was yawning when last seen. A few words exchanged among the passengers, as they roused themselves from their half-slumbers, or dreamy, slumber-like abstraction. Meantime dawn broke, our faces became partially visible, the morning air grew colder, and finally cloudy day came on. We found ourselves driving through quite a romantic country, with hills or mountains on all sides, a stream on one side, bordered by a high, precipitous bank, up which would have grown pines, only that, losing their footholds, many of them had slipped downward. The road was not the safest in the world; for often the carriage approached within two or three feet of a precipice; but the driver, a merry fellow, lolled on his box, with his feet protruding horizontally, and rattled on at the rate of ten miles an hour. Breakfast between four and five,—newly caught trout, salmon, ham, boiled eggs, and other niceties,—truly excellent. A bunch of pickerel, intended for a tavern-keeper farther on, was carried by the stage-driver. The drivers carry a "time-watch" enclosed in a small wooden case, with a lock, so that it may be known in what time they perform their stages. They are allowed so many hours and minutes to do their work, and their desire to go as fast as possible, combined with that of keeping their horses in good order, produces about a right medium.

One of the passengers was a young man who had been in Pennsylvania, keeping a school,—a genteel enough young man, but not a gentleman. He took neither supper nor breakfast, excusing himself from one as being weary with riding all day, and from the other because it was so early, he attacked me for a subscription for "building up a destitute church," of which he had taken an agency, and had collected two or three hundred dollars, but wanted as many thousands. Betimes in the morning, on the descent of a mountain, we arrived at a house where dwelt the married sister of the young man, whom he was going to visit. lie alighted, saw his trunk taken off, and then, having perceived his sister at the door, and turning to bid us farewell, there was a broad smile, even a laugh of pleasure, which did him more credit with me than anything else: for hitherto there had been a disagreeable scornful twist upon his face, perhaps, however, merely superficial. I saw. as the stage drove off, his comely sister approaching with a lighted-up face to greet him, and one passenger on the front seat beheld them meet. "Is it an affectionate greeting?" inquired I. "Yes," said he, "I should like to share it": whereby I concluded that there was a kiss exchanged.

The highest point of our journey was at Windsor, where we could see leagues around over the mountain, a terribly bare, bleak spot, fit for nothing but sheep, and without shelter of woods. We rattled downward into a warmer region, beholding as we went the sun shining on portions of the landscape, miles ahead of us, while we were yet in dullness and gloom. It is probable that during a part of the stage the mists around us looked like sky clouds to those in the lower regions. Think of driving a stage-coach through the clouds! Seasonably in the forenoon we arrived at Pittsfield.

Pittsfield is a large village, quite shut in. by mountain walls, generally extending like a rampart on all sides of it, but with insulated great hills rising here and there in the outline. The area of the town is level; its houses are handsome, mostly wooden and white; but some are of brick, painted deep red, the bricks being not of a healthy, natural color. There are handsome churches, Gothic and others, and a court-house and an academy; the court-house having a marble front. There is a small mall in the centre of the town, and in the centre of the mall rises an elm of the loftiest and straightest stem that ever I beheld, without a branch or leaf upon it till it has soared seventy or perhaps a hundred feet into the air. The top branches unfortunately have been shattered somehow or other, so that it does not cast a broad shade; probably they were broken by their own ponderous foliage. The central square of Pittsfield presents all the bustle of a thriving village,—the farmers of the vicinity in light wagons, sulkies, or on horseback; stages at the door of the Berkshire Hotel, under the stoop of which sit or lounge the guests, stage-people, and idlers, observing or assisting in the arrivals and departures. Huge trunks and bandboxes unladed and laded. The courtesy shown to ladies in aiding them to alight, in a shower, under umbrellas. The dull looks of passengers, who have driven all night, scarcely brightened by the excitement of arriving at a new place. The- stage agent demanding the names of those who are going on,—some to Lebanon Springs, some to Albany. The toddy-stick is still busy at these Berkshire public-houses. At dinner soup preliminary, in city style. Guests: the court people; Briggs, member of Congress, attending a trial here; horse-dealers, country squires, store-keepers in the village, etc. My room, a narrow crib overlooking a back courtyard, where a young man and a lad were drawing water for the maid-servants,.—their jokes, especially those of the lad, of whose wit the elder fellow, being a blockhead himself, was in great admiration, and declared to another that he knew as much as them both. Yet he was not very witty. Once in a while the maid-servants would come to the door, and hear and respond to their jokes, with a kind of restraint, yet both permitting and enjoying them.

After or about sunset there was a heavy shower, the thunder rumbling round and round the mountain wall, and the clouds stretching from rampart to rampart. When it abated, the clouds in all parts of the visible heavens were tinged with glory from the west; some that hung low being purple and gold, while the higher ones were gray. The slender curve of the new moon was also visible, brightening amidst the fading brightness of the sunny part of the sky. There are marble: quarries in and near Pittsfield, which accounts for the fact that there are none but marble gravestones in the burial-grounds; some of the monuments well carved; but the marble does not withstand the wear and tear of time and weather so well as the imported, marble, and the sculpture soon loses its sharp outline. The door of one tomb, a wooden door, opening in the side of a green mound, surmounted by a marble obelisk, having been shaken from its hinges by the late explosion of the powder-house, and incompletely repaired, I peeped in at the crevices, and saw the coffins. It was the tomb of Rev. Thomas Allen, first minister of Pittsfield, deceased in 1810. It contained three coffins, all with white mould on their tops: one, a small child's, rested upon another, and the other was on the opposite side of the tomb, and the lid was considerably displaced; but the tomb being dark, I could see neither corpse nor skeleton.

Marble also occurs here in North Adams, and thus some very ordinary houses have marble doorsteps, and even the stone walls are built of fragments of marble.

Wednesday, 26th.—Left Pittsfield at about eight o'clock in the Bennington stage, intending to go to Williamstown. Inside passengers,—a new-married couple taking a jaunt. The lady, with a clear, pale complexion, and a rather pensive cast of countenance, slender, and with a genteel figure; the bridegroom, a shopkeeper in New York probably, a young man with a stout black beard, black eyebrows, which formed one line across his forehead. They were very loving; and while the stage stopped, I watched them, quite entranced in each other, both leaning sideways against the back of the coach, and perusing their mutual comeliness, and apparently making complimentary observations upon it to one another. The bride appeared the most absorbed and devoted, referring her whole being to him. The gentleman seemed in a most paradisiacal mood, smiling ineffably upon his bride, and, when she spoke, responding to her with a benign expression of matrimonial sweetness, and, as it were, compassion for the "weaker vessel," mingled with great love and pleasant humor. It was very droll. The driver peeped into the coach once, and said that he had his arm round her waist. He took little freedoms with her, tapping her with his cane,—love-pats; and she seemed to see nothing amiss. They kept eating gingerbread all along the road, and dined heartily notwithstanding.

Our driver was a slender, lathe-like, round-backed, rough-bearded, thin-visaged, middle-aged Yankee, who became very communicative during our drive. He was not bred a stage-driver, but had undertaken the business temporarily, as a favor to his brother-in-law. He was a native of these Berkshire mountains, but had formerly emigrated to Ohio, and had returned for a time to try the benefit of her native air on his wife's declining health,—she having complaints of a consumptive nature. He pointed out the house where he was married to her, and told the name of the country squire who tied the knot. His wife has little or no chance of recovery, and he said he would never marry again,—this resolution being expressed in answer to a remark of mine relative to a second marriage. He has no children. I pointed to a hill at some distance before us, and asked what it was. "That, sir," said he, "is a very high hill. It is known by the name of Graylock." He seemed to feel that this was a more poetical epithet than Saddleback, which is a more usual name for it. Graylock, or Saddleback, is quite a respectable mountain; and I suppose the former name has been given to it because it often has a gray cloud, or lock of gray mist, upon its head. It does not ascend into a peak, but heaves up a round ball, and has supporting ridges on each side. Its summit is not bare, like that of Mount Washington, but covered with forests. The driver said, that several years since the students of Williams College erected a building for an observatory on the top of the mountain, and employed him to haul the materials for constructing it; and he was the only man who bad driven an ox-team up Graylock. It was necessary to drive the team round and round, in ascending. President Griffin rode up on horseback.

Along our road we passed villages, and often factories, the machinery whirring, and girls looking out of the windows at the stage, with heads averted from their tasks, but still busy. These factories have two, three, or more boarding-houses near them, two stories high, and of double length,—often with bean-vines running up round the doors, and with altogether a domestic look. There are several factories in different parts of North Adams, along the banks of a stream,—a wild, highland rivulet, which, however, does vast work of a civilized nature. It is strange to see such a rough and untamed stream as it looks to be so subdued to the purposes of man, and making cottons and woollens, sawing boards and marbles, and giving employment to so many men and girls. And there is a sort of picturesqueness in finding these factories, supremely artificial establishments, in the midst of such wild scenery. For now the stream will be flowing through a rude forest, with the trees erect and dark, as when the Indians fished there; and it brawls and tumbles and eddies over its rock-strewn current. Perhaps there is a precipice, hundreds of feet high, beside it, down which, by heavy rains, or the melting of snows, great pine-trees have slid or fallen headlong, and lie at the bottom, or half-way down, while their brethren seem to be gazing at their fall from the summit, and anticipating a like fate. And then, taking a turn in the road, behold these factories and their range of boarding-houses, with the girls looking out of the windows, as aforesaid! And perhaps the wild scenery is all around the very site of the factory, and mingles its impression strangely with those opposite ones. These observations were made during a walk yesterday.

I bathed in a pool of the stream that was out of sight, and where its brawling waters were deep enough to cover me, when I lay at length. A part of the road along which I walked was on the edge of a precipice, falling down straight towards the stream; and in one place the passage of heavy loads had sunk it, so that soon, probably, there will be an avalanche, perhaps carrying a stage-coach or heavy wagon down into the bed of the river.

I met occasional wayfarers; once two women in a cart,—decent, brown-visaged, country matrons,—and then an apparent doctor, of whom there are seven or thereabouts in North Adams; for though this vicinity is very healthy, yet the physicians are obliged to ride considerable distances among the mountain towns, and their practice is very laborious. A nod is always exchanged between strangers meeting on the road. This morning an underwitted old man met me on a walk, and held a pretty long conversation, insisting upon shaking hands (to which I was averse, lest his hand should not be clean), and insisting on his right to do so, as being "a friend of mankind." He was a gray, bald-headed, wrinkled-visaged figure, decently dressed, with cowhide shoes, a coat on one arm, and an umbrella on the other, and said that he was going to see a widow in the neighborhood. .Finding that I was not provided with a wife, he recommended a certain maiden of forty years, who had three hundred acres of land. He spoke of his children, who are proprietors of a circus establishment, and have taken a granddaughter to bring up in their way of life; and he gave me a message to tell them in ease we .should meet. While this old man is wandering among the hills, his children are the gaze of multitudes, lie told me the place where he was born, directing me to it by pointing to a wreath of mist which lay on the side of a mountain ridge, which he termed. "the smoke yonder." Speaking of the widow, he said: "My wife has been dead these seven years, and why should I not enjoy myself a little?" His manner was full of quirks and quips and eccentricities, waving his umbrella, and gesticulating strangely, with a great deal of action. I suppose, to help his natural foolishness, he had been drinking. We parted, he exhorting me not to forget his message to his sons, and I shouting after him a request to be remembered to the widow. Conceive something tragical to be talked about, and much might be made of this interview in a wild road among the hills, with Graylock, at a, great distance, looking sombre and angry, by reason of the gray, heavy mist upon his head.

The morning was cloudy, and all the near landscape lay unsunned; but there was sunshine on distant tracts, in the valleys, and in specks upon tins mountain-tops. Between the ridges of hills there are long, wide, deep valleys, extending for miles and miles, with houses scattered along them. A bulky company of mountains, swelling round head over round head, rises insulated by such broad vales from the surrounding ridges.

I ought to have mentioned that I arrived at North Adams in the forenoon of the 26th, and, liking the aspect of matters indifferently well, determined to make my headquarters here for a short time.

On the road to Northampton, we passed a tame crow, which was sitting on the peak of a barn. The crow flew down from its porch, and followed us a groat distance, hopping along the road, and flying with its large, black, flapping wings, from post to post of the fence, or from tree to tree. At last he gave; up the pursuit with a, croak of disappointment. The driver said, perhaps correctly, that the crow had scented some salmon which was in a basket under the seat, and that this was the secret of his pursuing us. This would be a terrific incident if it were a dead body that the crow scented, instead of a basket of salmon. Suppose, for instance, in a coach travelling along, that one of the passengers suddenly should die, and that one of the indications of his death would be this deportment of the crow.

July 29th.—Remarkable characters:—A disagreeable figure, waning from middle age, clad in a pair of tow homespun pantaloons, and a very soiled shirt, barefoot, and with one of his feet maimed by an axe; also an arm amputated two or three inches below the elbow. His beard, of a week's growth, grim and grisly, with a general effect of black; altogether a disgusting object. Yet he has the signs of having been a handsome man in his idea, though now such a beastly figure that probably no living thing but his great dog would touch him without an effort. Coming to the stoop, where several persons were sitting, "Good morning, gentlemen," said the wretch. Nobody answered for a time, till at last one said, "I don't know whom you speak to: not to me, I'm sure" (meaning that he did not claim to be a gentleman). "Why I thought I spoke to you all at once," replied the figure, laughing. So he sat himself down on the lower step of the stoop, and began to talk; and, the conversation being turned upon his bare feet by one of the company, he related the story of his losing his toes by the glancing aside of an axe, and with what great fortitude he bore it. Then he made a transition to the loss of his arm, and, setting his teeth and drawing in his breath, said that the pain was dreadful; but this, too, he seems to have borne like an Indian; and a person testified to his fortitude by saying that he did not suppose there was any feeling in him, from observing how he bore it. The man spoke of the pain of cutting the muscles, and the particular agony at one moment, while the bone was being sawed asunder; and there was a strange expression of remembered anguish, as he shrugged his half-limb, and described the matter. Afterwards, in a reply to a question of mine, whether he still seemed to feel the hand that had been amputated, he answered that he did always; and, baring the stump, he moved the severed muscles, saying, "There is the thumb, there the forefinger," and so on. Then he talked to me about phrenology, of which he seems a firm believer and skilful practitioner, telling how he had hit upon the true character of many people. There was a great deal of sense and acuteness in his talk, and something of elevation in his expressions,—perhaps a studied elevation,—and a sort of courtesy in his manner; but his sense had something out of the way in it; there was something wild and ruined and desperate in his talk, though I can hardly say what it was. There was a trace of the gentleman and man of intellect through his deep degradation; and a pleasure in intellectual pursuits, and an acuteness and trained judgment, which bespoke a mind once strong and cultivated. "My study is man," said he. And, looking at me, "I do not know your name," he said, "but there is something of the hawk-eye about you, too."

This man was formerly a lawyer in good practice; but, taking to drinking, was reduced to the lowest state. Yet not the lowest; for after the amputation of his arm, being advised by divers persons to throw himself upon the public for support, he told them that, even if he should lose his other arm, he would still be able to support himself and a servant. Certainly he is a strong-minded and iron-constitutioned man; but, looking at the stump of his arm, he said that the pain of the mind was a thousand times greater than the pain of the body. "That hand could make the pen go fast," said he. Among people in general, he does not seem to have any greater consideration in his ruin because of his former standing in society. He supports himself by making soap; and, on account of the offals used in that business, there is probably rather an evil odor in his domicile. Talking about a dead horse near his house, he said that he could not bear the scent of it. "I should not think you could smell carrion in *that* house," said a stage agent. Whereupon the soap-maker dropped his head, with a little snort, as it were, of wounded feeling; but immediately said that he took all in good part. There was an old squire of the village, a lawyer probably, whose demeanor was different,—with a distance, yet with a kindliness; for he remembered the times when they met on equal terms. "You and I," said the squire, alluding to their respective troubles and sicknesses, "would have died long ago, if we had not had the courage to live." The poor devil kept talking to me long after everybody else had left the stoop, giving vent to much practical philosophy, and just observation on the ways of men, mingled with rather more assumption of literature and cultivation than belonged to the present condition of his mind. Meantime his great dog, a cleanly looking and not ill-bred dog, being the only decent attribute appertaining to his master,—a well-natured dog, too, and receiving civilly any demonstration of courtesy from other people, though preserving a certain distance of deportment,—this great dog grew weary of his master's lengthy talk, and expressed his impatience to be gone by thrusting himself between his legs, rolling over on his back, seizing his ragged trousers, or playfully taking his maimed, bare foot into his mouth,—using, in short, the kindly and humorous freedom of a friend, with a wretch to whom all are free enough, but none other kind. His master rebuked him, but with kindness too, and not so that the dog felt himself bound to desist, though he seemed willing to allow his master all the time that could possibly be spared. And at last, having said many times that he must go and shave and dress himself,—and as his beard had been at least a week growing, it might have seemed almost a week's work to get rid of it,—he rose from the stoop and went his way,—a forlorn and miserable thing in the light of the cheerful summer morning. Yet he seems to keep his spirits up, and still preserves himself a man among men, asking nothing from them; nor is it clearly perceptible what right they have to scorn him, though he seems to acquiesce, in a manner, in their doing so. And yet he cannot wholly have, lost his self-respect; and doubtless there were persons on the stoop more grovelling than himself.

Another character:—A blacksmith of fifty or upwards, a corpulent figure, big in the paunch and enormous in the rear; yet there is such, an appearance of strength and robustness in his frame, that his corpulence appears very proper and necessary to him. A pound of flesh could not be spared from his abundance, any more than from the leanest man; and he walks about briskly, without any panting or symptom of labor or pain in his motion. He has a round, jolly face, always mirthful and humorous and shrewd, and the air of a man well to do, and well respected, yet not caring much about the opinions of men, because his independence is sufficient to itself. Nobody would take him for other than a man of some importance in the community, though his summer dress is a tow-cloth pair of pantaloons, a shirt not of the cleanest, open at the breast, and the sleeves rolled up at the elbows, and a straw hat. There is not such a vast difference between this costume and that of Lawyer H— above mentioned, yet never was there a greater diversity of appearance than between these two men; and a glance at them would be sufficient to mark the difference. The blacksmith loves his glass, and comes to the tavern for it, whenever it seems good to him, not calling for it slyly and shyly, but marching steadily to the bar, or calling across the room for it to be prepared. He speaks with great bitterness against the new license law, and vows if it be not repealed by fair means it shall be by violence, and that he will be as ready to cock his rifle for such a cause as for any other. On this subject his talk is really fierce; but as to all other matters he is good-natured and good-hearted, fond of joke, and shaking his jolly sides with frequent laughter. His conversation has much strong, unlettered sense, imbued with humor, as everybody's talk is in New England.

He takes a queer position sometimes,—queer for his figure particularly,—straddling across a chair, facing the back, with his arms resting thereon, and his chin on them, for the benefit of conversing closely with some one. When he has spent as much time in the bar-room or under the stoop as he chooses to spare, he gets up at once, and goes off with a brisk, vigorous pace. He owns a mill, and seems to be prosperous in the world. I know no man who seems more like a man, more indescribably human, than this sturdy blacksmith.

There came in the afternoon a respectable man in gray homespun cloth, who arrived in a wagon, I believe, and began to inquire, after supper, about a certain new kind of mill machinery. Being referred to the blacksmith, who owned one of these mills, the stranger said that he had come from Vermont to learn about the matter. "What may I call your name?" said he to the blacksmith. "My name is Hodge," replied the latter. "I believe I have heard of you," said the stranger. Then they colloquied at much length about the various peculiarities and merits of the new invention. The stranger continued here two or three days, making his researches, and forming acquaintance with several millwrights and others. He was a man evidently of influence in his neighborhood, and the tone of his conversation was in the style of one accustomed to be heard with deference, though all in a plain and homely way. Lawyer H— took notice of this manner; for the talk being about the nature of soap, and the evil odor arising from that process, the stranger joined in. "There need not be any disagreeable smell in making soap," said he. "Now we are to receive a lesson," said H—, and the remark was particularly apropos to the large wisdom of the stranger's tone and air.

Then he gave an account of the process in his domestic establishment, saying that he threw away the whole offals of the hog, as not producing any soap, and preserved the skins of the intestines for sausages. He seemed to be hospitable, inviting those with whom he did business to take "a mouthful of dinner" with him, and treating them with liquors; for he was not an utter temperance man, though moderate in his potations. I suspect he would turn out a pattern character of the upper class of New England yeomen, if I had an opportunity of studying him. Doubtless he had been selectman, representative, and justice, and had filled all but weighty offices. He was highly pleased with the new mill contrivance, and expressed his opinion that, when his neighbors saw the success of. his, it would be extensively introduced into that vicinity.

*Mem.* The hostlers at taverns call the money given them "pergasus,"—corrupted from "perquisites." Otherwise "knock-down money."

Remarkable character:—A travelling surgeon-dentist, who has taken a, room in the North Adams House, and sticks up his advertising bills on the pillars of the piazza, and all about the town. He is a tall, slim young man, six feet two, dressed in a country-made coat of light blue (taken, as he tells me, in exchange for dental operations), black pantaloons, and clumsy, cowhide hoots. Self-conceit is very strongly expressed in his air; and a doctor once told him that he owed his life to that quality; for, by keeping himself so stiffly upright, he opens his chest, and counteracts a consumptive tendency. He is not only a dentist, which trade he follows temporarily, but a licensed preacher of the Baptist persuasion, and is now on his way to the West to seek a place of settlement in his spiritual vocation. Whatever education he possesses, he has acquired by his own exertions since the age of twenty-one,—he being now twenty-four. We talk together very freely; and he has given me an account, among other matters, of all his love-affairs, which are rather curious, as illustrative of the life of a smart young country fellow in relation to the gentle sex. Nothing can exceed the exquisite self-conceit which characterizes these confidences, and which is expressed inimitably in his face, his upturned nose, and mouth, so as to be truly a caricature; and he seems strangely to find as much food for his passion in having been jilted once or twice as in his conquests. It is curious to notice his revengeful feeling against the false ones, hidden from himself, however, under the guise of religious interest, and desire that they may be cured of their follies.

A little boy named Joe, who haunts about the bar-room and the stoop, four years old, in a thin, short jacket, and full-breeched trousers, and bare feet. The men tease him, and put quids of tobacco in his mouth, under pretence of giving him a fig; and he gets enraged, and utters a peculiar, sharp, spiteful cry, and strikes at them with a stick, to their great mirth. He is always in trouble, yet will not keep away. They despatch him with two or three cents to buy candy and nuts and raisins. They set him down in a niche of the door, and tell him to remain there a day and a half: he sits down very demurely, as if he meant to fulfil his penance; hut a moment after, behold! there is little Joe capering across the street to join two or three boys who are playing in a wagon. Take this boy as the germ of a tavern-haunter, a country *roué,* to spend a wild and brutal youth, ten years of his prime in the State Prison, and his old age in the poor-house.

There are a great many dogs kept in the village, and many of the travellers also have dogs. Some are almost always playing about; and if a cow or a pig be passing, two or three of them scamper' forth for an attack. Some of the younger sort chase pigeons, wheeling as they wheel. If a contest arises between two dogs, a number of others come with huge barking to join the fray, though I believe that they do not really take any active part in the contest, but swell the uproar by way of encouraging the combatants. When a traveller is starting from the door, his dog often gets in front of the horse, placing his forefeet down, looking the horse in the face, and barking loudly; then, as the horse comes on, running a little farther, and repeating the process; and this he does in spite of his master's remonstrances, till, the horse being fairly started, the dog follows on quietly. One dog, a diminutive little beast, has been taught to stand on his hind legs, and rub his face with his paw, which he does with an aspect of much endurance and deprecation. Another springs at people whom his master points out to him, barking and pretending to bite. These tricks make much mirth in the bar-room. All dogs, of whatever different sizes and dissimilar varieties, acknowledge the common bond of species among themselves, and the largest one does not disdain to suffer his tail to be smelt of, nor to reciprocate that courtesy to the smallest. They appear to take much interest in one another; but there is always a degree of caution between two strange dogs when they meet.

July 31st—A visit to what is called "Hudson's Cave," or "Hudson's Falls," the tradition being that a man by the name of Henry Hudson, many years ago, chasing a deer, the deer fell over the place, which then first became known to white men. It is not properly a cave, but a fissure in a huge ledge of marble, through which a stream has been for ages forcing its way, and has left marks of its gradually wearing power on the tall crags, having made curious hollows from the summit down to the level which it has reached at the present day. The depth of the fissure in some places is at least fifty or sixty feet, perhaps more, and at several points it nearly closes over, and often the sight of the sky is hidden by the interposition of masses of the marble crags. The fissure is very irregular, so as not to be describable in words, and scarcely to be painted,—jutting buttresses, moss-grown, impending crags, with tall trees growing on their verge, nodding over the head of the observer at the bottom of the chasm, and rooted, as it were, in air. The part where the water works its way down is very narrow; but the chasm widens, after the descent, so as to form a spacious chamber between the crags, open to the sky, and its floor is strewn with fallen fragments of marble, and trees that have been precipitated long ago, and are heaped with drift-wood, left there by the freshets, when the scanty stream becomes a considerable waterfall. One crag, with a narrow ridge, which might be climbed without much difficulty, protrudes from the middle of the rock, and divides the fall. The passage through the cave made by the stream is very crooked, and interrupted, not only by fallen wrecks, but by deep pools of water, which probably have been forded by few. As the deepest pool occurs in the most uneven part of the chasm, where the hollows in the sides of the crag are deepest, so that each hollow is almost a cave by itself, I determined to wade through it. There was an accumulation of soft stuff on the bottom, so that the water did not look more than knee-deep; but, finding that my feet sunk in it, I took off my trousers, and waded through up to my middle. Thus I reached the most interesting part of the cave, where the whirlings of the stream had left the marks of its eddies in the solid marble, all up and down the two sides of the chasm. The water is now dammed for the construction of two marble sawmills, else it would have been impossible to effect the passage; and I presume that, for years after the cave was discovered, the waters roared and tore their way in a torrent through this part of the chasm. While I was there, I heard voices, and a small stone tumbled down; and looking up towards the narrow strip of bright light, and the sunny verdure that peeped over the top,—looking up thither from the deep, gloomy depth,—I saw two or three men; and, not liking to be to them the most curious part of the spectacle, I waded back, and put on my clothes. The marble crags are overspread with a concretion, which makes them look as gray as granite, except where the continual flow of water keeps them of a snowy whiteness. If they were so white all over, it would be a splendid show. There is a marble-quarry close in the rear, above the cave, and in process of time the whole of the crags will be quarried into tombstones, doorsteps, fronts of edifices, fireplaces, etc. That will be a pity. On such portions of the walls as are within reach, visitors have sculptured their initials, or names at full length; and the white letters showing plainly on the gray surface, they have more obvious effect than such inscriptions generally have. There was formerly, I believe, a complete arch of marble, forming a natural bridge over the top of the cave; but this is no longer so. At the bottom of the broad chamber of the cave, standing in its shadow, the effect of the morning sunshine on the dark or bright foliage of the pines and other trees that cluster on the summits of the crags was particularly beautiful; and it was strange how such great trees had rooted themselves in solid marble, for so it seemed.

After passing through this romantic and most picturesque spot, the stream goes onward to turn factories. Here its voice resounds within the hollow crags; there it goes onward, talking to itself, with, babbling din, of its own wild thoughts and fantasies,—the voice of solitude and the wilderness,—loud and continual, but which yet does not seem to disturb the thoughtful wanderer, so that he forgets there is a noise. It talks along its storm-strewn path; it talks beneath tall precipices and high banks,—a voice that has been the same for innumerable ages; and yet, if you listen, you will perceive a continual change and variety in its babble, and sometimes it seems to swell louder upon the ear than at others,—in the same spot, I mean. By and by man makes a dam for it, and it pours over it, still making its voice heard, while it labors. At one shop for manufacturing the marble, I saw the disk of a sundial as large as the top of a hogshead, intended for Williams College; also a small obelisk, and numerous gravestones. The marble is coarse-grained, but of a very brilliant whiteness. It is rather a pity that the cave is not formed of some worthless stone.

In the deep valleys of the neighborhood, where the shadows at sunset are thrown from mountain to mountain, the clouds have a beautiful effect, flitting high over them, bright with heavenly gold. It seems as if the soul might rise up from the gloom, and alight upon them and soar away. Walking along one of the valleys the other evening, while a pretty fresh breeze blew across it, the clouds that were skimming over my head seemed to conform themselves to the valley's shape.

At a distance, mountain summits look close together, almost as if forming one mountain, though in reality a village lies in the depths between them.

A steam-engine in a factory to be supposed to possess a malignant spirit. It catches one man's arm, and pulls it off; seizes another by the coat-tails, and almost grapples him bodily; catches a girl by the hair, and scalps her; and finally draws in a man and crushes him to death.

The one-armed soap-maker, Lawyer H—, wears an iron hook, which serves him instead of a hand for the purpose of holding on. They nickname him "Black Hawk."

North Adams still.—The village, viewed from the top of a hill to the westward at sunset, has a peculiarly happy and peaceful look. ' It lies on a level, surrounded by hills, and seems as if it lay in the hollow of a large hand. The Union Village may be seen, a manufacturing place, extending up a gorge of the hills. It is amusing to see all the distributed property of the aristocracy and commonalty, the various and conflicting interests of the town, the loves and hates, compressed into a space which the eye takes in as completely as the arrangement of a tea-table. The rush of the streams comes up the hill somewhat like the sound of a city.

The hills about the village appear very high and steep sometimes, when the shadows of the clouds are thrown blackly upon them, while there is sunshine elsewhere; so that, seen in front, the effect of their gradual slope is lost. These hills, surrounding the town on all sides, give it a snug and insulated air; and, viewed from certain points, it would be difficult to tell how to get out, without climbing the mountain ridges; but the roads wind away and accomplish the passage without ascending very high. Sometimes the notes of a horn or bugle may be heard sounding afar among these passes of the mountains, announcing the coming of the stage-coach from Bennington or Troy or Greenfield or Pittsfield.

There are multitudes of sheep among the hills, and they appear very tame and gentle; though sometimes, like the wicked, they "flee when no man pursueth." But, climbing a rude, rough, rocky, stumpy, ferny height yesterday, one or two of them stood and stared at me with great earnestness. I passed on quietly, but soon heard an immense baa-ing up the hill, and all the sheep came galloping and scrambling after me, baa-ing with all their might in innumerable voices, running in a compact body, expressing the utmost eagerness, as if they sought the greatest imaginable favor from me; and so they accompanied me down the hill-side,—a most ridiculous *cortège.* Doubtless they had taken it into their heads that I brought them salt.

The aspect of the village is peculiarly beautiful towards sunset, when there are masses of cloud about the sky,—the remnants of a thunder-storm. These clouds throw a shade upon large portions of the rampart of hills, and the hills towards the west are shaded of course; the clouds also make the shades deeper in the village, and thus the sunshine on the houses and trees, and along the street, is a bright, rich gold. The green is deeper in consequence of the recent rain.

The doctors walk about the village with their saddle-bags on their arms, one always with a pipe in his mouth.

A little dog, named Snapper, the same who stands on his hind legs, appears to be a roguish little dog, and the other day he stole one of the servant-girl's shoes, and ran into the street with it. Being pursued, he would lift the shoe in his mouth (while it almost dragged on the ground), and run a little way, then lie down with his paws on it and wait to be pursued again.

August 11th.—This morning, it being cloudy and boding of rain, the clouds had settled upon the mountains, both on the summits and ridges, all round the town, so that there seemed to be no way of gaining access to the rest of the world, unless by climbing above the clouds. By and by they partially dispersed, giving glimpses of the mountain ramparts through their obscurity, the separate clouds lying heavily upon the mountain's breast. In warm mornings, after rain, the mist breaks forth from the forests on the ascent of the mountains, like smoke,—the smoke of a volcano; then it soars up, and becomes a cloud in heaven. But these clouds to-day were real rain-clouds. Sometimes, it is said, while laboring up the mountain-side, they suddenly burst, and pour down their moisture in a cataract, sweeping all before it.

Every new aspect of the mountains, or view from a different position, creates a surprise in the mind.

Scenes and characters:—A young country fellow, twenty or thereabouts, decently dressed, pained with the toothache. A doctor, passing on horseback, with his black leather saddle-bags behind him, a thin, frosty-haired man. Being asked to operate, he looks at the tooth, lances the gum, and the fellow being content to be dealt with on the spot, he seats himself in a chair on the stoop with great heroism. The doctor produces a rusty pair of iron forceps; a man holds the patient's head; the doctor perceives that, it being a difficult tooth to get at, wedged between the two largest in his jaws, he must pull very hard; and the instrument is introduced. A turn of the doctor's hand; the patient begins to utter a cry, but the tooth comes out first, with four prongs. The patient gets up, half amazed, pays the doctor ninepence, pockets the tooth, and the spectators are in glee and admiration.

There was a fat woman, a stage-passenger to-day,—a wonder how she could possibly get through the door, which seemed not so wide as she. When she put her foot on the step, the stage gave a great lurch, she joking all the while. A great, coarse, red-faced dame. Other passengers,—three or four slender Williamstown students, a young girl, and a man with one leg and two crutches.

One of the most sensible men in this village is a plain, tall, elderly person, who is overseeing the mending of a road,—humorous, intelligent, with much thought about matters and things; and while at work he has a sort of dignity in handling the hoe or crowbar, which shows him to be the chief. In the evening he sits under the stoop, silent and observant from under the brim of his hat; but, occasion calling, he holds an argument about the benefit or otherwise of manufactories or other things. A simplicity characterizes him more than appertains to most Yankees.

A man in a pea-green frock-coat, with velvet collar. Another in a flowered chintz frock-coat. There is a great diversity of hues in garments. A doctor, a stout, tall, round-paunched, red-faced, brutal-looking old fellow, who gets drunk daily. He sat down on the step of our stoop, looking surly, and speaking to nobody; then got up and walked homeward, with a morose swagger and a slight unevenness of gait, attended by a fine Newfoundland dog.

A barouche with driver returned from beyond Greenfield or Troy empty, the passengers being left at the former place. The driver stops here for the night, and, while washing, enters into talk with an old man about the different roads over the mountain.

People washing themselves at a common basin in the bar-room! and using the common hair-brushes! perhaps with a consciousness of praiseworthy neatness!

A man with a cradle on his shoulder, having been cradling oats. I attended a child's funeral yesterday afternoon. There was an assemblage of people in a plain, homely apartment. Most of the men were dressed in their ordinary clothes, and one or two were in shirt-sleeves. The coffin was placed in the midst of us, covered with a velvet pall. A bepaid clergyman prayed (the audience remaining seated, while he stood up at the head of the coffin), read a passage of Scripture and commented upon it. While he read and prayed and expounded there was a heavy thunderstorm rumbling among the surrounding hills, and the lightning flashed fiercely through the gloomy room; and the preacher alluded to God's voice of thunder.

It is the custom in this part of the country—and perhaps extensively in the interior of New England—to bury the dead first in a charnel-house, or common tomb, where they remain till decay has so far progressed as to secure them from the resurrectionists. They are then reburied, with certain ceremonies, in their own peculiar graves.

O. E. S—, a widower of forty or upwards, with a son of twelve and a pair of infant twins. He is a sharp, shrewd Yankee, with a Yankee's license of honesty. He drinks sometimes more than enough, and is guilty of peccadilloes with the fair sex; yet speaks most affectionately of his wife, and is a fond and careful father. He is a tall, thin, hard-featured man, with a sly expression of almost hidden grave humor, as if there were some deviltry pretty constantly in his mind,—which is probably the case. His brother tells me that he was driven almost crazy by the loss of his wife. It appears to me that men are more affected by the deaths of their wives than wives by the deaths of their husbands. Orrin S— smokes a pipe, as do many of the guests.

A walk this forenoon up the mountain ridge that walls in the town towards the east. The road is cut zigzag, the mountain being generally as steep as the roof of a house; yet the stage to Greenfield passes over this road two or three times a week. Graylock rose up behind me, appearing, with its two summits and a long ridge between, like a huge monster crouching down slumbering, with its head slightly elevated. Graylock is properly the name for the highest elevation. It appeared to better advantage the higher the point from which I viewed it. There were houses scattered here and there up the mountain-side, growing poorer as I ascended; the last that I passed was a mean log-hut, rough, rude, and dilapidated, with the smoke issuing from a chimney of small stones, plastered with clay; around it a garden of beans, with some attempt at flowers, and a green creeper running over the side of the cottage. Above this point there were various excellent views of mountain scenery, far off and near, and one village lying below in the hollow vale.

Having climbed so far that the road seemed now to go downward, I retraced my steps. There was a wagon descending behind me; and as it followed the zigzag of the road I could hear the voices of the men high over my head, and sometimes I caught a glimpse of the wagon almost perpendicularly above me, while I was looking almost perpendicularly down to the log-hut aforementioned. Trees were thick on either hand,—oaks, pines, and others; and marble occasionally peeped up in the road; and there was a lime-kiln by the wayside, ready for burning.

Graylock had a cloud on his head this morning, the base of a heavy white cloud. The distribution of the sunshine amid mountain scenery is very striking; one does not see exactly why one spot should be in deep obscurity while others are all bright. The clouds throw their shadows upon the hill-sides as they move «lowly along,—a transitory blackness.

I passed a doctor high up the road in a sulky, with his black leather saddle-bags.

Hudson's Cave is formed by Hudson's Brook. There is a natural arch of marble still in one part of it. The cliffs are partly made verdant with green moss, chiefly gray with oxidation; on some parts the white of the marble is seen; in interstices grow brake and other shrubs, so that there is naked sublimity seen through a good deal of clustering beauty. Above, the birch, poplars, and pines grow on the utmost verge of the cliffs, which jut far over, so that they are suspended in air; and whenever the sunshine finds its way into the depths of the chasm, the branches wave across it. There is a lightness, however, about their foliage, which greatly relieves what would otherwise he a gloomy scene. After the passage of the stream through the cliffs of marble, the cliffs separate on either side, and leave it to flow onward; intercepting its passage, however, by fragments of marble, some of them huge ones, which the cliffs have flung down, thundering into the bed of the stream through numberless ages. Doubtless some of these immense fragments had trees growing on them, which have now mouldered away. Decaying trunks are heaped in various parts of the gorge. The pieces of marble that are washed by the water are of a snow-white, and partially covered with a bright green water-moss, making a beautiful contrast.

Among the cliffs, strips of earth-beach extend downward, and trees and large shrubs root themselves in that earth, thus further contrasting the nakedness of the stone with their green foliage. But the immediate part where the stream forces its winding passage through the rock is stern, dark, and mysterious.

Along the road, where it runs beneath a steep, there are high ridges, covered with trees,—the dew of midnight damping the earth, far towards midnoon. I observed the shadows of water-insects, as they swam in the pools of a stream. Looking down a streamlet, I saw a trunk of a tree, which has been overthrown by the wind, so as to form a bridge, yet sticking up all its branches, as if it were unwilling to assist anybody over.

Green leaves, following the eddies of the rivulet, were now borne deep under water, and now emerged. Great uprooted trees, adhering midway down a precipice of earth, hung with their tops downward.

There is an old man, selling the meats of butternuts under the stoop of the hotel. He makes that his station during a part of the season. He was dressed in a dark thin coat, ribbed velvet pantaloons, and a sort of moccasons, or shoes, appended to the legs of woollen stockings. He had on a straw hat, and his hair was gray, with a long, thin visage. His nuts were contained in a square tin box, having two compartments, one for the nuts, and another for maple sugar, which he sells in small cakes. He had three small tin measures for nuts,—one at one cent, others at two, four, and six cents; and as fast as they were emptied, he filled them again, and put them on the top of his box. He smoked a pipe, and talked with one man about whether, it would be worth while to grow young again, and the duty of being contented with old age; about predestination and freewill and other metaphysics. I asked him what his sales amounted to in the course of a day. He said that butternuts did not sell so well as walnuts, which are not yet in season; that he might to-day have sold fifty cents' worth of walnuts, never less than a dollar's worth, often more; and when he went round with a caravan, he had sold fifteen dollars' worth per day, and once as much as twenty dollars' worth. This promises to be an excellent year for walnuts. Chestnuts have been scarce for two or three years. He had one hundred chestnut-trees on his own land, and last year he offered a man twenty-five cents if he would find him a quart of good chestnuts on them. A bushel of walnuts would cost about ten dollars. He wears a pair of silver-rimmed spectacles.

A drunken fellow sat down by him, and bought a cent's worth of his butternuts, and inquired what he would sell out to him for. The old man made an estimate, though evidently in jest, and then reckoned his box, measures, meats, and what little maple sugar he had, at four dollars. He had a very quiet manner, and expressed an intention of going to the Commencement at Williamstown to-morrow. His name, I believe, is Captain Gavett.

Wednesday, August 15th.—I went to Commencement at Williams College,—five miles distant. At the tavern were students with ribbons, pink or blue, fluttering from their buttonholes, these being the badges of rival societies. There was a considerable gathering of people, chiefly arriving in wagons or buggies, some in barouches, and very few in chaises. The most characteristic part of the scene was where the pedlars, gingerbread-sellers, etc., were collected, a few hundred yards from the meeting-house. There was a pedlar there from New York State, who sold his wares by auction, and I could have stood and listened to him all day long. Sometimes he would put up a heterogeny[i] of articles in a lot,—as a paper of pins, a lead-pencil, and a shaving-box,—and knock them all down, perhaps for ninepence. Bunches of lead-pencils, steel-pens, pound-cakes of shaving-soap, gilt finger-rings, bracelets, clasps, and other jewelry, cards of pearl buttons, or steel ("there is some steel about them, gentlemen, for my brother stole 'em, and I bore him out in it"), bundles of wooden combs, boxes of matches, suspenders, and, in short, everything, —dipping his hand down into his wares, with the promise of a wonderful lot, and producing, perhaps, a bottle of opodeldoc, and joining it with a lead-pencil,—and when he had sold several things of the same kind, pretending huge surprise at finding "just one more," if the lads lingered; saying, "I could not afford to steal them for the price; for the remorse of conscience would be worth more,"—all the time keeping an eye upon those who bought, calling for the pay, making change with silver or bills, and deciding on the goodness of banks; and saying to the boys, who climbed upon his cart, "Fall down, roll down, tumble down, only get down"; and uttering everything in the queer, humorous recitative in which he sold his articles. Sometimes he would pretend that a person had bid, either by word or wink and raised a laugh thus; never losing his self-possession, nor getting out of humor. When a man asked whether a bill were good: "No! do you suppose I'd give you good money?" When he delivered an article, he exclaimed, "You' re the lucky man," setting off his wares with the most extravagant eulogies. The people bought very freely, and seemed also to enjoy the fun. One little boy bought a shaving-box, perhaps meaning to speculate upon it. This character could not possibly be overdrawn; and he was really excellent, with his allusions to what was passing, intermingled, doubtless, with a good deal that was studied. He was a man between thirty and forty, with a face expressive of other ability, as well as of humor.

A good many people were the better or the worse for liquor. There was one fellow, —named Randall, I think,—a round-shouldered, bulky, ill-hung devil, with a pale, sallow skin, black beard, and a sort of grin upon his face,—a species of laugh, yet not so much mirthful as indicating a strange mental and moral twist. He was very riotous in the crowd, elbowing, thrusting, seizing hold of people; and at last a ring was formed, and a regular wrestling-match commenced between him and a farmer-looking man. Randall brandished his legs about in the most ridiculous style, but proved himself a good wrestler, and finally threw his antagonist. He got up with the same grin upon his features,—not a grin of simplicity, but intimating knowingness. When more depth or force of expression was required, he could put on the most strangely ludicrous and ugly aspect (suiting his gesture and attitude to it) that can be imagined. I should like to see this fellow when he was perfectly sober.

There were a good many blacks among the crowd. I suppose they used to emigrate across the border, while New York was a slave State. There were enough of them to form a party, though greatly in the minority; and, a squabble arising, some of the blacks were knocked down, and otherwise maltreated. I saw one old negro, a genuine specimen of the slave negro, without any of the foppery of the race in our part of the State,—an old fellow, with a bag, I suppose, of broken victuals, on his shoulder, and his pockets stuffed out at his hips with the like provender; full of grimaces and ridiculous antics, laughing laughably, yet without affectation; then talking with a strange kind of pathos about the whippings he used to get while he was a slave;—a singular creature, of mere feeling, with some glimmering of sense. Then there was another gray old negro, but of a different stamp, politic, sage, cautious, yet with boldness enough, talking about the rights of his race, yet so as not to provoke his audience; discoursing of the advantage of living under laws, and the wonders that might ensue, in that very assemblage, if there were no laws; in the midst of this deep wisdom, turning off the anger of a half-drunken fellow by a merry retort, a leap in the air, and a negro's laugh. I was interested—there being a drunken negro ascending the meeting-house steps, and near him three or four well-dressed and decent negro wenches—to see the look of scorn and shame and sorrow and painful sympathy which one of them assumed at this disgrace of her color.

The people here show out their character much more strongly than they do with us; there was not the quiet, silent, dull decency of our public assemblages, but mirth, anger, eccentricity,—all manifesting themselves freely. There were many watermelons for sale, and people burying their muzzles deep in the juicy flesh of them. There were cider and beer. Many of the people had their mouths half opened in a grin, which, more than anything else, I think, indicates a low stage of refinement. A low-crowned hat—very low—is common. They are respectful to gentlemen.

A bat being startled, probably, out of the meetinghouse, by the commotion around, flew blindly about in the sunshine, and alighted on a sleeve. I looked at him,—a droll, winged,beast-insect, creeping up the man's arm, not over-clean, and scattering dust on the man's coat from his vampire wings. The man stared at him, and let the spectators stare for a minute, and then shook him gently off; and the poor devil took a flight across the green to the meetinghouse, and then, I believe, alighted on somebody else. Probably he was put to death. Bats are very numerous in these parts.

There was a drunken man, annoying people with his senseless talk and impertinences, impelled to perform eccentricities by an evil spirit in him; and a pale little boy, with a bandaged leg, whom his father brought out of the tavern and put into a barouche. Then the boy heedfully placed shawls and cushions about his leg to support it, his face- expressive of pain and care,—not transitory, but settled pain, of long and forcedly patient endurance; and this painful look, perhaps, gave his face more intelligence than it might otherwise have had, though it was naturally a sensitive face. Well-dressed ladies were in the meetinghouse in silks and cambrics,—the sunburnt necks in contiguity with the delicate fabrics of the dresses showing the yeoman's daughters.

Country graduates,—rough, brown-featured, schoolmaster-looking, half-bumpkin, half-scholarly figures, in black ill-cut broadcloth,—their manners quite spoilt by what little of the gentleman there was in them.

The landlord of the tavern keeping his eye on a man whom he suspected of an intention to bolt.[ii] The next day after Commencement was bleak and rainy from midnight till midnight, and a good many guests wore added to our table in consequence. Among them were some of the Williamstown students, gentlemanly young fellows, with a brotherly feeling for each other, a freedom about money concerns, a half-boyish, half-manly character; and my heart warmed to them. They took their departure—two for South Adams and two across the Green Mountains—in the midst of the rain. There was one of the graduates with his betrothed, and his brother-in-law and wife, who stayed during the day,—the graduate the very model of a country schoolmaster in his Sunday clothes, being his Commencement suit of black broadcloth and pumps. He is engaged as assistant teacher of the academy at Shelburne Falls. There was also the high sheriff of Berkshire, Mr. Twining, with a bundle of Writs under his aim, and some of them peeping out of his pockets. Also several Trojan men and women, who had been to Commencement. Likewise a young clergyman, graduate of Brown College, and student of the Divinity School at Cambridge. He had come across the Hoosic, or Green Mountains, about eighteen miles, on foot, from Charlemont, where he is preaching, and had been to Commencement. Knowing little of men and matters, and desiring to know more, he was very free in making acquaintance with people, but could not do it handsomely. A singular smile broke out upon his face on slight provocation. He was awkward in his manners, yet it was not an ungentlemanly awkwardness, —intelligent as respects book-learning, but much deficient in worldly tact. It was pleasant to observe his consciousness of this deficiency, and how he strove to remedy it by mixing as much as possible with people, and sitting almost all day in the bar-room to study character. Sometimes he would endeavor to contribute his share to the general amusement,—as by growling comically, to provoke and mystify a dog; and by some bashful and half-apropos observations.

In the afternoon there came a fresh bevy of students onward from Williamstown; but they made only a transient visit, though it was still raining. These were a rough-hewn, heavy set of fellows, from the hills and woods in this neighborhood, —great unpolished bumpkins, who had grown up farmer-boys, and had little of the literary man, save green spectacles and black broadcloth (which all of them had not), talking with a broad accent, and laughing clown-like, while sheepishness overspread all, together with a vanity at being students. One of the party was six feet seven inches high, and all his herculean dimensions were in proportion; his features, too, were cast in a mould suitable to his stature. This giant was not ill-looking, but of a rather intelligent aspect. His motions were devoid of grace, but yet had a rough freedom, appropriate enough to such a figure. These fellows stayed awhile, talked uncouthly about college matters, and started in the great open wagon which had brought them and their luggage hither. We had a fire in the bar-room almost all day,—a great, blazing fire,—and it was pleasant to have this day of bleak November weather, and cheerful fireside talk, and wet garments smoking in the fireside heat, still in the summer-time. Thus the day wore on with a sort of heavy, lazy pleasantness; and night set in, still stormy.

In the morning it was cloudy, but did not rain, and I went with the little clergyman to Hudson's Cave. The stream which they call North Branch, and into which Hudson's Brook empties, was much swollen, and tumbled and dashed and whitened over the rocks, and formed real cascades over the dams, and rushed fast along the side of the cliffs, which had their feet in it. Its color was deep brown, owing to the washing of the banks which the rain had poured into it. Looking back, we could see a cloud on Graylock; but on other parts of Saddle Mountain there were spots of sunshine, some of most glorious brightness, contrasting with the general gloom of the sky, and the deep shadow which lay on the earth.

We looked at the spot where the stream makes its entrance into the marble cliff, and it was (this morning, at least) the most striking view of the cave. The water dashed down in a misty cascade, through what looked like the portal of some infernal subterranean structure; and far within the portal we could see the mist and the falling water; and it looked as if, but for these obstructions of view, we might have had a deeper insight into a gloomy region.

After our return, the little minister set off for his eighteen" miles' journey across the mountains; and I was occupied the rest of the forenoon with an affair of stealing,—a woman of forty or upwards being accused of stealing a needle-case and other trifles from a factory-girl at a boarding-house. She came here to take passage in a stage; but Putnam, a justice of the peace, examined her and afterwards ordered her to be searched by Laura and Eliza, the chambermaid and table-waiter. Hereupon was much fun and some sympathy. They searched, and found nothing that they sought, though she gave up a pair of pantalets, which she pretended to have taken by mistake. Afterwards, she being in the parlor, I went in; and she immediately began to talk to me, giving me an account of the affair, speaking with the bitterness of a wronged person, with a sparkling eye, yet with great fluency and self-possession. She is a yellow, thin, and battered old thing, yet rather country-lady-like in aspect and manners. I heard Eliza telling another girl about it, under my window; and she seemed to think that the poor woman's reluctance to be searched arose from the poorness of her wardrobe and of the contents of her bandbox.

At parting, Eliza said to the girl, "What do you think I heard somebody say about you? That it was enough to make anybody's eyes start square out of their head to look at such red cheeks as yours." Whereupon the girl turned off the compliment with a laugh, and took her leave.

There is an old blind dog, recognizing his friends by the sense of smell. I observed the eager awkwardness with which he accomplishes the recognition, his carefulness in descending steps, and generally in his locomotion. He evidently has not forgotten that he once had the faculty of sight: for he turns his eyes with earnestness towards those who attract his attention, though the orbs are plainly sightless.

Here is an Englishman,—a thorough-going Tory and Monarchist,—upholding everything English, government, people, habits, education, manufactures, modes of living, and expressing his dislike of all Americanisms,—and this in a quiet, calm, reasonable way, as if it were quite proper to live in a country and draw his subsistence from it, and openly abuse it. He imports his clothes from England, and expatiates on the superiority of English boots, hats, cravats, etc. He is a man of unmalleable habits, and wears his dress of the same fashion as that of twenty years ago.

August 18th.—There has come one of the proprietors, or superintendents of a caravan of animals,—a large, portly-paunched, dark-complexioned, brandy-burnt, heavy-faced man of about fifty; with a diminutive nose in proportion to the size of his face,—thick lips; nevertheless he has the air of a man who has seen much, and derived such experience as was for his purpose. Also it is the air of a man not in a subordinate station, though vulgar and coarse. He arrived in a wagon, with a span of handsome gray horses, and ordered dinner. He had left his caravan at Worcester, and came from thence and over the mountain hither, to settle stopping-places for the caravan. The nearest place to this, I believe, was Charlemont; the penultimate at Greenfield. In stopping at such a village as this, they do not expect much profit, if any; but would be content with enough to pay their travelling expenses, while they look to gather gain at larger places. In this village, it seems, the selectmen had resolved not to license any public exhibition of the kind; and it was interesting to attend to the consultations whether it were feasible to overcome the objections, and what might be the best means. Orrin S— and the chance passers-by took part in the discussion. The scruple is that the factory-girls, having ready money by them, spend it for these nonsenses, quitting their work; whereas, were it a mere farming-town, the caravan would take little in proportion to their spendings. The opinion generally was that the license could not be obtained; and the portly man's face grew darker and downcast at the prospect; and he took out a travelling-map and looked it carefully over, to discover some other station. This is something like the planning of the march of an army. It was finally resolved to enlist the influence of a brother-in-law of the head selectman, and try to gain his consent. Whereupon the caravan-man and the brother-in-law (who, being a tavern-keeper, was to divide the custom of the caravan people with this house) went to make the attempt,—the caravan-man stalking along with stiff, awkward bulk and stature, yet preserving a respectability withal though with somewhat of the blackguard. Before he went, he offered a wager of "a drink of rum or a chaw of tobacco" that he did not succeed. When he came back there was a flush in his face and a sparkle in his eye that did not look like failure: but I know not what was the result He took a glass of wine with the brother-in-law,—a grave, thin, frosty-haired, shrewd-looking yeoman, in his shirt-sleeves,—then ordered his horses, paid his bill, and drove off, accompanied still by the same yeoman, perhaps to get the permission of the other two selectmen. If he does not get a license here, he will try at Cheshire.

A fellow appears with a pink guard-chain and two breast-pins in his shirt,—one a masonic one of gold, with compass and square, and the other of colored glass, set in filigree brass,—and the shirt a soiled one.

A tendency to obesity is more common in this part of the country than I have noticed it elsewhere.

August 19th.—I drove with Orrin S— last evening to an old farmer's house to get some chickens. Entering the kitchen, I observed a fireplace with rough stone jambs and back, and a marble hearth, cracked, and otherwise contrasting a roughness of workmanship with the value of the material. There was a clock without a case, the weights being visible, and the pendulum swinging in air,—and a coffee-mill fixed against the wall. A religious newspaper lay on the mantel-piece. The old farmer was reluctant to go after the fowls, declaring that it would be impossible to find them in the dark; but Orrin insisting, he lighted a lamp, and we all went together, and quickly found them, roosted about the wood-pile; whereupon Orrin speedily laid hands on five, and wrung their necks in a twinkling, they fluttering long after they should have been dead. When we had taken our departure, Orrin remarked, "How fainthearted these old fellows are!" and it was a good observation; for it was the farmer's timorous age that made him doubt the practicability of catching the chickens, and it contrasted well with the persevering energy of the middle-aged Orrin. But Orrin inquired, somewhat dolefully, whether I should suppose that he himself bewailed the advances of age. It is a grievous point with him.

In the evening there was a strange fellow in the bar-room,—a sort of mock Methodist,—a cattle-drover, who had stopped here for the night with two cows and a Durham bull. All his talk turned upon religion, and he would ever and anon burst out in some strain of scriptural-styled eloquence, chanted through his nose, like an exhortation at a camp-meeting. A group of universalists and no-religionists sat around him, making him their butt, and holding wild argument with him; and he strangely mingled humor, with his enthusiasm, and enthusiasm with his humor so that it was almost impossible to tell whether he were in jest or earnest. Probably it was neither, but an eccentricity, an almost monomania, that has grown upon him, —perhaps the result of strong religious excitement. And, having been a backslider, he is cursed with a half-frenzied humor. In the morning he talked in the same strain at breakfast, while quaffing fourteen cups of tea,—Eliza, all the while, as she supplied him, entreating him not to drink any more. After breakfast (it being the Sabbath) he drove his two cows and bull past the stoop, raising his staff, and running after them with strange, uncouth gestures; and the last word I heard from him was an exhortation: "Gentlemen, now all of you take your Bibles, and meditate on divine things,"—this being uttered with raised hands, and a Methodistical tone, intermingled, as was his expression, with something humorous; so that, to the last, the puzzle was still kept up, whether he was an enthusiast or a jester. He wore a suit of coarse brown cloth, cut in rather a Quaker fashion; and he had a large nose, and his face expressed enthusiasm and humor,—a sort of smile and twinkle of the eye, with wildness. He is excellent at a bargain; and if, in the midst of his ghostly exhortation, the talk were turned on cattle, he eagerly seized the topic and expatiated on it.

While this fellow was enumeratinog the Universalists in neighboring towns who had turned from their errors on their death-beds, some one exclaimed, "John Hodges! why, he isn't dead,—he's alive and well." Whereat there was a roar of laughter. While holding an argument at table, I heard him mutter to himself at something that his adversary said; and though I could not distinguish what it was, the tone did more to convince me of some degree of earnestness than aught beside. This character might be wrought into a strange portrait of something sad, terrific, and laughable.

The Sabbath wore away lazily, and therefore wickedly. The heavy caravan-man inquired for some book of *light* reading, and, having obtained an old volume of a literary paper, betook himself to the seat of his wagon, to read. At other times he smoked, and talked sensibly enough with anybody that offered. He is a man of sense, though not quick, and seems to be a fair man.

When he walks, he puts the thumb of each hand into the armhole of his waistcoat, and moves along stiffly, with a knock-kneed gait. His talk was chiefly of hotels, and such matters as a man, always travelling, without any purpose of observation for mental improvement, would be interested in. He spoke of his life as a hard one.

There was a Methodist quarterly meeting here, and a love-feast.

There is a fellow hereabout who refuses to pay six dollars for the coffin in which his wife was buried. She died about six months since, and I believe he is already engaged to another. He is young and rather comely, but has not a straightforward look.

One man plods along, looking always on the ground, without ever lifting his eyes to the mountain scenery, and forest, and clouds, above and around him. Another walks the street with a quick, prying eye, and sharp face,—the most expressive possible of one on the look-out for gain,—of the most disagreeable class of Yankees. There is also a sour-looking, unwholesome boy, the son of this man, whose voice is querulous and ill-natured, precisely suited to his aspect. So is his character.

We have another with Indian blood in him, and the straight, black hair,—something of the tawny skin and the quick, shining eye of the Indian. He seems reserved, but is not ill-natured when spoken to. There is so much of the white in him, that he gives the impression of belonging to a civilized race, which causes the more strange sensation on discovering that he has a wild lineage.

August 22d.—I walked out into what is called the Notch this forenoon, between Saddle Mountain and another. There are good farms in this Notch, although the ground is considerably elevated,—this morning, indeed, above the clouds; for I penetrated through one in reaching the higher region, although I found sunshine there. Graylock was hidden in clouds, and the rest of Saddle Mountain had one partially wreathed about it; but it was withdrawn! before long. It was very beautiful cloud-scenery. The clouds lay on the breast of the mountain, dense, white, well-defined, and some of them were in such close vicinity that it seemed as if I could infold myself in them: while others, belonging to the same fleet, were floating through the blue sky above. I had a view of Williamstown at the distance of a few miles,—two or three, perhaps,—a white village and steeple in a gradual hollow, with high mountainous swells heaving themselves up, like immense, subsiding waves, far and wide around it. On these high mountain-waves rested the white summer clouds, or they rested as still in the air above; and they were formed into such fantastic shapes that they gave the strongest possible impression of being confounded or intermixed with the sky. It was like a day-dream to look at it; and the students ought to he day-dreamers, all of them,—when cloud-land is one and the same thing with the substantial earth. By degrees all these clouds flitted away, and the sultry summer sun burned on hill and valley. As I was walking home, an old man came down the mountain-path behind me in a wagon, and gave me a drive to the village. Visitors being few in the Notch, the women and girls looked from the windows after me.; the men nodded and greeted me with a look of curiosity; and two little girls whom I met, bearing tin pails, whispered one another and smiled.

North Adams, August 23rd.—The county commissioners held a court in the bar-room yesterday afternoon, for the purpose of letting out the making of the new road over the mountain. The commissioners sat together in attitudes of some dignity, with one leg laid across another; and the people, to the number of twenty or thirty, sat round about with their hats on, in their shirt-sleeves, with but little, yet with some, formality. Several had come from a distance to bid for the job. They sat with whips in their hands. The first bid was three dollars,—then there was a long silence,—then a bid of two dollars eighty-live cents, and finally it was knocked down at two eighteen, per rod. A disposition to bid was evidenced in one man by his joking on the bid of another.

After supper, as the sun was setting, a man passed by the door with a hand-organ, connected with which was a row of figures, such as dancers, pirouetting and turning, a lady playing on a piano, soldiers, a negro wench dancing, and opening and shutting a huge red mouth,—all these keeping time to the lively or slow tunes of the organ. The man had a pleasant, but sly, dark face; he carried his whole establishment on his shoulder, it being fastened to a staff which he rested on the ground when he performed. A little crowd of people gathered about him on the stoop, peeping over each other's heads with huge admiration,—fat Otis Hodge, and the tall stage-driver, and the little boys all declaring that it was the masterpiece of sights. Some few coppers did the man obtain, as well as much praise. He had come over the high, solitary mountain, where for miles there could hardly be a soul to hear his music.

In the evening, a portly old commissioner, a cheerful man enough, was sitting reading the newspaper in the parlor, holding the candle between the newspaper and his eyes,—its rays glittering on his silver-bowed spectacles and silvery hair. A pensive mood of age had come upon him, and sometimes he heaved a long sigh, while he turned and re-turned the paper, and folded it for convenient reading. By and by a gentleman came to see him, and he talked with him cheerfully.

The fat old squire, whom I have mentioned more than once, is an odd figure, with his bluff, red face,—coarsely red,—set in silver hair,—his clumsy legs, which he moves in a strange straddle, using, I believe, a broomstick for a staff. The breadth of back of these fat men is truly a wonder.

A decent man, at table the other day, took the only remaining potato out of the dish, on the end of his knife, and offered his friend half of it!

The mountains look much larger and more majestic sometimes than at others,—partly because the mind may be variously disposed, so as to comprehend them more or less, and partly that an imperceptible (or almost so) haze adds a great deal to the effect. Saddleback often looks a huge, black mass,—black-green, or black-blue.

The cave makes a fresh impression upon me every time I visit it,—so deep, so irregular, so gloomy, so stern,—part of its walls the pure white of the marble,—others covered with a gray decomposition and with spots of moss, and with brake growing where there is a handful of earth. I stand and look into its depths at various points, and hear the roar of the stream re-echoing up. It is like a heart that has been rent asunder by a torrent of passion, which has raged and foamed, and left its ineffaceable traces; though now there is but a little rill of feeling at the bottom.

In parts, trees have fallen across the fissure,—trees with large trunks.

I bathed in the stream in this old, secluded spot, which I frequent for that purpose. To reach it, I cross one branch of the stream on stones, and then pass to the other side of a little island, overgrown with trees and underbrush. Where I bathe, the stream has partially dammed itself up by sweeping together tree-trunks and slabs and branches, and a thousand things that have come down its current for years perhaps; so that there is a deep pool, full of eddies and little whirlpools, which would carry me away, did I not take hold of the stem of a small tree that lies opportunely transversely across the water. The bottom is uneven, with rocks of various size, against which it is difficult to keep from stumbling, so rapid is the stream. Sometimes it bears along branches and strips of bark,—sometimes a green leaf, or perchance a dry one,—occasionally overwhelmed by the eddies and borne deep under water, then rushing atop the waves.

The forest, bordering the stream, produces its effect by a complexity of causes,—the old and stern trees, with stately trunks and dark foliage,—as the almost black pines,—the young trees, with lightsome green foliage,—as sapling oaks, maples, and poplars,—then the old, decayed trunks, that are seen lying here and there, all mouldered, so,, that the foot would sink into them. The sunshine, falling capriciously on a casual branch considerably within the forest verge, while it leaves nearer trees in shadow, leads the imagination into the depths. But it soon becomes bewildered there. Rocks strewn about, half hidden in the fallen leaves, must not be overlooked.

August 26th.—A funeral last evening, nearly at sunset,—a coffin of a boy about ten years old laid on a one-horse wagon among some straw,—two or three barouches and wagons following. As the funeral passed through the village street, a few men formed a short procession in front of the coffin, among whom were Orrin S— and I. The burial-ground (there are two in the town) is on the sides and summit of a round hill, which is planted with cypress and other trees, among which the white marble gravestones show pleasantly. The grave was dug on the steep slope of a hill; and the grave-digger was waiting there, and two or three other shirt-sleeved yeomen, leaning against the trees.

Orrin S—, a wanton and mirth-making middle-aged man, who would not seem to have much domestic feeling, took a chief part on the occasion, assisting in taking the coffin from the wagon and in lowering it into the grave. There being some superfluous earth at the bottom of the grave, the coffin was drawn up again after being once lowered, and the obstacle removed with a hoe; then it was lowered again for the last time. While this was going on, the father and mother stood weeping at the upper end of the grave, at the head of the little procession,—the mother sobbing with stifled violence, and peeping forth to discover why the coffin was drawn up again. It being fitted in its place, Orrin S— strewed some straw upon it,—this being the custom here, because "the clods on the coffin-lid have an ugly sound." Then the Baptist minister, having first whispered to the father, removed his hat, the spectators all doing the same, and thanked them "in the name of these mourners, for this last act of kindness to them."

In all these rites Orrin S— bore the chief part with real feeling and sadly decorous demeanor. After the funeral, I took a walk on the Williamstown road, towards the west. There had been a heavy shower in the afternoon, and clouds were brilliant all over the sky, around Graylock and everywhere else. Those over the hills of the west were the most splendid in purple and gold, and, there being a haze, it added immensely to their majesty and dusky magnificence.

This morning I walked a little way along the mountain road, and stood awhile in the shadow of some oak and chestnut-trees,—it being a warm, bright, sunshiny morning. The shades lay long from trees and other objects, as at sunset, but how different this cheerful and light radiance from the mild repose of sunset! Locusts, crickets, and other insects were making music. Cattle were feeding briskly, with morning appetites. The wakeful voices of children were heard in a neighboring hollow. The dew damped the road, and formed many-colored drops in the grass. In short, the world was not weary with a long, sultry day, but in a fresh, recruited state, fit to carry it through such a day.

A rough-looking, sunburnt, soiled-shirted, odd, middle-aged little man came to the house a day or two ago, seeking work. He had come from Ohio, and was returning to his native place, somewhere in New England, stopping occasionally to earn money to pay his way. There was something rather ludicrous in his physiognomy and aspect. He was very free to talk with all and sundry. He made a long eulogy on his dog Tiger, yesterday, insisting on his good moral character, his not being quarrelsome, his docility, and all other excellent qualities that a huge, strong, fierce mastiff could have. Tiger is the bully of the village, and keeps all the other dogs in awe. His aspect is very spirited, trotting massively along, with his tail elevated and his head likewise. "When he sees a dog that's anything near his size, he's apt to growl a little,"—Tiger had the marks of a battle on him,—"yet he's a good dog."

Friday, August 31st.—A drive on Tuesday to Shelburne Falls, twenty-two miles or thereabouts distant. Started at about eight o'clock in a wagon with Mr. Leach and Mr. Birch. Our road lay over the Green Mountains, the long ridge of which made awful by a dark, heavy, threatening cloud, apparently rolled and condensed along the whole summit. As we ascended the zigzag road, we looked behind, at every opening in the forest, and beheld a wide landscape of mountain-swells and valleys intermixed, and old Graylock and the whole of Saddleback. Over the wide scene there was a general gloom; but there was a continual vicissitude of bright sunshine flitting over it, now resting for a brief space on portions of the heights, now flooding the valleys with green brightness, now making out distinctly each dwelling, and the hotels, and then two small brick churches of the distant village, denoting its prosperity, while all around seemed under adverse fortunes. But we, who stood so elevated above mortal things, and saw so wide and far, could see the sunshine of prosperity departing from one spot and rolling towards another, so that we could not think it much matter which spot were sunny or gloomy at any one moment.

The top of this Hoosic Mountain is a long ridge, marked on the county map as two thousand one hundred and sixty feet above the sea; on this summit is a valley, not very deep, but one or two miles wide, in which is the town of L—. Here there are respectable farmers, though it is a rough, and must be a bleak place. The first house, after reaching the summit, is a small, homely tavern. We left our horse in the shed, and, entering the little unpainted bar-room, we heard a voice, in a strange, outlandish accent, exclaiming "Diorama." It was an old man, with a full, gray-bearded countenance, and Mr. Leach exclaimed, "Ah, here's the old Dutchman again!" And he answered, "Yes, Captain, here's the old Dutchman,"—though, by the way, he is a German, and travels the country with this diorama in a wagon, and had recently been at South Adams, and was now returning from Saratoga Springs. We looked through the glass orifice of his machine, while he exhibited a succession of the very worst scratches and daubings that can be imagined,—worn out, too, and full of cracks and wrinkles, dimmed with tobacco-smoke, and every other wise dilapidated. There were none in a later fashion than thirty years since, except some figures that had been cut from tailors' show-bills. There were views of cities and edifices in Europe, of Napoleon'a baffles and Nelson's sea-fights, in the midst of which would be seen a gigantic, brown, hairy hand (the Hand of Destiny) pointing at the principal points of the conflict, while the old Dutchman explained. He gave a good deal of dramatic effect to his descriptions, but his accent and intonation cannot be written. He seemed to take interest and pride in his exhibition; yet when the utter and ludicrous miserability thereof made us laugh, he joined in the joke very readily. When the last picture had been shown, he caused a country boor, who stood gaping beside the machine, to put his head within it, and thrust out his tongue. The head becoming gigantic, a singular effect was produced.

The old Dutchman's exhibition being over, a great, dog, apparently an elderly dog, suddenly made himself the object of notice, evidently in rivalship of the Dutchman. He had seemed to be a good-natured, quiet kind of dog, offering his head to be patted by those who were kindly disposed towards him. This great, old dog, unexpectedly, and of his own motion, began to run round after his not very long tail with the utmost eagerness; and, catching hold of it, he growled furiously at it, and still continued to circle round, growling and snarling with increasing rage, as if one half of his body were at deadly enmity with the other. Faster and faster went he, round and roundabout, growing still fiercer, till at last he ceased in a state of utter exhaustion; but no sooner had his exhibition finished than he became the same mild, quiet, sensible old dog as before; and no one could have suspected him of such nonsense as getting enraged with his own tail. He was first taught this trick by attaching a bell to the end of his tail; but he now commences entirely of his own accord, and I really believe he feels vain at the attention he excites.

It was chill and bleak on the mountain-top, and a fire was burning in the bar-room. The old Dutchman bestowed on everybody the title of "Captain," perhaps because such a title has a great chance of suiting an American.

Leaving the tavern, we drove a mile or two farther to the eastern brow of the mountain, whence we had a view, over the tops of a multitude of heights, into the intersecting valleys down which we were to plunge,—and beyond them the blue and indistinctive scene extended to the east and north for at least sixty miles. Beyond the hills it looked almost as if the blue ocean might be seen. Monadnock was visible, like a sapphire cloud against the sky. Descending, we by and by got a view of the Deerfield River, which makes a bend, in its course from about north and south to about east and west, coming out from one defile among the mountains, and flowing through another. The scenery on the eastern side of the Green Mountains is incomparably more striking than on the western, where the long swells and ridges have a flatness of effect; and even Graylock heaves itself so gradually that it does not much strike the beholder. But on the eastern part, peaks one or two thousand foot high rush up on either bank of the river in ranges, thrusting out their shoulders side by side. They are almost precipitous, clothed in woods, through which the naked rock pushes itself forth to view. Sometimes the, peak is bald, while the forest wraps the body of the hill, and the baldness gives it an indescribably stern effect. Sometimes the precipice rises with abruptness from the immediate side of the river; sometimes there is a cultivated valley on either side,—cultivated long, and with all the smoothness and antique rurality of a farm near cities,—this gentle picture strongly set off by the wild mountain-frame around it. Often it would seem a wonder how our road was to continue, the mountains rose so abruptly on either side, and stood, so direct a wall, across our onward course; while, looking behind., it would be an equal mystery how we had gotten thither, through the huge base of the mountain, that seemed to have reared itself erect after our passage. But, passing onward, a narrow defile would give us egress into a scene where new mountains would still appear to bar us. Our road was much of it level; but scooped out among mountains. The river was a brawling stream, shallow and roughened by rocks; now we drove on a plane with it; now there was a sheer descent down from the roadside upon it, often unguarded by any kind of fence, except by the trees that contrived to grow on the headlong interval. Between the mountains there were gorges, that led the imagination away into new scenes of wildness. I have never driven through such romantic scenery, where there was such a variety and boldness of mountain shapes as this; and though it was a broad sunny day, the mountains diversified the view with sunshine and shadow, and glory and gloom.

In Charlemont (I think), after passing a bridge, we saw a very curious rock on the shore of the river, about twenty feet from the roadside. Clambering down the bank, we found it a complete arch, hollowed out of the solid rock, and as high as the arched entrance of an ancient church, which it might be taken to be, though considerably dilapidated and weather-worn. The water flows through it, though the rock afforded standing room, beside the pillars. It was really like the archway of an enchanted palace, all of which has vanished except the entrance,—now only into nothingness and empty space. We climbed to the top of the arch, in which the traces of water having eddied are very perceptible. This curiosity occurs in a wild part of the river's course, and in a solitude of mountains.

Farther down, the river becoming deeper, broader, and more placid, little boats were seen moored along it, for the convenience of crossing. Sometimes, too, the well-beaten track of wheels and hoofs passed down to its verge, then vanished, and appeared on the other side, indicating a ford. We saw one house, pretty, small, with green blinds, and much quietness in its environments on the other side of the river, with a flat-bottomed boat for communication. It was a pleasant idea that the world was kept off by the river.

Proceeding onward, we reached Shelburne Falls. Here the river, in the distance of a few hundred yards, makes a descent of about a hundred and fifty feet over a prodigious bed of rock. Formerly it doubtless flowed unbroken over the rock, merely creating a rapid; and traces of water having raged over it are visible in portions of the rock that now lie high and dry. At present the river roars through a channel which it has worn in the stone, leaping in two or three distinct falls, and rushing downward, as from flight to flight of a broken and irregular staircase. The mist rises from the highest of these cataracts, and forms a pleasant object in the sunshine. The best view, I think, is to stand on the verge of the upper and largest fall, and look down through the whole rapid descent of the river, as it hurries, foaming, through its rock-worn path,—the rocks seeming to have been hewn away, as when mortals make a road. These falls are the largest in this State, and have a very peculiar character. It seems as if water had had more power at some former period than now, to hew and tear its passage through such an immense ledge of rock as here withstood it. In this crag, or parts of it, now far beyond the reach of the water, it has worn what are called pot-holes,—being circular hollows in the rock, where for ages stones have been whirled round and round by the eddies of the water; so that the interior of the pot is as circular and as smooth as it could have been made by art. Often the mouth of the pot is the narrowest part, the inner space being deeply scooped out. Water is contained in most of these pot-holes, sometimes so deep that a man might drown himself therein, and lie undetected at the bottom. Some of them are of a convenient size for cooking, which might be practicable by putting in hot stones.

The tavern at Shelburne Falls was about the worst I ever saw,—there being hardly anything to eat, at least nothing of the meat kind. There was a party of students from the Rensselaer school at Troy, who had spent the night there, a set of rough urchins, from sixteen to twenty years old, accompanied by the wagon-driver, a short, stubbed little fellow, who walked about with great independence, thrusting his hands into his breeches-pockets, beneath his frock. The queerness was, such a figure being associated with classic youth. They were on an excursion which is yearly made from that school in search of minerals. They seemed in rather better moral habits than students used to be, but wild-spirited, rude, and unpolished, somewhat like German students, which resemblance one or two of them increased by smoking pipes. In the morning, my breakfast being set in a corner of the same room with them, I saw their breakfast-table, with a huge wash-bowl of milk in the centre, and a basin and spoon placed for each guest.

In the bar-room of this tavern were posted up written advertisements, the smoked chimney-piece being thus made to serve for a newspaper: "I have rye for sale," "I have a fine mare colt," etc. There was one quaintly expressed advertisement of a horse that had strayed or been stolen from a pasture.

The students, from year to year, have been in search of a particular rock, somewhere on the mountains in the vicinity of Shelburne Falls, which is supposed to contain some valuable ore; but they cannot find it. One man in the bar-room observed that it must be enchanted; and spoke of a tinker, during the Revolutionary War, who met with a somewhat similar instance. Roaming along the Hudson River, he came to a precipice which had some bunches of singular appearance embossed upon it. He knocked off one of the bunches, and carrying it home, or to a camp, or wherever he lived, he put it on the fire, and melted it down into clear lead. He sought, for the spot again and again, but could never find it.

Mr. Leach's brother is a student at Shelburne Falls. He is about thirty-five years old, and married; and at this mature age he is studying for the ministry, and will not finish his course for two or three years. He was bred a farmer, but has sold his farm, and invested the money, and supports himself and wife by dentistry during his studies. Many of the academy students are men grown, and some, they say, well towards forty years old. Metbinks this is characteristic of American life,—these rough, weather-beaten, hard-handed, farmer-bred students. In nine cases out of ten they are incapable of any effectual cultivation; for men of ripe years, if they have any pith in them, will have long ago got beyond academy or even college instruction. I suspect nothing better than a very wretched smattering is to be obtained in these country academies.

Mr. Jenkins, an instructor at Amherst, speaking of the Western mounds, expressed an opinion that they were of the same nature and origin as some small circular hills which are of very frequent occurrence here in North Adams. The burial-ground is on one of them, and there is another, on the summit of which appears a single tombstone, as if there were something natural in making these hills the repositories of the dead. A question of old H— led to Mr. Jenkins's dissertation on this subject, to the great contentment of a large circle round the bar-room fireside on the hist rainy day.

A tailor is detected by Mr. Leach, because his coat had not a single wrinkle in it. I saw him exhibiting patterns of fashions to Randall, the village tailor. Mr. Leach has much tact in finding out the professions of people. He found out a blacksmith, because his right hand was much larger than the other.

A man getting subscriptions for a religious and abolition newspaper in New York, —somewhat elderly and gray-haired, quick in his movements, hasty in his walk, with an eager, earnest stare through his spectacles, hurrying about with a pocket-book of subscriptions in his hand,—seldom speaking, and then in brief expressions, —sitting down before the stage comes, to write a list of subscribers obtained to his employers in New York. Withal, a city and business air about him, as of one accustomed to hurry through narrow alleys, and dart across thronged streets, and speak hastily to one man and another at jostling corners, though now transiting his affairs in the solitude of mountains.

An old, gray man, seemingly astray and abandoned in this wide world, sitting in the bar-room, speaking to none, nor addressed by any one. Not understanding the meaning of the supper-bell till asked to supper by word of mouth. However, he called for a glass of brandy,

A pedlar, with girls' neckerchiefs,—or gauze,—men's silk pocket-handkerchiefs, red bandannas, and a variety of horn combs, trying to trade with the servant-girls of the house. One of them, Laura, attempts to exchange a worked Vandyke, which she values at two dollars and a half; Eliza, being reproached by the pedlar, "vows that she buys more of pedlars than any other person in the house."

A drove of pigs passing at dusk. They appeared not so much disposed to ramble and go astray from the line of march as in daylight, but kept together in a pretty compact body. There was a general grunting, not violent at all, but low and quiet, as if they were expressing their sentiments among themselves in a companionable way. Pigs, on a march, do not subject themselves to any leader among themselves, but pass on, higgledy-piggledy, without regard to age or sex.

September 1st.—Last evening, during a walk, Graylock and the whole of Saddleback were at first imbued with a mild, half-sunshiny tinge, then grew almost black,—a huge, dark mass lying on of the earth and encumbering it. Stretching up from behind the black mountain, over a third or more of the sky, there was a heavy, sombre blue heap or ledge of clouds, looking almost as solid as rocks. The volumes of which it was composed were perceptible by translucent lines and fissures; but the mass, as a whole, seemed as solid, bulky, and ponderous in the cloud-world as the mountain was on earth. The mountain and cloud together had an indescribably stern and majestic aspect. Beneath this heavy cloud, there was a fleet or flock of light, vapory mists, flitting in middle air; and these were tinted, from the vanished sun, with the most living purple that can be conceived,—a fringe upon the stern blue. In the opposite quarter of the heavens, a rose-light was reflected, whence I know not, which colored the clouds around the moon, then well above the horizon, so that the nearly round and silver moon appeared strangely among roseate clouds, —sometimes half obscured by them.

A man with a smart horse, upon which the landlord makes laudatory remarks. He replies that he has a better at home. Dressed in a brown, bright-buttoned coat, smartly cut. He immediately becomes familiar, and begins to talk of the license law, and other similar topics, making himself at home, as one who, being much of his time upon the road, finds himself at ease at any tavern. He inquired after a stage agent, named Brigham, who formerly resided here, but now has gone to the West. He himself was probably a horse-jockey.

An old lady, stopping here over the Sabbath, waiting for to-morrow's stage for Greenfield, having been deceived by the idea that she could proceed on her journey without delay. Quiet, making herself comfortable, taken into the society of the women of the house.

September 3d.—On the slope of .Bald Mountain a clearing, set in the frame of the forest on all sides,—a growth of clover upon it, which, having been mowed once this year, is now appropriated to pasturage. Stumps remaining in the ground; one tall, barkless stem of a tree standing upright, branchless, and with a shattered summit. One or two other stems lying prostrate and partly overgrown with bushes and shrubbery, some of them bearing a yellow flower,—a color which Autumn loves. The stumps and trunks fire-blackened, vet nothing about them that indicates a recent clearing, but the roughness of an old clearing, that, being removed from convenient labor, has none of the polish of the homestead. The field, with slight undulations, slopes pretty directly down. Near the lower verge, a rude sort of barn, or rather haystack roofed over, and with hay protruding and hanging out. An ox feeding, and putting up his muzzle to pull down a mouthful of hay; but seeing me, a stranger, in the upper part of the field, he remains long gazing, and finally betakes himself to feeding again. A solitary butterfly flitting to and fro, blown slightly on its course by a cool September wind,—the coolness of which begins to be tempered by a bright, glittering sun. There is dew on the grass. In front, beyond the lower spread of forest, Saddle Mountain rises, and the valleys, and long, swelling hills sweep away. But the impression of this clearing is solitude, as of a forgotten land.

It is customary here to toll the bell at the death of a person, at the hour of his death, whether a.m. or p.m. Not, however, I suppose, if it happen in deep night.

"There are three times in a man's life when he is talked about,—when he is born, when he is married, and when he dies." "Yes," said Orrin S—, "and only one of the times has he to pay anything for it out of his own pocket." (In reference to a claim by the guests of the bar-room on the man Amasa Richardson for a treat.)

A wood-chopper, travelling the country in search of jobs at chopping. His baggage a bundle, a handkerchief, and a pair of coarse boots. His implement an axe, most keenly ground and sharpened, which I had noticed standing in a corner, and thought it would almost serve as a razor. I saw another wood-chopper sitting down on the ascent of Bald Mountain, with his axe on one side and a jug and provisions on the other, on the way to his day's toil.

The Revolutionary pensioners come out into the sunshine to make oath that they are still above ground. One, whom Mr. S— saluted as "Uncle John," went into the bar-room, walking pretty stoutly by the aid of a long, oaken staff,—with an old, creased, broken and ashen bell-crowned hat on his head, and wearing a brown, old-fashioned suit of clothes. Pretty portly, fleshy in the face, and with somewhat of a paunch, cheerful, and his senses, bodily and mental, in no very bad order, though he is now in his ninetieth year. "An old withered and wilted apple," quoth Uncle John, "keeps a good while." Mr. S— says his grandfather lived to be a hundred, and that his legs became covered with moss, like the trunk of an old tree. Uncle John would smile and cackle at a little jest, and what; life there was in him seemed a good-natured and comfortable one enough. He can walk two or three miles, he says, "taking it moderate." I suppose his state is that of a drowsy man but partly conscious of life,—walking as through a dim dream, but brighter at some seasons than at others. By and by he will fall quite asleep, without any trouble. Mr. S—, unbidden, gave him a glass of gin, which the old man imbibed by the warm fireside, and grew the younger for it.

September 4th.—This day an exhibition of animals in the vicinity of the village, under a pavilion of sailcloth,—the floor being the natural grass, with here and there a rock partially protruding. A pleasant, mild shade; a strip of sunshine or a, spot of glimmering brightness in some parts. Crowded,—row above row of women, on an amphitheatre of seats, on one side. In an inner pavilion an exhibition of anacondas, —four,—which the showman took, one by one, from a large box, under some blankets, and hung round his shoulders. They seemed almost torpid when first taken out, but gradually began to assume life, to stretch, to contract, twine and writhe, about his neck and person, thrusting out their tongues and erecting their heads. Their weight was as much as he could bear, and they hung down almost to the ground when not contorted,—as big round as a man!s thigh, almost,—spotted and richly variegated. Then he put them into the box again, their heads emerging and writhing forth, which the showman thrust back again. He gave a descriptive and historical account of them, and a fanciful and poetical one also. A man put his arm and head into the lion's mouth,—all the spectators looking on so attentively that a breath could not be heard. That was impressive,—its effect on a thousand persons,—more so than the thing itself.

In the evening the caravan people were at the tavern, talking of their troubles in coming over the mountain,—the overturn of a cage containing two leopards and a hyena. They are a rough, ignorant set of men, apparently incapable of taking any particular enjoyment from the life of variety and adventure which they lead. There was the man who put his head into the lion's mouth, and, I suppose, the man about whom the anacondas twined, talking about their suppers, and blustering for hot meat, and calling for something to drink, without anything of the wild dignity of men familiar with the nobility of nature.

A character of a desperate young man, who employs high courage and strong faculties in this sort of dangers, and wastes his talents in wild riot, addressing the audience as a snake-man,—keeping the ring while the monkey rides the pony,—singing negro and other songs.

The country boors were continually getting within the barriers, and venturing too near the cages. The great lion lay with his fore paws extended, and a calm, majestic, but awful countenance. He looked on the people as if he had seen many such concourses. The hyena was the most ugly and dangerous looking beast, full of spite, and on ill terms with all nature, looking a good deal like a hog with the devil in him, the ridge of hair along his back bristling: He was in the cage with a leopard and a panther, and the latter seemed continually on the point of laying his paw on the hyena, who snarled, and showed his teeth. It is strange, though, to see how these wild beasts acknowledge and practise a degree of mutual forbearance, and of obedience to man, with their wild nature yet in them. The great white bear seemed in distress from the heat, moving his head and body in a peculiar, fantastic way, and eagerly drinking water when given it. He was thin and lank.

The caravan men were so sleepy, Orrin S— says, that he could hardly wake them in the morning. They turned over on their faces to show him.

Coming out of the caravansary, there were the mountains, in the quiet sunset, and many men drunk, swearing, and fighting. Shanties with liquor for sale.

The elephant lodged in the barn.

September 5th.—I took a walk of three miles from the village, which brought me into Vermont. The line runs athwart a bridge,—a rude bridge, which crosses a mountain stream. The stream runs deep at the bottom of a gorge, plashing downward, with rapids and pools, and bestrewn with large rocks, deep and shady, not to be reached by the sun except in its meridian, as well on account of the depth of the gorge as of the arch of wilderness trees above it. There was a stumpy clearing beyond the bridge, where some men were building a house. I went to them, and inquired if I were in Massachusetts or Vermont, and asked for some water. Whereupon they showed great hospitality, and the master-workman went to the spring, and brought delicious water in a tin basin, and produced another jug containing " new rum, and very good; and rum does nobody any harm if they make a good use of it," quoth he. I invited them to call on me at the hotel, if they should come to the village within two or three days. Then I took my way back through the forest, for this is a by-road, and is, much of its course, a sequestrated and wild one, with an unseen torrent roaring at an unseen depth, along the roadside.

My walk forth had been an almost continued ascent, and, returning, I had an excellent view of Graylock and the adjacent mountains, at such a distance that they were all brought into one group, and comprehended at one view, as belonging to the same company,—all mighty, with a mightier chief. As I drew nearer home, they separated, and the unity of effect was lost. The more distant then disappeared behind the nearer ones, and finally Graylock itself was lost behind the hill which immediately shuts in the village. There was a warm, autumnal haze, which, I think, seemed to throw the mountains farther off, and both to enlarge and soften them.

To imagine the gorges and deep hollows in among the group of mountains,—their huge shoulders and protrusions.

"They were just beginning to pitch over the mountains, as I came along,"—stage-driver's expression about the caravan.

A fantastic figure of a village coxcomb, striding through the bar-room, and standing with folded arms to survey the caravan men. There is much exaggeration and rattle-brain about this fellow.

A mad girl leaped from the top of a tremendous precipice in Pownall, hundreds of feet high, if the tale be true, and, being buoyed up by her clothes, came safely to the bottom.

Inquiries about the coming of the caravan, and whether the elephant had got to town, and reports that he had.

A smart, plump, crimson-faced gentleman, with a travelling-portmanteau of peculiar neatness and convenience. He criticises the road over the mountain, having come in the Greenfield stage; perhaps an engineer.

Bears still inhabit Saddleback and the neighboring mountains and forests. Six were taken in Pownall last year, and two hundred foxes. Sometimes they appear on the hills, in close proximity to this village.

September 7th.—Mr. Leach and I took a walk by moonlight last evening, on the road that leads over the mountain. Remote from houses, far up on the hill-side, we found a lime-kiln, burning near the road; and, approaching it, a watcher started from the ground, where he had been lying at his length. There are several of these limp-kilns in this vicinity. They are circular, built with stones, like a round tower, eighteen or twenty feet high, having a hillock heaped around in a great portion of their circumference, so that the marble may be brought and thrown in by cart-loads at the top. At the bottom there is a doorway, large enough to admit a man in a stooping posture. Thus an edifice of great solidity is constructed, which will endure for centuries, unless needless pains are taken to tear it down. There is one on the hill-side, close to the village, wherein weeds grow at the bottom, and grass and shrubs too are rooted in the interstices of the stones, and its low doorway has a dungeon-like aspect, and we look down from the top as into a roofless tower. It apparently has not been used for many years, and the lime and weather-stained fragments of marble are scattered about.

But in the one we saw last night a hard-wood fire was burning merrily, beneath the superincumbent marble,—the kiln being heaped full; and shortly after we came, the man (a dark, black-bearded figure, in shirt-sleeves) opened the iron door, through the chinks of which the fire was gleaming, and thrust in huge logs of wood, and stirred the immense coals with a long pole, and showed us the glowing limestone,—the lower layer of it. The heat of the fire was powerful, at the distance of several yards from the open door. He talked very sensibly with us, being doubtless glad to have two visitors to vary his solitary night-watch; for it would not do for him to fall asleep, since the fire should be refreshed as often as every twenty minutes. We ascended the hillock to the top of the kiln, and the marble was red-hot, and burning with a bluish, lambent flame, quivering up, sometimes nearly a yard high, and resembling the flame of anthracite coal, only, the marble being in large fragments, the flame was higher. The kiln was perhaps six or eight feet across.

Four hundred bushels of marble were then in a state of combustion. The expense of converting this quantity into lime is about fifty dollars, and it sells for twenty-five cents per bushel at the kiln. We asked the man whether he would run across the top of the intensely burning kiln, barefooted, for a thousand dollars; and he said he would for ten. He told us that the lime had been burning forty-eight hours, and would be finished in thirty-six more. He liked the business of watching it better by night than by day; because the days were often hot, but such a mild and beautiful night as the last was just right. Here a poet might make verses with moonlight in them, and a gleam of fierce fire-light flickering through. It is a shame to use this brilliant, white, almost transparent marble in this way. A man said of it, the other day, that into some pieces of it, when polished, one could see a good distance; and he instanced a certain gravestone.

Visited the cave. A large portion of it, where water trickles and falls, is perfectly white. The walls present a specimen of how Nature packs the stone, crowding huge masses, as it were, into chinks and fissures, and here we see it in the perpendicular or horizontal layers, as Nature laid it.

September 9th.—A walk yesterday forenoon through the Notch, formed between Saddle Mountain and another adjacent one. This Notch is otherwise called the Bellowspipe, being a long and narrow valley, with a steep wall on either side. The walls are very high, and the fallen timbers lie strewed adown the precipitous descent. The valley gradually descends from the narrowest part of the Notch, and a stream of water flows through the midst of it, which, farther onward in its coarse, turns a mill. The valley is cultivated, there being two or three farm-houses towards the northern end, and extensive fields of grass beyond, where stand the hay-mows of last year, with the hay cut away regularly around their bases. All the more distant portion of the valley is lonesome in the extreme; and on the hither side of the narrowest part the land is uncultivated, partly overgrown with forest, partly used as sheep-pastures, for which purpose it is not nearly so barren as sheep-pastures usually are. On the right, facing southward, rises Graylock, all beshagged with forest, and with headlong precipices of rock appearing among the black pines. Southward there is a most extensive view of the valley, in which Saddleback and its companion mountains are crouched,—wide and far,—a broad, misty valley, fenced in by a mountain wall, and with ullages scattered along it. and miles of forest, which appear but as patches scattered here and there upon the landscape. The descent from the Notch southward is much more abrupt than on the other side. A stream flows down through it; and along much of its course it has washed away all the earth from a ledge of rock, and then formed a descending pavement, smooth and regular, which the scanty flow of water scarcely suffices to moisten at this period, though a heavy rain, probably, would send down a torrent raging, roaring, and foaming. I descended along the course of the stream, and sometimes on the rocky path of it, and, turning off towards the south village, followed a cattle-path till I came to a cottage.

A horse was standing saddled near the door, but I did not see the rider. I knocked, and an elderly woman, of very pleasing and intelligent aspect, came at the summons, and gave me directions how to get to the south village through an orchard and "across lots," which would bring me into the road mar the Quaker meeting-house, with gravestones round it. While she talked, a young woman came into the pantry from the kitchen, with a dirty little brat, whose squalls I had heard all along; the reason of his outcry being that his mother was washing him,—a very unusual process, if I may judge by his looks. I asked the old lady for some water, and she gave me, I think, the most delicious I ever tasted. These mountaineers ought certainly to be temperance people; for their mountain springs supply them with a liquor of which the cities and the low countries can have no conception. Pure, fresh, almost sparkling, exhilarating,—such water as Adam and Eve drank.

I passed the south village on a by-road, without entering it, and was taken up by the stage from Pittsfield a mile or two this side of it. Platt, the driver, a friend of mine, talked familiarly about many matters, intermixing his talk with remarks on his team and addresses to the beasts composing it, who were three mares, and a horse on the near wheel,—all bays. The horse he pronounced "a dreadful nice horse to go; but if he could shirk off the work on the others, he would,"—which unfairness Platt corrected by timely strokes of the whip whenever the horse's traces were not tightened. One of the mares wished to go faster, hearing another horse tramp behind her; "and nothing made her so mad," quoth Platt, "as to be held in when she wanted to go." The near leader started. "On the little devil," said he, "how skittish she is!" Another stumbled, and Platt bantered her thereupon. Then he told of floundering through snow-drifts in winter, and carrying the mail on his back four miles from Bennington. And thus we jogged on, and got to "mine inn " just as the dinner-bell was ringing.

Pig-drover, with two hundred pigs. They are much more easily driven on rainy days than on fair ones. One of his pigs, a large one, particularly troublesome as to running off the road towards every object, and leading the drove. Thirteen miles about a day's journey, in the course of which the drover has to travel about thirty.

They have a dog, who runs to and fro indefatigably, barking at those who straggle on the flanks of the line of march, then scampering to the other side and barking there, and sometimes having quite an affair of barking and surly grunting with some refractory pig, who has found something to munch, and refuses to quit it. The pigs are fed on corn at their halts. The drove has some ultimate market, and individuals are peddled out on the march. Some die.

Merino sheep (which are much raised in Berkshire) are good for hardly anything to eat,—a fair-sized quarter dwindling down to almost nothing in the process of roasting.

The tavern-keeper in Stockbridge, an elderly bachelor,—a dusty, black-dressed, antiquated figure, with a white neck-cloth setting off a dim, yellow complexion, looking like one of the old wax-figures of ministers in a comer of the New England

Museum. He did not seem old, but like a middle-aged man, who had been preserved in some dark and cobwebby corner for a great while. He is asthmatic.

In Connecticut, and also sometimes in Berkshire, the villages are situated on the most elevated ground that can be found, so that they are visible for miles around. Litchfield is a remarkable instance, occupying a high plain, without the least shelter from the winds, and with almost as wide an expanse of view as from a mountain-top. The streets are very wide,—two or three hundred feet, at least,—with wide, green margins, and sometimes there is a wide green space between two road tracks. Nothing can be neater than the churches and houses. The graveyard is on the slope, and at the foot of a swell, filled with old and new gravestones, some of red freestone, some of gray granite, most of them of white marble, and one of cast-iron with an inscription of raised letters. There was one of the date of about 1770, on which was represented the third-length, bas-relief portrait of a gentleman in a wig and other costume of that day; and as a framework about this portrait was wreathed a garland of vine-leaves and heavy clusters of grapes. The deceased should have been a jolly bottleman; but the epitaph indicated nothing of the kind.

In a remote part of the graveyard,—remote from the main body of dead people,— I noticed a humble, mossy stone, on which I traced out "To the memory of Julia Africa, servant of Rev." somebody. There were also the half-obliterated traces of other graves, without any monuments, in the vicinity of this one. Doubtless the slaves here mingled their dark (day with the earth.

At Litchfield there is a doctor who undertakes to cure deformed people,—and humpbacked, lame, and otherwise defective folk go there. Besides these, there were many ladies and others boarding there, for the benefit of the air, I suppose.

At Canaan, Connecticut, before the tavern, there is a doorstep, two or three paces large in each of its dimensions; and on this is inscribed the date when the builder of the house came to the town,—namely, 1731. The house was built in 1751. Then follows the age and death of the patriarch (at over ninety) and his wife, and the births of, I think, eleven sons and daughters. It would seem as if they were buried underneath; and many people take that idea. It is odd to put a family record in a spot where it is sure to be trampled underfoot.

At Springfield, a blind man, who came in the stage,—elderly,—sitting in the reading-room, and, as soon as seated, feeling all around him with his cane, so as to find out his locality, and know where he may spit with safety! The cautious and scientific air with which he measures his distances. Then he sits still and silent a long while,—then inquires the hour,—then says, "I should like to go to bed." Nobody of the house being near, he receives no answer, and repeats impatiently, "I'll go to bed." One would suppose, that, conscious of his dependent condition, he would have learned a different sort of manner; but probably he has lived where he could command attention.

Two travellers, eating bread and cheese of their own in the bar-room at Stockbridge, and drinking water out of a tumbler borrowed from the landlord. Eating immensely, and, when satisfied, putting the relics in their trunk, and rubbing down the table.

Sample ears of various kinds of corn hanging over the looking-glass or in the bars of taverns. Four ears on a stalk (good ones) are considered a heavy harvest.

A withered, yellow, sodden, dead-alive looking woman,—an opium-eater. A deaf man, with a great fancy for conversation, so that his interlocutor is compelled to halloo and bawl over the rumbling of the coach, amid which he hears best. The sharp tones of a woman's voice appear to pierce his dull organs much better than a masculine voice. The impossibility of saying anything but commonplace matters to a deaf man, of expressing any delicacy of thought in a raised tone, of giving utterance to fine feelings in a bawl. This man's deafness seemed to have made his mind and feelings uncommonly coarse; for, after the opium-eater had renewed an old acquaintance with him, almost the first question he asked, in his raised voice, was, "Do you eat opium now?"

At Hartford, the keeper of a temperance hotel reading a Hebrew Bible in the bar by means of a lexicon and an English version.

A negro, respectably dressed, and well-mounted on horseback, travelling on his own hook, calling for oats, and drinking a glass of brandy-and-water at the bar, like any other Christian. A young man from Wisconsin said, "I wish I had a thousand such fellows in Alabama." It made a strange impression on me,—the negro was really so human!—and to talk of owning a thousand like him!

Left North Adams September 11th. Reached home September 24th, 1838.

October 24th.—View from a chamber of the Tremont of the brick edifice opposite, on the other side of Beacon Street. At one of the lower windows, a woman at work; at one above, a lady hemming a ruff or some such lady-like thing. She is pretty, young, and married; for a little boy comes to her knees, and she parts his hair, and caresses him in a motherly way. A note on colored paper is brought her; and she reads it, and puts it in her bosom. At another window, at some depth within the apartment, a gentleman in a dressing-gown, reading, and rocking in an easy-chair, etc., etc., etc. A rainy day, and people passing with umbrellas disconsolately between the spectator and these various scenes of indoor occupation and comfort. With this sketch might be mingled and worked up some story that was going on within the chamber where the spectator was situated.

All the dead that had ever been drowned in a certain lake to arise.

The history of a small lake from the first, till it was drained.

An autumnal feature,—boys had swept together the fallen leaves from the elms along the street in one huge pile, and had made a hollow, nest-shaped, in this pile, in which three or four of them lay curled, like young birds.

A tombstone-maker, whom Miss B—y knew, used to cut cherubs on the top of the tombstones, and had the art of carving the cherubs' faces in the likeness of the deceased.

A child of Rev. E. P— was threatened with total blindness. A week after the father had been informed of this, the child died; and, in the mean while, his feelings had become so much the more interested in the child, from its threatened blindness, that it was infinitely harder to give it up. Had he not been aware of it till after the child's death, it would probably have been a consolation.

Singular character of a gentleman (H. H—, Esq.) living in retirement in Boston,—esteemed a man of nicest honor, and his seclusion attributed to wounded feelings on account of the failure of his firm in business. Yet it was discovered that this man had been the mover of intrigues by which men in business had been ruined, and their property absorbed, none knew how or by whom; love-affairs had been broken off, and much other mischief done; and for years he was not in the least suspected. He died suddenly, soon after suspicion fell upon him. Probably it was the love of management, of having an influence on affairs, that produced these phenomena.

Character of a man who, in himself and his external circumstances, shall be equally and totally false: his fortune resting on baseless credit,—his patriotism assumed,—his domestic affections, his honor and honesty, all a sham. His own misery in the midst of it,—it making the whole universe, heaven and earth alike, an unsubstantial mockery to him.

Dr. Johnson's penance in Uttoxeter Market. A man who does penance in what might appear to lookers-on the most glorious and triumphal circumstance of his life. Each circumstance of the career of an apparently successful man to be a penance and torment to him on account of some fundamental error in early life.

A person to catch fire-flies, and try to kindle his household fire with them. It would be symbolical of something.

Thanksgiving at the Worcester Lunatic Asylum. A ball and dance of the inmates in the evening,—a furious lunatic dancing with the principal's wife. Thanksgiving in an almshouse might make a better sketch.

The house on the eastern corner of North and Essex Streets [Salem], supposed to have have been built about 1640, had, say sixty years later, a brick turret erected, wherein on e of the ancestors of the present occupants used to practise alchemy. He was the operative of a scientific person in Boston, the director. There have been other alchemists of old in this town,—one who kept his fire burning seven weeks, and then lost the elixir by letting it go out.

An ancient wineglass (Miss Ingersol's), long-stalked, with a small, cup-like bowl, round which is wreathed a branch of grape-vine, with a rich cluster of grapes, and leaves spread out. there is also some kind of a bird flying. The is excellently cut or engraved.

In the Duke of Buckingham's comedy, "The Chances," Don Frederic says of Don John (they are two noble Spanish gentlemen), "One bed contains us ever."

A person, while awake and in the business of life, to think highly of another, and place perfect confidence in him, but to be troubled with dreams in which this seeming friend appears to act the part of a most deadly enemy. Finally it is discovered that the dream-character is the true one. The explanation would be—the soul's instinctive perception.

Pandora's box for a child's story.

Moonlight is sculpture; sunlight is painting.

"A person to look back on a long life ill-spent, and to picture forth a beautiful life which he would live, if he could be permitted to begin his life over again. Finally to discover that he had only been dreaming of old age,—that he was really young, and could lire such a life as he had pictured."

A newspaper, purporting to be published in a family, and satirizing the political and general world by advertisements, remarks on domestic affairs,—advertisement of a lady's lost thimble, etc.

L. H—. She was unwilling to die, because she had no friends to meet her in the other world. Her little son F. being very ill, on his recovery she confessed a feeling of disappointment, having supposed that he would have gone before, and welcomed her into heaven!

H. L. C— heard from a French Canadian a story of a young couple in Acadie. On their marriage day, all the men of the Province were summoned to assemble in the church to hear a proclamation. When assembled, they were all seized and shipped off to be distributed through New England,—among them the new bridegroom. His bride set off in search of him,—wandered about new England all her lifetime, and at last, when she was old, she found her bridegroom on his death-bed. The shock was so great that it killed her likewise.

January 4th, 1839.—When scattered clouds are resting on the bosoms of hills, it seems as if one might climb into the heavenly region, earth being so intermixed with sky, and gradually transformed into it.

A stranger, dying, is buried; and after many years two strangers come in search of his grave, and open it.

The strange sensation of a person who feels himself an object of deep interest, and close observation, and various construction of all his actions, by another person.

Letters in the shape of figures of men, etc. At a distance, the words composed by the letters are alone distinguishable. Close at hand, the figures alone are seen, and not distinguished as letters. Thus things may have a positive, a relative, and a composite meaning, according to the point of view.

"Passing along the street, all muddy with puddles, and suddenly seeing the sky reflected in these puddles in such a way as quite to conceal the foulness of the street."

A young man in search of happiness,—to be personified by a figure whom he expects to meet in a crowd, and is to be recognized by certain signs. All these signs are given by a figure in various garbs and actions, but he does not recognize that this is the sought-for person till too late.

If cities were built by the sound of music, then some edifices would appear to be constructed by grave, solemn tones,—others to have danced forth to light, fantastic airs.

Familiar spirits, according to Lilly, used to be worn in rings, watches, sword-hilts. Thumb-rings were set with jewels of extraordinary size.

A very fanciful person, when dead, to have his burial in a cloud.

"A story there passeth of an Indian king that sent unto Alexander a fair woman, fed with aconite and other poisons, with this intent complexionally to destroy him!"—*Sir T. Browne.*

Dialogues of the unborn, like dialogues of the dead,—or between two young children.

A mortal symptom for a person being to lose his own aspect and to take the family lineaments, which were hidden deep in the healthful visage. Perhaps a seeker might thus recognize the man he had sought, after long intercourse with him unknowingly.

Some moderns to build a fire on Ararat with the remnants of the ark.

Two little boats of cork, with a magnet in one and steel in the other.

To have ice in one's blood.

To make a story of all strange and impossible things,—as the Salamander, the Phoenix.

The semblance of a human face to be formed on the side of a mountain, or in the fracture of a small stone, by a *lusus naturæ.* The face is an object of curiosity for years or centuries, and by and by a boy is born, whose features gradually assume the aspect of that portrait. At some critical juncture, the resemblance is found to be perfect. A prophecy may be connected.

A person to be the death of his beloved in trying to raise her to more than mortal perfection; yet this should be a comfort to him for having aimed so highly and holily.

1840.—A man, unknown, conscious of temptation to secret crimes, puts up a note in church, desiring the prayers of the congregation for one so tempted.

Some most secret thing, valued and honored between lovers, to be hung up in public places, and made the subject of remark by the city,—remarks, sneers, and laughter.

To make a story out of a scarecrow, giving it odd attributes. From different points of view, it should appear to change,—now an old man, now an old woman,—a gunner, a farmer, or the Old Nick.

A ground-sparrow's nest in the slope of a bank, brought to view by mowing the grass, but still sheltered and comfortably hidden by a blackberry-vine trailing over it. At first, four brown-speckled eggs,—then two little bare young ones, which, on the slightest noise, lift their heads, and open wide mouths for food,—immediately dropping their heads, after a broad gape. The action looks as if they were making a most earnest, agonized petition. In another egg, as in a coffin, I could discern the quiet, death-like form of the little bird. The whole thing had something awful and mysterious in it.

A coroner's inquest on a murdered man,—the gathering of the jury to be described, and the characters of the members,—some with secret guilt upon their souls.

To represent a man as spending life and the intensest labor in the accomplishment of some mechanical trifle,—as in making a miniature coach to be drawn by fleas, or a dinner-service to be put into a cherrystone.

A bonfire to be made of the gallows and of all symbols of evil.

The love of posterity is a consequence of the necessity of death. If a man were sure of living forever here, he would not care about his offspring.

The device of a sundial for a monument over a grave, with some suitable motto.

A man with the right perception of things,—a feeling within him of what is true and what is false. It might be symbolized by the talisman with which, in fairy tales, an adventurer was enabled to distinguish enchantments from realities.

A phantom of the old royal governors, or some such shadowy pageant, on the night of the evacuation of Boston by the British.

— taking my likeness, I said that such changes would come over my face that she would not know me when we met again in heaven. "See if I do not!" said she, smiling. There was the most peculiar and beautiful humor in the point itself, and in her manner, that can be imagined.

Little F. H— used to look into E—'s mouth to see where her smiles came from.

"There is no Measure for Measure to my affections. If the earth fails me, I can die, and go to God," said —.

Selfishness is one of the qualities apt to inspire love. This might be thought out at great length.

# EXTRACTS FROM HIS PRIVATE LETTERS

Boston, July 3d, 1839.—I do not mean to imply that I am unhappy or discontented, for this is not the case. My life only is a burden in the same way that it is to every toilsome man; and mine is a healthy weariness, such as needs only a night's sleep to remove it. But from henceforth forever I shall be entitled to call the sons of toil my brethren, and shall know how to sympathize with them, seeing that I likewise have risen at the dawn, and borne the fervor of the midday sun, nor turned my heavy footsteps homeward till eventide. Years hence, perhaps, the experience that my heart is acquiring now will flow out in truth and wisdom.

August 27th.—I have been stationed all day at the end of Long Wharf, and I rather think that I had the most eligible situation of anybody in Boston. I was aware that it must be intensely hot in the midst of the city; but there was only a short space of uncomfortable heat in my region, half-way towards the centre of the harbor; and almost all the time there was a pure and delightful breeze, fluttering and palpitating, sometimes shyly kissing my brow, then dying away, and then rushing upon me in livelier sport, so that I was fain to settle my straw hat more tightly upon my head. Late in the afternoon, there was a sunny shower, which came down so like a benediction that it seemed ungrateful to take shelter in the cabin or to put up an umbrella. Then there was a rainbow, or a large segment of one, so exceedingly brilliant and of such long endurance that I almost fancied it was stained into the sky, and would continue there permanently. And there were clouds floating all about,—great clouds and small, of all glorious and lovely hues (save that imperial crimson which was revealed to our united gaze),—so glorious, indeed, and so lovely, that I had a fantasy of heaven's being broken into fleecy fragments and dispersed through space, with its blest inhabitants dwelling blissfully upon those scattered islands.

February 7th, 1840.—What beautiful weather this is!—beautiful, at least, so far as sun, sky, and atmosphere are concerned, though a poor, wingless biped is sometimes constrained to wish that he could raise himself a little above the earth. How much mud and mire, how many pools of unclean water, how many slippery footsteps, and perchance heavy tumbles, might be avoided, if we could tread but six inches above the crust of this world. Physically we cannot do this; our bodies cannot; but it seems to me that our hearts and minds may keep themselves above moral mud-puddles and other discomforts of the soul's pathway.

February 11th.—I have been measuring coal all day, on board of a black little British schooner, in a dismal dock at the north end of the city. Most of the time I paced the deck to keep myself warm; for the wind (northeast, I believe) blew up through the dock, as if it had been the pipe of a pair of bellows. The vessel lying deep between two wharves, there was no more delightful prospect, on the right hand and on the left, than the posts and timbers, half immersed in the water, and covered with ice, which the rising and falling of successive tides bad left upon them, so that they looked like immense icicles. Across the water, however, not more than half a mile off, appeared the Bunker Hill Monument; and, what interested me considerably more, a church-steeple, with the dial of a clock upon it, whereby I was enabled to measure the march of the weary hours. Sometimes I descended into the dirty little cabin of the schooner, and warmed myself by a red-hot stove, among biscuit-barrels, pots and kettles, sea-chests, and innumerable lumber of all sorts,—my olfactories, meanwhile, being greatly refreshed by the odor of a pipe, which the captain, or some one of his crew, was smoking. But at last came the sunset, with delicate clouds, and a purple light upon the islands; and I blessed it, because it was the signal of my release.

February 12th.—All day long again have I been engaged in a very black business, —as black as a coal; and, though my face and hands have undergone a thorough purification, I feel not altogether fit to hold communion with doves. Methinks my profession is somewhat akin to that of a chimney-sweeper; but the latter has the advantage over me, because, after climbing up through the darksome flue of the chimney, he emerges into the midst of the golden air, and sings out his melodies far over the heads of the whole tribe of weary earth-plodders. My toil to-day has been cold and dull enough; nevertheless, I was neither cold nor dull.

March 15th.—I pray that in one year more I may find some way of escaping from this unblest Custom House; for it is a very grievous thraldom. I do detest all offices,—all, at least, that are held on a political tenure. And I want nothing to do with politicians. Their hearts wither away and die out of their bodies. Their consciences are turned to india-rubber, or to some substance as black as that, and which will stretch as much. One thing, if no more, I have gained by my custom house experience,—to know a politician. It is a knowledge which no previous thought or power of sympathy could have taught me, because the animal, or the machine rather, is not in nature.

March 23d.—I do think that it is the doom laid upon me, of murdering so many of the brightest hours of the day at the Custom House, that makes such havoc with my wits, for here I am again trying to write worthily,...yet with a sense as if all the noblest part of man had been left out of my composition, or had decayed out of it since my nature was given to my own keeping....Never comes any bird of Paradise into that dismal region. A salt or even a coal ship is ten million times preferable; for there the sky is above me, and the fresh breeze around me, and my thoughts, having hardly anything to do with my occupation, are as free as air.

Nevertheless, you are not to fancy that the above paragraph gives a correct idea of my mental and spiritual state.....It is only once in a while that the image and desire of a better and happier life makes me feel the iron of my chain; for, after all, a human spirit may find no insufficiency of food fit for it, even in the Custom House. And, with such materials as these, I do think and feel and learn things that are worth knowing, and which I should not know unless I had learned them there, so that the present portion of my life shall not be quite left out of the sum of my real existence....It is good for me, on many accounts, that my life has had this passage in it. I know much more than I did a year ago. I have a stronger sense of power to act as a man among men. I have gained worldly wisdom, and wisdom also that is not altogether of this world. And, when I quit this earthly cavern where I am now buried, nothing will cling to me that ought to be left behind. Men will not perceive, I trust, by my look, or the tenor of my thoughts and feelings, that I have been a custom house officer.

April 7th.—It appears to me to have been the most uncomfortable day that ever was inflicted on poor mortals....Besides the bleak, unkindly air, I have been plagued by *two* sets of coal-shovellers at the same time, and have been obliged to keep two separate tallies simultaneously. But I was conscious that all this was merely a vision and a fantasy, and that, in reality, I was not half frozen by the bitter blast, nor tormented by those grimy coal-heavers, but that I was basking quietly in the sunshine of eternity....Any sort of bodily and earthly torment may serve to make us sensible that we have a soul that is not within the jurisdiction of such shadowy demons,—it separates the immortal within us from the mortal. But the wind has blown my brains into such confusion that I cannot philosophize now.

April 19th.—...What a beautiful day was yesterday! My spirit rebelled against being confined in my darksome dungeon at the Custom House. It seemed a sin,—a murder of the joyful young day,—a quenching of the sunshine. Nevertheless, there I was kept a prisoner till it was too late to fling myself on a gentle wind, and be blown away into the country....When I shall be again free, I will enjoy all things with the fresh simplicity of a child of five years old. I shall grow young again, made all over anew. I will go forth and stand in a summer shower, and all the worldly dust that has collected on me shall be washed away at once, and my heart will be like a bank of fresh flowers for the weary to rest upon....

6 p.m.—I went out to walk about an hour ago, and found it very pleasant, though there was a somewhat cool wind. I went round and across the Common, and stood

on the highest point of it, where I could see miles and miles into the country. Blessed be God for this green tract, and the view which it affords, whereby we poor citizens may be put in mind, sometimes, that all his earth is not composed of blocks of brick houses, and of stone or wooden pavements. Blessed be God for the sky, too, though the smoke of the city may somewhat change its aspect,—but still it is better than if each street were covered over with a roof. There were a good many people walking on the mall,—mechanics apparently, and shopkeepers' clerks, with their wives; and boys were rolling on the grass, and I would have liked to lie down and roll too.

April 30th.—...I arose this morning feeling more elastic than I have throughout the winter; for the breathing of the ocean air has wrought a very beneficial effect....What a beautiful, most beautiful afternoon this has been! It was a real happiness to live. If I had been merely a vegetable,—a hawthorn-bush, for instance,—I must have been happy in such an air and sunshine; but, having a mind and a soul,...I enjoyed somewhat more than mere vegetable happiness....The footsteps of May can be traced upon the islands in the harbor, and I have been watching the tints of green upon them gradually deepening, till now they are almost as beautiful as they ever can be.

May 19th.—...Lights and shadows are continually flitting across my inward sky, and I know neither whence they come nor whither they go; nor do I inquire too closely into them. It is dangerous to look too minutely into such phenomena. It is apt to create a substance where at first there was a mere shadow....If at any time there should seem to be an expression unintelligible from one soul to another, it is best not to strive to interpret it in earthly language, but wait for the soul to make itself understood; and, were we to wait a thousand years, we need deem it no more time than we can spare....It is not that I have any love of mystery, but because I abhor it, and because I have often felt that words may be a thick and darksome veil of mystery between the soul and the truth which it seeks. Wretched were we, indeed, if we had no better means of communicating ourselves, no fairer garb in which to array our essential being, than these poor rags and tatters of Babel. Yet words are not without their use even for purposes of explanation,—but merely for explaining outward acts and all sorts of external things, leaving the soul's life and action to explain itself in its own way.

What a misty disquisition I have scribbled! I would not read it over for sixpence.

May 29th.—Rejoice with me, for I am free from a load of coal which has been pressing upon my shoulders throughout all the hot weather. I am convinced that Christian's burden consisted of coal; and no wonder he felt so much relieved, when it fell off and rolled into the sepulchre. His load, however, at the utmost, could not have been more than a few bushels, whereas mine was exactly one hundred and thirty-five chaldrons and seven tubs.

May 30th.—...On board my salt-vessels and colliers there are many things happening, many pictures which, in future years, when I am again busy at the loom of fiction, I could weave in; but my fancy is rendered so torpid by my ungenial way of life that I cannot sketch off the scenes and portraits that interest me, and I am forced to trust them to my memory, with the hope of recalling them at some more favorable period. For these three or four days I have been observing a little Mediterranean boy from Malaga, not more than ten or eleven years old, but who is already a citizen of the world, and seems to be just as gay and contented on the deck of a Yankee coal-vessel as he could be while playing beside his mother's door. It is really touching to see how free and happy he is,—how the little fellow takes the whole wide world for his home, and all mankind for his family. He talks Spanish,—at least that is his native tongue; but he is also very intelligible in English, and perhaps he likewise has smatterings of the speech of other countries, whither the winds may have wafted this little sea-bird. He is a Catholic: and yesterday being Friday he caught some fish and fried them for his dinner in sweet-oil, and really they looked so delicate that I almost wished he would invite me to partake. Every once in a while he undresses himself and leaps overboard, plunging down beneath the waves as if the sea were as native to him as the earth. Then he runs up the rigging of the vessel as if he meant to fly away through the air. I must remember this little boy, and perhaps I may make something more beautiful of him than these rough and imperfect touches would promise.

June 11th.—...I could wish that the east-wind would blow every day from ten o'clock till five; for there is great refreshment in it to us poor mortals that toil beneath the sun. We must not think too unkindly even of the east-wind. It is not. perhaps, a wind to be loved, even in its benignest moods: but there are seasons when I delight to feel its breath upon my cheek, though it be never advisable to throw open my bosom and take it into my heart, as I would its gentle sisters of the south and west. To-day, if I had been on the wharves, the slight chill of an east-wind would have been a blessing, like the chill of death to a world-weary man.

...But this has been one of the idlest days that I ever spent in Boston....In the morning, soon after breakfast, I went to the Athenæum gallery, and, during the hour or two that I stayed, not a single visitor came in. Some people were putting up paintings in one division of the room: but I had the other all to myself. There are two pictures there by our friend Sarah Clarke,—scenes in Kentucky.

From the picture-gallery I went to the reading-rooms of the Athenæum, and there read the magazines till nearly twelve: thence to the Custom House, and soon afterwards to dinner with Colonel Hall: then back to the Custom House, but only for a little while. There was nothing in the world to do, and so at two o'clock I came home and lay down, with the "Faerie Queene" in my hand.

August 21st.—Last night I slept like a child of five years old, and had no dreams at all,—unless just before it was time to rise, and I have forgotten what those dreams were. After I was fairly awake this morning, I felt very bright and airy, and was glad that I had been compelled to snatch two additional hours of existence from annihilation. The sun's disk was but half above the ocean's verge when I ascended the ship's side. These early morning hours are very lightsome and quiet. Almost the whole day I have been in the shade, reclining on a pile of sails, so that the life and spirit are not entirely worn out of me....The wind has been east this afternoon,—perhaps in the forenoon, too,—and I could not help feeling refreshed, when the gentle chill of its breath stole over any cheek. I would fain abominate the east-wind,...but it persists in doing me kindly offices now and then. What a perverse wind it is! Its refreshment is but another mode of torment.

Salem, Oct. 4th. Union Street [Family Mansion].—...Here I sit in my old accustomed chamber, where I used to sit in days gone by....Here I have written many tales,—many that have been burned to ashes, many that doubtless deserved the same fate. This claims to be called a haunted chamber, for thousands upon thousands of visions have appeared to me in it; and some few of them have become visible to the world. If ever I should have a biographer, he ought to make great mention of this chamber in my memoirs, because so much of my lonely youth was wasted here, and here my mind and character were formed; and here I have been hopeful, and here I have been despondent. And here I sat a long, long time, waiting patiently for the world to know me, and sometimes wondering why it did not know me sooner, or whether it would ever know me at all,—at least, till I were in my grave. And sometimes it seemed as if I were already in the grave, with only life enough to be chilled and benumbed. But oftener I was happy,—at least, as happy as I then knew how to be, or was aware of the possibility of being. By and by, the world found me out in my lonely chamber, and called me forth,—not, indeed, with a loud roar of acclamation, but rather with a still, small voice,—and forth I went, but found nothing in the world that I thought preferable to my old solitude till now....And now I begin to understand why I was imprisoned so many years in this lonely chamber, and why I could never break through the viewless bolts and bars; for if I had sooner made my escape into the world, I should have grown hard and rough, and been covered with earthly dust, and my heart might have become callous by rude encounters with the multitude....But living in solitude till the fulness of time was come, I still kept the dew of my youth and the freshness of my heart....I used to think I could imagine all passions, all feelings, and states of the heart and mind; but how little did I know!...Indeed, we are but shadows; we are not endowed with real life, and all that seems most real about as is but the thinnest substance of a dream,—till the heart be touched. That touch creates us,—then we begin to be,—thereby we are beings of reality and inheritors of eternity....

When we shall be endowed with our spiritual bodies, I think that they will be so constituted that we may send thoughts and feelings any distance in no time at all, and transfuse them warm and fresh into the consciousness of those whom we love....But, after all, perhaps it is not wise to intermix fantastic ideas with the reality of affection. Let us content ourselves to be earthly creatures, and hold communion of spirit in such modes as are ordained to us....

I was not at the end of Long Wharf to-day, but in a distant region,—my authority having been put in requisition to quell a rebellion of the captain and "gang" of shovellers aboard a coal-vessel. I would you could have beheld the awful sternness of my visage and demeanor in the execution of this momentous duty. Well,—I have conquered the rebels, and proclaimed an amnesty; so to-morrow I shall return to that paradise of measurers, the end of Long Wharf,—not to my former salt-ship, she being now discharged, but to another, which will probably employ me well-nigh a fortnight longer....Salt is white and pure,—there is something holy in salt....

I have observed that butterflies—very broad-winged and magnificent butterflies—frequently come on board of the salt-ship, where I am at work. What have these bright strangers to do on Long Wharf, where there are no flowers nor any green thing,—nothing but brick storehouses, stone piers, black ships, and the bustle of toilsome men, who neither look up to the blue sky, nor take note of these wandering gems of the air? I cannot account for them, unless they are the lovely fantasies of the mind.

November.—...How delightfully long the evenings are now! I do not get intolerably tired any longer, and my thoughts sometimes wander back to literature, and I have momentary impulses to write stories. But this will not be at present. The utmost that I can hope to do will be to portray some of the characteristics of the life which I am now living, and of the people with whom I am brought into contact, for future use....The days are cold now, the air eager and nipping, yet it suits my health amazingly. I feel as if I could run a hundred miles at a stretch, and jump over all the houses that happen to be in my way....

I have never had the good luck to profit much, or indeed any, by attending lectures, so that I think the ticket had better be bestowed on somebody who can listen to Mr. — more worthily. My evenings are very precious to me, and some of them are unavoidably thrown away in paying or receiving visits, or in writing letters of business, and therefore I prize the rest as if the sands of the hour-glass were gold or diamond dust.

I was invited to dine at Mr. Bancroft's yesterday, with Miss Margaret Fuller; but Providence had given me some business to do, for which I was very thankful.

Is not this a beautiful morning? The sun shines into my soul.

April 1841.—...I have been busy all day, from early breakfast-time till late in the afternoon; and old Father Time has gone onward somewhat less heavily than is his wont when I am imprisoned within the walls of the Custom House. It has been a brisk,breezy day, an effervescent atmosphere, and I have enjoyed it in all its freshness,—breathing air which had not been breathed in advance by the hundred thousand pairs of lungs which have common and invisible property in the atmosphere of this great city. My breath had never belonged to anybody but me. It came fresh from the wilderness of ocean....It was exhilarating to see the vessels, how they bounded over the waves, while a sheet of foam broke out around them. I found a good deal of enjoyment, too, in the busy scene around me; for several vessels were disgorging themselves (what an unseemly figure is this,—"disgorge," quotha, as if the vessel were sick) on the wharf, and everybody seemed to be working with might and main. It pleased me to think that I also had a part to act in the material and tangible business of this life, and that a portion of all this industry could not have gone on without my presence. Nevertheless, I must not pride myself too much on my activity and utilitarianism. I shall, doubtless, soon bewail myself at being compelled to earn my bread by taking some little share in the toils of mortal men....

Articulate words are a harsh clamor and dissonance. When man arrives at his highest perfection, he will again be dumb! for I suppose he was dumb at the Creation, and must go round an entire circle in order to return to that blessed state.

Brook Farm, Oak Hill, April 13th, 1841.—...Here I am in a polar Paradise! I know not how to interpret this aspect of nature,—whether it be of good or evil omen to our enterprise. But I reflect that the Plymouth pilgrims arrived in the midst of storm, and stepped ashore upon mountain snow-drifts; and, nevertheless, they prospered, and became a great people,—and doubtless it will be the same with us. I laud my stars, however, that you will not have your first impressions of (perhaps) our future home from such a day as this....Through faith, I persist in believing that Spring and Summer will come in their due season; but the unregenerated man shivers within me, and suggests a doubt whether I may not have wandered within the precincts of the Arctic Circle, and chosen my heritage among everlasting snows....Provide yourself with a good stock of furs, and, if you can obtain the skin of a polar bear, you will find it a very suitable summer dress for this region....

I have not yet taken my first lesson in agriculture, except that I went to see our cows foddered, yesterday afternoon. We have eight of our own; and the number is now increased by a transcendental heifer belonging to Miss Margaret Fuller. She is very fractious, I believe, and apt to kick over the milk-pail....I intend to convert myself into a milkmaid this evening, but I pray Heaven that Mr. Ripley may be moved to assign me the kindliest cow in the herd, otherwise I shall, perform my duty with fear and trembling.

I like my brethren in affliction very well; and, could you see us sitting round our table at meal-times, before the great kitchen fire, you would call it a cheerful sight. Mrs. B— is a most comfortable woman to behold. She looks as if her ample person were stuffed full of tenderness,—indeed, as if she were all one great, kind heart.

* * * * *

April 14th, 10 a.m.—...I did not milk the cows last night, because Mr. Ripley was afraid to trust them to my hands, or me to their horns, I know not which. But this morning I have done wonders. Before breakfast, I went out to the barn and began to chop hay for the cattle, and with such "righteous vehemence," as Mr. Ripley says, did I labor, that in the space of ten minutes I broke the machine. Then I brought wood and replenished the fires; and finally went down to breakfast, and ate up a huge mound of buckwheat cakes. After breakfast, Mr. Ripley put a four-pronged instrument into my hands, which he gave me to understand was called a pitchfork; and he and Mr. Farley being armed with similar weapons, we all three commenced a gallant attack upon a heap of manure. This office being concluded, and I having purified myself, I sit down to finish this letter....

Miss Fuller's cow hooks the other cows, and has made herself ruler of the herd, and behaves in a very tyrannical manner....I shall make an excellent husbandman,—I feel the original Adam reviving within me.

April 16th.—...Since I last wrote, there has been an addition to our community of four gentlemen in sables, who promise to be among our most useful and respectable members. They arrived yesterday about noon. Mr. Ripley had proposed to them to join us, no longer ago than that very morning. I had some conversation with them in the afternoon, and was glad to hear them express much satisfaction with their new abode and all the arrangements. They do not appear to be very communicative, however,—or perhaps it may be merely an external reserve, like my own, to shield their delicacy. Several of their prominent characteristics, as well as their black attire, lead me to believe that they are members of the clerical profession; but I have not yet ascertained from their own lips what has been the nature -of their past lives. I trust to have much pleasure in their society, and, sooner or later, that we shall all of us derive great strength from our intercourse with them. I cannot too highly applaud the readiness with which these four gentlemen in black have thrown aside all the fopperies and flummeries which have their origin in a false state of society. When I last saw them, they looked as heroically regardless of the stains and soils incident to our profession as I did when I emerged from the gold-mine....

I have milked a cow!!!...The herd has rebelled against the usurpation of Miss Fuller's heifer; and, whenever they are turned out of the barn, she is compelled to take refuge under our protection. So much did. she impede my labors by keeping close to me, that I found it necessary to give her two or three gentle pats with a shovel; but still she preferred to trust herself to my tender mercies, rather than venture among the horns of the herd. She is not an amiable cow; but she has a very intelligent face, and seems to be of a reflective cast of character. I doubt not that she will soon perceive the expediency of being on good terms with the rest of the sisterhood.

I have not yet been twenty yards from our house and barn; but I begin to perceive that this is a beautiful place. The scenery is of a mild and placid character, with nothing bold in its aspect; but I think its beauties will grow upon us, and make us love it the more, the longer we live here. There is a brook, so near the house that we shall be able to hear its ripple in the summer evenings,...but, for agricultural purposes, it has been made to flow in a straight and rectangular fashion, which does it infinite damage as a picturesque object....

It was a moment or two before I could think whom you meant by Mr. Dismal View. Why, he is one of the best of the brotherhood, so far as cheerfulness goes; for if he do not laugh himself, he makes the rest of us laugh continually. He is the quaintest and queerest personage yon ever saw,—full of dry jokes, the humor of which is so incorporated with the strange twistifications of his physiognomy, that his sayings ought to be written down, accompanied with illustrations by Cruikshank. Then he keeps quoting innumerable scraps of Latin, and makes classical allusions, while we are turning over the gold-mine: and the contrast between the nature of his employment and the character of his thoughts is irresistibly ludicrous.

I have written this epistle in the parlor, while Farmer Ripley, and Farmer Farley, and Farmer Dismal View were talking about their agricultural concerns. So you will not wonder if it is not a classical piece of composition, either in point of thought or expression.

* * * * *

Mr. Ripley has bought four black pigs.

*April 22d...*What an abominable hand do I scribble! but I have been chopping wood, and turning a grindstone all the forenoon; and such occupations are likely to disturb the equilibrium of the muscles and sinews. It is an endless surprise to me how much work there is to he done in the world; but, thank God, I am able to do my share of it,—and my ability increases daily. What a great, broad-shouldered, elephantine personage I shall become by and by!

* * * * *

I milked two cows this morning, and would send you some of the milk, only that it is mingled with that which was drawn forth by Mr. Dismal View and the rest of the brethren.

April 28th.—...I was caught by a cold during my visit to Boston. It has not affected my whole frame,, but took entire possession of my head, as being the weakest and most vulnerable part. Never did anybody sneeze with such vehemence and frequency; and my poor brain has been in a thick fog; or, rather, it seemed as if my head were staffed with coarse wool....Sometimes I wanted to wrench it off, and give it a great kick, like a football.

This annoyance has made me endure the bad weather with even less than ordinary patience; and my faith was so far exhausted that, when they told me yesterday that the sun was setting clear, I would not even torn my eyes towards the west But this morning I am made all over anew, and have no greater remnant of my cold than will serve as an excuse for doing no work to-day.

* * * * *

The family has been dismal and dolorous throughout the storm. The night before last, William Allen was stung by a wasp on the eyelid; whereupon the whole side of his face swelled to an enormous magnitude, so that, at the breakfast-table, one half of him looked like a blind giant (the eye being closed), and the other half had such a sorrowful and ludicrous aspect that I was constrained to laugh out of sheer pity.

The same day, a colony of wasps was discovered in my chamber, where they had remained throughout the winter, and were now just bestirring themselves, doubtless with the intention of stinging me from head to foot....A similar discovery was made in Mr. Farley's room. In short, we seem to have taken up our abode in a wasps' nest. Thus you see a rural life is not one of unbroken quiet and serenity.

If the middle of the day prove warm and pleasant, I promise myself to take a walk....I have taken one walk with Mr. Farley; and I could not have believed that there was such seclusion at so short a distance from a great city. Many spots seem hardly to have been visited for ages,—not since John Eliot preached to the Indians here. If we were to travel a thousand miles, we could not escape the world more completely than we can here.

* * * * *

I read no newspapers, and hardly remember who is President, and feel as if I had no more concern with what other people trouble themselves about than if I dwelt in another planet.

May 1st.—...Every day of my life makes me feel more and more how seldom a fact is accurately stated; how, almost invariably, when a story has passed through the mind of a third person, it becomes, so far as regards the impression that it makes in further repetitions, little better than a falsehood, and this, too, though the narrator be the most truth-seeking person in existence. How marvellous the tendency is!...Is truth a fantasy which we are to pursue forever and never grasp?

* * * * *

My cold has almost entirely departed. Were it a sunny day, I should consider myself quite fit for labors out of doors; but as the ground is so damp, and the atmosphere so chill, and the sky so sullen, I intend to keep myself on the sick-list this one day longer, more especially as I wish to read Carlyle on Heroes.

* * * * *

There has been but one flower found in this vicinity,—and that was an anemone, a poor,, pale, shivering little flower, that had crept under a stone-wall for shelter. Mr. Farley found it, while taking a walk with me.

...This is May-Day! Alas, what a difference between the ideal and the real!

May 4th.—...My cold no longer troubles me, and all the morning I have been at work under the clear, blue sky, on a hill-side. Sometimes it almost seemed as if I were at work in the sky itself, though the material in which I wrought was the ore from our gold-mine. Nevertheless, there is nothing so unseemly and disagreeable in this sort' of toil as you could think. It denies the hands, indeed, but not the soul. This gold ore is a pure and wholesome substance, else our mother Nature would not devour it so readily, and derive so much nourishment from it, and return such a rich abundance of good grain and roots in requital of it.

The farm is growing very beautiful now,—not that we yet see anything of the peas and potatoes which we have planted; but the grass blushes green on the slopes and hollows. I wrote that word "blush" almost unconsciously; so we will let it go as an inspired utterance. When I go forth afield,...I look beneath the stone-walls, where the verdure is richest, in hopes that a little company of violets, or some solitary bud, prophetic of the summer, may be there....

But not a wild-flower have I yet found. One of the boys gathered some yellow cowslips last Sunday; but I am well content not to have found them, for they are not precisely what I should like to send to you, though they deserve honor and praise, because they come to us when no others will. We have our parlor here dressed in evergreen as at Christmas. That beautiful little flower-vase...stands on Mr. Ripley's study-table, at which I am now writing, It contains some daffodils and some willow-blossoms. I brought it here rather than keep it in my chamber, because I never sit there, and it gives me many pleasant emotions to look round and be surprised—for it is often a surprise, though I well know that it is there—by something connected with the idea [of a friend].

* * * * *

I do not believe that I should be patient here if I were not engaged in a righteous and heaven-blessed way of life. When I was in the Custom House and then at Salem I was not half so patient....

We had some tableaux last evening, the principal characters being sustained by Mr. Farley and Miss Ellen Slade, They went off very well....

I fear it is time for me—sod-compelling as I am—to take the field again.

May 11th.—...This morning I arose at milking-time in good trim for work; and we have been employed partly in an Augean labor of clearing out a wood-shed, and partly in carting loads of oak. This afternoon I hope to have something to do in the field, for these jobs about the house are not at all to my taste.

June 1st.—...I have been too busy to write a long letter by this opportunity, for I think this present life of mine gives me an antipathy to pen and ink, even more than my Custom House experience did....In the midst of toil, or after a hard day's work in the gold-mine, my soul obstinately refuses to be poured out on paper. That abominable gold-mine! Thank God, we anticipate getting rid of its treasures in the course of two or three days! Of all hateful places that is the worst, and I shall never comfort myself for having spent so many clays of blessed sunshine there. It is my opinion that a man's soul may be buried and perish under a dung-heap, or in a furrow of the field, just as well as under a pile of money.

Mr. George Bradford will probably be here to-day. so that there will be no danger of my being under the necessity of laboring more than I like hereafter. Meantime my health is perfect, and my spirits buoyant, even in the gold-mine.

August 12th.—...I am very well, and not at all weary, for yesterday's rain gave us a holiday; and, moreover, the labors of the farm are not so pressing as they have been. And, joyful thought! in a little more than a fortnight I shall be free from my bondage,—...free to enjoy Nature,—free to think and feel!...Even my Custom House experience was not such a thraldom and weariness: my mind and heart were free. Oh, labor is the curse of the world, and nobody can meddle with it without becoming proportionably brutified! Is it a praiseworthy matter that I have spent five golden months in providing food for cows and horses? It is not so.

August 18th.—I am very well, only somewhat tired with walking half a dozen miles immediately after breakfast, and raking hay ever since. We shall quite finish haying this week, and then there will be no more very hard or constant labor during the one other week that I shall remain a slave.

August 22d.—...I had an indispensable engagement in the bean-field, whither, indeed, I was glad to betake myself, in order to escape a parting scene with —. He was quite out of his wits the night before, and I sat up with him till long past midnight. The farm is pleasanter now that he is gone; for his unappeasable wretchedness threw a gloom over everything. Since I last wrote, we have done haying, and the remainder of my bondage will probably be light. It will be a long time, however, before I shall know how to make a good use of leisure, either as regards enjoyment or literary occupation....

It is extremely doubtful whether Mr. Ripley will succeed in locating his community on this farm. He can bring Mr. E— to no terms, and the more they talk about the matter, the further they appear to be from a settlement. We must form other plans for ourselves; for I can see few or no signs that Providence purposes to give us a home here. I am weary, weary, thrice weary, of waiting so many ages. Whatever may be my gifts, I have not hitherto shown a single one that may avail to gather gold. I confess that I have strong hopes of good from this arrangement with M—; but when I look at the scanty avails of my past literary efforts, I do not feel authorized to expect much from the future. Well, we shall see. Other persons have bought large estates and built splendid mansions with such little books as I mean to write; so that perhaps it is not unreasonable to hope that mine may enable me to build a little cottage, or, at least, to buy or hire one. But I am becoming more and more convinced that we must not lean upon this community. Whatever is to be done must be done by my own undivided strength. I shall not remain here through the winter, unless with an absolute certainty that there will be a house ready for us in the spring. Otherwise, I shall return to Boston,—still, however, considering myself an associate of the community, so that we may take advantage of any more favorable aspect of affairs. How much depends on these little books! Methinks if anything could draw out my whole strength, it would be the motives that now press upon me. Yet, after all, I must keep these considerations out of my mind, because an external pressure always disturbs instead of assisting me.

Salem, September 3d.—...But really I should judge it to be twenty years since I left Brook Farm; and I take this to be one proof that my life there was an unnatural and unsuitable, and therefore an unreal, one. It already looks like a dream behind me. The real Me was never an associate of the community; there has been a spectral Appearance there, sounding the horn at daybreak, and milking the cows, and hoeing potatoes, and raking hay, toiling in the sun, and doing me the honor to assume my name. But this spectre was not myself. Nevertheless, it is somewhat remarkable that my hands have, during the past summer, grown very brown and rough, insomuch that many people persist in believing that I, after all, was the aforesaid spectral horn-sounder, cow-milker, potato-hoer, and hay-raker. But such people do not know a reality from a shadow. Enough of nonsense. I know not exactly how soon I shall return to the farm. Perhaps not sooner than a fortnight from to-morrow.

Salem, September 14th.—... Master Cheever is a very good subject for a sketch, especially if he be portrayed in the very act of executing judgment on an evil-doer. The little urchin may be laid across his knee, and his arms and legs, and whole person indeed, should be flying all abroad, in an agony of nervous excitement and corporeal smart. The Master, on the other hand, must be calm, rigid, without anger or pity, the very personification of that immitigable law whereby suffering follows sin. Meantime the lion's head should have a sort of sly twist on one side of its mouth, and a wink of one eye, in order to give the impression that, after all, the crime and the punishment are neither of them the most serious things in the world. I could draw the sketch myself, if I had but the use of —'s magic fingers.

Then the Acadians will do very well for the second sketch. They might be represented as just landing on the wharf; or as presenting themselves before Governor Shirley, seated in the great chair. Another subject might be old Cotton Mather, venerable in a three-cornered hat and other antique attire, walking the streets of Boston, and lifting up his hands to bless the people, while they all revile him. An old dame should be seen, flinging water, or emptying some vials of medicine, on his head from the latticed window of an old-fashioned house; and all around must be tokens of pestilence and mourning,—as a coffin borne along,—a woman or children weeping on a doorstep. Can the tolling of the Old South bell be painted?

If not this, then the military council, holden at Boston by the Earl of Loudon and other captains and governors, might be taken,—his lordship in the great chair, an old-fashioned, military figure, with a star on his breast. Some of Louis XV.'s commanders will give the costume. On the table, and scattered about the room, must be symbols of warfare,—swords, pistols, plumed hats, a drum, trumpet, and rolled-up banner in one heap. It were not amiss to introduce the armed figure of an Indian chief, as taking part in the council,—or standing apart from the English, erect and stern.

Now for Liberty Tree. There is an engraving of that famous vegetable in Snow's History of Boston. If represented, I see not what scene can be beneath it, save poor Mr. Oliver, taking the oath. He must have on a bag-wig, ruffled sleeves, embroidered coat, and all such ornaments, because he is the representative of aristocracy and an artificial system. The people may be as rough and wild as the fancy can make them; nevertheless, there must be one or two grave, puritanical figures in the midst. Such an one might sit in the great chair, and be an emblem of that stern, considerate spirit which brought about the Revolution. But this would be a hard subject.

But what a dolt am I to obtrude my counsel....

September 16th.—....I do not very well recollect Monsieur du Miroir, but, as to Mrs. Bullfrog, I give her up to the severest reprehension. The story was written as a mere experiment in that style; it did not come from any depth within me,—neither my heart nor mind had anything to do with it. I recollect that the Man of Adamant seemed a fine idea to me when I looked at it prophetically; but I failed in giving shape and substance to the vision which I saw. I don't think it can be very good....

I cannot believe all these stories about —, because such a rascal never could be sustained and countenanced by respectable men. I take him to be neither better nor worse than the average of his tribe. However, I intend to have all my copyrights taken out in my own name; and, if he cheat me once, I will have nothing more to do with him, but will straightway be cheated by some other publisher,—that being, of course, the only alternative.

* * * * *

Governor Shirley's young French wife might be the subject of one of the cuts. She should sit in the great chair,—perhaps with a dressing-glass before her,—and arrayed in all manner of fantastic finery, and with an *outré* French air, while the old Governor is leaning fondly over her, and a puritanic councillor or two are manifesting their disgust in the background. A negro footman and a French waiting-maid might be in attendance.

* * * * *

In Liberty Tree might be a vignette, representing the chair in a very shattered, battered, and forlorn condition, after it had been ejected from Hutchinson's house. This would serve to impress the reader with the woful vicissitudes of sublunary things....Did you ever behold such a vile scribble as I write since I became a farmer? My chirography always was abominable, but now it is outrageous.

Brook Farm, September 22d, 1841.—...Here I am again, slowly adapting myself to the life of this queer community, whence I seem to have been absent half a lifetime,—so utterly have I grown apart from the spirit and manners of the place....I was most kindly received; and the fields and woods looked very pleasant in the bright sunshine of the day before yesterday. I have a friendlier disposition towards the farm, now that I am no longer obliged to toil in its stubborn furrows. Yesterday and to-day, however, the weather has been intolerable,—cold, chill, sullen, so that it is impossible to be on kindly terms with Mother Nature....

I doubt whether I shall succeed in writing another volume of Grandfather's Library while I remain here. I have not the sense of perfect seclusion which has always been essential to my power of producing anything. It is true, nobody intrudes into my room; but still I cannot be quiet. Nothing here is settled; everything is but beginning to arrange itself, and though I would seem to have little to do with aught beside my own thoughts, still I cannot but partake of the ferment around me. My mind will not be abstracted. I must observe, and think, and feel, and content myself with catching glimpses of things which may be wrought out hereafter. Perhaps it will be quite as well that I find myself unable to set seriously about literary occupation for the present. It will be good to have a longer interval between my labor of the body and that of the mind. I shall work to the better purpose after the beginning of November. Meantime I shall see these people and their enterprise under a new point of view, and perhaps be able to determine whether we have any call to cast in our lot among them.

* * * * *

I do wish the weather would put off this sulky mood. Had it not been for the warmth and brightness of Monday, when I arrived here, I should have supposed that all sunshine had left Brook Farm forever. I have no disposition to take long walks in such a state of the sky; nor have I any buoyancy of spirit. I am a very dull person just at this time.

September 25th.—...One thing is certain. I cannot and will not spend the winter here. The time would be absolutely thrown away so far as regards any literary labor to be performed....

The intrusion of an outward necessity into labors of the imagination and intellect is, to me, very painful....

I had rather a pleasant walk to a distant meadow a day or two ago, and we found white and purple grapes in great abundance, ripe, and gushing with rich, pure juice when the hand pressed the clusters. Did you know what treasures of wild grapes there are in this land? If we dwell here, we will make our own wine....

September 27th.—...Now, as to the affair with —, I fully confide in your opinion that he intends to make an unequal bargain with poor, simple, innocent me,—never having doubted this myself. But how is he to accomplish it? I am not, nor shall be, the least in his power, whereas he is, to a certain extent, in mine. He might announce his projected Library, with me for the editor, in all the newspapers in the universe: but still I could not be bound to become the editor, unless by my own act; nor should I have the slightest scruple in refusing to be so, at the last moment, if he persisted in treating me with injustice. Then, as for his printing "Grandfather's Chair," I have the copyright in my own hands, and could and would prevent the sale, or make him account to me for the profits, in case of need. Meantime he is making arrangements for publishing the Library, contracting with other booksellers, and with printers and engravers, and, with every step, making it more difficult for himself to draw back. I, on the other hand, do nothing which I should not do if the affair with — were at an end; for, if I write a book, it will be just as available for some other publisher as for him. Instead of getting me into his power by this delay, he has trusted to my ignorance and simplicity, and has put *himself* in *my* power.

He is not insensible of this. At our last interview, he himself introduced the subject of the bargain, and appeared desirous to close it. But I was not prepared,—among other reasons, because I do not yet see what materials I shall have for the republications in the Library; the works that he has shown me being ill adapted for that purpose; and I wish first to see some French and German books which he has sent for to New York. And, before concluding the bargain, I have promised George Hillard to consult him, and let him do the business. Is not this consummate discretion? and am I not perfectly safe?...I look at the matter with perfect composure, and see all round my own position, and know that it is impregnable.

* * * * *

I was elected to two high offices last night,—viz. to be a trustee of the Brook Farm estate, and Chairman of the Committee of Finance!...From the nature of my office, I shall have the chief direction of all the money affairs of the community, the making of bargains, the supervision of receipts and expenditures, etc., etc., etc....

My accession to these august offices does not at all decide the question of my remaining here permanently. I told Mr. Ripley that I could not spend the winter at the farm, and that it was quite uncertain whether I returned in the spring....

Take no part, I beseech you, in these magnetic miracles. I am unwilling that a power should be exercised on you of which we know neither the origin nor consequences, and the phenomena of which seem rather calculated to bewilder us than to teach us any truths about the present or future state of being....Supposing that the power arises from the transfusion of one spirit into another, it seems to me that the sacredness of an individual is violated by it; there would be an intruder into the holy of holies....I have no faith whatever that people are raised to the seventh or to any heaven at all, or that they gain any insight into the mysteries of life beyond death, by means of this strange science. Without distrusting that the phenomena have really occurred, I think that they are to be accounted for as the result of a material and physical, not of a spiritual, influence. Opium has produced many a brighter vision of heaven, I fancy, and just as susceptible of proof, as these. They are dreams....And what delusion can be more lamentable and mischievous, than to mistake the physical and material for the spiritual? What so miserable as to lose the soul's true, though hidden, knowledge of heaven in the mist of an earth-born vision? If we would know what heaven is before we come thither, let us retire into the depths of our own spirits, and we shall find it there among holy thoughts and feelings; but let us not degrade high heaven and its inhabitants into any such symbols and forms as Miss L— describes; do not let an earthly effluence from Mrs. P—'s corporeal system bewilder and perhaps contaminate, something spiritual and sacred. I should as soon think of seeking revelations of the future state in the rottenness of the grave,—where so many do seek it....

The view which I take of this matter is caused by no want of faith in mysteries; but from a deep reverence of the soul, and of the mysteries which it knows within itself, but never transmits to the earthly eye and ear. Keep the imagination sane,—that is one of the truest conditions of communion with heaven.

# PASSAGES FROM THE NOTE-BOOKS

Brook Farm, September 26th.—A walk this morning along the Needham road. A clear, breezy morning, after nearly a week of cloudy and showery weather. The grass is much more fresh and vivid than it was last month, and trees still retain much of their verdure, though here and there is a shrub or arrayed in scarlet and gold. Along the road, in the midst of a beaten track, I saw mushrooms or toadstools which had sprung up probably during the night.

The houses in this vicinity are, many of them, quite antique, with long, sloping roofs, commencing at a few feet from the ground, and ending in a lofty peak. Some of them have huge old elms overshadowing the yard. One may see the family sleigh near the door, it having stood there all through the summer sunshine, and perhaps with weeds sprouting through the crevices of its bottom, the growth of the months since snow departed. Old barns, patched and supported by timbers leaning against the sides, and stained with the excrement of past ages.

In the forenoon I walked along the edge of the meadow towards Cow Island. Large trees, almost a wood, principally of pine with the green pasture-glades intermixed, and cattle feeding. They cease grazing when an intruder appears, and look at him with long and wary observation, then bend their heads to the pasture again. Where the firm ground of the pasture ceases, the meadow begins,—loose, spongy, yielding to the tread, sometimes permitting the foot to sink into black mud, or perhaps over ankles in water. Cattle-paths, somewhat firmer than the general surface, traverse the dense shrubbery which has overgrown the meadow. This shrubbery consists of small birch, elders, maples, and other trees, with here and there white-pines of larger growth. The whole is tangled and wild and thick-set, so that it is necessary to part the nestling stems and branches, and go crashing through. There are creeping plants of various sorts which clamber up the trees; and some of them have changed color in the slight frosts which already have befallen these low grounds, so that one sees a spiral wreath of scarlet leaves twining up to the top of a green tree, intermingling its bright hues with their verdure, as if all were of one piece. Sometimes, instead of scarlet, the spiral wreath is of a golden yellow.

Within the verge of the meadow, mostly near the firm shore of pasture ground, I found several grapevines, hung with an abundance of large purple grapes. The vines had caught hold of maples and alders, and climbed to the summit, curling round about and interwreathing their twisted folds in so intimate a manner that it was not easy to tell the parasite from the supporting tree or shrub. Sometimes the same vine had enveloped several shrubs, and caused a strange, tangled confusion, converting all these poor plants to the purpose of its own support, and hindering their growing to their own benefit and convenience. The broad vine-leaves, some of them yellow or yellowish-tinged, were seen apparently growing on the same stems with the silver-mapled leaves, and those of the other shrubs, thus married against their will by the conjugal twine; and the purple clusters of grapes hung down from above and in the midst, so that one might "gather grapes," if not "of thorns," yet of as alien bushes.

One vine had ascended almost to the tip of a large white-pine, spreading its leaves and hanging its purple clusters among all its boughs,—still climbing and clambering, as if it would not be content till it had crowned the very summit with a wreath of its own foliage and bunches of grapes. I mounted high into the tree, and ate the fruit there, while the vine wreathed still higher into the depths above my head. The grapes were sour, being not yet fully ripe. Some of them, however, were sweet and pleasant.

September 27th.—A ride to Brighton yesterday morning, it being the day of the weekly cattle-fair. William Allen and myself went in a wagon, carrying a calf to be sold at the fair. The calf had not had his breakfast, as his mother had preceded him to Brighton, and he kept expressing his hunger and discomfort by loud, sonorous baas, especially when we passed any cattle in the fields or in the road. The cows, grazing within hearing, expressed great interest, and some of them came galloping to the roadside to behold the calf. Little children, also, on their way to school, stopped to laugh and point at poor little Bossie. He was a prettily behaved urchin, and kept thrusting his hairy muzzle between William and myself, apparently wishing to be stroked and patted. It was an ugly thought that his confidence in human nature, and nature in general, was to be so ill rewarded as by cutting his throat, and selling him in quarters. This, I suppose, has been his fate before now!

It was a beautiful morning, clear as crystal, with an invigorating, but not disagreeable coolness. The general aspect of the country was as green as summer, —greener indeed than mid or latter summer,—and there were occasional interminglings of the brilliant hues of autumn, which made the scenery more beautiful, both visibly and in sentiment. We saw no absolutely mean nor poor-looking abodes along the road. There were warm and comfortable farm-houses, ancient, with the porch, the sloping roof, the antique peak, the clustered chimney, of old times; and modern cottages, smart and tasteful; and villas, with terraces before them, and dense shade, and wooden urns on pillars, and other such tokens of gentility. Pleasant groves of oak and walnut, also, there were, sometimes stretching along valleys, sometimes ascending a hill and clothing it all round, so as to make it a great clump of verdure. Frequently we passed people with cows, oxen, sheep, or pigs for Brighton Fair.

On arriving at Brighton, we found the village thronged with people, horses, and vehicles. Probably there is no place in New England where the character of an agricultural population may be so well studied. Almost all the farmers within a reasonable distance make it a point, I suppose, to attend Brighton Pair pretty frequently, if not on business, yet as amateurs. Then there are all the cattle-people and butchers who supply the Boston market, and dealers from far and near; and every man who has a cow or a yoke of oxen, whether to sell or buy, goes to Brighton on Monday. There were a thousand or two of cattle in the extensive pens belonging to the tavern-keeper, besides many that were standing about. One could hardly stir a step without running upon the horns of one dilemma or another, in the shape of ox, cow, bull, or ram. The yeomen appeared to be more in their element than I have ever seen them anywhere else, except, indeed, at labor,—more so than at musterings and such gatherings of amusement. And yet this was a sort of festal day, as well as a day of business. Most of the people were of a bulky make, with much bone and muscle, and some good store of fat, as if they had lived on flesh-diet; with mottled faces, too, hard and red, like those of persons who adhered to the old fashion of spirit-drinking. Great, round-paunched country squires were there too, sitting under the porch of the tavern, or waddling about, whip in hand, discussing the points of the cattle. There were also gentlemen-farmers, neatly, trimly, and fashionably dressed, in handsome surtouts, and trousers strapped under their boots. Yeomen, too, in their black or blue Sunday suits, cut by country tailors, and awkwardly worn. Others (like myself) had on the blue stuff frocks which they wear in the fields, the most comfortable garments that ever were invented. Country loafers were among the throng,—men who looked wistfully at the liquors in the bar, and waited for some friend to invite them to drink,—poor, shabby, out-at-elbowed devils. Also, dandies from the city, corseted and buckramed, who had come to see the humors of Brighton Fair. All these, and other varieties of mankind, either thronged the spacious bar-room of the hotel, drinking, smoking, talking, bargaining, or walked about among the cattle-pens, looking with knowing eyes at the horned people. The owners of the cattle stood near at hand, waiting for offers. There was something indescribable in their aspect, that showed them to be the owners, though they mixed among the crowd. The cattle, brought from a hundred separate farms, or rather a thousand, seemed to agree very well together, not quarrelling in the least. They almost all had a history, no doubt, if they could but have told it. The cows had each given her milk to support families,—had roamed the pastures, and come home to the barn-yard, had been looked upon as a sort of member of the domestic circle, and was known by a name, as Brindle or Cherry. The oxen, with their necks bent by the heavy yoke, had toiled in the plough-field and in haying-time for many years, and knew their master's stall as well as the master himself knew his own table. Even the young steers and the little calves had something of domestic sacredness about them; for children had watched their growth, and petted them, and played with them. And here they all were, old and young, gathered from their thousand homes to Brighton Fair; whence the great chance was that they would go to the slaughter-house, and thence be transmitted, in surloins, joints, and such pieces, to the tables of the Boston folk.

William Allen had come to buy four little pigs to take the places of four who have now grown large at our farm, and are to be fatted and killed within a few weeks. There were several hundreds, in pens appropriated to their use, grunting discordantly, and apparently in no very good humor with their companions or the world at large. Most or many of these pigs had been imported from the State of New York. The drovers set out with a large number, and peddle them along the road till they arrive at Brighton with the remainder. William selected four, and bought them at five cents per pound. These poor little porkers were forthwith seized by the tails, their legs tied, and they thrown into our wagon, where they kept up a continual grunt and squeal till we got home. Two of them were yellowish, or light gold-color, the other two were black and white speckled; and all four of very piggish aspect and deportment. One of them snapped at William's finger most spitefully and bit it to the bone.

All the scene of the Fair was very characteristic and peculiar,—cheerful and lively, too, in the bright, warm sun. I must see it again; for it ought to be studied.

September 28th.—A picnic party in the woods, yesterday, in honor of little Frank Dana's birthday, he being six years old. I strolled out, after dinner, with Mr. Bradford, and in a lonesome glade we met the apparition of an Indian chief, dressed in appropriate costume of blanket, feathers, and paint, and armed with a musket. Almost at the same time, a young gypsy fortune-teller came from among the trees, and proposed to tell my fortune. While she was doing this, the goddess Diana let fly an arrow, and hit me smartly in the hand. The fortune-teller and goddess were in fine contrast, Diana being a blonde, fair, quiet, with a moderate composure; and the gypsy (O. G.) a bright, vivacious, dark-haired, rich-complexioned damsel,—both of them very pretty, at least pretty enough to make fifteen years enchanting. Accompanied by these denizens of the wild wood, we went onward, and came to a company of fantastic figures, arranged in a ring for a dance or a game. There was a Swiss girl, an Indian squaw, a negro of the Jim Crow order, one or two foresters, and several people in Christian attire, besides children of all ages. Then followed childish games, in which the grown people took part with mirth enough,—while I, whose nature it is to be a mere spectator both of sport and serious business, lay under the trees and looked on. Meanwhile, Mr. Emerson and Miss Fuller, who arrived an hour or two before, came forth into the little glade where we were assembled. Here followed much talk. The ceremonies of the day concluded with a cold collation of cakes and fruit. All was pleasant enough,—an excellent piece of work,—"would't were done!" It has left a fantastic impression on my memory, this intermingling of wild and fabulous characters with real and homely ones, in the secluded nook of the woods. I remember them, with the sunlight breaking through overshadowing branches, and they appearing and disappearing confusedly,—perhaps starting out of the earth; as if the every-day laws of nature were suspended for this particular occasion. There were the children, too, laughing and sorting about, as if they were at home among such strange shapes,—and anon bursting into loud uproar of lamentation, when the rude gambols of the merry archers chanced to overturn them. And apart, with a shrewd, Yankee observation of the scene, stands our friend Orange, a thickset, sturdy figure, enjoying the fun well enough, yet, rather laughing with a perception of its nonsensicalness than at all entering into the spirit of the thing.

This morning I have been helping to gather apples. The principal farm labors at this time are ploughing for whiter rye, and breaking up the greensward for next year's crop of potatoes, gathering squashes, and not much else, except such year-round employments as milking. The crop of rye, to be sure, is in process of being threshed, at odd intervals.

I ought to have mentioned among the diverse and incongruous growths of the picnic party our two Spanish boys from Manilla,—Lucas, with his heavy features and almost mulatto complexion; and José, slighter, with rather a feminine face,—not a gay, girlish one, but grave, reserved, eying you sometimes with an earnest but secret expression, and causing you to question what sort of person he is.

Friday, October 1st.—I have been looking at our four swine,—not of the last lot, but those in process of fattening. They lie among the clean rye straw in the sty, nestling close together; for they seem to be beasts sensitive to the cold, and this is a clear, bright, crystal morning, with a cool northwest-wind. So there lie these four black swine, as deep among the straw as they can burrow, the very symbols of slothful ease and sensuous comfort. They seem to be actually oppressed and overburdened with comfort. They are quick to notice any one's approach, and utter a low grunt thereupon,—not drawing a breath for that particular purpose, but grunting with their ordinary breath,—at the same time turning an observant, though dull and sluggish eye upon the visitor. They seem to be involved and buried in their own corporeal substance, and to look dimly forth at the outer world. They breathe not easily, and yet not with difficulty nor discomfort; for the very unreadiness and oppression with which their breath comes appears to make them sensible of the deep sensual satisfaction which they feel. Swill, the remnant of their last meal, remains in the trough, denoting that their food is more abundant than even a hog can demand. Anon they fall asleep, drawing short and heavy breaths, which heave their huge sides up and down; but at the slightest noise they sluggishly unclose their eyes, and give another gentle grunt. They also grunt among themselves, without any external cause; but merely to express their swinish sympathy. I suppose it is the knowledge that these four grunters are doomed to die within two or three weeks that gives them a sort of awfulness in my conception. It makes me contrast their present gross substance of fleshly life with the nothingness speedily to come. Meantime the four newly bought pigs are running about the cow-yard, lean, active, shrewd, investigating everything, as their nature is. "When I throw an apple among them, they scramble with one another for the prize, and the successful one scampers away to eat it at leisure. They thrust their snouts into the mud, and pick a grain of corn out of the rubbish. Nothing within their sphere do they leave unexamined, grunting all the time with infinite variety of expression. Their language is the most copious of that of any quadruped, and, indeed, there is something deeply and indefinably interesting in the swinish race. They appear the-more a mystery the longer one gazes at them. It seems as if there were an important meaning to them, if one could but find it out. One interesting trait in them is their perfect independence of character. They care not for man, and will not adapt themselves to his notions, as other beasts do; but are true to themselves, and act out their hoggish nature.

October 7th.—Since Saturday last (it being now Thursday), I have been in Boston and Salem, and there has been a violent storm and rain during the whole time. This morning shone as bright as if it meant to make up for all the dismalness of the past days. Our brook, which in the summer was no longer a running stream, but stood in pools along its pebbly course, is now full from one grassy verge to the other, and hurries along with a murmuring rush. It will continue to swell, I suppose, and in the winter and spring it will flood all the broad meadows through which it flows.

I have taken a long walk this forenoon along the Needham road, and across the bridge, thence pursuing a cross-road through the woods, parallel with the river, which I crossed again at Dedham. Most of the road lay through a growth of young oaks principally. They still retain their verdure, though, looking closely in among them, one perceives the broken sunshine falling on a few sere or bright-hued tufts of shrubbery. In low, marshy spots, on the verge-of the meadows or along the river-side, there is a much more marked autumnal change. Whole ranges of bushes are there painted with many variegated hues, not of the brightest tint, but of a sober cheerfulness. I suppose this is owing more to the late rains than to the frost; for a heavy rain changes the foliage somewhat at this season. The first marked frost was seen last Saturday morning. Soon after sunrise it lay, white as snow, over all the grass, and on the tops of the fences, and in the yard, on the heap of firewood. On Sunday, I think, there was a fall of snow, which, however, did not lie on the ground a moment.

There is no season when such pleasant and sunny spots may be lighted on, and produce so pleasant an effect on the feelings, as now in October. The sunshine is peculiarly genial; and in sheltered places, as on the side of a bank, or of a barn or house, one becomes acquainted and friendly with the sunshine. It seems to be of a kindly and homely nature. And the green grass, strewn with a few withered leaves, looks the more green and beautiful for them. In summer or spring, Nature is farther from one's sympathies.

October 8th.—Another gloomy day, lowering with portents of rain close at hand. I have walked up into the pastures this morning, and looked about me a little. The woods present a very diversified appearance just now, with perhaps more varieties of tint than they are destined to wear at a somewhat later period. There are some strong yellow hues, and some deep red; there are innumerable shades of green, some few having the depth of summer; others, partially changed towards yellow, look freshly verdant with the delicate tinge of early summer or of May. Then there is the solemn and dark green of the pines. The effect is, that every tree in the wood and every bush among the shrubbery has a separate existence, since, confusedly intermingled, each wears its peculiar color, instead of being lost in the universal emerald of summer. And yet there is a oneness of effect likewise, when we choose to look at a whole sweep of woodland instead of analyzing its component trees. Scattered over the pasture, which the late rams have kept tolerably green, there are spots or islands of dusky red,—a deep, substantial hue, very well fit to be close to the ground,—while the yellow, and light, fantastic shades of green soar upward to the sky. These red spots are the blueberry and whortleberry bushes. The sweet-fern is changed mostly to russet, but still retains its wild and delightful fragrance when pressed in the hand. Wild China asters are scattered about, but beginning to wither. A little while ago, mushrooms or toadstools were very numerous along the wood-paths and by the roadsides, especially after rain. Some were of spotless white, some yellow, and some scarlet. They are always mysteries and objects of interest to me. springing as they do so suddenly from no root or seed, and growing one wonders why. I think, too, that some varieties are pretty objects, little fairy tables, centre-tables, standing on one leg. But their growth appears to be checked now, and they are of a brown tint and decayed.

The farm business to-day is to dig potatoes. I worked a little at it. The process is to grasp all the stems of a hill and pull them up. A great many of the potatoes are thus pulled, clinging to the steins and to one another in curious shapes,—long red things, and little round ones, imbedded in the earth which clings to the roots. These being plucked off. the rest of the potatoes are dug out of the hill with a hoe. the tops being flung into a heap for the cow-yard. On my way home, I paused to inspect the squash-bold. Some of the squashes lay in heaps as they were gathered, presenting much variety of shape and hue,—as golden yellow, like great lumps of gold, dark green, striped and variegated; and some were round, and some lay curling their long necks, nestling, as it were, and seeming as if they had life.

In my walk yesterday forenoon I passed an old house which seemed to be quite deserted. It was a two-story, wooden house, dark and weather-beaten. The front windows, some of them, were shattered and open, and others were boarded up. Trees and shrubbery were growing neglected, so as quite to block up the lower part. There was an aged barn near at hand, so ruinous that it had been necessary to prop it up. There were two old carts, both of which had lost a wheel. Everything was in keeping. At first I supposed that there would be no inhabitants in such a dilapidated place; but, passing on, I looked back, and saw a decrepit and infirm old man at the angle of the house, its fit occupant. The grass, however, was very green and beautiful around this dwelling, and, the sunshine falling brightly on it, the whole effect was cheerful and pleasant. It seemed as if the world was so glad that this desolate old place, where there was never to be any more hope and happiness, could not at all lessen the general effect of joy.

I found a small turtle by the roadside, where he had crept to warm himself in the genial sunshine. He had a sable back, and underneath his shell was yellow, and at the edges bright scarlet. His head, tail, and claws were striped yellow, black, and red. He withdrew himself as far as he possibly could into his shell, and absolutely refused to peep out, even when I put him into the water. Finally, I threw him into a deep pool and left him. These mailed gentlemen, from the size of a foot or more down to an inch, were very numerous in the spring; and now the smaller kind appear again.

Saturday, October 9th.—Still dismal weather. Our household, being composed in great measure of children and young people, is generally a cheerful one enough, even in gloomy weather. For a week past we have been especially gladdened with a little seamstress from Boston, about seventeen years old; but of such a *petite* figure, that, at first view, one would take her to be hardly in her teens. She is very vivacious and smart, laughing and singing and talking all the time,—talking sensibly; but still, taking the view of matters that a city girl naturally would. If she were larger than she is, and of less pleasing aspect, I think she might be intolerable; but being so small, and with a fair skin, and as healthy as a wild-flower, she is really very agreeable; and to look at her face is like being shone upon by a ray of the sun. She never walks, but bounds and dances along, and this motion, in her diminutive person, doe"s not give the idea of violence. It is like a bird, hopping from twig to twig, and chirping merrily all the time. Sometimes she is rather vulgar, but even that works well enough into her character, and accords with it. On continued observation, one discovers that she is not a little girl, but really a little woman, with all the prerogatives and liabilities of a woman. This gives a new aspect to her, while the girlish impression still remains, and is strangely combined with the sense that this frolicsome maiden has the material for the sober bearing of a wife. She romps with the boys, runs races with them in the yard, and up and down the stairs, and is heard scolding laughingly at their rough play. She asks William Allen to place her "on top of that horse," whereupon he puts his large brown hands about her waist, and, swinging her to and fro, lifts her on horseback. William threatens to rivet two horseshoes round her neck, for having clambered, with the other, girls and boys, upon a load of hay, whereby the said load lost its balance and slid off the cart. She strings the seed-berries of roses together, making a scarlet necklace of them, which she fastens about her throat. She gathers flowers of everlasting to wear in her bonnet, arranging them with the skill of a dress-maker. In the evening, she sits singing by the hour, with the musical part of the establishment, often breaking into laughter, whereto she is incited by the tricks of the boys. The last thing one hears of her, she is tripping up stairs to bed, talking lightsomely or warbling; and one meets her in the morning, the very image of bright morn itself, smiling briskly at you, so that one takes her for a promise of cheerfulness through the day. Be it said, with all the rest, that there is a perfect maiden modesty in her deportment. She has just gone away, and the last I saw of her was her vivacious face peeping through the curtain of the cariole, and nodding a gay farewell to the family, who were shouting their adieus at the door. With her other merits, she is an excellent daughter, and supports her mother by the labor of her hands. It would be difficult to conceive beforehand how much can be added to the enjoyment of a household by mere sunniness of temper and liveliness of disposition; for her intellect is very ordinary, and she never says anything worth hearing, or even laughing at, in itself. But she herself is an expression well worth studying.

Brook Farm, October 9th.—A walk this afternoon to Cow Island. The clouds had broken away towards noon, and let forth a few sunbeams, and more and more blue sky ventured to appear, till at last it was really warm and sunny,—indeed, rather too warm in the sheltered hollows, though it is delightful to be too warm now, after so much stormy chillness. Oh the beauty of grassy slopes, and the hollow ways of paths winding between hills, and the intervals between the road and wood-lots, where Summer lingers and sits down, strewing dandelions of gold, and blue asters, as her parting gifts and memorials! I went to a grapevine, which I have already visited several times, and found some clusters of grapes still remaining, and now perfectly ripe. Coming within view of the river, I saw several wild ducks under the shadow of the opposite shore, which was high, and covered with a grove of pines. I should not have discovered the ducks had they not risen and skimmed the surface of the glassy stream, breaking its dark water with a bright streak, and, sweeping round, gradually rose high enough to fly away. I likewise started a partridge just within the verge of the woods, and in another place a large squirrel ran across the wood-path from one shelter of trees to the other. Small birds, in flocks, were flitting about the fields, seeking and finding I know not what sort of food. There were little fish, also, darting in shoals through the pools and depths of the brooks, which are now replenished to their brims, and rush towards the river with a swift, amber-colored current.

Cow Island is not an island,—at least, at this season,—though, I believe, in the time of freshets, the marshy Charles floods the meadows all round about it, and extends across its communication with the mainland. The path to it is a very secluded one, threading a wood of pines, and just wide enough to admit the loads of meadow hay which are drawn from the splashy shore of the river. The island has a growth of stately pines, with tall and ponderous stems, standing at distance enough to admit the eye to travel far among them; and, as there is no underbrush, the effect is somewhat like looking among the pillars of a church.

I returned home by the high-road. On my right, separated from the road by a level field, perhaps fifty yards across, was a range of young forest-trees, dressed in their garb of autumnal glory. The sun shone directly upon them; and sunlight is like the breath of life to the pomp of autumn. In its absence, one doubts whether there be any truth in what poets have told about the splendor of an American autumn; but when this charm is added, one feels that the effect is beyond description. As I beheld it to-day, there was nothing dazzling; it was gentle and mild, though brilliant and diversified, and had a most quiet and pensive influence. And yet there were some trees that seemed really made of sunshine, and others were of a sunny red, and the whole picture was painted with but little relief of darksome hues, only a few evergreens. But there was nothing inharmonious; and, on closer examination, it appeared that all the tints had a relationship among themselves. And this, I suppose, is the reason that, while nature seems to scatter them so carelessly, they still never shock the beholder by their contrasts, nor disturb, but only soothe. The brilliant scarlet and the brilliant yellow are different hues of the maple leaves, and the first changes into the last. I saw one maple-tree, its centre yellow as gold, set in a framework of red. The native poplars have different shades of green, verging towards yellow, and are very cheerful in the sunshine. Most of the oak-leaves have still the deep verdure of summer; but where a change has taken place, it is into a russet-red, warm, but sober. These colors, infinitely varied by the progress which different trees have made in their decay, constitute almost the whole glory of autumnal woods; but it is impossible to conceive how much is done with such scanty materials. In my whole walk I saw only one man, and he was at a distance, in the obscurity of the trees, He had a horse and a wagon, and was getting a load of dry brushwood.

Sunday, October 10th.—I visited my grapevine this afternoon, and ate the last of its clusters. This vine climbs around a young maple-tree, which has now assumed the yellow leaf. The leaves of the vine are more decayed than those of the maple. Thence to Cow Island, a solemn and thoughtful walk. Returned by another path, of the width of a wagon, passing through a grove of hard wood, the lightsome hues of which make the walk more cheerful than among the pines. The roots of oaks emerged from the soil, and contorted themselves across the path. The sunlight, also, broke across in spots, and otherwheres the shadow was deep; but still there was intermingling enough of bright hues to keep off the gloom from the whole path.

Brooks and pools have a peculiar aspect at this season. One knows that the water must be cold, and one shivers a little at the sight of it; and yet the grass about the pool may be of the deepest green, and the sun maybe shining into it. The withered leaves which overhanging trees shed upon its surface contribute much to the effect.

Insects have mostly vanished in the fields and woods. I hear locusts yet, singing in the sunny hours, and crickets have not yet finished their song. Once in a while I see a caterpillar,—this afternoon, for instance, a red, hairy one, with black head and tail. They do not appear to be active, and it makes one rather melancholy to look at them.

Tuesday, October 12th.—The cawing of the crow resounds among the woods. A sentinel is aware of your approach a great way off, and gives the alarm to his comrades loudly and eagerly,—Caw, caw, caw! Immediately the whole conclave replies, and you behold them rising above the trees, flapping darkly, and winging their way to deeper solitudes. Sometimes, however, they remain till you come near enough to discern their sable gravity of aspect, each occupying a separate bough, or perhaps the blasted tip-top of a pine. As you approach, one after another, with loud cawing, flaps his wings and throws himself upon the air.

There is hardly a more striking feature in the landscape nowadays than the red patches of blueberry and whortleberry bushes, as seen on a sloping hill-side, like islands among the grass, with trees growing in them; or crowning the summit of a bare, brown hill with their somewhat russet liveliness; or circling round the base of an earth-imbedded rock. At a distance, this hue, clothing spots and patches of the earth, looks more like a picture than anything else,—yet such a picture as I never saw painted.

The oaks are now beginning to look sere, and their leaves have withered borders. It is pleasant to notice the wide circle of greener grass beneath the circumference of an overshadowing oak. Passing an orchard, one hears an uneasy rustling in the trees, and not as if they were struggling with the wind. Scattered about are barrels to contain the gathered apples; and perhaps a great heap of golden or scarlet apples is collected in one place.

Wednesday, October 13th.—A good view, from an upland swell of our pasture, across the valley of the river Charles. There is the meadow, as level as a floor, and carpeted with green, perhaps two miles from the rising ground on this side of the river to that on the opposite side. The stream winds through the midst of the flat space, without any banks at all; for it fills its bed almost to the brim, and bathes the meadow grass on either side. A tuft of shrubbery, at broken intervals, is scattered along its border; and thus it meanders sluggishly along, without other fife than what it gains from gleaming in the sun. Now, into the broad, smooth meadow, as into a lake, capes and headlands put themselves forth, and shores of firm woodland border it, covered with variegated foliage, making the contrast so much the stronger of their height and rough outline with the even spread of the plain. And beyond, and far away, rises a long, gradual swell of country, covered with an apparently dense growth of foliage for miles, till the horizon terminates it; and here and there is a house, or perhaps two, among the contiguity of trees. Everywhere the trees wear their autumnal dress, so that the whole landscape is red, russet, orange, and yellow, blending in the distance into a rich tint of brown-orange, or nearly that, —except the green expanse so definitely hemmed in by the higher ground.

I took a long walk this morning, going first nearly to Newton, thence nearly to Brighton, thence to Jamaica Plain, and thence home. It was a fine morning, with a northwest-wind; cool when facing the wind, hot warm and most genially pleasant in sheltered spots; and warm enough everywhere while I was in motion. I traversed most of the by-ways which offered themselves to me; and, passing through one in which there was a double line of grass between the wheel-tracks and that of the horses' feet, I came to where had once stood a farmhouse, which appeared to have been recently torn down. Most of the old timber and boards had been carted away; a pile of it, however, remained. The cellar of the house was uncovered, and beside it stood the base and middle height of the chimney. The oven, in which household bread had been baked for daily food, and puddings and cake and jolly pumpkin-pies for festivals, opened its mouth, being deprived of its iron door. The fireplace was close at hand. All round the site of the house was a pleasant, sunny, green space, with old fruit-trees in pretty fair condition, though aged. There was a barn, also aged, but in decent repair; and a ruinous shed, on the corner of which was nailed a boy's windmill, where it had probably been turning and clattering for years together, till now it was black with time and weather-stain. It was broken, but still it went round whenever the wind stirred. The spot was entirely secluded, there being no other house within a mile or two.

No language can give an idea of the beauty and glory of the trees, just at this moment. It would be easy, by a process of word-daubing, to set down a confused group of gorgeous colors, like a bunch of tangled skeins of bright silk; but there is nothing of the reality in the glare which would thus be produced. And yet the splendor both of individual clusters and of whole scenes is unsurpassable. The oaks are now far advanced in their change of hue; and, in certain positions relatively to the sun, they light up and gleam with a most magnificent deep gold, varying according as portions of the foliage are in shadow or sunlight. On the sides which receive the direct rays, the effect is altogether rich; and in other points of view it is equally beautiful, if less brilliant. This color of the oak is more superb than the lighter yellow of the maples and walnuts. The whole landscape is now covered with this indescribable pomp; it is discerned on the uplands afar off; and Blue Hill in Milton, at the distance of several miles, actually glistens with rich, dark light,—no, not glistens, nor gleams,—but perhaps to say glows subduedly will be a truer expression for it.

Met few people this morning; a grown girl, in company with a little boy, gathering barberries in a secluded lane; a portly, autumnal gentleman, wrapped in a great-coat, who asked the way to Mr. Joseph Goddard's; and a fish-cart from the city, the driver of which sounded his horn along the lonesome way.

Monday, October 18th.—There has been a succession of days which were cold and bright in the forenoon, and gray, sullen, and chill towards night. The woods have now taken a soberer tint than they wore at my last date. Many of the shrubs which looked brightest a little while ago are now wholly bare of leaves. The oaks have generally a russet-brown shade, although some of them are still green, as are likewise other scattered trees in the forests. The bright yellow and the rich scarlet are no more to be seen. Scarcely any of them will now bear a close examination; for this shows them to be rugged, wilted, and of faded, frost-bitten hue; but at a distance, and in the mass, and enlivened by the sun, they have still somewhat of the varied splendor which distinguished them a week ago. It is wonderful what a difference the sunshine makes; it is like varnish, bringing out the hidden veins in a piece of rich wood. In the cold, gray atmosphere, such as that of most of our afternoons now, the landscape lies dark,—brown, and in a much deeper shadow than if it were clothed in green. But, perchance, a gleam of sun falls on a certain spot of distant shrubbery or woodland, and we see it brighten with many hues, standing forth prominently from the dimness around it. The sunlight gradually spreads, and the whole sombre scene is changed to a motley picture,—the sun bringing out many shades of color, and converting its gloom to an almost laughing cheerfulness. At such times I almost doubt whether the foliage has lost any of its brilliancy. But the clouds intercept the sun again, and lo! old Autumn appears, clad in his cloak of russet-brown.

Beautiful now, while the general landscape lies in shadow, looks the summit of a distant hill (say a mile off), with the sunshine brightening the trees that cover it. It is noticeable that the outlines of hills, and the whole bulk of them at the distance of several miles, become stronger, denser, and more substantial in this autumn atmosphere and in these autumnal tints than in summer. Then they looked blue, misty, and dim. Now they show their great humpbacks more plainly, as if they had drawn nearer to us.

A waste of shrubbery and small trees, such as overruns the borders of the meadows for miles together, looks much more rugged, wild, and savage in its present brown color than when clad in green.

I passed through a very pleasant wood-path yesterday, quite shut in and sheltered by trees that had not thrown off their yellow robes. The sun shone strongly in among them, and quite kindled them; so that the path was brighter for their shade than if it had. been quite exposed to the sun. .

In the village graveyard, which lies contiguous to the street, I saw a man digging a grave, and one inhabitant after another turned aside from his way to look into the grave and talk with the digger. I heard him laugh, with the traditionary mirthfulness of men of that occupation.

In the hollow of the woods, yesterday afternoon, I lay a long while watching a squirrel, who was capering about among the trees over my head (oaks and white-pines, so close together that their branches intermingled). The squirrel seemed not to approve of my presence, for he frequently uttered a sharp, quick, angry noise, like that of a scissors-grinder's wheel. Sometimes I could see him sitting on an impending bough, with his tail over his back, looking down pryingly upon me. It seems to be a natural posture with him, to sit on his hind legs, holding up his fore paws. Anon, with a peculiarly quick start, he would scramble along the branch, and be lost to sight in another part of the tree, whence his shrill chatter would again be heard. Then I would see him rapidly descending the trunk, and running along the ground; and a moment afterwards, casting my eye upward, I beheld him flitting like a bird among the high limbs at the summit, directly above me. Afterwards, be apparently became accustomed to my society, and set about some business of his own. He came down to the ground, took up a piece of a decayed bough (a heavy burden for such a small personage), and, with this in his mouth, again climbed up and passed from the branches of one tree to those of another, and thus onward and onward till he went out of sight. Shortly afterwards he returned for another burden, and this he repeated several times. I suppose he was building a nest,—at least, I know not what else could have been his object. Never was there such an active, cheerful, choleric, continually-in-motion fellow as this little red squirrel, talking to himself, chattering at me, and as sociable in his own person as if he had half a dozen companions, instead of being alone in the lonesome wood. Indeed, he flitted about so quickly, and showed himself in different places so suddenly, that I was in some doubt whether there were not two or three of them.

I must mention again the very beautiful effect produced by the masses of berry-bushes, lying like scarlet islands in the midst of withered pasture-ground, or crowning the tops of barren hills. Their hue, at a distance, is lustrous scarlet, although it does not look nearly as bright and gorgeous when examined close at hand. But at a proper distance it is a beautiful fringe on Autumn's petticoat.

Friday, October 22d.—A continued succession of unpleasant, Novembery days, and autumn has made rapid progress in the work of decay. It is now somewhat of a rare good fortune to find a verdant, grassy spot, on some slope, or in a dell; and even such seldom-seen oases are bestrewn with dried brown leaves,—which, however, methinks, make the short, fresh grass look greener around them. Dry leaves are now plentiful everywhere, save where there are none but pine-trees. They rustle beneath the tread, and there is nothing more autumnal than that sound. Nevertheless, in a walk this afternoon, I have seen two oaks which retained almost the greenness of summer. They grew close to the huge Pulpit Rock, so that portions of their trunks appeared to grasp the rough surface; and they were rooted beneath it, and, ascending high into the air, overshadowed the gray crag with verdure. Other oaks, here and there, have a few green leaves or boughs among their rustling and rugged shade.

Yet, dreary as the woods are in a bleak, sullen day, there is a very peculiar sense of warmth and a sort of richness of effect in the slope of a bank and in sheltered spots, where bright sunshine falls, and the brown oaken foliage is gladdened by it. There is then a feeling of comfort, and consequently of heart-warmth, which cannot be experienced in summer.

I walked this afternoon along a pleasant wood-path, gently winding, so that but little of it could be seen at a time, and going up and down small mounds, now plunging into a denser shadow, and now emerging from it. Part of the way it was strewn with the dusky, yellow leaves of white-pines,—the cast-off garments of last year; part of the way with green grass, close-cropped, and very fresh for the season. Sometimes the trees met across it; sometimes it was bordered on one side by an old rail-fence of moss-grown cedar, with bushes sprouting beneath it, and thrusting their branches through it; sometimes by a stone-wall of unknown antiquity, older than the wood it closed in. A stone-wall, when shrubbery has grown around it, and thrust its roots beneath it, becomes a very pleasant and meditative object. It does not belong too evidently to man, having been built so long ago. It seems a part of nature.

Yesterday I found two mushrooms in the woods, probably of the preceding night's growth. Also I saw a mosquito, frost-pinched, and so wretched that I felt avenged for all the injuries which his tribe inflicted upon me last summer, and so did not molest this lone survivor.

Walnuts in their green rinds are falling from the trees, and so are chestnut-burrs.

I found a maple-leaf to-day, yellow all over, except its extremest point, which was bright scarlet. It looked as if a drop of blood were hanging from it. The first change of the maple-leaf is to scarlet; the next, to yellow. Then it withers, wilts, and drops off, as most of them have already done.

October 27th.—Fringed gentians,—I found the last, probably, that will be seen this year, growing on the margin of the brook.

1842.—Some man of powerful character to command a person, morally subjected to him, to perform some act. The commanding person suddenly to die; and, for all the rest of his life, the subjected one continues to perform that act.

"Solomon dies during the building of the temple, but his body remains leaning on a staff, and overlooking the workmen, as if it were alive."

A tri-weekly paper, to be called the Tertian Ague.

Subject for a picture,—Satan's reappearance in Pandemonium, shining out from a mist with "shape star-bright."

Five points of Theology,—Five Points at New York.

It seems a greater pity that an accomplished worker with the hand should perish prematurely, than a person of great intellect; because intellectual arts may be cultivated in the next world, but not physical ones.

To trace out the influence of a frightful and disgraceful crime in debasing and destroying a character naturally high and noble, the guilty person being alone conscious of the crime.

A man, virtuous in his general conduct, but committing habitually some monstrous crime,—as murder,—and doing this without the sense of guilt, but with a peaceful conscience,—habit, probably, reconciling him to it; but something (for instance, discovery) occurs to make him sensible of his enormity. His horror then.

The strangeness, if they could be foreseen and forethought, of events which do not seem so strange after they have happened. As, for instance, to muse over a child's cradle, and foresee all the persons in different parts of the world with whom he would have relations.

A man to swallow a small snake,—and it to be a symbol of a cherished sin.

Questions as to unsettled points of history, and mysteries of nature, to be asked of a mesmerized person.

Gordier, a young man of the island of Jersey, was paying his addresses to a young lady of Guernsey. He visited the latter island, intending to be married. He disappeared on his way from the beach to his mistress's residence, and was afterwards found dead in a cavity of the rocks. After a time, Galliard, a merchant of Guernsey, paid his addresses to the young lady; but she always felt a strong, unaccountable antipathy to him. He presented her with a beautiful trinket. the mother of Gordier, chancing to see the trinket, recognised it as having been bought by her dead son as a present for his mistress. She expired on learning this; and Galliard, being suspected of the murder, committed suicide.

The *curé* of Montreux in Switzerland, ninety-six years old, still vigorous in mind and body, and able to preach. He had a twin-brother, also a preacher, and the exact likeness of himself. Sometimes strangers have beheld a white-haired, venerable, clerical personage, nearly a century old; and, upon riding a few miles farther, have been astonished to meet again this white-haired, venerable, century-old personage.

When the body of Lord Mohun (killed in a duel) was carried home, bleeding, to his house, Lady Mohun was very angry because it was "flung upon the best bed."

A prophecy, somehat in the style of Swift's about Partridge, but bracing various events and personages.

An incident that befell Dr. Harris, while a Junior at college. Being in great want of money to buy shirts or other necessaries, and not knowing how to obtain it, hc sct out on a walk from Cambridge to Boston. On the way he cut a stick, and, after walking a short distance, perceived that something had become attached to the end of it. It proved to be a gold ring, with the motto, "God speed thee, friend."

Brobdingnag lay on the northwest coast of the American continent.

A gush of violets along a wood-path.

People with false hair and other artifices maybe supposed to deceive Death himself, so that he does not know when their hour is come.

Bees are sometimes drowned (or suffocated) in the honey which they collect. So some writers are lost in their collected learning.

Advice of Lady Pepperell's father on her marriage,—never to work one moment after Saturday sunset,—never to lay down her knitting except in the middle of the needle,—always to rise with the sun,—to pass an hour daily with the housekeeper,—to visit every room daily from garret to cellar,—to attend herself to the brewing of beer and the baking of bread,—and to instruct every member of the family in their religious duties.

Service of plate, presented by the city of London to Sir William Pepperell, together with a table of solid silver, The table very narrow, but long; the articles of plate numerous, but of small dimensions,—the tureen not holding more than three pints. At the close of the Revolution, when the Pepperell and Sparhawk property was confiscated, this plate was sent to the grandson of Sir William, in London, It was so valuable, that Sheriff Moulton, of old York, with six well-armed men, accompanied it to Boston. Pepperell's only daughter married Colonel Sparhawk, a fine gentleman of the day. Andrew Pepperell, the son, was rejected by a young lady (afterwards the mother of Mrs. General Knox), to whom he was on the point of marriage, as being addicted to low company and low pleasures. The lover, two days afterwards, in the streets of Portsmouth, was sun-struck, and fell down dead. Sir William had built an elegant house for bis son and his intended wife; but after the death of the former he never entered it. He lost his cheerfulness and social qualities, and gave up intercourse with people, except on business. Very anxious to secure his property to his descendants by the provisions of his will, which was drawn up by Judge Sewall, then a young lawyer. Yet the Judge lived to see two of Sir William's grandchildren so reduced that they were to have been numbered among the town's poor, and were only rescued from this fate by private charity.

The arms and crest of the Pepperell family were displayed over the door of every room in Sir William's house. In Colonel Sparhawk's house there were forty portraits, most of them in full length. The house built for Sir William's son was occupied as barracks during the Revolution, and much injured. A few years after the peace, it was blown down by a violent tempest, and finally no vestige of it was left, but there remained only a summer-house and the family tomb.

At Sir William's death, his mansion was hung with black, while the body lay in state for a week, All the Sparhawk portraits were covered with black crape, and the family pew was draped with black. Two oxen were roasted, and liquid hospitality dispensed in proportion.

Old lady's dress seventy or eighty years ago. Brown brocade gown, with a nice lawn handkerchief and apron,—short sleeves, with a little ruffle, just below the elbow,—black mittens,—a lawn cap, with rich lace border,—a black velvet hood on the back of the head, tied with black ribbon under the chin. She sat in an old-fashioned easy-chair, in a small, low parlor,—the wainscot painted entirely black, and the walls hung with a dark velvet paper.

A table, stationary ever since the house was built, extending the whole length of a room. One end was raised two steps higher than the rest. The Lady Ursula, an early Colonial heroine, was wont to dine at the upper end, while her servants sat below. This was in the kitchen. An old garden and summer-house, and roses, currant-bushes, and tulips, which Lady Ursula had brought from Grondale Abbey, in Old England. Although a hundred and fifty years before, and though their roots were propagated all over the country, they were still flourishing in the original garden. This Lady Ursula was the daughter of Lord Thomas Cutts, of Grondale Abbey, in England. She had been in love with an officer named Fowler, who was supposed to have been slain in battle. After the death of her rather and mother. Lady Ursula came to Kittery, bringing twenty men-servants and several women. After a time, a letter arrived from her lover, who was not killed, but merely a prisoner to the French. He announced his purpose to come to America, where he would arrive in October. A few days after the letter came, she went out in a low carriage to visit her work-people, and was blessing the food for their luncheon, when she fell dead, struck by an Indian tomahawk, as did all the rest save one. They were buried where the massacre took place, and a stone was erected, which (possibly) still remains. The lady's family had a grant from Sir Ferdinando Gorges of the territory thereabout, and her brother had likewise come over and settled in the vicinity. I believe very little of this story. Long afterwards, at about the commencement of the Revolution, a descendant of Fowler came from England, and applied to the Judge of Probate to search the records tor a will, supposed to have been made by Lady Ursula in favor of her lover as soon as she heard of his existence. In the mean time the estate had been sold to Colonel Whipple. No will could be found. (Lady Ursula was old Mrs. Cutts, widow of President Cutts.)

The mode of living of Lady Ursula's brother in Kittery. A drawbridge to the house, which was raised every evening, and lowered in the morning, for the laborers and the family to pass out. They kept thirty cows, a hundred sheep, and several horses. The house spacious,—one room large enough to contain forty or fifty guests, Two silver branches for candles,—the walls ornamented with paintings and needlework. The floors were daily rubbed with wax, and shone like a mahogany table. A domestic chaplain, who said prayers every morning and evening in a small apartment called the chapel. Also a steward and butler. The family attended the Episcopal Church at Christmas, Easter, and Good Friday, and gave a grand entertainment once a year.

Madam Cutts, at the last of these entertainments, wore a black damask gown, and cuffs with double knee ruffles, velvet shoes, blue silk stockings, white and silver stomacher. The daughter and granddaughters in rich brocades and yellow satin. Old Major Cutts in brown velvet, laced with gold, and a large wig. The parson in his silk cassock, and his helpmate in brown damask. Old General Atkinson in scarlet velvet, and his wife and daughters in white damask. The Governor in black velvet, and his lady in crimson tabby trimmed with silver. The ladies wore bell-hoops, high-heeled shoes, paste buckles, silk stockings, and enormously high head-dresses, with lappets of Brussels lace hanging thence to the waist.

Among the eatables, a silver tub of the capacity of four gallons, holding a pyramid of pancakes powdered with white sugar.

The date assigned to all this about 1690.

What is the price of a day's labor in Lapland, where the sun never sets tor six months?

Miss Asphyxia Davis!

A life, generally of a grave hue, may be said to be *embroidered* with occasional sports and fantasies.

A father confessor,—his reflections on character, and the contrast of the inward man with the outward, as he looks around on his congregation, all whose secret sins are known to him.

A person with an ice-cold hand,—his right hand, which people ever afterwards remember when once they have grasped it.

A stove possessed by a Devil.

June 1st, 1842.—One of my chief amusements is to see the boys sail their miniature vessels on the Frog Pond. There is a great variety of shipping owned among the young people, and they appear to have a considerable knowledge of the art of managing vessels. There is a full-rigged man-of-war, with, I believe, every spar, rope, and sail, that sometimes makes its appearance; and, when on a voyage across the pond, it so identically resembles a great ship, except in size, that it has the effect of a picture. All its motions,—its tossing up and down on the small waves, and its sinking and rising in a calm swell, its heeling to the breeze,—the whole effect, in short, is that of a real ship at sea; while, moreover, there is something that kindles the imagination more than the reality would do. If we see a real, great ship, the mind grasps and possesses, within its real clutch, all that there is of it; while here the mimic ship is the representation of an ideal one, and so gives us a more imaginative pleasure. There are many schooners that ply to and fro on the pond, and pilot-boats, all perfectly rigged. I saw a race, the other day, between the ship above mentioned and a pilot-boat, in which the latter came off conqueror. The boys appear to be well acquainted with all the ropes and sails, and can call them by their nautical names. One of the owners of the vessels remains on one side of the pond, and the other on the opposite side, and so they send the little bark to and fro, like merchants of different countries, consigning their vessels to one another.

Generally, when any vessel is on the pond, there are full-grown spectators, who look on with as much interest as the boys themselves. Towards sunset, this is especially the case: for then are seen young girls and their lovers; mothers, with their little boys in hand; school-girls, beating hoops round about, and occasionally running to the side of the pond; rough tars, or perhaps masters or young mates of vessels, who make remarks about the miniature shipping, and occasionally give professional ad Wee to the navigators; visitors from the country; gloved and caned young gentlemen,—in short, everybody stops to take a look. In the mean time, dogs are continually plunging into the pond, and swimming about, with noses pointed upward, and snatching at floating chips; then emerging, they shake themselves, scattering a horizontal shower on the clean gowns of ladies and trousers of gentlemen; then scamper to and fro on the grass, with joyous barks.

Some boys cast off lines of twine with pin-hooks, and perhaps pull out a horned-pout,—that being, I think, the only kind of fish that inhabits the Frog Pond.

The ship-of-war above mentioned is about three feet from stem to stern, or possibly a few inches more. This, if I mistake not, was the size of a ship-of-the-line in the navy of Liliput.

Fancy pictures of familiar places which one has never been in, as the green-room of a theatre, etc.

The famous characters of history,—to imagine their spirits now extant on earth, in the guise of various public or private personages.

The case quoted in Combe's "Physiology" of a young man of great talents and profound knowledge of chemistry, who had in view some new discovery of importance. In order to put his mind into the highest possible activity, he shut himself up for several successive days, and used various methods of excitement. He had a singing-girl, he drank spirits, smelled penetrating odors, sprinkled Cologne-water round the room, etc., etc. Eight days thus passed, when he was seized with a fit of frenzy which terminated in mania.

Flesh and Blood,—a firm of butchers.

Miss Polly Syllable,—a schoolmistress.

Mankind are earthen jugs with spirits in them.

A spendthrift,—in one sense he has his money's worth by the purchase of large lots of repentance and other dolorous commodities.

To symbolize moral or spiritual disease by disease of the body; as thus,—when a person committed any sin, it might appear in some form on the body,—this to be wrought out.

"Shrieking fish," a strange idea of Leigh Hunt.

In my museum, all the ducal rings that have been thrown into the Adriatic.

An association of literary men in the other world, or dialogues of the dead, or something of that kind.

Imaginary diseases to be cured by impossible remedies,—as a dose of the Grand Elixir, in the yolk of a Phoenix's egg. The disease may be either moral or physical.

A physician for the cure of moral diseases.

To point out the moral slavery of one who deems himself a free man.

A stray leaf from the book of fate, picked up in the street.

Concord, August 5th.—A rainy day,—a rainy day. I am commanded to take pen in hand, and 1 am therefore banished to the little ten-foot-square apartment misnamed my study; but perhaps the dismalness of the day and the dulness of my solitude will be the prominent characteristics of what I write. And what is there to write about? Happiness has no succession of events, because it is a part of eternity; and we have been living in eternity ever since we came to this old manse. Like Enoch, we seem to have been translated to the other state of being without having passed through death. Our spirits must have flitted away unconsciously, and we can only perceive that we have cast off. our mortal part by the more real and earnest life of our souls. Externally, our Paradise has very much the aspect of a pleasant old domicile on earth. This antique house—for it looks antique, though it was created by Providence expressly for our use, and at the precise time when we wanted it—stands behind a noble avenue of balm-of-Gilead trees; and when we chance to observe a passing traveller through the sunshine and the shadow of this long avenue, his figure appeal's too dim and remote to disturb the sense of blissful seclusion. Few, indeed, are the mortals who venture within our sacred precincts. George Prescott, who has not yet grown earthly enough, I suppose, to be debarred from occasional visits to Paradise, comes daily to bring three pints of milk from some ambrosial cow; occasionally, also, he makes an offering of mortal flowers. Mr. Emerson comes sometimes, and has been feasted on our nectar and ambrosia. Mr. Thoreau has twice listened to the music of the spheres, which, for our private convenience, we have packed into a musical-box. E— H—, who is much more at home among spirits than among fleshly bodies, came hither a few times merely to welcome us to the ethereal world; but latterly she has vanished into some other region of infinite space. One rash mortal, on the second Sunday after our arrival, obtruded himself upon us in a gig. There have since been three or four callers, who preposterously think that the courtesies of the lower world are to be responded to by people whose home is in Paradise. I must not forget to mention that the butcher comes twice or thrice a week; and we have so far improved upon the custom of Adam and Eve, that we generallv furnish forth our feasts with portions of some delicate calf or lamb, whose unspotted innocence entitles them to the happiness of becoming our sustenance. Would that I were permitted to record the celestial dainties that kind Heaven provided for us on the first day of our arrival! Never, surely, was such food heard of on earth,—at least, not by me. Well, the above-mentioned persons are nearly all that have entered into the hallowed shade of our avenue; except, indeed, a certain sinner who came to bargain for the grass in our orchard, and another who came with a new cistern. For it is one of the drawbacks upon our Eden that it contains no water fit either to drink or to bathe in; so that the showers have become, in good truth, a godsend. I wonder why Providence does not cause a clear, cold fountain to bubble up at our doorstep; me-thinks it would not be unreasonable to pray for such a favor. At present we are under the ridiculous necessity of sending to the outer world for water. Only imagine Adam trudging out of Paradise with a bucket in each hand, to get water to drink, or for Eve to bathe in! Intolerable! (though our stout handmaiden really fetches our water.) In other respects Providence has treated us pretty tolerably well; but here I shall expect something further to be done. Also, in the way of future favors, a kitten would be very acceptable. Animals (except, perhaps, a pig) seem never out of place, even in the most paradisiacal spheres. And, by the way, a young colt comes up our avenue, now and then, to crop the seldom-trodden herbage; and so does a company of cows, whose sweet breath well repays us for the food which they obtain. There are likewise a few hens, whose quiet cluck is heard pleasantly about the house. A black dog sometimes stands at the farther extremity of the avenue, and looks wistfully hitherward; but when I whistle to him, he puts his tail between his legs, and trots away. Foolish dog! if he had more faith, he should have bones enough.

Saturday, August 6th.—Still a dull day, threatening rain, yet without energy of character enough to rain outright. However, yesterday there were showers enough to supply us well with their beneficent outpouring. As to the new cistern, it seems to be bewitched; for, while the spout pours into it like a cataract, it still remains almost empty. I wonder where Mr. Hosmer got it; perhaps from Tantalus, under the eaves of whose palace it must formerly have stood; for, like his drinking-cup in Hades, it has the property of filling itself forever, and never being full.

After breakfast I took my fishing-rod, and went down through our orchard to the river-side; but as three or four boys were already in possession of the best spots along the shore, I did not fish. This river of ours is the most sluggish stream that I ever was acquainted with. I had spent three weeks by its side, and swam across it every day, before I could determine which way its current ran; and then I was compelled to decide the question by the testimony of others, and not by my own observation. Owing to this torpor of the stream, it has nowhere a bright, pebbly shore, nor is there so much as a narrow strip of glistening sand in any part of its course; but it slumbers along between broad meadows, or kisses the tangled grass of mowing-fields and pastures, or bathes the overhanging boughs of elder-bushes and other water-loving plants. Flags and rushes grow along its shallow margin. The yellow water-lily spreads its broad flat leaves upon its surface; and the fragrant white pond-lily occurs in many favored spots,—generally selecting a situation just so far from the river's brink that it cannot be grasped except at the hazard of plunging in. But thanks be to the beautiful flower for growing at any rate. It is a marvel whence it derives its loveliness and perfume, sprouting as it does from the black mud over which the river sleeps, and from which the yellow lily likewise draws its unclean life and noisome odor. So it is with many people in this world; the same soil and circumstances may produce the good and beautiful, and the wicked and ugly. Some have the faculty of assimilating to themselves only what is evil, and so they become as noisome as the yellow water-lily. Some assimilate none but good influences, and their emblem is the fragrant and spotless pond-lily, whose very breath is a blessing to all the region round about....Among the productions of the river's margin, I must not forget the pickerel-weed, which grows just on the edge of the water, and shoots up a long stalk crowned with a blue spire, from among large green leaves. Both the flower and the leaves look well in a vase with pond-lilies, and relieve the unvaried whiteness of the latter; and, being all alike children of the waters, they are perfectly in keeping with one another....

I bathe once, and often twice, a day in our river; but one dip into the salt sea would be worth more than a whole week's soaking in such a lifeless tide. I have read of a river somewhere (whether it be in classic regions or among our Western Indians I know not) which seemed to dissolve and steal away the vigor of those who bathed in it. Perhaps our stream will be found to have this property. Its water, however, is pleasant in its immediate effect, being as soft as milk, and always warmer than the air. Its hue has a slight tinge of gold, and my limbs, when I behold them through its medium, look tawny. I am not aware that the inhabitants of Concord resemble their native river in any of their moral characteristics. Their forefathers, certainly, seem to have had the energy and impetus of a mountain torrent, rather than the torpor of this listless stream,—as it was proved by the blood with which they stained their river of Peace. It is said there are plenty of fish in it; but my most important captures hitherto have been a mud-turtle and an enormous eel. The former made his escape to his native element,—the latter we ate; and truly he had the taste of the whole river in his flesh, with a very prominent flavor of mud. On the whole, Concord River is no great favorite of mine; but I am glad to have any river at all so near at hand, it being just at the bottom of our orchard. Neither is it without a degree and kind of picturesqueness, both in its nearness and in the distance, when a blue gleam from its surface, among the green meadows and woods, seems like an open eye in Earth's countenance. Pleasant it is, too, to behold a little flat-bottomed skiff gliding over its bosom, which yields lazily to the stroke of the paddle, and allows the boat to go against its current almost as freely as with it. Pleasant, too, to watch an angler, as he strays along the brink, sometimes sheltering himself behind a tuft of bushes, and trailing his line along the water, in hopes to catch a pickerel. But, taking the river for all in all, I can find nothing more fit to compare it with than one of the half-torpid earthworms which I dig up for bait. The worm is sluggish, and so is the river,—the river is muddy, and so is the worm. You hardly know whether either of them be alive or dead; but still, in the course of time, they both manage to creep away. The best aspect of the Concord is when there is a northwestern breeze curling its surface, in a bright, sunshiny day. It then assumes a vivacity not its own. Moonlight, also, gives it beauty, as it does to all scenery of earth or water.

Sunday, August 7th.—At sunset last evening I ascended the lull-top opposite our house: and, looking downward at the long extent of the river, it struck me that I had done it some in justice in my remarks. Perhaps, like other gentle and quiet characters, it will be better appreciated the longer I am acquainted with it. Certainly, as I beheld it then, it was one of the loveliest features in a scene of great rural beauty. It was visible through a course of two or three miles, sweeping in a semicircle round the hill on which I stood, and being the central line of a broad vale on either side. At a distance, it looked like a strip of sky set into the earth, which it so etherealized and idealized that it seemed akin to the upper regions. Nearer the base of the hill, I could discern the shadows of every tree and rock, imaged with a distinctness that made them even more charming than the reality; because, knowing them to be unsubstantial, they assumed the ideality which the soul always craves in the contemplation of earthly beauty. All the sky, too, and the rich clouds of sunset, were reflected in the peaceful bosom of the river; and surely, if its bosom can give back such an adequate reflection of heaven, it cannot be so gross and impure as I described it yesterday. Or, if so, it shall be a symbol to me that even a human breast, which may appear least spiritual in some aspects, may still have the capability of reflecting an infinite heaven in its depths, and therefore of enjoying it. It is a comfortable thought, that the smallest and most turbid mud-puddle can contain its own picture of heaven. Let us remember this, when we feel inclined to deny all spiritual life to some people, in whom, nevertheless, our Father may perhaps see the image of His face. This dull river has a deep religion of its own; so, let us trust, has the dullest human soul, though, perhaps, unconsciously.

The scenery of Concord, as I beheld it from the summit of the hill, has no very marked characteristics, but has a great deal of quiet beauty, in keeping with the river. There are broad and peaceful meadows, which, I think, are among the most satisfying objects in natural scenery. The heart reposes on them with a feeling that few things else can give, because almost all other objects are abrupt and clearly defined; but a meadow stretches out like a small infinity, yet with a secure homeliness which we do not find either in an expanse of water or of air. The hills which border these meadows are wide swells of land, or long and gradual ridges, some of them densely covered with wood. The white village, at a distance on the left, appears to be embosomed among wooded hills. The verdure of the country is much more perfect than is usual at this season of the year, when the autumnal hue has generally made considerable progress over trees and grass. Last evening, after the copious showers of the preceding two days, it was worthy of early June, or, indeed, of a world just created. Had I not then been alone, I should have had a far deeper sense of beauty, for I should have looked through the medium of another spirit. Along the horizon there were masses of those deep clouds in which the fancy may see-images of all things that ever existed or were dreamed of. Over our old manse, of which I could catch but a glimpse among its embowering trees, appeared the immensely gigantic figure of a hound, crouching down with head erect, as if keeping watchful guard while the master of the mansion was away....How sweet it was to draw near my own home, after having lived homeless in the world so long!...With thoughts like these, I descended the hill, and clambered over the stone-wall, and crossed the road, and passed up our avenue, while the quaint old house put on an aspect of welcome.

Monday, August 8th.—I wish I could give a description of our house, for it really has a character of its own, which is more than can be said of most edifices in these days. It is two stories high, with a third story of attic chambers in the gable-roof. When I first visited it, early in June, it looked pretty much as it did during the old clergyman's lifetime, showing all the dust and disarray that might be supposed to have gathered about him in the course of sixty years of occupancy. The rooms seemed never to have been painted; at all events, the walls and panels, as well as the huge cross-beams, had a venerable and most dismal tinge of brown. The furniture consisted of high-backed, short-legged, rheumatic chairs, small, old tables, bedsteads with lofty posts, stately chests of drawers, looking-glasses in antique black frames, all of which were probably fashionable in the days of Dr. Ripley's predecessor. It required some energy of imagination to conceive the idea of transforming this ancient edifice into a comfortable modern residence. However, it has been successfully accomplished. The old Doctor's sleeping-apartment, which was the front room on the ground-floor, we have converted into a parlor; and by the aid of cheerful paint and paper, a gladsome carpet, pictures and engravings, new furniture, *bijouterie,* and a daily supply of flowers, it has become one of the prettiest and pleasantest rooms in the whole world. The shade of our departed host will never haunt it; for its aspect has been changed as completely as the scenery of a theatre. Probably the ghost gave one peep into it, uttered a groan, and vanished forever. The opposite room has been metamorphosed into a store-room. Through the house, both in the first and second story, runs a spacious hall or entry, occupying more space than is usually devoted to such a purpose in modern times. This feature contributes to give the whole house an airy, roomy, and convenient appearance; we can breathe the freer by the aid of the broad passageway. The front door of the hall looks up the stately avenue, which I have already mentioned; and the opposite door opens into the orchard, through which a path descends to the river. In the second story we have at present fitted up three rooms,—one being our own chamber, and the opposite one a guest-chamber, which contains the most presentable of the old Doctor's ante-Revolutionary furniture. After all, the moderns have invented nothing better, as chamber furniture, than these chests of drawers, which stand on four slender legs, and rear an absolute tower of mahogany to the ceiling, the whole terminating in a fantastically carved summit. Such a venerable structure adorns our guest-chamber. In the rear of the house is the little room which I call my study, and which, in its day, has witnessed the intellectual labors of better students than myself. It contains, with some additions and alterations, the furniture of my bachelor-room in Boston; but there is a happier disposal of things now. There is a little vase of flowers on one of the bookcases, and a larger bronze vase of graceful ferns that surmounts the bureau. In size the room is just what it ought to be; for I never could compress my thoughts sufficiently to write in a very spacious room. It has three windows, two of which are shaded by a large and beautiful willow-tree, which sweeps against the overhanging eaves. On this side we have a view into the orchard, and, beyond, a glimpse of the river. The other window is the one from which Mr. Emerson, the predecessor of Dr. Ripley, beheld the first fight of the Revolution,—which he might well do, as the British troops were drawn up within a hundred yards of the house; and on looking forth just now, I could still perceive the western abutments of the old bridge, the passage of which was contested. The new monument is visible from base to summit.

Notwithstanding all we have done to modernize the old place, we seem scarcely to have disturbed its air of antiquity. It is evident that other wedded pairs have spent their honeymoons here, that children have been born here, and people have grown old and died in these rooms, although for our behoof the same apartments have consented to look cheerful once again. Then there are dark closets, and strange nooks and corners, where the ghosts of former occupants might hide themselves in the daytime, and stalk forth when night conceals all our sacrilegious improvements. We have seen no apparitions as yet; but we hear strange noises, especially in the kitchen, and last night, while sitting in the parlor, we heard a thumping and pounding as of somebody at work in my study. Nay, if I mistake not (for I was half asleep), there was a sound as of some person crumpling paper in his hand in our very bedchamber. This must have been old Dr. Ripley with one of his sermons. There is a whole chest of them in the garret; but he need have no apprehensions of our disturbing them. I never saw the old patriarch myself, which I regret, as I should have been glad to associate his venerable figure at ninety years of age with the house in which he dwelt.

Externally the house presents the same appearance as in the Doctor's day. It had once a coat of white paint; but the storms and sunshine of many years have almost obliterated it, and produced a sober, grayish hue, which entirely suits the antique form of the structure. To repaint its reverend face would be a real sacrilege. It would look like old Dr. Ripley in a brown wig. I hardly know why it is that our cheerful and lightsome repairs and improvements in the interior of the house seem to be in perfectly good taste, though the heavy old beams and high wainscoting of the walls speak of ages gone by. But so it is. The cheerful paper-hangings have the air of belonging to the old walls; and such modernisms as astral lamps, card-tables, gilded Cologne-bottles, silver taper-stands, and bronze and alabaster flower-vases, do not seem at all impertinent. It is thus that an aged man may keep his heart warm for new things and new friends, and often furnish himself anew with ideas; though it would not be graceful for him to attempt to suit his exterior to the passing fashions of the day.

August 9th.—Our orchard in its day has been a very productive and profitable one; and we were told that in one year it returned Dr. Ripley a hundred dollars, besides defraying the expense of repairing the house. It is now long past its prime: many of the trees are moss-grown, and have dead and rotten branches intermixed among the green and fruitful ones. And it may well be so; for I suppose some of the trees may have been set out by Mr. Emerson, who died in the first year of the Revolutionary War. Neither will the fruit, probably, bear comparison with the delicate productions of modern pomology. Most of the trees seem to have abundant burdens upon them; but they are homely russet apples, fit only for baking and cooking. (But we are yet to have practical experience of our fruit.) Justice Shallow's orchard, with its choice pippins and leather-coats, was doubtless much superior. Nevertheless, it pleases me to think of the good minister, walking in the shadows of these old, fantastically shaped apple-trees, here plucking some of the fruit to taste, there pruning away a too luxuriant branch, and all the while computing how many barrels may be filled, and how large a sum will be added to his stipend by their sale. And the same trees offer their fruit to me as freely as they did to him,—their old branches, like withered hands and arms, holding out apples of the same flavor as they held out to Dr. Ripley in his lifetime. Thus the trees, as living existences, form a peculiar link between the dead and us. My fancy has always found something very interesting in an orchard. Apple-trees, and all fruit-trees, have a domestic character which brings them into relationship with man. They have lost, in a great measure, the wild nature of the forest-tree, and have grown humanized by receiving the care of man, and by contributing to his wants. They have become a part of the family; and their individual characters are as well understood and appreciated as those of the human members. One tree is harsh and crabbed, another mild; one is churlish and illiberal, another exhausts itself with its free-hearted bounties. Even the shapes of apple-trees have great individuality, into such strange postures do they put themselves, and thrust their contorted branches so grotesquely in all directions. And when they have stood around a house for many years, and held converse with successive dynasties of occupants, and gladdened their hearts so often in the fruitful autumn, then it would seem almost sacrilege to cut them down.

Besides the apple-trees, there are various other kinds of fruit in close vicinity to the house. When we first arrived, there were several trees of ripe cherries, but so sour that we allowed them to wither upon the branches. Two long rows of currant-bushes supplied us abundantly for nearly four weeks. There are a good many peach-trees, but all of an old date,— their branches rotten, gummy, and mossy,— and their fruit, I fear, will be of very inferior quality. They produce most abundantly, however,—the peaches being almost as numerous as the leaves; and even the sprouts and suckers from the roots of the old trees have fruit upon them. Then there are pear-trees of various kinds, and one or two quince-trees. On the whole, these fruit-trees, and the other items and adjuncts of the place, convey a very agreeable idea of the outward comfort in which the good old Doctor must have spent his life. Everything seems to have fallen to his lot that could possibly be supposed to render the life of a country clergyman easy and prosperous. There is a barn, which probably used to be filled annually with his hay and other agricultural products. There are sheds, and a hen-house, and a pigeon-house, and an old stone pigsty, the open portion of which is overgrown with tall weeds, indicating that no grunter has recently occupied it....I have serious thoughts of inducting a new incumbent in this part of the parsonage. It is our duty to support a pig, even if we have no design of feasting upon him; and, for my own part, I have a great sympathy and interest for the whole race of porkers, and should have much amusement in studying the character of a pig. Perhaps I might try to bring out his moral and intellectual nature, and cultivate his affections. A cat, too, and perhaps a dog, would be desirable additions to our household.

August 10th.—The natural taste of man for the original Adam's occupation is fast developing itself in me. I find that I am a good deal interested in our garden, although, as it was planted before we came here, I do not feel the same affection for the plants that I should if the seed had been sown by my own hands. It is something like nursing and educating another person's children. Still, it was a very pleasant moment when I gathered the first string-beans, which were the earliest esculent that the garden contributed to our table. And I love to watch the successive development of each new vegetable, and mark its daily growth, which always affects me with surprise. It is as if something were being created under my own inspection, and partly by my own aid. One day, perchance, I look at my bean-vines, and see only the green leaves clambering up the poles; again, to-morrow, I give a second glance, and there are the delicate blossoms; and a third day, on a somewhat closer observation, I discover the tender young beans, hiding among the foliage. Then, each morning, I watch the swilling of the pods and calculate how soon they will he ready to yield their treasures. All this gives a pleasure and an ideality, hitherto unthought of, to the business of providing sustenance for my family. I suppose Adam bit it in Paradise; and, of merely and exclusively earthly enjoyments, there are few purer and more harmless to be experienced. Speaking of beans, by the way, they are a classical food, and their culture must have been the occupation of many ancient sages and heroes. Summer-squashes are a very pleasant vegetable to be acquainted with. They grow in the forms of urns and vases,—some shallow, others deeper, and all with a beautifully scalloped edge. Almost any squash in our garden might be copied by a sculptor, and would look lovely in marble, or in china; and, if I could afford it, I would have exact imitations of the real vegetable as portions of my dining-service. They would be very appropriate dishes for holding garden-vegetables. Besides the summer-squashes, we have the crook-necked winter-squash, which I always delight to look at, when it turns up its big rotundity to ripen in the autumn sun. Except a pumpkin, there is no vegetable production that imparts such an idea of warmth and comfort to the beholder. Our own crop, however, does not promise to be very abundant; for the leaves formed such a superfluous shade over the young blossoms, that most of them dropped off without producing the germ of fruit Yesterday and to-day I have cut off an immense number of leaves, and have thus given the remaining blossoms a chance to profit by the air and sunshine; hut the season is too far advanced, I am afraid, for the squashes to attain any great bulk, and grow yellow in the sun. We have muskmelons and watermelons, which promise to supply us with as many as we can eat. After all, the greatest interest of these vegetables does not seem to consist in their being articles of food. It is rather that we love to see something born into the world; and when a great squash or melon is produced, it is a large and tangible existence, which the imagination can seize hold of and rejoice in. I love, also, to see my own works contributing to the life and well-being of animate nature. It is pleasant to have the bees come and suck honey out of my squash-blossoms, though, when they have laden themselves, they fly away to some unknown hive, which will give me back nothing in return for what my garden has given them. But there is much more honey in the world, and so I am content. Indian corn, in the prime and glory of its verdure, is a very beautiful vegetable, both considered in the separate plant, and in a mass in a broad field, rustling and waving, and surging up and down in the breeze and sunshine of a summer afternoon. We have as many as fifty hills, I should think, which will give us an abundant supply. Pray Heaven that we may be able to eat it all! for it is not pleasant to think that anything which Nature has been at the pains to produce should be thrown away. But the hens will be glad of our superfluity, and so will the pigs, though we have neither hens nor pigs of our own. But hens we must certainly keep. There is something very sociable and quiet, and soothing, too, in their soliloquies and converse among themselves; and, in an idle and half-meditative mood, it is very pleasant to watch a party of hens picking up their daily subsistence, with a gallant chanticleer in the midst of them. Milton had evidently contemplated such a picture with delight.

I find that I have not given a very complete idea of our garden, although it certainly deserves an ample record in this chronicle, since my labors in it are the only present labors of my life. Besides what I have mentioned, we have cucumber-vines, which to-day yielded us the first cucumber of the season, a bed of beets, and another of carrots, and another of parsnips' and turnips, none of which promise us a very abundant harvest. In truth, the soil is worn out, and, moreover, received very little manure this season. Also, we have cabbages in superfluous abundance, inasmuch as we neither of us have the least affection for them; and it would be unreasonable to expect Sarah, the cook, to eat fifty head of cabbages. Tomatoes, too, we shall have by and by. At our first arrival, we found green peas ready for gathering, and these, instead of the string-beans, were the first offering of the garden to our board.

Saturday, August 13th.—My life, at this time, is more like that of a boy, externally, than it has been since I was really a boy. It is usually supposed that the cares of life come with matrimony; but I seem to have cast off all care, and live on with as much easy trust in Providence as Adam could possibly have felt before he had learned that there was a world beyond Paradise. My chief anxiety consists in watching the prosperity of my vegetables, in observing how they are affected by the rain or sunshine, in lamenting the blight of one squash and rejoicing at the luxurious growth of another. It is as if the original relation between man and Nature were restored in my case, and as if I were to look exclusively to her for the support of my Eve and myself,—to trust to her for food and clothing, and all things needful, with the full assurance that she would not fail me. The fight with the world,—the struggle of a man among men,—the agony of the universal effort to wrench the means of living from a host of greedy competitors,—all this seems like a dream to me. My business is merely to five and to enjoy; and whatever is essential to life and enjoyment will come as naturally as the dew from heaven. This is, practically at least, my faith. And so I awake in the morning with a boyish thoughtlessness as to how the outgoings of the day are to be provided for, and its incomings rendered certain. After breakfast, I go forth into my garden, and gather whatever the bountiful Mother has made fit for our present sustenance; and of late days she generally gives me two squashes and a cucumber, and promises me green corn and shell-beans very soon. Then I pass down through our orchard to the river-side, and ramble along its margin in search of flowers. Usually I discern a fragrant white lily, here and there along the shore, growing, with sweet prudishness, beyond the grasp of mortal arm. But it does not escape me so. I know what is its fitting destiny better than the silly flower knows for itself; so I wade in, heedless of wet trousers, and seize the shy lily by its slender stem. Thus I make prize of five or six, which are as many as usually blossom within my reach in a single morning;—some of them partially worm-eaten or blighted, like virgins with an eating sorrow at the heart; others as fair and perfect as Nature's own idea was, when she first imagined this lovely flower. A perfect pond-lily is the most satisfactory of flowers. Besides these, I gather whatever else of beautiful chances to be growing in the moist soil by the river-side,—an amphibious tribe, yet with more richness and grace than the wild-flowers of the deep and dry woodlands and hedgerows,—sometimes the white arrow-head, always the blue spires and broad green leaves of the pickerel-flower, which contrast and harmonize so well with the white lilies. For the last two or three days, I have found scattered stalks of the cardinal-flower, the gorgeous scarlet of which it is a joy even to remember. The world is made brighter and sunnier by flowers of such a hue. Even perfume, which otherwise is the soul and spirit of a flower, may be spared when it arrays itself in this scarlet glory. It is a flower of thought and feeling, too: it seems to have its roots deep down in the hearts of those who gaze at it. Other bright flowers sometimes impress me as wanting sentiment: but it is not so with this.

Well, having made up my bunch of flowers, I return home with them....Then I ascend to my study, and generally read, or perchance scribble in this journal, and otherwise suffer Time to loiter onward at his own pleasure, till the dinner-hour. In pleasant days, the chief event of the afternoon, and the happiest one of the day, is our walk....So comes the night; and I look back upon a day spent in what the world would call idleness, and for which I myself can suggest no more appropriate epithet, but which, nevertheless, I cannot feel to have been spent amiss. True, it might be a sin and shame, in such a world as ours, to spend a lifetime in this manner; but for a few summer weeks it is good to live as if this world were heaven. And so it is, and so it shall be, although, in a little while, a flitting shadow of earthly care and toil will mingle itself with our realities.

Monday, August 15th.—George Hillard and his wife arrived from Boston in the dusk of Saturday evening, to spend Sunday with us. It was a pleasant sensation, when the coach rumbled up our avenue, and wheeled round at the door; for I felt that I was regarded as a man with a household,—a man having a tangible existence and locality in the world,—when friends came to avail themselves of our hospitality. It was a sort of acknowledgment and reception of us into the corps of married people,—a sanction by no means essential to our peace and well-being, but yet agreeable enough to receive. So we welcomed them cordially at the door, and ushered them into our parlor, and soon into the supper-room....The night flitted over us all, and passed away, and up rose a gray and sullen morning,...and we had a splendid breakfast of flapjacks, or slapjacks, and whortleberries, which I gathered on a neighboring hill, and perch, bream, and pout, which I hooked out of the river the evening before. About nine o'clock, Hillard and I set out for a, walk to Walden Pond, calling by the way at Mr. Emerson's, to obtain his guidance or directions, and he accompanied us in his own illustrious person. We turned aside a little from our way, to visit Mr. —, a yeoman, of whose homely and self-acquired wisdom Mr. Emerson has a very high opinion. We found him walking in his fields, a short and stalwart and sturdy personage of middle age, with a face of shrewd and kind expression, and manners of natural courtesy. He had a very free flow of talk; for, with a little induction from Mr. Emerson, he began to discourse about the state of the nation, agriculture, and business in general, uttering thoughts that had come to him at the plough, and which had a sort of flavor of the fresh earth about them. His views were sensible and characteristic, and had grown in the soil where we found them;...and he is certainly a man of intellectual and moral substance, a sturdy fact, a reality, something to be felt and touched, whose ideas seem to be dug out of his mind as he digs potatoes, beets, carrots, and turnips out of the ground.

After leaving Mr. —, we proceeded through wood-paths to Walden Pond, picking blackberries of enormous size along the way. The pond itself was beautiful and refreshing to my soul, after such long and exclusive familiarity with our tawny and sluggish river. It lies embosomed among wooded hills,—it is not very extensive, but large enough for waves to dance upon its surface, and to look like a piece of blue firmament, earth-encircled. The shore has a narrow, pebbly strand, which it was worth a day's journey to look at, for the sake of the contrast between it and the weedy, oozy margin of the river. Farther within its depths, you perceive a bottom of pure white sand, sparkling through the transparent water, which, methought, was the very purest liquid in the world. After Mr. Emerson left us, Hillard and I bathed in the pond, and it does really seem as if my spirit, as well as corporeal person, were refreshed by that bath. A good deal of mud and river slime had accumulated on my soul; but these bright waters washed them all away.

We returned home in due season for dinner....To my misfortune, however, a box of Mediterranean wine proved to have undergone the acetous fermentation; so that the splendor of the festival suffered some diminution. Nevertheless, we ate our dinner with a good appetite, and afterwards went universally to take our several siestas. Meantime there came a shower, which so besprinkled the grass and shrubbery as to make it rather wet for our after-tea ramble. The chief result of the walk was the bringing home of an immense burden of the trailing clematis-vine, now just in blossom, and with which all our flower-stands and vases are this morning decorated. On our return we found Mr. and Mrs. S—, and E. H—, who shortly took their leave, and we sat up late, telling ghost-stories. This morning, at seven, our friends left us. We were both pleased with the visit, and so, I think, were our guests.

* * * * *

Monday, August 22d.—I took a walk through the woods yesterday afternoon, to Mr. Emerson's, with a book which Margaret Fuller had left, after a call on Saturday eve. I missed the nearest way, and wandered into a very secluded portion of the forest; for forest it might justly be called, so dense and sombre was the shade of oaks and pines. Once I wandered into a tract so overgrown with bushes and underbrush that I could scarcely force a passage through. Nothing is more annoying than a walk of this kind, where one is tormented by an innumerable host of petty impediments. It incenses and depresses me at the same time. Always when I flounder into the midst of bushes, which cross and intertwine themselves about my legs, and brush my face, and seize hold of my clothes, with their multitudinous grip,—always, in such a difficulty, I feel as if it were almost as well to lie down and die in rage and despair as to go one step farther. It is laughable, after I have got out of the moil, to think how miserably it affected me for the moment; but I had better learn patience betimes, for there are many such bushy tracts in this vicinity, on the margins of meadows, and my walks will often lead me into them. Escaping from the bushes, I soon came to an open space among the woods,— a very lovely spot, with the tall old trees standing around as quietly as if no one had intruded there throughout the whole summer. A company of crows Were holding their Sabbath on their summits. Apparently they felt themselves injured or insulted by my presence; for, with one consent, they began to Caw 1 caw! caw! and, launching themselves sullenly on the air, took flight to some securer solitude. Mine, probably, was the first human shape that they had seen all day long,—at least, if they had been stationary in that spot; but perhaps they had winged their way over miles and miles of country, had breakfasted on the summit of Graylock, and dined at the base of Wachusett, and were merely come to sup and sleep among the quiet woods of Concord. But it was my impression at the time, that they had sat still and silent on the tops of the trees all through the Sabbath day, and I felt like one who should unawares disturb an assembly of worshippers. A crow, however, has no real pretensions to religion, in spite of his gravity of mien and black attire. Crows are certainly thieves, and probably infidels. Nevertheless, their voices yesterday were in admirable accordance with the influences of the quiet, sunny, warm, yet autumnal afternoon. They were so far above my head that their loud clamor added to the quiet of the scene, instead of disturbing it. There was no other sound, except the song of the cricket, which is but an audible stillness; for, though it be very loud and heard afar, yet the mind does not take note of it as a sound, so entirely does it mingle and lose its individuality among the other characteristics of coming autumn. Alas for the summer! The grass is still verdant on the hills and in the valleys; the foliage of the trees is as dense as ever, and as green; the flowers are abundant along the margin of the river, and in the hedge-rows, and deep among the woods; the days, too, are as fervid as they were a month ago; and yet in every breath of wind and in every beam of sunshine there is an autumnal influence. I know not how to describe it. Methinks there is a sort of coolness amid all the heat, and a mildness in the brightest of the sunshine. A breeze cannot stir without thrilling me with the breath of autumn, and I behold its pensive glory in the far, golden gleams among the long shadows of the trees. The flowers, even the brightest of them,—the golden-rod and the gorgeous cardinals,—the most glorious flowers of the year,—have this gentle sadness amid their pomp. Pensive autumn is expressed in the glow of every one of them. I have felt this influence earlier in some years than in others. Sometimes autumn may be perceived even in the early days of July. There is no other feeling like that caused by this faint, doubtful, yet real perception, or rather prophecy, of the year's decay, so deliciously sweet and sad at the same time.

After leaving the book at Mr. Emerson's I returned through the woods, and, entering Sleepy Hollow, I perceived a lady reclining near the path which bends along its verge. It was Margaret herself. She had been there the whole afternoon, meditating or reading; for she had a book in her hand, with some strange title, which I did not understand, and have forgotten. She said that nobody had broken her solitude, and was just giving utterance to a theory that no inhabitant of Concord ever visited Sleepy Hollow, when we saw a group of people entering the sacred precincts. Most of them followed a path which led them away from us; but an old man passed near us, and smiled to see Margaret reclining on the. ground, and me sitting by her side. He made some remark about the beauty of the afternoon, and withdrew himself into the shadow of the wood. Then we talked about autumn, and about the pleasures of being lost in the woods, and about the crows, whose voices Margaret had heard; and about the experiences of early childhood, whose influence remains upon the character after the recollection of them has passed away; and about the sight of mountains from a distance, and the view from their summits; and .about other matters of high and low philosophy. In the midst of our talk, we heard footsteps above us, on the high bank; and while the person was still hidden among the trees, he called to Margaret, of whom he had gotten a glimpse. Then he emerged from the green shade, and, behold! it was Mr. Emerson. He appeared to have had a pleasant time; for he said that there were Muses in the woods to-day, and whispers to be heard in the breezes. It being now nearly six o'clock, we separated,—Margaret and Mr. Emerson towards his home, and I towards mine....

Last evening there was the most beautiful moonlight that ever hallowed this earthly world; and when I went to bathe in the river, which was as calm as death, it seemed like plunging down into the sky. But I had rather be on earth than even in the seventh heaven, just now.

Wednesday, August 24th.—I left home at five o'clock this morning to catch some fish for breakfast. I shook our summer apple-tree, and ate the golden apple which fell from it. Methinks these early apples, which come as a golden promise before the treasures of autumnal fruit, are almost more delicious than anything that comes afterwards. We have but one such tree in our orchard; but it supplies us with a daily abundance, and probably will do so for at least a week to come. Meantime other trees begin to cast their ripening windfalls upon the grass; and when I taste them, and perceive their mellowed flavor and blackening seeds, I feel somewhat overwhelmed with the impending bounties of Providence. I suppose Adam, in Paradise, did not like to see his fruits decaying on the ground, after he had watched them through the sunny days of the world's first summer. However, insects, at the worst, will hold a festival upon them, so that they will not be thrown away, in the great scheme of Nature. Moreover, I have one advantage over the primeval Adam, inasmuch as there is a chance of disposing of my superfluous fruits among people who inhabit no Paradise of their own.

Passing a little way down along the river-side, I threw in my line, and soon drew out one of the smallest possible of fishes. It seemed to be a pretty good morning for the angler,—an autumnal coolness in the air, a clear sky, but with a fog across the lowlands and on the surface of the river, which a gentle breeze sometimes condensed into wreaths. At first, I could barely discern the opposite shore of the river; but, as the sun arose, the vapors gradually dispersed, till only a warm, smoky tint was left along the water's surface. The farm-houses across the river made their appearance out of the dusky cloud; the voices of boys were heard, shouting to the cattle as they drove them to the pastures; a man whetted his scythe, and set to work in a neighboring meadow. Meantime, I continued to stand on the oozy margin of the stream, beguiling the little fish; and though the scaly inhabitants of our river partake somewhat of the character of their native element, and are but sluggish biters, still I contrived to pull out not far from two dozen. They were all bream, a broad, flat, almost circular fish, shaped a good deal like a flounder, but swimming on their edges, instead of on their sides. As far as mere pleasure is concerned, it is hardly worth while to fish, in our river, it is so much like angling in a mud-puddle; and one does not attach the idea of freshness and purity to the fishes, as we do to those which inhabit swift, transparent streams, or haunt the shores of the great briny deep. Standing on the weedy margin, and throwing the line over the elder-bushes that dip into the water, it seems as if we could catch nothing but frogs and mud-turtles, or reptiles akin to them. And even when a fish of reputable aspect is drawn out, one feels a shyness about touching him. As to our river, its character was admirably expressed last night by some one who said "it was too lazy to keep itself clean." I might write pages and pages, and only obscure the impression which this brief sentence conveys. Nevertheless, we made bold to eat some of my fish for breakfast, and found them very savory; and the rest shall meet with due entertainment at dinner, together with some shell-beans, green corn, and cucumbers from our garden; so this day's food comes directly and entirely from beneficent Nature, without the intervention of any third person between her and us.

Saturday, August 27th.—A peach-tree, which grows beside our house and brushes against the window, is so burdened with fruit that I have had to prop it up. I never saw more splendid peaches in appearance,—great, round, crimson-cheeked beauties, clustering all over the tree. A pear-tree, likewise, is maturing a generous burden of small, sweet fruit, which will require to be eaten at about the same time as the peaches. There is something pleasantly annoying in this superfluous abundance; it is like standing under a tree of ripe apples, and giving it a shake, with the intention of bringing down a single one, when, behold, a dozen come thumping about our ears. But the idea of the infinite generosity and exhaustless bounty of our Mother Nature is well worth attaining; and I never had it so vividly as now, when I find myself, with the few mouths which I am to feed, the sole inheritor of the old clergyman's wealth of fruits. His children, his friends in the village, and the clerical guests who came to preach in his pulpit, were all wont to eat and be filled from these trees. Now, all these hearty old people have passed away, and in their stead is a solitary pair, whose appetites are more than satisfied with the windfalls which the trees throw down at their feet. Howbeit, we shall have now and then a guest to keep our peaches and pears from decaying.

G. B—, my old fellow-laborer at the community at Brook Farm, called on me last evening, and dined here to-day. He has been cultivating vegetables at Plymouth this summer, and selling them in the market. What a singular mode of life for a man of education and refinement,—to spend his days in hard and earnest bodily toil, and then to convey the products of his labor, in a wheelbarrow, to the public market, and there retail them out,—a peck of peas or beans, a bunch of turnips, a squash, a dozen ears of green corn! Few men, without some eccentricity of character, would have the moral strength to do this; and it is very striking to find such strength combined with the utmost gentleness, and an uncommon regularity of nature. Occasionally he returns for a day or two to resume his place among scholars and idle people, as, for instance, the present week, when he has thrown aside his spade and hoe to attend the Commencement at Cambridge. He is a rare man,—a perfect original, yet without any one salient point; a character to be felt and understood, but almost impossible to describe; for, should you seize upon any characteristic, it would inevitably be altered and distorted in the process of writing it down.

Our few remaining days of summer have been latterly grievously darkened with clouds. To-day there has been an hour or two of hot sunshine; but the sun rose amid cloud and mist, and before he could dry up the moisture of last night's shower upon the trees and grass, the clouds have gathered between him and us again. This afternoon the thunder rumbles in the distance, and I believe a few drops of rain have fallen; but the weight of the shower has burst elsewhere, leaving us nothing but its sullen gloom. There is a muggy warmth in the atmosphere, which takes all the spring and vivacity out of the mind and body.

Sunday, August 28th.—Still another rainy day,—the heaviest rain, I believe, that has fallen since we came to Concord (not two months ago). There never was a more sombre aspect of all external nature. I gaze from the open window of my study somewhat disconsolately, and observe the great willow-tree which shades the house, and which has caught and retained a whole cataract of rain among its leaves and boughs; and all the fruit-trees, too, are dripping continually, even in the brief intervals when the clouds give us a respite. If shaken to bring down the fruit, they will discharge a shower upon the head of him who stands beneath. The rain is warm, coming from some southern region; but the willow attests that it is an autumnal spell of weather, by scattering down no infrequent multitude of yellow leaves, which rest upon the sloping roof of the house, and strew the gravel-path and the grass. The other trees do not yet shed their leaves, though in some of them a lighter tint of verdure, tending towards yellow, is perceptible. All day long we hear the water drip, drip, dripping, splash, splash, splashing, from the eaves, and babbling and foaming into the tubs which have been set out to receive it. The old unpainted shingles and boards of the mansion and out-houses are black with the moisture which they have imbibed. Looking at the river, we perceive that its usually smooth and mirrored surface is blurred by the infinity of rain-drops; the whole landscape—grass, trees, and houses—has a completely water-soaked aspect, as if the earth were wet through. The wooded hill, about a mile distant, whither we went to gather whortleberries, has a mist upon its summit, as if the demon of the rain were enthroned there; and if we look to the sky, it seems as if all the water that had been poured down upon us were as nothing to what is to come. Once in a while, indeed, there is a gleam of sky along the horizon, or a half-cheerful, half-sullen lighting up of the atmosphere; the rain-drops cease to patter down, except when the trees shake off a gentle shower; but soon we hear the broad, quiet, slow, and sure recommencement of the rain. The river, if I mistake not, has risen considerably during the day, and its current will acquire some degree of energy.

In this sombre weather, when some mortals almost forget that there ever was any golden sunshine, or ever will be any hereafter, others seem absolutely to radiate it from their own hearts and minds. The gloom cannot pervade them; they conquer it, and drive it quite out of their sphere, and create a moral rainbow of hope upon the blackest cloud. As for myself, I am little other than a cloud at such seasons, but such persons contrive to make me a sunny one, shining all through me. And thus, even without the support of a stated occupation, I survive these sullen days and am happy.

This morning we read the Sermon on the Mount. In the course of the forenoon, the rain abated for a season, and I went out and gathered some corn and summer-squashes, and picked up the windfalls of apples and pears and peaches. Wet, wet, wet,—everything was wet; the blades of the corn-stalks moistened me; the wet grass soaked my boots quite through; the trees threw their reserved showers upon my head; and soon the remorseless rain began anew, and drove me into the house. When shall we be able to walk again to the far hills, and plunge into the deep woods, and gather more cardinals along the river's margin? The track along which we trod is probably under water now. How inhospitable Nature is during a rain! In the fervid heat of sunny days, she still retains some degree of mercy for us; she has shady spots, whither the sun cannot come; but she provides no shelter against her storms. It makes one shiver to think how dripping with wet are those deep, umbrageous nooks, those overshadowed banks, where we find such enjoyment during sultry afternoons. And what becomes of the birds in such a soaking rain as this? Is hope and an instinctive faith so mixed up with their nature that they can be cheered by the thought that the sunshine will return? or do they think, as I almost do, that there is to be no sunshine any more? Very disconsolate must they be among the dripping leaves; and when a single summer makes so important a portion of their lives, it seems hard that so much of it should be dissolved in rain. I, likewise, am greedy of the summer days for my own sake; the life of man does not contain so many of them that one can be spared without regret.

Tuesday, August 30th.—I was promised, in the midst of Sunday's rain, that Monday should be fair, and, behold! the sun came back to us, and brought one of the most perfect days ever made since Adam was driven out of Paradise. By the by, was there ever any rain in Paradise? If so, how comfortless must Eve's bower have been! and what a wretched and rheumatic time must they have had on their bed of wet roses! It makes me shiver to think of it. Well, it seemed as if the world was newly created yesterday morning, and I beheld its birth; for I had risen before the sun was over the hill, and had gone forth to fish. How instantaneously did all dreariness and heaviness of the earth's spirit flit away before one smile of the beneficent sun! This proves that all gloom is but a dream and a shadow, and that cheerfulness is the real truth. It requires many clouds, long brooding over us, to make us sad, but one gleam of sunshine always suffices to cheer up the landscape. The banks of the river actually laughed when the sunshine fell upon them; and the river itself was alive and cheerful, and, by way of fun and amusement, it had swept away many wreaths of meadow-hay, and old, rotten branches, of trees, and all such trumpery. These matters came floating downwards, whirling round and round in the eddies, or hastening onward in the main current; and many of them, before this time, have probably been carried into the Merrimack, and will be borne onward to the sea. The spots where I stood to fish, on my preceding excursion, were now under water; and the tops of many of the bushes, along the river's margin, barely emerged from the stream. Large spaces of meadow are overflowed.

There was a northwest-wind throughout the day; and as many clouds, the remnants of departed gloom, were scattered about the sky, the breeze was continually blowing them across the sun. For the most part, they were gone again in a moment; but sometimes the shadow remained long enough to make me dread a return of sulky weather. Then would come the burst of sunshine, making me feel as if a rainy day were henceforth an impossibility....

In the afternoon Mr. Emerson called, bringing Mr. —. He is a good sort of humdrum parson enough, and well fitted to increase the stock of manuscript sermons, of which there must be a fearful quantity already in the world. Mr. —, however, is probably one of the best and most useful of his class, because no suspicion of the necessity of his profession, constituted as it now is, to mankind, and of his own usefulness and success in it, has hitherto disturbed him; and therefore, he labors with faith and confidence, as ministers did a hundred years ago.

After the visitors were gone, I sat at the gallery window, looking down the avenue; and soon there appeared an elderly woman,—a homely, decent old matron, dressed in a dark gown, and with what seemed a manuscript book under her arm. The wind sported with her gown, and blew her veil across her face, and seemed to make game of her, though on a nearer view she looked like a sad old creature, with a pale, thin countenance, and somewhat of a wild and wandering expression. She had a singular gait, reeling, as it were, and yet not quite reeling, from one side of the path to the other; going onward as if it were not much matter whether she went straight or crooked. Such were my observations as she approached through the scattered sunshine and shade of our long avenue, until, reaching the door, she gave a knock, and inquired for the lady of the house. Her manuscript contained a certificate, stating that the old woman was a widow from a foreign land, who had recently lost her son, and was now utterly destitute of friends and kindred, and without means of support. Appended to the certificate there was a list of names of people who had bestowed charity on her, with the amounts of the several donations,—none, as I recollect, higher than twenty-five cents. Here is a strange life, and a character fit for romance and poetry. All the early part of her life, I suppose, and much of her widowhood, were spent in the quiet of a home, with kinsfolk around her, and children, and the lifelong gossiping acquaintances that some women always create about them. But in her decline she has wandered away from all these, and from her native country itself, and is a vagrant, yet with something of the homeliness and decency of aspect he-longing to one who has been a wife and mother, and has had a roof of her own above her head,—and, with all this, a wildness proper to her present life. I have a liking for vagrants of all sorts, and never, that I know of, refused my mite to a wandering beggar, when I had anything in my own pocket. There is so much wretchedness in the world, that we may safely take the word of any mortal professing to need our assistance; and, even should we be deceived, still the good to ourselves resulting from a kind act is worth more than the trifle by which we purchase it. It is desirable, I think, that such persons should be permitted to roam through our land of plenty, scattering the seeds of tenderness and charity, as birds of passage bear the seeds of precious plants from land to land, without even dreaming of the office which they perform.

Thursday, September 1st.—Mr. Thoreau dined with us yesterday....He is a keen and delicate observer of nature,—a genuine observer,—which, I suspect, is almost as rare a character as even an original poet; and Nature, in return for his love, seems to adopt him as her especial child, and shows him secrets which few others are allowed to witness. He is familiar with beast, fish, fowl, and reptile, and has strange stories to tell of adventures and friendly passages with these lower brethren of mortality. Herb and flower, likewise, wherever they grow, whether in garden or wildwood, are his familiar friends. He is also on intimate terms with the clouds, and can tell the portents of storms. It is a characteristic trait, that he has a great regard for the memory of the Indian tribes, whose wild life would have suited him so well; and, strange to say, he seldom walks over a ploughed field without picking up an arrow-point, spear-head, or other relic of the red man, as if their spirits willed him to be the inheritor of their simple wealth.

With all this he has more than a tincture of literature,—a deep and true taste for poetry, especially for the elder poets, and he is a good writer,—at least he has written a good article, a rambling disquisition on Natural History, in the last "Dial," which, he says, was chiefly made up from journals of his own observations. Methinks this article gives a very fair image of his mind and character,—so true, innate, and literal in observation, yet giving the spirit as well as letter of what he sees, even as a lake reflects its wooded banks, showing every leaf, yet giving the wild beauty of the whole scene. Then there are in the article passages of cloudy and dreamy metaphysics, and also passages where his thoughts seem to measure and attune themselves into spontaneous verse, as they rightfully may, since there is real poetry in them. There is a basis of good sense and of moral truth, too, throughout the article, which also is a reflection of his character; for he is not unwise to think and feel, and I find him a healthy and wholesome man to know.

After dinner (at which we cut the first watermelon and muskmelon that our garden has grown), Mr. Thoreau and I walked up the bank of the river, and at a certain point he shouted for his boat. Forthwith a young man paddled it across, and Mr. Thoreau and I voyaged farther up the stream, which soon became more beautiful than any picture, with its dark and quiet sheet of water, half shaded, half sunny, between high and wooded banks. The late rains have swollen the stream so much that many trees are standing up to their knees, as it were, in the water, and boughs, which lately swung high in air, now dip and drink deep of the passing wave. As to the poor cardinals which glowed upon the bank a few days since, I could see only a few of their scarlet hats, peeping above the tide. Mr. Thoreau managed the boat so perfectly, either with two paddles or with one, that it seemed instinct with his own will, and to require no physical effort to guide it. He said that, when some Indians visited Concord a few years ago, he found that he had acquired, without a teacher, their precise method of propelling and steering a canoe. Nevertheless he was desirous of selling the boat of which he was so fit a pilot, and which was built by his own hands; so I agreed to take it, and accordingly became possessor of the Musketaquid. I wish I could acquire the aquatic skill of the original owner.

September 2d.—Yesterday afternoon Mr. Thoreau arrived with the boat. The adjacent meadow being overflowed by the rise of the stream, he had rowed directly to the foot of the orchard, and landed at the bars, after floating over forty or fifty yards of water where people were lately making hay. I entered the boat with him, in order to have the benefit of a lesson in rowing and paddling....I managed, indeed, to propel the boat by rowing with two oars, but the use of the single paddle is quite beyond my present skill. Mr. Thoreau had assured me that it was only necessary to will the boat to go in any particular direction, and she would immediately take that course, as if imbued with the spirit of the steersman. It may be so with him, but it is certainly not so with me. The boat seemed to be bewitched, and turned its head to every point of the compass except the right one. He then took the paddle himself, and, though I could observe nothing peculiar in his management of it, the Musketaquid immediately became as docile as a trained steed. I suspect that she has not yet transferred her affections from her old master to her new one. By and by, when we are better acquainted, she will grow more tractable....We propose to change her name from Musketaquid (the Indian name of the Concord River, meaning the river of meadows) to the Pond-Lily, which will be very beautiful and appropriate, as, during the summer season, she will bring home many a cargo of pond-lilies from along the river's weedy shore. It is not very likely that I shall make such long voyages in her as Mr. Thoreau has made. He once followed our river down to the Merrimack, and thence, I believe, to Newburyport in this little craft.

In the evening, — — called to see us, wishing to talk with me about a Boston periodical, of which he had heard that I was to be editor, and to which he desired to contribute. He is an odd and clever young man, with nothing very peculiar about him,—some originality and self-inspiration in his character, but none, or, very little, in his intellect. Nevertheless, the lad himself seems to feel as if he were a genius. I like him well enough, however; but, after all, these originals in a small way, after one has seen a few of them, become more dull and commonplace than even those who keep the ordinary pathway of life. They have a rule and a routine, which they follow with as little variety as other people do their rule and routine; and when once we have fathomed their mystery, nothing can be more wearisome. An innate perception and reflection of truth give the only sort of originality that does not finally grow intolerable.

September 4th.—I made a voyage in the Pond-Lily all by myself yesterday morning, and was much encouraged by my success in causing the boat to go whither I would. I have always liked to be afloat, but I think I have never adequately conceived of the enjoyment till now, when I begin to feel a power over that which supports me. I suppose I must have felt something like this sense of triumph when I first learned to swim; but I have forgotten it. Oh that I could run wild!—that is, that I could put myself into a true relation with Nature, and be on friendly terms with all congenial elements.

We had a thunder-storm last evening; and to-day was been a cool, breezy, autumnal day, such as my soul and body love.

September 18th.—How the summer-time flits away, even while it seems to be loitering onward, arm in arm with autumn! Of late I have walked but little over the hills and through the woods, my leisure being chiefly occupied with my boat, which I have now learned to manage with tolerable skill. Yesterday afternoon I made a voyage alone up the North Branch of Concord River. There was a strong west-wind blowing dead against me, which, together with the current, increased by the height of the water, made the first part of the passage pretty toilsome. The black river was all dimpled over with little eddies and whirlpools; and the breeze, moreover, caused the billows to beat against the bow of the boat, with a sound like the flapping of a bird's wing. The water-weeds, where they were discernible through the tawny water, were straight outstretched by the force of the current, looking as if they were forced to hold on to their roots with all their might. If for a moment I desisted from paddling, the head of the boat was swept round by the combined might of wind and tide. However. I toiled onward stoutly, and, entering the North Branch, soon found myself floating quietly along a tranquil stream, sheltered from the breeze by the woods and a lofty hill. The current, likewise, lingered along so gently that it was merely a pleasure to propel the boat against it. I never could have conceived that there was so beautiful a river-scene in Concord as this of the North Branch. The stream flows through the midmost privacy and deepest heart of a wood, which, as if but half satisfied with its presence, calm, gentle, and unobtrusive as it is, seems to crowd upon it, and barely to #1-low it passage; for the trees are rooted on the very verge of the water, and dip their pendent branches into it. On one side there is a high bank, forming the side of a hill, the Indian name of which I have forgotten, though Mr. Thoreau told it to me; and here, in some instances, the trees stand leaning over the river, stretching out their arms as if .about to plunge in headlong. On the other side, the bank is almost on a level with the water; and there the quiet congregation of trees stood with feet in the flood, and fringed with foliage down to its very surface. Vines here and there twine themselves about bushes or aspens or alder-trees, and hang their clusters (though scanty and infrequent this season) so that I can reach them from my boat. I scarcely remember a scene of more complete and lovely seclusion than the passage of the river through this wood. Even an Indian canoe, in olden times, could not hare floated onward in deeper solitude than my boat. I have never elsewhere had such an opportunity to observe how much more beautiful reflection is than what we call reality. The sky, and the clustering foliage on either hand, and the effect of sunlight as it found its way through the shade, giving lightsome hues in contrast with the quiet depth of the prevailing tints,—all these seemed unsurpassably beautiful when beheld in upper air. But on gazing downward, there they were, the same even to the minutest particular, yet arrayed in ideal beauty, which satisfied the spirit incomparably more than the actual scene. I am half convinced that the reflection is indeed the reality, the real thing which Nature imperfectly images to our grosser sense. At any rate, the disembodied shadow is nearest to the soul.

There were many tokens of autumn in this beautiful picture. Two or three of the trees were actually dressed in their coats of many colors,—the real scarlet and gold which they wear before they put on mourning. These stood on low, marshy spots, where a frost has probably touched them already. Others were of a light, fresh green, resembling the hues of spring, though this, likewise, is a token of decay. The great mass of the foliage, however, appears unchanged; but ever and anon down came a yellow leaf, half flitting upon the air, half falling through it, and finally settling upon the water. A multitude of these were floating here and there along the river, many of them curling upward, so as to form little boats, fit for fairies to voyage in. They looked strangely pretty, with yet a melancholy prettiness, as they floated along. The general aspect of the river, however, differed but little from that of summer,—at least the difference defies expression. It is more in the character of the rich yellow sunlight than in aught else. The water of the stream has now a thrill of autumnal coolness; yet whenever a broad gleam fell across it, through an interstice of the foliage, multitudes of insects were darting to and fro upon its surface. The sunshine, thus falling across the dark river, has a most beautiful effect. It burnishes it, as it were, and yet leaves it as dark as ever.

On my return, I suffered the boat to float almost of its own will down the stream, and caught fish enough for this morning's breakfast. But, partly from a qualm of conscience, I finally put them all into the water again, and saw them swim away as if nothing had happened.

Monday, October 10th.—A long while, indexed, since my last date. But the weather has been generally sunny and pleasant, though often very cold; and I cannot endure to waste anything so precious as autumnal sunshine by staying in the house. So I have spent almost all the daylight hours in the open air. My chief amusement has been boating up and down the river. A week or two ago (September 27 and 28) I went on a pedestrian excursion with Mr. Emerson, and was gone two days and one night, it being the first and only night that I have spent away from home. We were that night at the village of Harvard, and the next morning walked three miles farther, to the Shaker village, where we breakfasted. Mr. Emerson had a theological discussion with two of the Shaker brethren; but the particulars of it have faded from my memory; and all the other adventures of the tour have now so lost their freshness that I cannot adequately recall them. Wherefore let them rest untold. I recollect nothing so well as the aspect of some fringed gentians, which we saw growing by the roadside, and which were so beautiful that I longed to turn back and pluck them. After an arduous journey, we arrived safe home in the afternoon of the second day,—the first time that I ever came home in my life; for I never had a home before. On Saturday of the same week, my friend D. R— came to see us, and stayed till Tuesday morning. On Wednesday there was a cattle-show in the village, of which I would give a description, if it had possessed any picturesque points. The foregoing are the chief outward events of our life.

In the mean time autumn has been advancing, and is said to be a month earlier than usual. We had frosts, sufficient to kill the bean and squash vines, more than a fortnight ago; but there has since been some of the most delicious Indian-summer weather that I ever experienced,—mild, sweet, perfect days, in which the warm sunshine seemed to embrace the earth and all earth's children with love and tenderness. Generally, however, the bright days have been vexed with winds from the northwest, somewhat too keen and high for comfort. These winds have strewn our avenue with withered leaves, although the trees still retain some density of foliage, which is now imbrowned or otherwise variegated by autumn. Our apples, too, have been falling, falling, falling: and we have picked the fairest of them from the dewy grass, and put them in our store-room and elsewhere. On Thursday, John Flint began to gather those which remained on the trees; and I suppose they will amount to nearly twenty barrels, or perhaps more. As usual when I have anything to sell, apples are very low indeed in price, and will not fetch me more than a dollar a barrel. I have sold my share of the potato-field for twenty dollars and ten bushels of potatoes for my own use. This may suffice for the economical history of our recent life.

12 o'clock, m.—Just now I heard a sharp tapping at the window of my study, and, looking up from my book (a volume of Rabelais), behold! the head of a little bird, who seemed to demand admittance! He was probably attempting to get a fly, which was on the pane of glass against which he rapped; and on my first motion the feathered visitor took wing. This incident had a curious effect on me. It impressed me as if the bird had been a spiritual visitant, so strange was it that this little wild thing should seem to ask our hospitality.

November 8th.—I am sorry that our journal has fallen so into neglect; but I see no chance of amendment. All my scribbling propensities will be far more than gratified in writing nonsense for the press; so that any gratuitous labor of the pen becomes peculiarly distasteful. Since the last date, we have paid a visit of nine days to Boston and Salem, whence we returned a week ago yesterday. Thus we lost above a week of delicious autumnal weather, which should have been spent in the woods or upon the river. Ever since our return, however, until to-day, there has been a succession of genuine Indian-summer days, with gentle winds, or none at all, and a misty atmosphere, which idealizes all nature, and a mild, beneficent sunshine, inviting one to lie down in a nook and forget all earthly care. To-day the sky is dark and lowering, and occasionally lets fall a few sullen tears. I suppose we must bid farewell to Indian summer now, and expect no more love and tenderness from Mother Nature till next spring be well advanced. She has already made herself as unlovely in outward aspect as can well be. We took a walk to Sleepy Hollow yesterday, and beheld scarcely a green thing, except the everlasting verdure of the family of pines, which, indeed, are trees to thank God for at this season. A range of young birches had retained a pretty liberal coloring of yellow or tawny leaves, which became very cheerful in the sunshine. There were one or two oak-trees whose foliage still retained a deep, dusky red, which looked rich and warm; but most of the oaks had reached the last stage of autumnal decay,—the dusky brown hue. Millions of their leaves strew the woods and rustle underneath the foot; but enough remain upon the boughs to make a melancholy harping when the wind sweeps over them. We found some fringed gentians in the meadow, most of them blighted and withered; but a few were quite perfect. The other day, since our return from Salem, I found a violet; yet it was so cold that day, that a large pool of water, under the shadow of some trees, had remained frozen from morning till afternoon. The ice was so thick as not to be broken by some sticks and small stones which I threw upon it. But ice and snow too will soon be no extraordinary matters with us.

During the last week we have had three stoves put up, and henceforth no light of a cheerful fire will gladden us at eventide. Stoves are detestable in every respect, except that they keep us perfectly comfort able.

Thursday, November 24th.—This is Thanksgiving Day, a good old festival, and we have kept it with our hearts, and, besides, have made good cheer upon our turkey and pudding, and pies and custards, although none sat at our board but our two selves. There was a new and livelier sense, I think, that we have at last found a home, and that a new family has been gathered since the last Thanksgiving Day. There have been many bright, cold days latterly,—so cold that it has required a pretty rapid pace to keep one's self warm a-walking. Day before yesterday I saw a party of boys skating on a pond of water that has overflowed a neighboring meadow. Running water has not yet frozen. Vegetation has quite come to a stand, except in a few sheltered spots. In a deep ditch we found a tall plant of the freshest and healthiest green, which looked as if it must have grown within the last few weeks. We wander among the wood-paths, which are very pleasant in the sunshine of the afternoons, the trees looking rich and warm,—such of them, I mean, as have retained their russet leaves; and where the leaves are strewn along the paths, or heaped plentifully in some hollow of the hills, the effect is not without a charm. To-day the morning rose with rain, which has since changed to snow and sleet; and now the landscape is as dreary as can well be imagined,—white, with the brownness of the soil and withered grass everywhere peeping out. The swollen river, of a leaden hue, drags itself sullenly along; and this may be termed the first winter's day.

Friday, March 21st, 1843.—The first month of spring is already gone; and still the snow lies deep on hill and valley, and the river is still frozen from bank to bank, although a late rain has caused pools of water to stand on the surface of the ice, and the meadows are overflowed into broad lakes. Such a protracted winter has not been known for twenty years, at least I have almost forgotten the wood-paths and shady places which I used to know so well last summer; and my views are so much confined to the interior of our mansion, that sometimes, looking out of the window, I am surprised to catch a glimpse of houses, at no great distance, which had quite passed out of my recollection. From present appearances, another month may scarcely suffice to wash away all the snow from the open country: and in the woods and hollows it may linger yet longer. The winter will not have been a day less than five months long; and it would not be unfair to call it seven. A great space, indeed, to miss the smile of Nature, in a single year of human life. Even out of the midst of happiness I have sometimes sighed and groaned; for I love the sunshine and the green woods, and the sparkling blue water; and it seems as if the picture of our inward bliss should be set in a beautiful frame of outward nature.... As to the daily course of our life, I have written with pretty commendable diligence, averaging from two to four hours a day; and the result is seen in various magazines. I might have written more, if it had seemed worth while, but I was content to earn only so much gold as might suffice for our immediate wants, halving prospect of official station and emolument which would do away with the necessity of writing for bread. Those prospects have not yet had their fulfilment: and we are well content to wait, because an office would inevitably remove us from our present happy home,—at least from an outward home; for there is an inner one that will accompany us wherever we go. Meantime, the magazine people do not pay their debts; so that we taste some of the inconveniences of poverty. It is an annoyance, not a trouble.

Every day, I trudge through snow and slosh to the village, look into the post-office, and spend an hour at the reading-room; and then return home, generally without having spoken a word to a human being....In the way of exercise I saw and split wood, and, physically, I never was in a better condition than now. This is chiefly owing, doubtless, to a satisfied heart, in aid of which comes the exercise above mentioned, and about a fair proportion of intellectual labor.

On the 9th of this month, we left home again on a visit to Boston and Salem. I alone went to Salem, where I resumed all my bachelor habits for nearly a fortnight, leading the same life in which ten years of my youth flitted away like a dream. But how much changed was I! At last I had caught hold of a reality which never could be taken from me. It was good thus to get apart from my happiness, for the sake of contemplating it. On the 21st, I returned to Boston, and went out to Cambridge to dine with Longfellow, whom I had not seen since his return from Europe. The next day we came back to our old house, which had been deserted all this time; for our servant had gone with us to Boston.

Friday. April 7th.—My wife has gone to Boston to see her sister M—, who is to be married in two or three weeks, and then immediately to visit Europe for six months....I betook myself to sawing and splitting wood; there being an inward unquietness which demanded active exercise, and I sawed, I think, more briskly than ever before. When I reëntered the house, it was with somewhat of a desolate feeling; yet not without an intermingled pleasure, as being the more conscious that all separation was temporary, and scarcely real, even for the little time that it may last. After my solitary dinner, I lay down, with the "Dial" in my hand, and attempted to sleep; but sleep would not come....So I arose, and began this record in the journal, almost at the commencement of which I was interrupted by a visit from Mr. Thoreau, who came to return a book, and to announce his purpose of going to reside at Staten Island, as private tutor in the family of Mr. Emerson's brother. We had some conversation upon this subject, and upon the spiritual advantages of change of place, and upon the "Dial," and upon Mr. Alcott, and other kindred or concatenated subjects. I am glad, on Mr. Thoreau's own account, that he is going away, as he is out of health, and may be benefited by his removal; but, on my account, I should like to have him remain here, he being one of the few persons, I think, with whom to hold intercourse is like hearing the wind among the boughs of a forest-tree; and, with all this wild freedom, there is high and classic cultivation in him too....

I had a purpose, if circumstances would permit, of passing the whole term of my wife's absence without speaking a word to any human being; but now my Pythagorean vow has been broken, within three or four hours after her departure.

Saturday, April 8th.—After journalizing yesterday afternoon, I went out and sawed and split wood till tea-time, then studied German (translating "Lenore"), with an occasional glance at a beautiful sunset, which I could not enjoy sufficiently by myself to induce me to lay aside the book. After lamplight, finished "Lenore," and drowsed over Voltaire's "Candide," occasionally refreshing myself with a tune from Mr. Thoreau's musical-box, which he had left in my keeping. The evening was but a dull one.

I retired soon after nine, and felt some apprehension that the old Doctor's ghost would take this opportunity to visit me; but I rather think his former visitations have not been intended for me, and that I am not sufficiently spiritual for ghostly communication. At all events, I met with no disturbance of the kind, and slept soundly enough till six o'clock or thereabouts. The forenoon was spent with the pen in my hand, and sometimes r»had the glimmering of an idea, and endeavored to materialize it in words; but on the whole my mind was idly vagrant, and refused to work to any systematic purpose. Between eleven and twelve I went to the post-office, but found no letter; then spent above an hour reading at the Athenæum. On my way home, I encountered Mr. Flint, for the first time these many weeks, although he is our next neighbor in one direction. I inquired if he could sell us some potatoes, and he promised to send half a bushel for trial. Also, he encouraged me to hope that he might buy a barrel of our apples. After my encounter with Mr. Flint, I returned to our lonely old abbey, opened the door without the usual heart-spring, ascended to my study, and began to read a tale of Tieck. Slow work, and dull work too! Anon, Molly, the cook, rang the bell for dinner,—a sumptuous banquet of stewed veal and macaroni, to which I sat down in solitary state. My appetite served me sufficiently to eat with, but not for enjoyment. Nothing has a zest in my present widowed state. [Thus far I had written, when Mr. Emerson called.] After dinner, I lay down on the couch, with the "Dial" in my hand as a soporific, and had a short nap; then began to journalize.

Mr. Emerson came, with a sunbeam in his face; and we had as good a talk as I ever remember to have had with him. He spoke of Margaret Fuller, who, he says, has risen perceptibly into a higher state since their last meeting. [There rings the tea-bell.] Then we discoursed of Ellery Channing, a volume of whose poems, is to be immediately published, with revisions by Mr. Emerson himself and Mr. Sam G. Ward....He calls them "poetry for poets." Next Mr. Thoreau was discussed, and his approaching departure: in respect to which we agreed pretty well....We talked of Brook Farm, and the singular moral aspects which it presents, and the great desirability that its progress and developments should be observed and its history written; also of C. N—, who, it appears, is passing through a new moral phasis. He is silent, inexpressive, talks little or none, and listens without response, except a sardonic laugh; and some of his friends think that he is passing into permanent eclipse. Various other matters were considered or glanced at, and finally, between five and six o'clock, Mr. Emerson took his leave. I then went out to chop wood, my allotted space for which had been very much abridged by his visit; but I was not sorry. I went on with the journal for a few minutes before tea, and have finished the present record in the setting sunshine and gathering dusk....

Salem.—...Here I am, in my old chamber, where I produced those stupendous works of fiction which have since impressed the universe with wonderment and awe! To this chamber, doubtless, in all succeeding ages, pilgrims will come to pay their tribute of reverence; they will put off their shoes at the threshold for fear of desecrating the tattered old carpets! "There," they will exclaim, "is the very bed in which he slumbered, and where he was visited by those ethereal visions which he afterwards fixed forever in glowing words! There is the wash-stand at which this exalted personage cleansed himself from the stains of earth, and rendered his outward man a fitting exponent of the pure soul within. There, in its mahogany frame, is the dressing-glass, which often reflected that noble brow, those hyacinthine locks, that mouth bright with smiles or tremulous with feeling, that flashing or melting eye, that—in short, every item of the magnanimous face of this unexampled man. There is the pine table,—there the old flag-bottomed chair on which he sat, and at which he scribbled, during his agonies of inspiration! There is the old chest of drawers in which he kept what shirts a poor author may be supposed to have possessed! There is the closet in which was reposited his threadbare suit of black! There is the worn-out shoe-brush with which this polished writer polished his boots. There is"—but I believe this will be pretty much all, so here I close the catalogue....

A cloudy veil stretches over the abyss of my nature. I have, however, no love of secrecy and darkness. I am glad to think that God sees through my heart, and, if any angel has power to penetrate into it, he is welcome to know everything that is there. Yes, and so may any mortal who is capable of full sympathy, and therefore worthy to come into my depths. But, he must find his own way there. I can neither guide nor enlighten him. It is this involuntary reserve, I suppose, that has given the objectivity to my writings; and when people think that I am pouring myself out in a tale or an essay, I am merely telling what is common to human nature, not what is peculiar to myself. I sympathize with them, not they with me....

I have recently been both lectured about and preached about here in my native city; the preacher was Rev. Mr. Fox, of Newburyport; but how he contrived to put me into a sermon I know not. I trust he took for his text, "Behold an Israelite indeed, in whom there is no guile."

Salem, March 12th.—...That poor home! how desolate it is now! Last night, being awake,...my thoughts travelled back to the lonely old manse; and it seemed as if I were wandering up stairs and down stairs all by myself. My fancy was almost afraid to be there alone. I could see every object in a dim, gray light,—our chamber, the study, all in confusion; the parlor, with the fragments of that abortive breakfast on the table, and the precious silver forks, and the old bronze image, keeping its solitary stand upon the mantel-piece. Then, methought, the wretched Vigwiggie came, and jumped upon the window-sill, and clung there with her fore paws, mewing dismally for admittance, which I could not grant, her, being there myself only in the spirit. And then camw the ghost of the old Doctor, stalking through the gallery, and down the staircase, and poking into the parlor; and though I was wide awake, and conscious of being so many miles from the spot, still it was quite awful to think of the ghost having sole possession of our home; for I could not quite separate myself from it, after all. Somehow the Doctor and I seemed to be there *tête-à-tête*....I believe I did not have any fantasies about the ghostly kitchen-maid; but I trust Mary left the flat-irons within her reach, so that she may do all her ironing while we are away, and never disturb us more at midnight. I suppose she comes thither to iron her shroud, and perhaps, likewise, to smooth the Doctor's band. Probably, during her lifetime, she allowed him to go to some ordination or other grand clerical celebration with rumpled linen; and ever since, and throughout all earthly futurity (at least, as long as the house shall stand), she is doomed to exercise a nightly toil with a spiritual flat-iron. Poor sinner!—and doubtless Satan heats the irons for her. What nonsense is all this! but, really, it does make me shiver to think of that poor home of ours.

March 16th.—...As for this Mr. —, I wish he would not be so troublesome. His scheme is well enough, and might possibly become popular; but it has no peculiar advantages with reference to myself, nor do the subjects of his proposed books particularly suit my fancy as themes to write upon. Somebody else will answer his purpose just as well; and I would rather write books of my own imagining than be hired to develop the ideas of an engraver; especially as the pecuniary prospect is not better, nor so good, as it might be elsewhere. I intend to adhere to my former plan of writing one or two mythological story-books, to be published under O'Sullivan's auspices in New York,—which is the only place where books can be published with a chance of profit. As a matter of courtesy, I may call on Mr. — if I have time; but I do not intend to be connected with this affair.

Sunday, April 9th.—...After finishing my record in the journal, I sat a long time in grandmother's chair, thinking of many things....My spirits were at a lower ebb than they ever descend to when I am not alone; nevertheless, neither was I absolutely sad. Many times I wound and re-wound Mr. Thoreau's little musical-box; but certainly its peculiar sweetness had evaporated, and I am pretty sure that I should throw it out of the window were I doomed to hear it long and often. It has not an infinite soul. When it was almost as dark as the moonlight would let it be, I lighted the lamp, and went on with Tieck's tale, slowly and painfully, often wishing for help in my difficulties. At last I determined to learn a little about pronouns and verbs before proceeding further, and so took up the phrase-book, with which I was commendably busy, when, at about a quarter to nine, came a knock at my study door, and, behold, there was Molly with a letter! How she came by it I did not ask, being content to suppose it was brought by a heavenly messenger. I had not expected a letter; and what a comfort it was to me in my loneliness and sombreness! I called Molly to take her note (enclosed), which she received with a face of delight as broad and bright as the kitchen fire. Then I read, and re-read, and re-re-read, and quadruply, quintuply, and sextuply re-read my epistle, until I had it all by heart, and then continued to re-read it for the sake of the penmanship. Then I took up the phrase-book again; but could not study, and so bathed and retired, it being now not far from ten o'clock. I lay awake a good deal in the night, but saw no ghost.

I arose about seven, and found that the upper part of my nose, and the region round about, was grievously discolored; and at the angle of the left eve there is a great spot of almost black purple, and a broad streak of the same hue semicircling beneath either eye, while green, yellow, and orange overspread the circumjacent country. It looks not unlike a gorgeous sunset, throwing its splendor over the heaven of my countenance. It will behoove me to show myself as little as possible, else people will think I have fought a pitched battle....The Devil take the stick of wood! What had I done, that it should bemaul me so? However, there is no pain, though, I think, a very slight affection of the eyes.

This forenoon I began to write, and caught an idea by the skirts, which I intend to hold fast, though it struggles to get free. As it was not ready to be put upon paper, however, I took up the "Dial," and finished reading the article on Mr. Alcott. It is not very satisfactory, and it has not taught me much. Then I read Margaret's article on Canova, which is good. About this time the dinner-bell rang, and I went down without much alacrity, though with a good appetite enough....It was in the angle of my *right* eye, not my left, that the blackest purple was collected. But they both look like the very Devil.

Half past five o'clock.—After writing the above....I again set to work on Tieck's tale, and worried through several pages; and then, at half past four, threw open one of the western windows of my study, and sallied forth to take the sunshine. I went down through the orchard to the river-side. The orchard-path is still deeply covered with snow; and so is the whole visible universe, except streaks upon the hillsides, and spots in the sunny hollows, where the brown earth peeps through. The river, which a few days ago was entirely imprisoned, has now broken its fetters; but a tract of ice extended across from near the foot of the monument to the abutment of the old bridge, and looked so solid that I supposed it would yet remain for a day or two. Large cakes and masses of ice came floating down the current, which, though not very violent, hurried along at a much swifter pace than the ordinary one of our sluggish river-god. These ice-masses, when they struck the barrier of ice above mentioned, acted upon it like a battering-ram, and were themselves forced high out of the water, or sometimes carried beneath the main sheet of ice. At last, down the stream came an immense mass of ice, and, striking the barrier about at its centre, it gave way, and the whole was swept onward together, leaving the river entirely free, with only here and there a cake of ice floating quietly along. The great accumulation, in its downward course, hit against a tree that stood in mid-current, and caused it to quiver like a reed; and it swept quite over the shrubbery that bordered what, in summer-time, is the river's bank, but which is now nearly the centre of the stream. Our river in its present state has quite a noble breadth. The little hillock which formed the abutment of the old bridge is now an island with its tuft of trees. Along the hither shore a row of trees stand up to their knees, and the smaller ones to their middles, in the water; and afar off, on the surface of the stream, we see tufts of bushes emerging, thrusting up their heads, as it were, to breathe. The water comes over the stone-wall, and encroaches several yards on the boundaries of our orchard. [Here the supper-bell rang.] If our boat were in good order, I should now set forth on voyages of discovery, and visit nooks on the borders of the meadows, which by and by will be a mile or two from the water's edge. But she is in very bad condition, full of water, and, doubtless, as leaky as a sieve. On coming from supper, I found that little Puss had established herself in the study, probably with intent to pass the night here. She now lies on the footstool between my feet, purring most obstreperously. The day of my wife's departure; she came to me, talking with the greatest earnestness; but whether it was to condole with me on my loss, or to demand my redoubled care for herself, I could not well make out. As Puss now constitutes a third part of the family, this mention of her will not appear amiss. How Molly employs herself, I know not. Once in a while, I hear a door slam like a thunder-clap; but she never shows her face, nor speaks a word, unless to announce a visitor or deliver a letter. This day, on my part, will have been spent without exchanging a syllable with any human being, unless something unforeseen should yet call for the exercise of speech before bedtime.

Monday, April 10th.—I sat till eight o'clock, meditating upon this world and the next,...and sometimes dimly shaping out scenes of a tale. Then betook myself to the German phrase-book. Ah! these are but dreary evenings. The lamp would not brighten my spirits, though it was duly filled....This forenoon was spent in scribbling, by no means to my satisfaction, until past eleven, when I went to the village.. Nothing in our box at the post-office. I read during the customary hour, or more, at the Athenæum, and returned without saying a word to mortal. I gathered from some conversation that I heard, that a son of Adam is to be buried this afternoon from the meeting-house; but the name of the deceased escaped me. It is no great matter, so it be but written in the Book of Life.

My variegated face looks somewhat more human today; though I was unaffectedly ashamed to meet anybody's gaze, and therefore turned my back or my shoulder as much as possible upon the world. At dinner, behold an immense joint of roast veal! I would willingly have had some assistance in the discussion of this great piece of calf. I am ashamed to eat alone; it becomes the mere gratification of animal appetite,—the tribute which we are compelled to pay to our grosser nature; whereas, in the company of another it is refined and moralized and spiritualized; and over our earthly victuals (or rather *vtitles,* for the former is a very foolish mode of spelling),—over our earthly vittles is diffused a sauce of lofty and gentle thoughts, and tough meat is mollified with tender feelings. But oh! these solitary meals are the dismallest part of my present experience. When the company rose from table, they all, in my single person, ascended to the study, and employed themselves in reading the article on Oregon in the "Democratic Review." Then they plodded onward in the rugged and bewildering depths of Tieck's tale until five o'clock, when, with one accord, they went out to split wood. This has been a gray day, with now and then a sprinkling of snow-flakes through the air....To-day no more than yesterday have I spoken a word to mortal....It is now sunset, and I must meditate till dark.

April 11th.—I meditated accordingly, but without any very wonderful result. Then at eight o'clock bothered myself till after nine with this eternal tale of Tieck. The forenoon was spent in scribbling; but at eleven o'clock my thoughts ceased to flow, —indeed, their current has been wofully interrupted all along,—so I threw down my pen, and set out on the daily journey to the village. Horrible walking! I wasted the customary hour at the Athenæum, and returned home, if home it may now be called. Till dinner-time I labored on Tieck's tale, and resumed that agreeable employment after the banquet.

Just when I was on the point of choking with a huge German word, Molly announced Mr. Thoreau. He wished to take a row in the boat, for the last time, perhaps, before he leaves Concord. So we emptied the water out of her, and set forth on our voyage. She leaks, but not more than she did in the autumn. We rowed to the foot of the hill which borders the North Branch, and there landed, and climbed the moist and snowy hill-side for the sake of the prospect. Looking down the river, it might well have been mistaken for an arm of the sea, so broad is now its swollen tide; and I could have fancied that, beyond one other headland, the mighty ocean would outspread itself before the eye. On our return we boarded a large cake of ice, which was floating down the river, and were borne by it directly to our own landing-place, with the boat towing behind.

Parting with Mr. Thoreau, I spent half an hour in chopping wood, when Molly informed me that Mr. Emerson wished to see me. He had brought a letter of Ellery Channing, written in a style of very pleasant humor. This being read and discussed, together with a few other matters, he took his leave, since which I have been attending to my journalizing duty; and thus this record is brought down to the present moment.

April 25th.—Spring is advancing, sometimes with sunny days, and sometimes, as is the case now, with chill, moist, sullen ones. There is an influence in the season that makes it almost impossible for me to bring my mind down to literary employment; perhaps because several months' pretty constant work has exhausted that species of energy,—perhaps because in spring it is more natural to labor actively than to think. But my impulse now is to be idle altogether,—to lie in the sun, or wander about and look at the revival of Nature from her death-like slumber, or to be borne down the current of the river in my boat. If I had wings, I would gladly fly; yet would prefer to be wafted along by a breeze, sometimes alighting on a patch of green grass, then gently whirled away to a still sunnier spot....Oh, how blest should I be were there nothing to do! Then I would watch every inch and hair's-breadth of the progress of the season; and not a leaf should put itself forth, in the vicinity of our old mansion, without my noting it. But now, with the burden of a continual task upon me, I have not freedom of mind to make such observations. I merely see what is going on in a very general way. The snow, which, two or three weeks ago, covered hill and valley, is now diminished to one or two solitary specks in the visible landscape; though doubtless there are still heaps of it in the shady places in the woods. There have been no violent rains to carry it off: it has diminished gradually, inch by inch, and day after day; and I observed, along the roadside, that the green blades of grass had sometimes sprouted on the very-edge of the snowdrift the moment that the earth was uncovered.

The pastures and grass-fields have not yet a general effect of green; nor have they that cheerless brown tint which they wear in later autumn, when vegetation has entirely ceased. There is now a suspicion of verdure,—the faint shadow of it,—but not the warm reality. Sometimes, in a happy exposure,—there is one such tract across the river, the carefully cultivated mowing-field, in front of an old red homestead,—such patches of land wear a beautiful and tender green, which no other season will equal; because, let the grass be green as it may hereafter, it will not be so set off by surrounding barrenness. The trees in our orchard, and elsewhere, have as yet no leaves; yet to the most careless eye they appear full of life and vegetable blood. It seems as if, by one magic touch, they might instantaneously put forth all their foliage, and the wind, which now sighs through their naked branches, might all at once find itself impeded by innumerable leaves. This sudden development would he scarcely more wonderful than the gleam of verdure which often brightens, in a moment, as it were, along the slope of a bank or roadside. It is like a gleam of sunlight. Just now it was brown, like the rest of the scenery: look again, and there is an apparition of green grass. The Spring, no doubt, comes onward with fleeter footsteps, because Winter has lingered so long that, at best, she can hardly retrieve half the allotted term of her reign.

The river, this season, has encroached farther on the land than it has been known to do for twenty years past. It has formed along its coarse a succession of lakes, with a current through the midst My boat has lain at the bottom of the orchard, in very convenient proximity to the house. It has borne me over stone fences; and, a few days ago, Ellery Channing and I passed through two rails into the great northern road, along which we paddled for some distance. The trees have a singular appearance in the midst of waters. The curtailment of their trunks quite destroys the proportions of the whole tree; and we become conscious of a regularity and propriety in the forms of Nature, by the effect of this abbreviation. The waters are now subsiding, bat gradually. Islands become annexed to the mainland, and other islands emerge from the flood, and will soon, likewise, be connected with the continent We have seen on a small scale the process of the deluge, and can now witness that of the reappearance of the earth.

Crows visited us long before the snow was off. They seem mostly to have departed now, or else to have betaken themselves to remote depths of the woods, which they haunt all summer long. Ducks came in great numbers, and many sportsmen went iu pursuit of them along the river; but they also have disappeared. Gulls come up from seaward, and soar high overhead, flapping their broad wings in the upper sunshine. They are among the most picturesque birds that I am acquainted with; indeed, quite the most so, because the manner of their flight makes them almost stationary parts of the landscape. The imagination has time to rest upon them; they have not flitted away in a moment You go up among the clouds, and lay hold of these soaring gulls, and repose with them upon the sustaining atmosphere. The smaller birds,—the birds that build their nests in our trees, and sing for us at morning-red,—I will not describe....But I must mention the great companies of blackbirds—more than the famous "four-and-twenty" who were baked in a pie—that congregate on the tops of contiguous trees, and vociferate with all the clamor of a turbulent political meeting. Politics must certainly be the subject of such a tumultuous debate; but still there is a melody in each individual utterance, and a harmony in the general effect. Mr. Thoreau tells me that these noisy assemblages consist of three different species of blackbirds; hut I forget the other two. Robins have been long among us, and swallows have more recentlv arrived.

April 26th.—Here is another misty day, muffling the sun. The lilac-shrubs under my study window are almost in leaf. In two or three days more, I may put forth my hand and pluck a green hough. These lilacs appear to be very aged, and have lost the luxuriant foliage of their prime. Old age has a singular aspect in lilacs, rose-bushes, and other ornamental shrubs. It seems as if such things, as they grow only for beauty, ought to flourish in immortal youth, or at least to die before their decrepitude. They are trees of Paradise, and therefore not naturally subject to decay; but have lost their birthright by being transplanted hither. There is a kind of ludicrous unfitness in the idea of a venerable rose-hush-, and there is something analogous to this in human life. Persons who can only be graceful and ornamental —who can give the world nothing but flowers—should die young, and never be seen with gray hairs and wrinkles, any more than the flower-shrubs with mossy hark and scanty foliage, like the lilacs under my window. Not that beauty is not worthy of immortality. Nothing else, indeed, is worthy of it; and thence, perhaps, the sense of impropriety when we see it triumphed over by time. Apple-trees, on the other hand, grow old without reproach. Let them live as long as they may, and contort themselves in whatever fashion they please, they are still respectable, even if they afford us only an apple or two in a season, or none at all. Human flower-shrubs, if they will grow old on earth, should, beside their lovely blossoms, bear some hind of fruit that will satisfy earthly appetites; else men will not be satisfied that the moss should gather on them.

Winter and Spring are now struggling for the mastery in my study; and I yield somewhat to each, and wholly to neither. The window is open, and there is a fire in the stove. The day when the window is first thrown open should be an epoch in the year; but I have forgotten to record it. Seventy or eighty springs have visited this old house; and sixty of them found old Dr. Ripley here,—not always old, it is true, but gradually getting wrinkles and gray hairs, and looking more and more the picture of winter. But he was no flower-shrub, but one of those fruit-trees or timber-trees that acquire a grace with their old age. Last Spring found this house solitary for the first time since it was built; and now again she peeps into our open windows and finds new faces here....

It is remarkable how much uncleanness winter brings with it, or leaves behind it....The yard, garden, and avenue, which should be my department, require a great amount of labor. The avenue is strewed with withered leaves,—the whole crop, apparently, of last year,—some of which are now raked into heaps; and we intend to make a bonfire of them....There are quantities of decayed branches, which one tempest after another has flung down, black and rotten. In the garden are the old cabbages which we did not think worth gathering last autumn, and the dry bean-vines, and the withered stalks of the asparagus bed; in short, all the wrecks of the departed year, its mouldering relics, its dry bones. It is a pitv that the world cannot be made over anew every spring. Then, in the yard, there are the piles of firewood, which I ought to have sawed and thrown into the shed long since, but which will cumber the earth, I fear, till June, at least. Quantities of chips are strewn about, and on removing them we find the yellow stalks of grass sprouting underneath. Nature does her best to beautify this disarray. The grass springs up most industriously, especially in sheltered and sunny angles of the buildings, or round the doorsteps, a locality which seems particularly favorable to its growth; for it is already high enough to bend over and wave in the wind. I was surprised to observe that some weeds (especially a plant that stains the lingers with its yellow juice) had lived, and retained their freshness and sap as perfectly as in summer, through all the frosts and snows of last winter. I saw them, the last green thing, in the autumn; and here they are again, the first in the spring.

Thursday, April 27th. I took a walk into the fields, and round our opposite hill, yesterday noon, hut made no very remarkable observation. The frogs have begun their concerts, though not as yet with a full choir. I found no violets nor anemones, nor anything in the likeness of a flower, though I looked carefully along the shelter of the stone-walls, and in all spots apparently propitious. I ascended the hill, and had a wide prospect of a swollen river, extending around me in a semicircle of three or four miles, and rendering the view much finer than in summer, had there only been foliage. It seemed like the formation of a new world; for islands were everywhere emerging, and capes extending forth into the flood; and these tracts, which were thus won from the watery empire, were among the greenest in the landscape. The moment the deluge leaves them Nature asserts them to be her property by covering them with verdure; or perhaps the grass had been growing under the water. On the hill-top where I stood, the grass had scarcely begun to sprout: and I observed that even those places which looked greenest in the distance were but scantily grass-covered when I actually reached them. It was hope that painted them so bright.

Last evening we saw a bright light on the river, betokening that a boat's party were engaged in spearing fish. It looked like a descended star,—-like red Mars,—and, as the water was perfectly smooth, its gleam was reflected downward into the depths. It is a very picturesque sight. In the deep quiet of the night I suddenly heard the light and lively note of a bird from a neighboring tree,—a real song, such as those which greet the purple dawn, or mingle with the yellow sunshine. What could the little bird mean by pouring it forth at midnight? Probably the note gushed out from the midst of a dream, in which he fancied himself in Paradise with his mate; and, suddenly awakening, he found he was on a cold, leafless bough, with a New England mist penetrating through his feathers. That was a sad exchange of imagination for reality: but if he found his mate beside him, all was well.

This is another misty morning; ungenial in aspect, but kinder than it looks; for it paints the hills and valleys with a richer brush than the sunshine could. There is more verdure now than when I looked out of the window an hear ago. The willow-tree opposite my study window is ready to put forth its leaves. There are some objections to willows. It is not a dry and cleanly tree; it impresses me with an association of sliminess; and no trees, I think, are perfectly satisfactory, which have not a firm and hard texture of trunk and branches. But the willow is almost the earliest to put forth its leaves, and the last to scatter them on the ground: and during the whole winter its yellow twigs give it a sunny aspect, which is not without a cheering influence in a proper point of view. Our old house would lose much were this willow to be cut down, with its golden crown over the roof in winter, and its heap of summer verdure. The present Mr. Ripley planted it, fifty years ago, or thereabouts.

Friday, June 2d.—Last night there came a frost, which has done great damage to my garden. The beans have suffered very much, although, luckily, not more than half that I planted have come up. The squashes, both summer and winter, appear to be almost killed. As to the other vegetables, there is little mischief done,—the potatoes not being yet above ground, except two or three; and the peas and corn are of a hardier nature. It is sad that Nature will so sport with us poor mortals, inviting us with sunny smiles to confide in her; and then, when we are entirely in her power, striking us to the heart. Our summer commences at the latter end of June, and terminates somewhere about the first of August. There are certainly not more than six weeks of the whole year when a frost may be deemed anything remarkable.

Friday, June 23d.—Summer has come at last,—the longest days, with blazing sunshine, and fervid heat. Yesterday glowed like molten brass. Last night was the most uncomfortably and unsleepably sultry that we have experienced since our residence in Concord; and to-day it scorches again. I have a sort of enjoyment in these seven-times-heated furnaces of midsummer, even though they make me droop like a thirsty plant. The sunshine can scarcely be too burning for my taste; but I am no enemy to summer showers. Could I only have the freedom to be perfectly idle now,—no duty to fulfil, no mental or physical labor to perform,—I should be as happy as a squash, and much in the same mode; but the necessity of keeping my brain at work eats into my comfort, as the squash-bugs do into the heart of the vines. I keep myself uneasy and produce little, and almost nothing that is worth producing.

The garden looks well now: the potatoes flourish; the early corn waves in the wind; the squashes, both for summer and winter use, are more forward, I suspect, than those of any of my neighbors. I am forced, however, to carry on a continual warfare with the squash-bugs, who, were I to let them alone for a day, would perhaps quite destroy the prospects of the whole summer. It is impossible not to feel angry with these unconscionable insects, who scruple not to do such excessive mischief to me, with only the profit of a meal or two to themselves. For their own sakes they ought at least to wait till the squashes are better grown. Why is it, I wonder, that Nature has provided such a host of enemies for every useful esculent, while the weeds are suffered to grow unmolested, and are provided with such tenacity of life, and such methods of propagation, that the gardener must maintain a continual struggle or they will hopelessly overwhelm him? What hidden virtue is in these things, that it is granted them to sow themselves with the wind, and to grapple the earth with this immitigable stubbornness, and to flourish in spite of obstacles, and never to suffer blight beneath any sun or shade, but always to mock their enemies with the same wicked luxuriance? It is truly a mystery, and also a symbol. There is a sort of sacredness about them. Perhaps, if we could penetrate Nature's secrets, we should find that what we call weeds are more essential to the well-being of the world than the most precious fruit or grain. This may be doubted, however, for there is an unmistakable analogy between these wicked weeds and the bad habits and sinful propensities which have overrun the moral world; and we may as well imagine that there is good in one as in the other.

Our peas are in such forwardness that I should not wonder if we had some of them on the table within a week. The beans have come up ill, and I planted a fresh supply only the day before yesterday. We have watermelons in good advancement, and muskmelons also within three or four days. I set out some tomatoes last night, also some capers. It is my purpose to plant some more corn at the end of the month, or sooner. There ought to be a record of the flower-garden, and of the procession of the wild-flowers, as minute, at least, as of the kitchen vegetables and potherbs. Above all, the noting of the appearance of the first roses should not be omitted; nor of the Arethusa, one of the delicatest, gracefullest, and in every manner sweetest, of the whole race of flowers. For a fortnight past I have found it in the swampy meadows, growing up to its chin in heaps of wet moss. Its hue is a delicate pink, of various depths of shade, and somewhat in the form of a Grecian helmet. To describe it is a feat beyond my power. Also the visit of two friends, who may fitly enough be mentioned among flowers, ought to have been described. Mrs. F. S— and Miss A. S—. Also I have neglected to mention the birth of a little white dove.

I never observed, until the present season, how long and late the twilight lingers in these longest days. The orange hue of the western horizon remains till ten o'clock, at least, and how much later I am unable to say. The night before last, I could distinguish letters by this lingering gleam between nine and ten o'clock. The dawn, I suppose, shows itself as early as two o'clock, so that the absolute dominion of night has dwindled to almost nothing. There seems to be also a diminished necessity, or, at all events, a much less possibility, of sleep than at other periods of the year. I get scarcely any sound repose just now. It is summer, and not winter, that steals away mortal life. Well, we get the value of what is taken from us.

Saturday, July 1st.—We had our first dish of green peas (a very small one) yesterday. Every day for the last week has been tremendously hot; and our garden flourishes like Eden itself, only Adam could hardly have been doomed to contend with such a ferocious banditti of weeds.

Sunday, July 9th.—I know not what to say, and yet cannot be satisfied without marking with a word or two this anniversary....But life now swells and heaves beneath me like a brim-full ocean; and the endeavor to comprise any portion of it in words is like trying to dip up the ocean in a goblet....God bless and keep us! for there is something more awful in happiness than in sorrow,—the latter being earthly and finite, the former composed of the substance and texture of eternity, so that spirits still embodied may well tremble at it.

July 18th.—This morning I gathered our first summer-squashes. We should have had them some days earlier, but for the loss of two of the vines, either by a disease of the roots or by those infernal bugs. We have had turnips and carrots several times. Currants are now ripe, and we are in the full enjoyment of cherries, which turn out much more delectable than I anticipated. George Hillard and Mrs. Hillard paid us a visit on Saturday last. On Monday afternoon he left us, and Mrs. Hillard still remains here.

Friday, July 28th.—We had green corn for dinner 'yesterday, and shall have some more to-day, not quite full grown, but sufficiently so to be palatable. There has been no rain, except one moderate shower, for many weeks; and the earth appears to be wasting away in a slow fever. This weather, I think, affects the spirits very unfavorably. There is an irksomeness, a restlessness, a pervading dissatisfaction, together with an absolute incapacity to bend the mind to any serious effort. With me, as regards literary production, the summer has been unprofitable; and I only hope that my forces are recruiting themselves for the autumn and winter. For the future, I shall endeavor to be so diligent nine months of the year that I may allow myself a full and free vacation of the other three.

Monday, July 31st.—We had our first cucumber yesterday. There were symptoms of rain on Saturday, and the weather has since been as moist as the thirstiest soul could desire.

Wednesday, September 13th.—There was a frost the night before last, according to George Prescott; but no effects of it were visible in our garden. Last night, however, there was another, which has nipped the leaves of the winter-squashes and cucumbers, but seems to have done no other damage. This is a beautiful morning, and promises to be one of those heavenly days that render autumn, after all, the most delightful season of the year. We mean to make a voyage on the river this afternoon.

Sunday, September 23d.—I have gathered the two last of our summer-squashes to-day. They have lasted ever since the 18th of July, and have numbered fifty-eight edible ones, of excellent quality. Last Wednesday, I think, I harvested our winter-squashes, sixty-three in number, and mostly of fine size. Our last series of green corn, planted about the 1st of July, was good for eating two or three days ago. We still have beans; and our tomatoes, though backward, supply us with a dish every day or two. My potato-crop promises well; and, on the whole, my first independent experiment of agriculture is quite a successful one.

This is a glorious day,—bright, very warm, yet with an unspeakable gentleness both in its warmth and brightness. On such days it is impossible not to love Nature, for she evidently loves us. At other seasons she does not give me this impression, or only at very rare intervals; but in these happy, autumnal days, when she has perfected the harvests, and accomplished every necessary thing that she had to do, she overflows with a blessed superfluity of love. It is good to be alive now. Thank God for breath,—yes, for mere breath! when it is made up of such a heavenly breeze as this. It comes to the cheek with a real kiss; it would linger fondly around us, if it might; but, since it must be gone, it caresses us with its whole kindly heart, and passes onward, to caress likewise the next thing that it meets. There is a pervading blessing diffused over all the world. I look out of the window and think, "O perfect day! O beautiful world! O good God!" And such a day is the promise of a blissful eternity. Our Creator would never have made such weather, and given us the deep heart to enjoy it, above and beyond all thought, if he had not meant us to be immortal. It opens the gates of heaven and gives us glimpses far inward.

Bless me! this flight has carried me a great way; so now let me come back to our old abbey. Our orchard is fast ripening; and the apples and great thumping pears strew the grass in such abundance that it becomes almost a trouble—though a pleasant one—to gather them. This happy breeze, too, shakes them down, as if it flung fruit to us out of the sky; and often, when the air is perfectly still, I hear the quiet fall of a great apple. Well, we are rich in blessings, though poor in money....

Friday, October 6th.—Yesterday afternoon I took a solitary walk to Walden Pond. It was a cool, windy day, with heavy clouds rolling and tumbling about the sky, but still a prevalence of genial autumn sunshine. The fields are still green, and the great masses of the woods have not yet assumed their many-colored garments; but here and there are solitary oaks of deep, substantial red, or maples of a more brilliant hue, or chestnuts either yellow or of a tenderer green than in summer. Some trees seem to return to their hue of May or early June before they put on the brighter autumnal tints. In some places, along the borders of low and moist land, a whole range of trees were clothed in the perfect gorgeousness of autumn, of all shades of brilliant color, looking like the palette on which Nature was arranging the tints wherewith to paint a picture. These hues appeared to be thrown together without design; and yet there was perfect harmony among them, and a softness and a delicacy made up of a thousand different brightnesses. There is not, I think, so much contrast among these colors as might at first appear. The more you consider them, the more they seem to have one element among them all, which is the reason that the most brilliant display of them soothes the observer, instead of exciting him. And I know not whether it be more a moral effect or a physical one, operating merely on the eye; but it is a pensive gayety, which causes a sigh often, and never a smile. We never fancy, for instance, that these gayly clad trees might be changed into young damsels in holiday attire, and betake themselves to dancing on the plain. If they were to undergo such a transformation, they would surely arrange themselves in funeral procession, and go sadly along, with their purple and scarlet and golden garments trailing over the withering grass. When the sunshine falls upon them, they seem to smile; but it is as if they were heart-broken. But it is in vain for me to attempt to describe these autumnal brilliancies, or to convey the impression which they make on me. I have tried a thousand times, and always without the slightest self-satisfaction. Fortunately there is no need of such a record, for Nature renews the picture year after year; and even when we shall have passed away from the world, we can spiritually create these scenes, so that we may dispense with all efforts to put them into words,

Walden Pond was clear and beautiful as usual. It tempted me to bathe; and, though the water was thrillingly cold, it was like the thrill of a happy death. Never was there such transparent water as this, I threw sticks into it, and saw them float suspended on an almost invisible medium. It seemed as if the pure air were beneath them, as well as above. It is fit for baptisms; but one would not wish it to be polluted by having sins washed into it. None but angels should bathe in it; but blessed babies might be dipped into its bosom.

In a small and secluded dell that opens upon the most beautiful cove of the whole lake, there is a little hamlet of huts or shanties inhabited by the Irish people who are at work upon the railroad. There are three or four of these habitations, the very rudest, I should imagine, that civilized men ever made for themselves,—constructed of rough boards, with the protruding ends. Against some of them the earth is heaped up to the roof, or nearly so; and when the grass has had time to sprout upon them, they will look like small natural hillocks, or a species of ant-hills,—something in which Nature has a larger share than man. These huts are placed beneath the trees, oaks, walnuts, and white-pines, wherever the trunks give them space to stand; and by thus adapting themselves to natural interstices, instead of making new ones, they do not break or disturb the solitude and seclusion of the place. Voices are heard, and the shouts and laughter of children, who play about like the sunbeams that come down through the branches. Women are washing in open spaces, and long lines of whitened clothes are extended from tree to tree, fluttering and gambolling in the breeze. A pig, in a sty even more extemporary than the shanties, is grunting and poking his snout through the clefts of his habitation. The household pots and kettles are seen at the doors; and a glance within shows the rough benches that serve for chairs, and the bed upon the floor. The visitor's nose takes note of the fragrance of a pipe. And yet, with all these homely items, the repose and sanctity of the old wood do not seem to be destroyed or profaned. It overshadows these poor people, and assimilates them somehow or other to the character of its natural inhabitants. Their presence did not shock me any more than if I had merely discovered a squirrel's nest in a tree. To be. sure, it is a torment to see the great, high, ugly embankment of the railroad, which is here thrusting itself into the lake, or along its margin, in close vicinity to this picturesque little hamlet. I have seldom seen anything more beautiful than the cove on the border of which the huts are situated; and the more I looked, the lovelier it grew. The trees overshadowed it deeply; but on one side there was some brilliant shrubbery which seemed to light up the whole picture with the effect of a sweet and melancholy smile.

I felt as if spirits were there,—or as if these shrubs had a spiritual life. In short, the impression was indefinable; and, after gazing and musing a good while, I retraced my steps through the Irish hamlet, and plodded on along a wood-path.

According to my invariable custom, I mistook my way, and, emerging upon the road, I turned my back instead of my face towards Concord, and walked on very diligently till a guide-board informed me of my mistake. I then turned about, and was shortly overtaken by an old yeoman in a chaise, who kindly offered me a drive, and soon set me down in the village. extracts from letters.

## EXTRACTS FROM LETTERS

Salem, April 14th, 1844.—...I went to George Hillard's office, and he spoke with immitigable resolution of the necessity of my going to dine with Longfellow before returning to Concord; but I have an almost miraculous power of escaping from necessities of this kind. Destiny itself has often been worsted in the attempt to get me out to dinner. Possibly, however, I may go. Afterwards, I called on Colonel Hall, who held me long in talk about politics and other sweetmeats? Then I stepped into a book auction, not to buy, but merely to observe, and, after a few moments, who should come in, with a smile as sweet as sugar (though savoring rather of molasses), but, to my horror and petrifaction, — —! I anticipated a great deal of bore and botheration; but, through Heaven's mercy, he merely spoke a few words, and left me. This is so unlike his deportment in times past, that I suspect "The Celestial Railroad" must have given him a pique; and, if so, I shall feel as if Providence had sufficiently rewarded me for that pious labor.

In the course of the forenoon I encountered Mr. Howes in the street. He looked most exceedingly depressed, and, pressing my hand with peculiar emphasis, said that he was in great affliction, having just heard of his son George's death in Cuba. He seemed encompassed and overwhelmed by this misfortune, and walks the street as in a heavy cloud of his own grief, forth from which he extended his hand to meet my grasp. I expressed my sympathy, which I told him I was now the more capable of feeling in a father's suffering, as being myself the father of a little girl, —and, indeed, the being a parent does give one the freedom of a wider range of sorrow as well as of happiness. He again pressed my hand, and left me....

When I got to Salem, there was great joy, as yon may suppose....Mother hinted an apprehension that poor baby would be spoilt, whereupon I irreverently observed that, having spoiled her own three children, it was natural for her to suppose that all other parents would do the same; when she averred that it was impossible to spoil such children as E— and I, because she had never been able to do anything with us....I could hardly convince them that Una had begun to smile so soon. It surprised my mother, though her own children appear to have been bright specimens of babyhood. E— could walk and talk at nine months old. I do not understand that I was quite such a miracle of precocity, but should think it not impossible, inasmuch as precocious boys are said to make stupid men.

May 27th, 1844.—...My cook fills his office admirably. He prepared what I must acknowledge to be the best dish of fried fish and potatoes for *dinner* to-day that I ever tasted in this house. I scarcely recognized the fish of our own river. I make him get all the dinners, while I confine myself to the much lighter task of breakfast and tea. He also takes his turn in washing the dishes.

We had a very pleasant dinner at Longfellow's, and I liked Mrs. Longfellow very much. The dinner was late and we sat long; so that C— and I did not get to Concord till half past nine o'clock, and truly the old manse seemed somewhat dark and desolate. The next morning George Preseott came with Una's Lion, who greeted me very affectionately, but whined and moaned as if he missed somebody who should have been here. I am not quite so strict as I should be in keeping him out of the house; but I commiserate him and myself, for are we not both of us bereaved? C—, whom I can no more keep from smoking than I could the kitchen chimney, has just come into the study with a cigar, which might perfume this letter and make you think it came from my own enormity, so I may as well stop here.

May 29th.—C— is leaving me, to my unspeakable relief; for he has had a bad cold, which caused him to be much more troublesome and leas amusing than might otherwise have been the case.

May 31st.—...I get along admirably, and am at this moment superintending the corned beef, which has been on the fire, as it appears to me, ever since the beginning of time, and shows no symptom of being done before the crack of doom. Mrs. Hale says it must boil till it becomes tender; and so it shall, if I can find wood to keep the fire a-going.

Meantime, I keep my station in the dining-room, and read or write as composedly as in my own study. Just now, there came a very important rap at the front door, and I threw down a smoked herring which I had begun to eat, as there is no hope of the corned beef to-day, and went to admit the visitor. Who should it be but Ben B—, with a very peculiar and mysterious grin upon his face! He put into my hand a missive directed to "Mr. and Mrs. Hawthorne." It contained a little bit of card, signifying that Dr. L. F— and Miss C. B— receive their friends Thursday eve, June 6. I am afraid I shall be too busy washing my dishes to pay many visits. The washing of dishes does seem to me the most absurd and unsatisfactory business that I ever undertook. If, when once washed, they would remain clean forever and ever (which they ought in all reason to do, considering how much trouble it is), there would be less occasion to grumble; but no sooner is it done, than it requires to be done again. On the whole, I have come to the resolution not to use more than one dish at each meal. However, I moralize deeply on this and other matters, and have discovered that all the trouble and affliction in the world come from the necessity of cleansing away our earthly stains.

I ate the last morsel of bread yesterday, and congratulate myself on being now reduced to the fag-end of necessity. Nothing worse can happen, according to ordinary modes of thinking, than to want bread; but like most afflictions, it is more in prospect than reality. I found one cracker in the tureen, and exulted over it as if it had been so much gold. However, I have sent a petition to Mrs. P— stating my destitute condition, and imploring her succor; and, till it arrive, I shall keep myself alive on herrings and apples, together with part of a pint of milk, which I share with Leo. He is my great trouble now, though an excellent companion too. But it is not easy to find food for him, unless I give him what is fit for Christians,—though, for that matter, he appears to be as good a Christian as most laymen, or even as some of the clergy. I fried some pouts and eels yesterday, on purpose for him, for he does not like raw fish. They were very good, but I should hardly have taken the trouble on my own account.

George P— has just come to say that Mrs. P— has no bread at present, and is gone away this afternoon, but that she will send me some to-morrow. I mean to have a regular supply from the same source....You cannot imagine how much the presence of Leo relieves the feeling of perfect loneliness. He insists upon being in the room with me all the time, except at night, when he sleeps in the shed, and I do not find myself severe enough to drive him out. He accompanies me likewise in all my walks to the village and elsewhere; and, in short, keeps at my heels, all the time, except when I go down cellar. Then he stands at the head of the stairs and howls, as if he never expected to see me again. He is evidently impressed with the present solitude of our old abbey, both on his own account and mine, and feels that he may assume a greater degree of intimacy than would be otherwise allowable. He will be easily brought within the old regulations after your return.

*P.S.* 3 o'clock.—The beef is done!!!

Concord. The Old Manse. June 2d.—...Everything goes on well with me. At the time of writing my last letter, I was without bread. Well, just at supper time xame Mrs. B— with a large covered dish, which proved to contain a quantity of specially good flapjacks, piping hot, prepared, I suppose, by the fair hands of Miss Martha or Miss Abby, for Mrs. P— was not at home. They served me both for supper and breakfast; and I thanked Providence, and the young ladies, and compared myself to the prophet fed by ravens,—though the simile does rather more than justice to myself, and not enough to the generous donors of the flapjacks. The next morning, Mrs. P— herself brought two big loaves of bread, which will last me a week, unless I have some guests to provide for. I have likewise found a board of crackers in one of the covered dishes; so that the old castle is sufficiently provisioned to stand a long siege. The corned beef is exquisitely done, and as tender as a young lady's heart, all owing to my skilful cookery; for I consulted Mrs. Hale at every step, and precisely followed her directions. To say the truth, I look upon ,it as such a masterpiece in its way, that it seems irreverential to eat it. Things on which so much thought and labor are bestowed should surely be immortal....Leo and I attended divine services this morning in a temple not made with hands. We went to the farthest extremity of Peter's path, and there lay together under an oak, on the verge of the broad meadow.

Concord, June 6th.—...Mr. F— arrived yesterday, and appeared to be in most excellent health, and as happy as the sunshine. About the first thing he did was to wash the dishes; and he is really indefatigable in the kitchen, so that I am quite a gentleman of leisure. Previous to his arrival, I had kindled no fire for four entire days, and had lived all that time on the corned beef, except one day, when Ellery and I went down the river on a fishing excursion. Yesterday, we boiled some lamb, which we shall have cold for dinner to-day. This morning, Mr. F— fried a sumptuous dish of eels for breakfast. Mrs. P. — continues to be the instrument of Providence, and yesterday sent us a very nice plum-pudding. I have told Mr. F— that I shall be engaged in the forenoons, and he is to manage his own occupations and amusements during that time....

Leo, I regret to say, has fallen under suspicion of a very great crime,—nothing less than murder,—a fowl crime it may well be called, for it is the slaughter of one of Mr. Hay ward's hens. He has been seen to chase the hens, several times, and the other day one of them was found dead. Possibly he may be innocent, and, as there is nothing but circumstantial evidence, it must be left with his own conscience.

Meantime, Mr. Hayward, or somebody else, seems to have given him such a whipping that he is absolutely stiff, and walks about like a rheumatic old gentleman. I am afraid, too, that he is an incorrigible thief. Ellery says he has seen him coming up the avenue with a calf's whole head in his mouth. How he came by it is best known to Leo himself. If he were a dog of fair character, it would be no more than charity to conclude that he had either bought it, or had it given to him; but with the other charges against him, it inclines me to great distrust of his moral principles. Be that as it may, he managed his stock of provisions very thriftily,—burying it in the earth, and eating a portion of it whenever he felt an appetite. If he insists upon living by highway robbery, it would be well to make him share his booty with us....

June 10th.—...Mr. F-is in perfect health, and absolutely in the seventh heaven, and he talks and talks and talks and talks; and I listen and listen and listen with a patience for which, in spite of all my sins, I firmly expect to be admitted to the mansions of the blessed. And there is really a contentment in being able to make this poor, world-worn, hopeless, half-crazy man so entirely comfortable as he seems to be here. He is an admirable cook. We had some roast veal and a baked rice-pudding on Sunday, really a fine dinner, and cooked in better style than Mary can equal; and George Curtis came to dine with us. Like all male cooks, he is rather expensive, and has a tendency to the consumption of eggs in his various concoctions....I have had my dreams of splendor; but never expected to arrive at the dignity of keeping a man-cook. At first we had three meals a day, but now only two....

* * * * *

We dined at Mr. Emerson's the other day, in company with Mr. Hedge. Mr. Bradford has been to see us two or three times....He looks thinner than ever.

# PASSAGES FROM NOTE-BOOKS

May 5th, 1850.—I left Portsmouth last Wednesday, at the quarter past twelve, by the Concord Railroad, which at Newcastle unites with the Boston and Maine Railroad about ten miles from Portsmouth. The station at Newcastle is a small wooden building, with one railroad passing on one side, and another on another, and the two crossing each other at right angles. At a little distance stands a black, large, old wooden church, with a square tower, and broken windows, and a great rift through the middle of the roof, all in a stage of dismal ruin and decay. A farm-house of the old style, with a long sloping roof, and as black as the church, stands on the opposite side of the road, with its barns; and these are all the buildings in sight of the railroad station. On the Concord rail is the train of cars, with the locomotive puffing, and blowing off its steam, and making a great blaster in that lonely place, while along the other railroad stretches the desolate track, with the withered weeds growing up betwixt the two lines of iron, all so desolate. And anon you hear a low thunder running along these iron rails: it grows louder; an object is seen afar off; it approaches rapidly, and comes down upon you like fate, swift and inevitable. In a moment, it dashes along in front of the station-house, and comes to a pause, the locomotive hissing and fuming in its eagerness to go on. How much life has come at once into this lonely place! Four or five long cars, each, perhaps, with fifty people in it, reading newspapers, reading pamphlet novels, chattering, sleeping; all this vision of passing life! A moment passes, while the luggage-men are putting on the trunks and packages; then the bell strikes a few times, and away goes the train again, quickly out of sight of those who remain behind, while a solitude of hours again broods over the station-house, which, for an instant, has thus been put in communication with far-off cities, and then remains by itself, with the old, black, ruinous church, and the black old farm-house, both built years and years ago, before railroads were over dreamed of. Meantime, the passenger, stepping from the solitary station into the train, finds himself in the midst of a new world all in a moment. He rushes out of the solitude into a village; thence, through woods and hills, into a large inland town; beside the Merrimack, which has overflowed its banks, and eddies along, turbid as a vast mud-puddle, sometimes almost laving the doorstep of a house, and with trees standing in the flood half-way up their trunks. Boys, with newspapers to sell, or apples and lozenges; many passengers departing and entering, at each new station; the more permanent passenger, with his check or ticket stuck in his hatband, where the conductor may see it. A party of girls, playing at ball with a young man. Altogether it is a scene of stirring life, with which a person who had been waiting long for the train to come might find it difficult at once to amalgamate himself.

It is a sombre, brooding day, and begins to rain as the cars pass onward. In a little more than two hours we find ourselves in Boston surrounded by eager hack-men.

Yesterday I went to the Athenæum, and, being received with great courtesy by Mr. Folsom, was shown all over the edifice from the very bottom to the very top, whence I looked out over Boston. It is an admirable point of view; but, it being an overcast and misty day, I did not get the full advantage of it. The library is in a noble hall, and looks splendidly with its vista of alcoves. The most remarkable sight, however, was Mr. Hildreth, writing his history of the United States. He sits at a table, at the entrance of one of the alcoves, with his books and papers before him, as quiet and absorbed as he would be in the loneliest study; now consulting an authority; now penning a sentence or paragraph, without seeming conscious of anything but his subject. It is very curious thus to have a glimpse of a book in process of creation under one's eye. I know not how many hours he sits there; but while I saw him he was a pattern of diligence and unwandering thought. He had taken himself out of the age, and put himself, I suppose, into that about which he was writing. Being deaf, he finds it much the easier to abstract himself. Nevertheless, it is a miracle. He is a thin, middle-aged man, in black, with an intelligent face, rather sensible than scholar-like.

Mr. Folsom accompanied me to call upon Mr. Ticknor, the historian of Spanish literature. He has a fine house, at the corner of Park and Beacon Streets, perhaps the very best position in Boston. A marble hall, a wide and easy staircase, a respectable old man-servant, evidently long at home in the mansion, to admit us. We entered the library, Mr. Folsom considerably in advance, as being familiar with the house; and I heard Mr. Ticknor greet him in friendly tones, their scholar-like and bibliographical pursuits, I suppose, bringing them into frequent conjunction. Then I was introduced, and received with great distinction, but yet without any ostentatious flourish of courtesy. Mr. Ticknor has a great head, and his hair is gray or grayish. You recognize in him at once the man who knows the world, the scholar, too, which probably is his more distinctive character, though a little more under the surface. He was in his slippers; a volume of his book was open on a table, and apparently he had been engaged in revising or annotating it. His library is a stately and beautiful room for a private dwelling, and itself looks large and rich. The fireplace has a white marble frame about it, sculptured with figures and reliefs. Over it hung a portrait of Sir Walter Scott, a copy, I think, of the one that represents him hi Melrose Abbey.

Mr. Ticknor was most kind in his alacrity to solve the point on which Mr. Folsom, in my behalf, had consulted him (as to whether there had been any English translation of the Tales of Cervantes); and most liberal in his offers of books from his library. Certainly, he is a fine example of a generous-principled scholar, anxious to assist the human intellect in its efforts and researches. Methinks he must have spent a happy life (as happiness goes among mortals), writing his great three-volumed book for twenty years: writing it, not for bread, nor with any uneasy desire of fame, but only with a purpose to achieve something true and enduring. He is, I apprehend, a man of great cultivation and refinement, and with quite sulk-stance enough to be polished and refined, without being worn too thin in the process,—a man of society. He related a singular story of an attempt of his to become acquainted with me years ago, when he mistook my kinsman Eben for me.

At half past four, I went to Mr. Thompson's, the artist who has requested to paint my picture. This was the second sitting. The portrait looked dimly out from tile canvas, as from a cloud, with something that I could recognize as my outline, but no strong resemblance as yet, I have had three portraits taken before this,—an oil picture, a miniature, and a crayon sketch,—neither of them satisfactory to those most familiar with my physiognomy. In fact, there is no such thing as a true portrait; they are all delusions, and I like, nor hardly any two that I would recognize merely by the portraits themselves, as being of the same man. A bust has more reality. This artist is a man of thought, and with no mean idea of his art; a Swedenborgian, or, as he prefers to call it, a member of the New Church; and I have generally found something marked in men who adopt that faith. He had painted a good picture of Bryant. He seems to me to possess truth in himself, and to aim at it in his artistic endeavors.

May 6th.—This morning it is an easterly rain (south-easterly, I should say just now at twelve o'clock), and I went at nine, by appointment, to sit for my picture. The artist painted awhile, but soon found that he had not so much light as was desirable, and complained that his tints were as muddy as the weather. Further sitting was therefore postponed till to-morrow at eleven. It will be a good picture: but I see no assurance, as yet, of the likeness. An artist's apartment is always very interesting to me, with its pictures, finished and unfinished: its little fancies in the pictorial way,—as here two sketches of children among flowers and foliage, representing Spring and Summer, Winter and Autumn being yet to come out of the artist's mind: the portraits of his wife and children; here a clergyman, there a poet: here a woman with the stamp of reality upon her, there a feminine conception which we feel not to have existed. There was an infant Christ, or rather a child Christ, not unbeautiful, but scarcely divine. I love the odor of paint in an artist's room: his palette and all his other tools have a mysterious charm for me. The pursuit has always interested my imagination mow than any other, and I remember, before having my first portrait taken, there was a great bewitchery in the idea, as if it were a magic process. Even now, it is not without interest to me.

I left Mr. Thompson before ten, and took my way through the sloppy streets to the Athenæum, where I looked over the newspapers and periodicals, and found two of my old stories ("Peter Goldthwaite" and the "Shaker Bridal") published as original in the last "London Metropolitan!" The English are much more unscrupulous and dishonest pirates than ourselves. However, if they are poor enough to perk themselves in such false feathers as these, Heaven help them! I glanced over the stories, and they seemed painfully cold and dull. It is the more singular that these should be so published, inasmuch as the whole book was republished in London, only a few months ago. Mr. Fields tells me that two publishers in London had advertised the "Scarlet Letter" as in press, each book at a shilling.

* * * * *

Certainly life is made much more tolerable, and man respects himself far more, when he takes his meals with a certain degree of order and state. There should be a sacred law in these matters; and, as consecrating the whole business, the preliminary prayer is a good and real ordinance. The advance of man from a savage and animal state may be as well measured by his mode and morality of dining, as by any other circumstance. At Mr. Fields's, soon after entering the house, I heard the brisk and cheerful notes of a canary-bird, singing with great vivacity, and making its voice echo through the large rooms. It was very pleasant at the close of the rainy, east-windy day, and seemed to fling sunshine through the dwelling.

May 7th.—I did not go out yesterday afternoon, but after tea I went to Parker's. The drinking and smoking shop is no bad place to see one kind of life. The front apartment is for drinking. The door opens into Court Square, and is denoted, usually, by some choice specimens of dainties exhibited in the windows, or hanging beside the door-post; as, for instance, a pair of canvas-back ducks, distinguishable by their delicately mottled feathers; an admirable cut of raw beefsteak; a ham, ready boiled, and with curious figures traced in spices on its outward fat; a half, or perchance the whole, of a large salmon, when in season; a bunch of partridges, etc., etc. A screen stands directly before the door, so as to conceal the interior from an outside barbarian. At the counter stand, at almost all hours,—certainly at all hours when I have chanced to observe,—tipplers, either taking a solitary glass, or treating all round, veteran topers, flashy young men, visitors from the country, the various petty officers connected with the law, whom the vicinity of the Court-House brings hither. Chiefly, they drink plain liquors, gin, brandy, or whiskey, sometimes a Tom and Jerry, a gin cocktail (which the bar-tender makes artistically, tossing it in a large parabola from one tumbler to another, until fit for drinking), a brandy-smash, and numerous other concoctions. All this toping goes forward with little or no apparent exhilaration of spirits; nor does this seem to be the object sought,—it being rather, I imagine, to create a titillation of the coats of the stomach and a general sense of invigoration, without affecting the brain. Very seldom does a man grow wild and unruly.

The inner room is hung round with pictures and engravings of various kinds,—a painting of a premium ox, a lithograph of a Turk and of a Turkish lady,...and various showily engraved tailors' advertisements, and other shop-bills; among them all, a small painting of a drunken toper, sleeping on a bench beside the grog-shop,

—a ragged, half-hatless, bloated, red-nosed, jolly, miserable-looking devil, very well done, and strangely suitable to the room in which it hangs. Round the walls are placed some half a dozen marble-topped tables, and a centre-table in the midst; most of them strewn with theatrical and other show-bills; and the large theatre-bills, with their type of gigantic solidity and blackness, hung against the walls.

Last evening, when I entered, there was one guest somewhat overcome with liquor, and slumbering with his chair tipped against one of the marble tables. In the course of a quarter of an hour, he roused himself (a plain, middle-aged man), and went out with rather an unsteady step, and a hot, red face. One or two others were smoking, and looking over the papers, or glancing at a play-bill. From the centre of the ceiling descended a branch with two gas-burners, which sufficiently illuminated every corner of the room. Nothing is so remarkable in these bar-rooms and drinking-places, as the perfect order that prevails: if a man gets drunk, it is no otherwise perceptible than by his going to sleep, or his inability to walk.

Pacing the sidewalk in front of this grog-shop of Parker's (or sometimes, on cold and rainy days, taking his station inside), there is generally to be observed an elderly ragamuffin, in a dingy and battered hat, an old surtout, and a more than shabby general aspect; a thin face and red nose, a patch over one eye, and the other half drowned in moisture. He leans in a slightly stooping posture on a stick, forlorn and silent, addressing nobody, but fixing bis one moist eye on you with a certain intentness. He is a man who has been in decent circumstances at some former period of his life, but, falling into decay (perhaps by dint of too frequent visits at Parker's bar), he now haunts about the place, as a ghost haunts the spot where he was murdered, "to collect his rents," as Parker says,—that is, to catch an occasional nine-pence from some charitable acquaintances, or a glass of liquor at the bar. The word "ragamuffin," which I have used above, does not accurately express the man, because there is a sort of shadow or delusion of respectability about him, and a sobriety too, and a kind of decency in his groggy and red-nosed destitution.

Underground, beneath the drinking and smoking rooms, is Parker's eating-hall, extending all the way to Court Street. All sorts of good eating may be had there, and a gourmand may feast at what expense he will.

I take an interest in all the nooks and crannies and every development of cities; so here I try to make a description of the view from the back windows of a house in the centre of Boston, at which I now glance in the intervals of writing. The view is bounded, at perhaps thirty yards' distance, by a row of opposite brick dwellings, standing, I think, on Temple Place; houses of the better order, with tokens of genteel families visible in all the rooms betwixt the basements and the attic windows in the roof; plate-glass in the rear drawing-rooms, flower-pots in some of the windows of the upper stories. Occasionally, a lady's figure, either seated or appearing with a flitting grace, or dimly manifest farther within the obscurity of the room. A balcony, with a wrought-iron fence running along under the row of drawing-room windows, above the basement. In the space betwixt the opposite row of dwellings and that in which I am situated are the low out-houses of the above-described houses, with flat roofs; or solid brick walls, with walks on them, and high railings, for the convenience of the washerwomen in hanging out their clothes. In the intervals are grass-plots, already green, because so sheltered; and fruit-trees, now beginning to put forth their leaves, and one of them, a cherry-tree, almost in full blossom. Birds flutter and sing among these trees. I should judge it a good site for the growth of delicate fruit; for, quite enclosed on all sides by houses, the blighting winds cannot molest the trees. They have sunshine on them a good part of the day, though the shadow must come early, and I suppose there is a rich soil about the roots. I see grapevines clambering against one wall, and also peeping over another, where the main body of the vine is invisible to me, In another place, a frame is erected for a grapevine, and probably it will produce as rich clusters as the vines of Madeira here in the heart of the city, in this little spot of fructifying earth, while the thunder of wheels rolls about it on every side. The trees are not all fruit-trees. One pretty well-grown buttonwood-tree aspires upward above the roofs of the houses. In the full verdure of summer, there will be quite a mass or curtain of foliage between the hither and the thither row of houses.

Afternoon.—At eleven, I went to give Mr. Thompson a sitting for my picture. 1 like the painter. He seems to reverence his art, and to aim at truth in it, as I said before; a man of gentle disposition too, and simplicity of life and character. I seated myself in the pictorial chair, with the only light in the room descending upon me from a high opening, almost at the ceiling, the rest of the sole window being shuttered. He began to work, and we talked in an idle and desultory way,—neither of us feeling very conversable,— which he attributed to the atmosphere, it being a bright, westwindy, bracing day, We talked about the pictures of Christ, and how inadequate and untrue they are. He said he thought artists should attempt only to paint child-Christs, human powers being inadequate to the task of painting such purity and holiness in a manly development. Then he said that an idea of a picture had occurred to him that morning while reading a chapter in the New Testament,—how "they parted his garments among them, and for his vesture did cast lots." His picture was to represent the soldier to whom the garment without a seam had fallen, after taking it home and examining it, and becoming impressed with a sense of the former holiness. I do not quite see how he would make such a picture tell its own story;—but I find the idea suggestive to my own own mind, and I think I could make something of it. We talked of physiognomy and impressions of character,—first impressions,—and how apt they are to come aright in the face of the closest subsequent observation.

There were several visitors in the course of the sitting, one a gentleman, a connection from the country, with whom the artist talked about family matters and personal affairs,—observing on the poorness of his own business, and that he had thoughts of returning to New York. I wish he would meet with better success. Two or three ladies also looked in. Meanwhile Mr. Thompson had been painting with more and more eagerness, casting quick, keen glances at me, and then making hasty touches on the picture, as if to secure with his brush what he had caught with his eye. He observed that he was just getting interested in the work, and I could recognize the feeling that was in him as akin to what I have experienced myself in the glow of composition. Nevertheless, he seemed able to talk about foreign matters, through it all. He continued to paint in this rapid way, up to the moment of closing the sitting; when he took the canvas from the easel, without giving me time to mark what progress he had made, as he did the last time.

The artist is middle-sized, thin, a little stooping, with a quick, nervous movement. He has black hair, not thick, a beard under his chin, a small head, but well-developed forehead, black eyebrows, eyes keen, but kindly, and a dark face, not indicating robust health, but agreeable in its expression. His voice is gentle and sweet, and such as comes out from amidst refined feelings. He dresses very simply and unpictorially in a gray frock or sack, and does not seem to think of making a picture of himself in his own person.

At dinner to-day there was a young Frenchman,whom-befriended a year or so ago, when he had not another friend in America, and obtained employment for him in a large dry-goods establishment. He is a young man of eighteen or thereabouts, with smooth black hair, neatly dressed; his face showing a good disposition, but with nothing of intellect or character. It is funny to think of this poor little Frenchman, a Parisian too, eating our most un-French victuals,— our beefsteaks, and roasts, and various homely puddings, and hams, and all things most incongruent to his hereditary stomach; but nevertheless he eats most cheerfully and uncomplainingly. He has not a large measure of French vivacity, never rattles, never dances, nor breaks into ebullitions of mirth and song; on the contrary, I have never known a youth of his age more orderly and decorous. He is kind-hearted and grateful, and evinces his gratitude to the mother of the family and to his benefactress by occasional presents, not trifling when measured by his small emolument of five dollars per week. Just at this time he is confined to his room by indisposition, caused, it is suspected, by a spree on Sunday last. Our gross Saxon orgies would soon be the ruin of his French constitution.

A thought to-day. Great men need to be lifted upon the shoulders of the whole world, in order to conceive their great ideas or perform their great deeds. That is, there must be an atmosphere of greatness round about them. A hero cannot be a hero unless in an heroic world.

May 8th.—I went last evening to the National Theatre to see a pantomime. It was Jack the Giant-Killer, and somewhat heavy and tedious. The audience was more noteworthy than the play. The theatre itself is for the middling and lower classes, and I had not taken my seat in the most aristocratic part of the house; so that I found myself surrounded chiefly by young sailors, Hanover Street shopmen, mechanics, and other people of that class. It is wonderful! the difference that exists in the personal aspect and dress, and no less in the manners, of people in this quarter of the city, as compared with other parts of it.

One would think that Oak Hall should give a common garb and air to the great mass of the Boston population; but it seems not to be so; and perhaps what is most singular is, that the natural make of the men has a conformity and suitableness to the dress. Glazed caps and Palo Alto hats were much worn. It is a pity that this picturesque and comparatively graceful hat should not have been generally adopted, instead of falling to the exclusive use of a rowdy class.

In the next box to me were two young women, with an infant, but to which of them appertaining I could not at first discover. One was a large, plump girl, with a heavy face, a snub nose, coarse-looking, but good-natured, and with no traits of evil,—save, indeed, that she had on the vilest gown of dirty white cotton, so pervadingly dingy that it was white no longer, as it seemed to me. The sleeves were short, and ragged at the borders, and her shawl, which she took off on account of the heat, was old and faded,—the shabbiest and dirtiest dress that I ever saw a woman wear. Yet she was plump, and looked comfortable in body and mind. I imagine that she must have had a better dress at home, but had come to the theatre extemporaneously, and, not going to the dress circle, considered her ordinary gown good enough for the occasion. The other girl seemed as young or younger than herself. She was small, with a particularly intelligent and pleasant face, not handsome, perhaps, but as good or better than if it were. It was mobile with whatever sentiment chanced to be in her mind, as quick and vivacious a face in its movements as I have ever seen; cheerful, too, and indicative of a sunny, though I should think it might be a hasty, temper. She was dressed in a dark gown (chintz, I suppose, the women call it), a good, homely dress, proper enough for the fireside, hut a strange one to appear in at a theatre. Both these girls appeared to enjoy themselves very much,—the large and heavy one in her own duller mode; the smaller manifesting her interest by gestures, pointing at the stage, and with so vivid a talk of countenance that it was precisely as if she had spoken. She was not a brunette, and this made the vivacity of her expression the more agreeable. Her companion, on the other hand, was so dark, that I rather suspected her to have a tinge of African blood.

There were two men who seemed to have some connection with these girls,—one an elderly, gray-headed personage, well-stricken in liquor, talking loudly and foolishly, but good-humoredly; the other a young man, sober, and doing his best to keep his elder friend quiet. The girls seemed to give themselves no uneasiness about the matter. Both the men wore Palo Alto hats. I could not make out whether either of the men were the father of the child, though I was inclined to set it down as a family party.

As the play went on, the house became crowded and oppressively warm, and the poor little baby grew dark red, or purple almost, with the uncomfortable heat in its small body. It must have been accustomed to discomfort, and have concluded it to be the condition of mortal life, else it never would have remained so quiet. Perhaps it had been quieted with a sleeping-potion. The two young women were not negligent of it; but passed it to and fro between them, each willingly putting herself to inconvenience for the sake of tending it. But I really feared it might die in some kind of a fit, so hot was the theatre, so purple with heat, yet strangely quiet, was the child. I was glad to hear it cry at last; but it did not cry with any great rage and vigor, as it should, but in a stupid kind of way. Hereupon the smaller of the two girls, after a little inefficacious dandling, at once settled the question of maternity by nursing her baby. Children must be hard to kill, however injudicious the treatment. The two girls and their cavaliers remained till nearly the close of the play. I should like well to know who they are,—of. what condition in life, and whether reputable as members of the class to which they belong. My own judgment is that they are so. Throughout the evening, drunken young sailors kept stumbling into and out of the boxes, calling to one another from different parts of the house, shouting to the performers, and singing the burden of songs. It was a scene of life in the rough.

May 14th.—A stable opposite the house,—an old wooden construction, low, in three distinct parts; the centre being the stable proper, where the horses are kept, and with a chamber over it for the hay. On one side is the department for chaises and carriages; on the other, the little office where the books are kept. In the interior region of the stable everything is dim and undefined,—half-traceable outlines of stalls, sometimes the shadowy aspect of a horse. Generally a groom is dressing a horse at the stable door, with a care and accuracy that leave no part of the animal unvisited by the currycomb and brush; the horse, meanwhile, evidently enjoying it, but sometimes, when the more sensitive parts are touched, giving a half-playful kick with his hind legs, and a little neigh. If the men bestowed half as much care on their own personal cleanliness, they would be all the better and healthier men therefor. They appear to be busy men, these stablers, yet have a lounging way with them, as if indolence were somehow diffused through their natures. The apparent head of the establishment is a sensible, thoughtful-looking, large-featured, and homely man, past the middle age, clad rather shabbily in gray, stooping somewhat, and without any smartness about him. There is a groom, who seems to be a very comfortable kind of personage,—a man of forty-five or thereabouts (R. W. Emerson says he was one of his schoolmates), but not looking so old; corpulent, not to say fat, with a white frock, which his goodly bulk almost fills, enveloping him from neck nearly to ankles. On his head he wears a cloth cap of a jockey shape; his pantaloons are turned up an inch or two at bottom, and he wears brogans on his feet. His hair, as may be seen when he takes off his cap to wipe bis brow, is black and in perfect preservation, with not exactly a curl, yet a vivacious and elastic kind of twist in it. His face is fresh-colored, comfortable, sufficiently vivid in expression, not at all dimmed by his fleshly exuberance, because the man possesses vigor enough to carry it off. His bodily health seems perfect; so, indeed, does his moral and intellectual. He is very active and assiduous in his duties, currycombing and rubbing down the horses with alacrity and skill; and, when not otherwise occupied, you may see him talking jovially with chance acquaintances, or observing what is going forward in the street. If a female acquaintance happens to pass, he touches his jockey cap, and bows, accomplishing this courtesy with a certain smartness that proves him a man of the world. Whether it be his greater readiness to talk, or the wisdom of what he says, he seems usually to be the centre talker of the group. It is very pleasant to see such an image of earthly comfort as this. A fat man who feels his flesh as a disease and encumbrance, and on whom it presses so as to make him melancholy with dread of apoplexy, and who moves heavily under the burden of himself,—such a man is a doleful and disagreeable object. But if he have vivacity enough to pervade all his earthiness, and bodily force enough to move lightly under it, and if it be not too unmeasured to have a trimness and briskness in it, then it is good and wholesome to look at him.

In the background of the house, a cat, occasionally stealing along on the roofs of the low out-houses: descending a flight of wooden steps into the brick area; investigating the shed, and entering all dark and secret places; cautious, circumspect, as if in search of something; noiseless, attentive to every noise. Moss grows on spots of the roof; there are little boxes of earth here and there, with plants in them. The grass-plots appertaining to each of the houses whose rears are opposite ours (standing in Temple Place) are perhaps ten or twelve feet broad, and three times as long. Here and there is a large, painted garden-pot, half buried in earth. Besides the large trees in blossom, there are little ones, probably of last year's setting out. Early in the day chambermaids are seen hanging the bedclothes out of the upper windows; at the window of the basement of the same house, I see a woman ironing. Were I a solitary prisoner, I should not doubt to find occupation of deep interest for my whole day in watching only one of the houses. One house seems to be quite shut up; all the blinds in the three windows of each of the four stories being closed, although in the roof-windows of the attic story the curtains are hung carelessly upward, instead of being drawn. I think the house is empty, perhaps for the summer. The visible side of the whole row of houses is now in the shade,—they looking towards, I should say, the southwest. Later in the day, they are wholly covered with sunshine, and continue so through the afternoon; and at evening the sunshine slowly withdraws upward, gleams aslant upon the windows, perches on the chimneys, and so disappears. The upper part of the spire and the weathercock of the Park Street Church appear over one of the houses, looking as if it were close behind. It shows the wind to be east now. At one of the windows of the third story sits a woman in a colored dress, diligently sewing on something white. She sews, not like a lady, but with an occupational air. Her dress, I observe, on closer observation, is a kind of loose morning sack, with, I think, a silky gloss on it; and she seems to have a silver comb in her hair,—no, this latter item is a mistake. Sheltered as the space is between the two rows of houses, a puff of the east-wind finds its way in, and shakes off some of the withering blossoms from the cherry-trees.

Quiet as the prospect is, there is a continual and near thunder of wheels proceeding from Washington Street. In a building not far off, there is a hall for exhibitions; and sometimes, in the evenings, loud music is heard from it; or, if a diorama be shown (that of Bunker Hill, for instance, or the burning of Moscow), an immense racket of imitative cannon and musketry.

May 16th.—It has been an easterly rain yesterday and to-day, with occasional fightings up, and then a heavy downfall of the gloom again.

Scenes out of the rear windows,—the glistening roof of the opposite houses; the chimneys, now and then choked with their own smoke, which a blast drives down their throats. The church-spire has a mist about it. Once this morning a solitary dove came and alighted on the peak of an attic window, and looked down into the areas, remaining in this position a considerable time. Now it has taken a flight, and alighted on the roof of this house, directly over the window at which I sit, so that I can look up and see its head and beak, and the tips of its claws. The roofs of the low out-houses are black with moisture; the gutters are full of water, and there is a little puddle where there is a place for it in the hollow of a board. On the grass-plot are strewn the fallen blossoms of the cherry-tree, and over the scene broods a parallelogram of sombre sky. Thus it will be all day as it was yesterday; and, in the evening, one window after another will be lighted up in the drawing-rooms. Through the white curtains may be seen the gleam of an astral-lamp, like a fixed star. In the basement rooms, the work of the kitchen going forward; in the upper chambers, here and there a light.

In a bar-room, a large, oval basin let into the counter, with a brass tube rising from the centre, out of which gushes continually a miniature fountain, and descends in a soft, gentle, never-ceasing rain into the basin, where swim a company of gold-fishes. Some of them gleam brightly in their golden armor; others have a dull white aspect, going through some process of transformation. One would think that the atmosphere, continually filled with tobacco-smoke, might impregnate the water unpleasantly for the scaly people; but then it is continually flowing away and being renewed. And what if some toper should be seized with the freak of emptying his glass of gin or brandy into the basin,—would the fishes die or merely get jolly?

I saw, for a wonder, a man pretty drunk at Parker's the other evening,—a well-dressed man, of not ungentlemanly aspect. He talked loudly and foolishly, but in good phrases, with a great flow of language, and he was no otherwise impertinent than in addressing his talk to strangers. Finally, after sitting a long time staring steadfastly across the room in silence, he arose, and staggered away as best he might, only showing, his very drunken state when he attempted to walk.

Old acquaintances,—a gentleman whom I knew ten years ago, brisk, active, vigorous, with a kind of fire of physical well-being and cheerful spirits glowing through him. Now, after a course, I presume, of rather free living, pale, thin, oldish, with a grave and care or pain worn brow,—yet still lively and cheerful in his accost, though with something invincibly saddened in his tones. Another, formerly commander of a revenue vessel,—a man of splendid epaulets and very aristocratic equipment and demeanor; now out of service and without position, and changed into a brandy-burnt and rowdyish sort of personage. He seemed as if he might still be a gentleman if he would; but his manners show a desperate state of mind by their familiarity, recklessness, the lack of any hedge of reserve about himself, while still he is evidently a man of the world, accustomed to good society. He has latterly, I think, been in the Russian service, and would very probably turn pirate on fair occasion.

Lenox, July 14th.—The tops of the chestnut-trees have a whitish appearance, they being, I suppose, in bloom. Red raspberries are just through the season.

Language,—human language,—after all, is but little better than the croak and cackle of fowls and other utterances of brute nature,—sometimes not so adequate.

July 16th.—The tops of the chestnut-trees are peculiarly rich, as if a more luscious sunshine were falling on them than anywhere else. "Whitish," as above, don't express it.

The queer gestures and sounds of a hen looking about for a place to deposit her egg; her self-important gait; the sideway turn of her head and cock of her eye, as she pries into one and another nook, croaking all the while,—evidently with the idea that the egg in question is the most important thing that has been brought to pass since the world began. A speckled black and white and tufted hen of ours does it to most ludicrous perfection; and there is something laughably womanish in it too.

July 25th.—As I sit in my study, with the windows open, the occasional incident of the visit of some winged creature,—wasp, hornet, or bee,—entering out of the warm, sunny atmosphere, soaring round the room in large sweeps, then buzzing against the glass, as not satisfied with the place, and desirous of getting out. Finally, the joyous uprising curve with which, coming to the open part of the window, it emerges into the cheerful glow of the outside.

August 4th.—Dined at hotel with J. T. Fields and wife. Afternoon, drove with them to Pittsfield and called on Dr. Holmes.

August 5th.—Drove with Fields and his wife to Stockbridge, being thereto invited by Mr. Field of Stockbridge, in order to ascend Monument Mountain. Found at Mr. Field's Dr. Holmes and Mr. Duyckinck of New York; also Mr. Cornelius Matthews and Herman Melville. Ascended the mountain: that is to say, Mrs. Fields and Miss Jenny Field, Mr. Field and Mr. Fields, Dr. Holmes, Messrs. Duyckinck, Matthews, Melville, Mr. Henry Sedgewick, and I, and were caught in a shower. Dined at Mr. Field's. Afternoon, under guidance of J. T. Headley, the party scrambled through the ice-glen.

August 7th.—Messrs. Duyckinck, Matthews, Melville, and Melville, Junior, called in the forenoon. Gave them a couple of bottles of Mr. Mansfield's champagne, and walked down to the lake with them. At twilight Mr. Edwin P. Whipple and wife called.

August 8th.—Mr. and Mrs. Whipple took tea with us.

August 12th.—Seven chickens hatched. J. T. Headley and brother called. Eight chickens.

August 19th.—Monument Mountain, in the early sunshine; its base enveloped in mist, parts of which are floating in the sky, so that the great hill looks really as if it were founded on a cloud. Just emerging from the mist is seen a yellow field of rye, and, above that, forest.

August 21st—Eight more chickens hatched. Ascended a mountain with my wife; a beautiful, mellow, autumnal sunshine.

August 24th.—In the afternoons, nowadays, this valley in which I dwell seems like a vast basin filled with golden sunshine as with wine.

August 31st.—J. R. Lowell called in the evening.

September 1st.—Mr. and Mrs. Lowell called in the forenoon, on their way to Stockbridge or Lebanon, to meet Miss Bremer.

September 2d.—"When I grow up," quoth J—, in illustration of the might to which he means to attain,—"when I grow up, I shall be two men."

September 3d.—Foliage of maples begins to change. Julian, after picking up a handful of autumnal maple-leaves the other day,—"Look, papa, here's a bunch of fire!"

September 7th.—In a wood, a heap or pile of logs and sticks, that had been cut for firewood, and piled up square, in order to be carted away to the house when convenience served,—or, rather, to be sledded in sleighing time. But the moss had accumulated on them, and leaves falling over them from year to year and decaying, a kind of soil had quite covered them, although the softened outline of the woodpile was perceptible in the green mound. It was perhaps fifty years—perhaps more—since the woodman had cut and piled those logs and sticks, intending them for his winter fires. But lie probably needs no fire now. There was something strangely interesting in this simple circumstance. Imagine the long-dead woodman, and his long-dead wife and family, and the old man who was a little child when the wood was cut, coming back from their graves, and trying to make a fire with this mossy fuel.

September 19th.—Lying by the lake yesterday afternoon, with my eyes shut, while the waves and sunshine were playing together on the water, the quick glimmer of the wavelets was perceptible through my closed eyelids.

October 13th.—A windy day, with wind northwest, cool, with a prevalence of dull gray clouds over the sky, but with brief, quick glimpses of sunshine.

The foliage having its autumn hues, Monument Mountain looks like a headless sphinx, wrapped in a rich Persian shawl. Yesterday, through a diffused mist, with the sun shining on it, it had the aspect of burnished copper. The sun-gleams on the hills are peculiarly magnificent just in these days.

One of the children, drawing a cow on the blackboard, says, "I'll kick this leg out a little more,"—a very happy energy of expression, completely identifying herself with the cow; or perhaps, as the cow's creator, conscious of full power over its movements.

October 14th.—The brilliancy of the foliage has passed its acme; and indeed it has not been so magnificent this season as in some others, owing to the gradual approaches of cooler weather, and there having been slight frosts instead of severe ones. There is still a shaggy richness on the hill-sides.

October 16th.—A morning mist, filling up the whole length and breadth of the valley betwixt my house and Monument Mountain, the summit of the mountain emerging. The mist reaches almost to my window, so dense as to conceal everything, except that near its hither boundary a few ruddy or yellow tree-tops appear, glorified by the early sunshine, as is likewise the whole mist-cloud.

There is a glen between this house and the lake, through which winds a little brook with pools and tiny waterfalls over the great roots of trees. The glen is deep and narrow, and filled with trees; so that, in the summer, it is all a dense shadow of obscurity. Now, the foliage of the trees being almost entirely a golden yellow, instead of being full of shadow, the glen is absolutely full of sunshine, and its depths are more brilliant than the open plain or the mountain-tops. The trees are sunshine, and, many of the golden leaves being freshly fallen, the glen is strewn with sunshine, amid which winds and gurgles the bright, dark little brook.

December 1st.—I saw a dandelion in bloom near the lake.

December 19th.—If the world were crumbled to the finest dust, and scattered through the universe, there would not be an atom of the dust for each star.

"Generosity is the flower of justice."

The print in blood of a naked foot to be traced through the street of a town.

Sketch of a personage with the malignity of a witch, and doing the mischief attributed to one,—but by natural means; breaking off love-affairs, teaching children vices, ruining men of wealth, etc.

Ladislaus, King of Naples, besieging the city of Florence, agreed to show mercy, provided the inhabitants would deliver to him a certain virgin of famous beauty, the daughter of a physician of the city. When she was sent to the king, every one contributing something to adorn her in the richest manner, her father gave her a perfumed handkerchief, at that time a universal decoration, richly wrought. This handkerchief was poisoned with his utmost art,...and they presently died in one another's arms.

Of a bitter satirist,—of Swift, for instance,—it might be said, that the person or thing on which his satire fell shrivelled up as if the Devil had spit on it.

The Fount of Tears,—a traveller to discover it,—and other similar localities.

Benvenuto Cellini saw a Salamander in the household fire. It was shown him by his father, in childhood.

For the virtuoso's collection,—the pen with which Faust signed away his salvation, with a drop of blood dried in it.

An article on newspaper advertisements,—a country newspaper, methinks, rather than a city one.

An eating-house, where all the dishes served out, even to the bread and salt, shall be poisoned with the adulterations that are said to be practised. Perhaps Death himself might be the cook.

Personify the century,—talk of its present middle age, of its youth, and its adventures and prospects.

An uneducated countryman, supposing he had a live frog in his stomach, applied himself to the study of medicine in order to find a cure for this disease; and he became a profound physician. Thus misfortune, physical or moral, may be the means of educating and elevating us.

"Mather's Manuductio ad Ministerium,"—or, "Directions for a Candidate" for the ministry,—with the autographs of four successive clergymen in it, all of them, at one time or another, residents of the Old Manse,—Daniel Bliss, 1734; William Emerson, 1770; Ezra Ripley, 1781; and Samuel Ripley, son of the preceding. The book, according to a Latin memorandum, was sold to Daniel Bliss by Daniel Bremer, who, I suppose, was another student of divinity. Printed at Boston "for Thomas Hancock, and sold at his shop in Ann St. near the Draw Bridge, 1726." William Emerson was son-in-law of Daniel Bliss. Ezra Ripley married the widow of said William Emerson, and Samuel Ripley was their son.

Mrs. Prescott has an ox whose visage bears a strong resemblance to Daniel Webster,—a majestic brute.

The spells of witches have the power of producing meats and viands that have the appearance of a sumptuous feast, which the Devil furnishes. But a Divine Providence seldom permits the meat to be good, but it has generally some bad taste or smell,—mostly wants salt,—and the feast is often without bread.

An article on cemeteries, with fantastic ideas of monuments; for instance, a sundial;—a large, wide carved stone chair, with some such motto as "Rest and Think," and others, facetious or serious.

"Mamma, I see a part of your smile,"—a child to her mother, whose mouth was partly covered by her hand.

"The syrup of my bosom,"—an improvisation of a little girl, addressed to an imaginary child.

"The wind-turn," "the lightning-catch," a child's phrases for weathercock and lightning-rod.

"Where's the man-mountain of these Liliputs?" cried a little boy, as he looked at a small engraving of the Greeks getting into the wooden horse.

When the sun shines brightly on the new snow, we discover ranges of hills, miles away towards the south, which we have never seen before.

To have the North Pole for a fishing-pole, and the Equinoctial Line for a fishing-line.

If we consider the lives of the lower animals, we shall see in them a close parallelism to those of mortals,—toil, struggle, danger, privation, mingled with glimpses of peace and ease; enmity, affection, a continual hope of bettering themselves, although their objects lie at less distance before them than ours can do. Thus, no argument for the imperfect character of our existence and its delusory promises, and its apparent injustice, can be drawn in reference to our immortality, without, in a degree, being applicable to our brute brethren.

Lenox, February 12th, 1851.—A walk across the lake with Una. A heavy rain, some days ago, has melted a good deal of the snow on the intervening descent between our house and the lake; but many drifts, depths, and levels yet remain; and there is a frozen crust, sufficient to bear a man's weight, and very slippery. Adown the slopes there are tiny rivulets, which exist only for the winter. Bare, brown spaces of grass here and there, but still so infrequent as only to diversify the scene a little. In the woods, rocks emerging, and, where there is a slope immediately towards the lake, the snow is pretty much gone, and we see partridge-berries frozen, and outer shells of walnuts, and chestnut-burrs, heaped or scattered among the roots of the trees. The walnut-husks mark the place where the boys, after nutting, sat down to clear the walnuts of their outer shell. The various species of pine look exceedingly brown just now,— less beautiful than those trees which shed their leaves. An oak-tree, with almost all its brown foliage still rustling on it. We clamber down the bank, and step upon the frozen lake. It was snow-covered for a considerable time; but the rain overspread it with a surface of water, or imperfectly melted snow, which is now hard frozen again; and the thermometer having been frequently below zero, I suppose the ice may be four or five feet thick. Frequently there are great cracks across it, caused, I suppose, by the air beneath, and giving an idea of greater firmness than if there were no cracks; round holes, which have been hewn in the marble pavement by fishermen, and are now frozen over again, looking darker than the rest of the surface; spaces where the snow was more imperfectly dissolved than elsewhere; little crackling spots, where a thin surface of ice, over the real mass, crumples beneath one's foot; the track of a line of footsteps, most of them vaguely formed, but some quite perfectly, where a person passed across the lake while its surface was in a state of slush, but which are now as hard as adamant, and remind one of the traces discovered by geologists in rocks that hardened thousands of ages ago. It seems as if the person passed when the lake was in an intermediate state between ice and water. In one spot some pine boughs, which somebody had cut and heaped there for an unknown purpose. In the centre of the lake, we see the surrounding hills in a new attitude, this being a basin in the midst of them. Where they are covered with wood, the aspect is gray or black; then there are bare slopes of unbroken snow, the outlines and indentations being much more hardly and firmly defined than in summer. We went southward across, the lake, directly towards Monument Mountain, which reposes, as I said, like a headless sphinx. Its prominences, projections, and roughnesses are very evident; and it does not present a smooth and placid front, as when the grass is green and the trees in leaf. At one end, too, we are sensible of precipitous descents, black and shaggy with the forest that is likely always to grow there; and, in one streak, a headlong sweep downward of snow. We just set our feet on the farther shore, and then immediately returned, facing the northwest-wind, which blew very sharply against us.

After landing, we came homeward, tracing up the little brook so far as it lay in our course. It was considerably swollen, and rushed fleetly on its course between overhanging banks of snow and ice, from which depended adamantine icicles. The little waterfalls with which we had impeded it in the summer and autumn could do no more than form a large ripple, so much greater was the volume of water. In some places the crust of frozen snow made a bridge quite over the brook; so that you only knew it was there by its brawling sound beneath.

The sunsets of winter are incomparably splendid, and when the ground is covered with snow, no brilliancy of tint expressible by words can come within an infinite distance of the effect. Our southern view at that time, with the clouds and atmospherical hues, is undescribable and unimaginable; and the various distances of the hills which lie between us and the remote dome of Taconic are brought out with an accuracy unattainable in summer. The transparency of the air at this season has the effect of a telescope in bringing objects apparently near, while it leaves the scene all its breadth. The sunset sky, amidst its splendor, had a softness and delicacy that impart themselves to a white marble world.

February, 18th.—A walk, yesterday afternoon, with the children; a bright, and rather cold day, breezy from the north and westward. There has been a good deal of soaking rain lately, and it has, in great measure, cleared hills and plains of snow, only it may be seen lying in spots, and on each side of stone-walls, in a pretty broad streak. The grass is brown and withered, and yet, scattered all amongst it, on close inspection, one finds a greenness,—little shrubs that have kept green under all the severity of winter, and seem to need no change to fit them for midsummer. In the woods we see stones covered with moss that retains likewise a most lively green. Where the trees are dense, the snow still lies under them. On the sides of the mountains, some miles off, the black pines and the white snow among them together produce a gray effect. The little streams are most interesting objects at this time; some that have an existence only at this season,—Mississippis of the moment,—yet glide and tumble along as if they were perennial. The familiar ones seem strange by their breadth and volume; their little waterfalls set off by glaciers on a small scale. The sun has by this time force enough to make sheltered nooks in the angles of woods, or on banks, warm and comfortable, The lake is still of adamantine substance, but all round the borders there is a watery margin, altogether strewed or covered with thin and broken ice, so that I could not venture on it with the children. A chickadee was calling in the woods yesterday,—the only small bird I have note of yet; but crows have been cawing in the woods for a week past, though not in very great numbers.

February 22d.—For the last two or three days there has been a warm, soaking, southeasterly rain, with a spongy moisture diffused through the atmosphere. The snow has disappeared, except in spots which are the ruins of high drifts, and patches far up on the hill-sides. The mists rest all day long on the brows of the hills that shut in our valley. The road over which I walk every day to and from the village is in the worst state of mud and mire, soft, slippery, nasty to tread upon; while the grass beside it is scarcely better, being so oozy and so overflowed with little streams, and sometimes an absolute bog. The rivulets race along the road, adown the hills; and wherever there is a permanent brooklet, however generally insignificant, it is now swollen into importance, and the rumble and tumble of its waterfalls may be heard a long way off. The general effect of the day and scenery is black, black, black. The streams are all as turbid as mud-puddles.

Imitators of original authors might be compared to plaster casts of marble statues, or the imitative book to a cast of the original marble.

March 11th.—After the ground had been completely freed of snow, there has been a snow-storm for the two days preceding yesterday, which made the earth all white again. This morning at sunrise, the thermometer stood at about 18° above zero. Monument Mountain stands out in great prominence, with its dark forest-covered sides, and here and there a large, white patch, indicating tillage or pasture land; but making a generally dark contrast with the white expanse of the frozen and snow-covered lake at its base, and the more undulating white of the surrounding country. Yesterday, under the sunshine of midday, and with many voluminous clouds hanging over it, and a mist of wintry warmth in the air, it had a kind of visionary aspect, although still it was brought out in striking relief. But though one could see all its bulgings, round swells, and precipitous abruptnesses, it looked as much akin to the clouds as to solid earth and rock substance. In the early sunshine of the morning, the atmosphere being very clear, I saw the dome of Taconic with more distinctness than ever before, the snow-patches, and brown, uncovered soil on its round head, being fully visible. Generally it is but a dark blue unvaried mountain-top. All the ruggedness of the intervening hill-country was likewise effectively brought out. There seems to be a sort of illuminating quality in new snow, which it loses after being exposed for a day or two to the sun and atmosphere.

For a child's story,—the voyage of a little boat made of a chip, with a birch-bark sail, down a river.

March 31st—A walk with the children yesterday forenoon. We went through the wood, where we found partridge-berries, half hidden among the dry, fallen leaves; thence down to the brook. This little brook has not cleansed itself from the disarray of the past autumn and winter, and is much embarrassed and choked up with brown leaves, twigs, and bits of branches. It rushes along merrily and rapidly, gurgling cheerfully, and tumbling over the impediments of stones with which the children and I made little waterfalls last year. At many spots, there are small basins or pools of calmer and smoother depth,—three feet, perhaps, in diameter, and a foot or two deep,—in which little fish are already sporting about; all else- where is tumble and gurgle and mimic turbulence. I sat on the withered leaves at the foot of a tree, while the children played, a little brook being the most fascinating plaything that a child can have. Una jumped to and fro across it; Julian stood beside a pool fishing with a stick, without hook or line, and wondering that he caught nothing. Then he made new waterfalls with mighty labor, pulling big stones out of the earth, and flinging them into the current. Then they sent branches of trees, or the outer shells of walnuts, sailing down the stream, and watched their passages through the intricacies of the way,—how they were hurried over in a cascade, hurried dizzily round in a whirlpool, or brought quite to a stand-still amongst the collected rubbish. At last Julian tumbled into the brook, and was wetted through and through, so that we were obliged to come home; he squelching along all the way, with his india-rubber shoes full of water.

There are still patches of snow on the hills; also in the woods, especially on the northern margins. The lake is not yet what we may call thawed out, although there is a large space of blue water, and the ice is separated from the shore everywhere, and is soft, water-soaked, and crumbly. On favorable slopes and exposures, the earth begins to look green; and almost anywhere, if one looks closely, one sees the greenness of the grass, or of little herbage, amidst the brown. Under the nut-trees are scattered some of the nuts of last year; the walnuts have lost their virtue, the chestnuts do not seem to have much taste, but the butternuts are in no manner deteriorated. The warmth of these days has a mistiness, and in many respects resembles the Indian summer, and is not at all provocative of physical exertion. Nevertheless, the general impression is of life, not death. One feels that a new season has begun.

Wednesday, April 9th.–There was a great rain yesterday,—wind from the southeast, and the last visible vestige of snow disappeared. It was a small patch near the summit of Bald Mountain, just on the upper verge of a grove of trees. I saw a slight remnant of it yesterday afternoon, but to-day it is quite gone. The grass comes up along the roadside and on favorable exposures, with a sort of green blush. Frogs have been melodious for a fortnight, and the birds sing pleasantly.

April 20th.—The children found Houstonias more than a week ago. There have been easterly wind, continual cloudiness, and occasional rain, for a week. This morning opened with a great snow-storm from the northeast, one of the most earnest snow-storms of the year, though rather more moist than in midwinter. The earth is entirely covered. Now, as the day advances towards noon, it shows some symptoms of turning to rain.

April 28th.—For a week we have found the trailing arbutus pretty abundant in the woods. A day or two since, Una found a few purple violets, and yesterday a dandelion in bloom. The fragrance of the arbutus is spicy and exquisite.

May 16th.—In our walks now, the children and I find blue, white, and golden violets, the former, especially, of great size and richness. Houstonias are abundant, blue-whitening some of the pastures. They are .a very sociable little flower, and dwell close together in communities,—sometimes covering a space no larger than the palm of the hand, but keeping one another in cheerful heart and life,—sometimes they occupy a much larger space. Lobelia, a pink flower, growing in the woods. Columbines, of a pale red, because they have lacked sun, growing in rough and rocky places on banks in the copses, precipitating towards the lake. The leaves of the trees are not yet out, but are so apparent that the woods are getting a very decided shadow. Water-weeds on the edge of the lake, of a deep green, with roots that seem to have nothing to do with earth, but with water only.

May 23d.—I think the face of nature can never look more beautiful than now, with this so fresh and youthful green,—the trees not being fully in leaf, yet enough so to give airy shade to the woods. The sunshine fills them with green light. Monument Mountain and its brethren are green, and the lightness of the tint takes away something from their massiveness and ponderosity, and they respond with livelier effect to the shine and shade of the sky. Each tree now within sight stands out in its own individuality of hue. This is a very windy day, and the light shifts with magical alternation. In a walk to the lake just now with the children, we found abundance of flowers,—wild geranium, violets of all families, red columbines, and many others known and unknown, besides innumerable blossoms of the wild strawberry, which has been in bloom for the past fortnight. The Houstonias seem quite to overspread some pastures, when viewed from a distance. Not merely the flowers, but the various shrubs which one sees, seated, for instance, on the decayed trunk of a tree,—are well worth looking at, such a variety and such enjoyment they have of their new growth- Amid these fresh creations, we see others that have already run their course, and have done with warmth and sunshine, —the hoary periwigs, I mean, . of dandelions gone to seed.

August 7th.—Fourier states that, in the progress of the world, the ocean is to lose its saltness, and acquire the taste of a peculiarly flavored lemonade.

October 13th.—How pleasant it is to see a human countenance which cannot be insincere,—in reference to baby's smile.

The best of us being unfit to die, what an inexpressible absurdity to put the worst to death!

"Is that a burden of sunshine on Apollo's back?" asked one of the children,—of the chlamys on our Apollo Belvedere.

October 21st.—Going to the village yesterday afternoon, I saw the face of a beautiful woman, gazing at me from a cloud. It was the full face, not the bust. It had a sort of mantle on the head, and a pleasant expression of countenance. The vision lasted while I took a few steps, and then vanished. I never before saw nearly so distinct a cloud-picture, or rather sculpture; for it came out in alto-rilievo on the body of the cloud.

October 27th.—The ground this morning is white with a thin covering of snow. The foliage has still some variety of hue. The dome of Taconic looks dark, and seems to have no snow on it, though I don't understand how that can be. I saw, a moment ago, on the lake, a very singular spectacle. There is a high northwest-wind ruffling the lake's surface, and making it blue, lead-colored, or bright, in stripes or at intervals; but what I saw was a boiling up of foam, which began at the right bank of the lake, and passed quite across it; and the mist flew before it, like the cloud out of a steam-engine. A fierce and narrow blast of wind must have ploughed the water in a straight line, from side to side of the lake. As fast as it went on, the foam subsided behind it, so that it looked somewhat like a sea-serpent, or other monster, swimming very rapidly.

October 29th.—On a walk to Scott's pond, with Ellery Channing, we found a wild strawberry in the woods, not quite ripe, but beginning to redden. For a week or two, the cider-mills have been grinding apples. Immense heaps of apples lie piled near them, and the creaking of the press is heard as the horse treads on. Farmers are repairing cider-barrels; and the wayside brook is made to pour itself into the bunghole of a barrel, in order to cleanse it for the new cider.

November 3d.—The face of the country is dreary now in a cloudy day like the present. The woods on the hill-sides look almost black, and the cleared spaces a kind of gray brown.

Taconic, this morning (4th), was a black purple, as dense and distinct as Monument Mountain itself. I hear the creaking of the cider-press; the patient horse going round and round, perhaps thirsty, to make the liquor which he never can enjoy.

We left Lenox Friday morning, November 21, 1851, in a storm of snow and sleet, and took the cars at Pittsfield, and arrived at West Newton that evening.

Happiness in this world, when it comes, comes incidentally. Make it the object of pursuit, and it leads us a wild-goose chase, and is never attained. Follow some other object, and very possibly we may find that we have caught happiness without dreaming of it; but likely enough it is gone the moment we say to ourselves, "Here it is!" like the chest of gold that treasure-seekers find.

West Newton, April 13th, 1852.—One of the severest snow-storms of the winter.

April 30th.—Wrote the last page (199th MS.) of "The Blithedale Romance."

May 1st.—Wrote Preface. Afterwards modified the conclusion, and lengthened it to 201 pages. First proof-sheets, May 14.

Concord, Mass., August 20th.—A piece of land contiguous to and connected with a handsome estate, to the adornment and good appearance of which it was essential. But the owner of the strip of land was at variance with the owner of the estate, so he always refused to sell it at any price, but let it lie there, wild and ragged, in front of and near the mansion-house.

When he dies, the owner of the estate, who has rejoiced at the approach of the event all through his enemy's illness, hopes at last to buy it; hut, to his infinite discomfiture, the enemy enjoined in his will that his body should be buried in the centre of this strip of land. All sorts of ugly weeds grow most luxuriantly out of the grave in poisonous rankness.

The Isles of Shoals, Monday, August 30th.—Left Concord at a quarter of nine a.m. Friday, September 3, set sail at about half past ten to the Isles of Shoals. The passengers were an old master of a vessel; a young, rather genteel man from Greenland, N. H.; two Yankees from Hamilton and Danvers; and a country trader (I should judge) from some inland town of New Hampshire. The old sea-captain, preparatory to sailing, bought a bunch of cigars (they cost ten cents), and occasionally puffed one. The two Yankees had brought guns on board, and asked questions about the fishing of the Shoals. They were young men, brothers, the youngest a shopkeeper in Danvers, the other a farmer, I imagine, at Hamilton, and both specimens of the least polished kind of Yankee, and therefore proper to those localities. They were at first full of questions, and greatly interested in whatever was going forward; but anon the shopkeeper began to grow, first a little, then very sick, till he lay along the boat, longing, as he afterwards said, for a little fresh water to be drowned in. His brother attended him in a very kindly way, but became sick himself before he reached the end of the voyage.

The young Greenlander talked politics, or rather discussed the personal character of Pierce. The New Hampshire trader said not a word, or hardly one, all the way. A Portsmouth youth (whom I forgot to mention) sat in the stern of the boat, looking very white. The skipper of the boat is a Norwegian, a good-natured fellow, not particularly intelligent, and speaking in a dialect somewhat like Irish. He had a man with him, a silent and rather sulky fellow, who, at the captain's bidding, grimly made himself useful.

The wind not being favorable, we had to make several tacks before reaching the islands, where we arrived at about two o'clock. We landed at Appledore, on which is Laighton's Hotel,—a large building with a piazza or promenade before it, about an hundred and twenty feet in length, or more,—yes, it must be more. It is an edifice with a centre and two wings, the central part upwards of seventy feet. At one end of the promenade is a covered veranda, thirty or forty feet square, so situated that the breeze draws across it from the sea on one side of the island to the sea on the other, and it is the breeziest and comfortablest place in the world on a hot day. There are two swings beneath it, and here one may sit or walk, and enjoy life, while all other mortals are suffering.

As I entered the door of the hotel, there met me a short, corpulent, round, and full-faced man, rather elderly, if not old. He was a little lame. He addressed me in a hearty, hospitable tone, and, judging that it must be my landlord, I delivered a letter of introduction from Pierce. Of course it was fully efficient in obtaining the best accommodations that were to be had. I found that we were expected, a man having brought the news of our intention the day before. Here ensued great inquiries after the General, and wherefore he had not come. I was looked at with considerable curiosity on my own account, especially by the ladies, of whom there were several, agreeable and pretty enough. There were four or five gentlemen, most of whom had not much that was noteworthy.

After dinner, which was good and abundant, though somewhat rude in its style, I was introduced by Mr. Laighton to Mr. Thaxter, his son-in-law, and Mr. Weiss, a clergyman of New Bedford, who is staying here for his health. They showed me some of the remarkable features of the island, such as a deep chasm in the cliffs of the shore, towards the southwest; also a monument of rude stones, on the highest point of the island, said to have been erected by Captain John Smith before the settlement at Plymouth. The tradition is just as good as truth. Also, some ancient cellars, with thistles and other weeds growing in them, and old fragmentary bricks scattered about. The date of these habitations is not known; but they may well be the remains of the settlement that Cotton Mather speaks about; or perhaps one of them was the house where Sir William Pepperell was born, and where he went when he and somebody else set up a stick, and travelled to seek their fortunes in the direction in which it fell.

In the evening, the company at the hotel made up two whist parties, at one of which I sat down,—my partner being an agreeable young lady from Portsmouth. We played till I, at least, was quite weary. It had been the beautifullest of weather all day, very hot on the mainland, but a delicious climate under our veranda.

Saturday, September 4th.—Another beautiful day, rather cooler than the preceding, but not too cool. I can bear this coolness better than that of the interior. In the forenoon, I took passage for Star Island, in a boat that crosses daily whenever there are passengers. My companions were the two Yankees, who had quite recovered from yesterday's sickness, and were in the best of spirits and the utmost activity of mind of which they were capable. Never was there such a string of questions as they directed to the boatman,—questions that seemed to have no gist, so far as related to any use that could be made of the answers. They appear to be very good young men, however, well-meaning, and with manners not disagreeable, because their hearts are not amiss. Star Island is less than a mile from Appledore. It is the most populous island of the group,—has been, for three or four years, an incorporated township, and sends a representative to the New Hampshire legislature. The number of voters is variously represented as from eighteen to twenty-eight. The inhabitants are all, I presume, fishermen. Their houses stand in pretty close neighborhood to one another, scattered about without the slightest regularity or pretence of a street, there being no wheel-carriages on the island. Some of the houses are very comfortable two-story dwellings. I saw two or three, I think, with flowers. There are also one or two trees on the island. There is a strong odor of fishiness, and the little cove is full of mackerel-boats, and other small craft for fishing, in some of which little boys of no growth at all were paddling about. Nearly in the centre of this insular metropolis is a two-story house, with a flag-staff in the yard. This is the hotel.

On the highest point of Star Island stands the church,—a small, wooden structure; and, sitting in its shadow, I found a red baize-shirted fisherman, who seemed quite willing to converse. He said that there was a minister here, who was also the schoolmaster; but that he did not keep school just now, because his wife was very much out of health. The school-house stood but a little way from the meeting-house, and near it was the minister's dwelling; and by and by I had a glimpse of the good man himself, in his suit of black, which looked in very decent condition at the distance from which I viewed it. His clerical air was quite distinguishable, and it was rather curious to See it, when everybody else wore red-baize shirts and fishing-boots, and looked of the scaly genus. He did not approach me, and I saw him no nearer. I soon grew weary of Gosport, and was glad to reëmbark, although I intend to revisit the island with Mr. Thaxter, and see more of its peculiarities and inhabitants. I saw one old witch-looking woman creeping about with a cane, and stooping down, seemingly to gather herbs. On mentioning her to Mr. Thaxter, after my return, he said that it was probably "the bearded woman." I did not observe her beard; but very likely she may have had one.

The larger part of the company at the hotel returned to the mainland to-day. There remained behind, however, a Mr. T— from Newburyport,—a man of natural refinement, and a taste for reading that seems to point towards the writings of Emerson, Thoreau, and men of that class. I have had a good deal of talk with him, and at first doubted whether he might not be a clergyman; but Mr. Thaxter tells me that he has made his own way in the world,—was once a sailor before the mast, and is now engaged in mercantile pursuits. He looks like nothing of this kind, being tall and slender, with very quiet manners, not beautiful, though pleasing from the refinement that they indicate. He has rather a precise and careful pronunciation, but yet a natural way of talking.

* * * * *

In the afternoon I walked round a portion of the island that I had not previously visited, and in the evening went with Mr. Titcomb to Mr. Thaxter's to drink apple-toddy. We found Mrs. Thaxter sitting in a neat little parlor, very simply furnished, but in good taste. She is not now, I believe, more than eighteen years old, very pretty, and with the manners of a lady,—not prim and precise, but with enough of freedom and ease. The books on the table were "Pre-Raphaelitism," a tract on spiritual mediums, etc. There were several shelves of books on one side of the room, and engravings on the walls. Mr. Weiss was there, and I do not know but he is an inmate of Mr. Thaxter's. By and by came in Mr. Thaxter's brother, with a young lady whose position I do not know,—either a sister or the brother's wife. Anon, too, came in the apple-toddy, a very rich and spicy compound; after which we had some glees and negro melodies, in which Mr. Thaxter sang a noble bass, and Mrs. Thaxter sang like a bird, and Mr. Weiss sang, I suppose, tenor, and the brother took some other part, and all were very mirthful and jolly. At about ten o'clock Mr. Titcomb and myself took leave, and emerging into the open air, out of that room of song, and pretty youthfulness of woman, and gay young men, there was the sky, and the three-quarters waning moon, and the old sea moaning all round about the island.

Sunday, September 5th.—To-day I have done little or nothing except to roam along the shore of the island, and to sit under the piazza, talking with Mr. Laighton or some of his half-dozen guests; and about an hour before dinner I came up to my room, and took a brief nap. Since dinner I have been writing the foregoing journal. I observe that the Fanny Ellsler, our passenger and mail boat, has arrived from Portsmouth, and now lies in a little cove, moored to the rocky shore, with a flag flying at her main-mast. We have been watching her for some hours, but she stopped to fish, and then went to some other island, before putting in here. I must go and see what news she has brought.

"What did you fire at?" asked one of the Yankees just now of a boy who had been firing a gun. "Nothing," said the boy. "Did you hit it?" rejoined the Yankee.

The farmer is of a much ruder and rougher mould than his brother,—heavier in frame and mind, and far less cultivated. It was on this account, probably, that he labored as a farmer, instead of setting up a shop. When it is warm, as yesterday, he takes off his coat, and, not minding whether or no his shirtsleeves be soiled, goes in this guise to meals or wherever else,—not resuming his coat as long as he is more comfortable without it. His shoulders have a stoop, and altogether his air is that of a farmer in repose. His brother is handsome, and might have quite the aspect of a smart, comely young man, if well dressed.

This island is said to be haunted by a spectre called "Old Bab," He was one of Captain Kidd's men, and was slain for the protection of the treasure. Mr. Laighton said that, before he built his house, nothing would have induced the inhabitant of another island to come to this after nightfall. The ghost especially haunts the space between the hotel and the cove in front. There has, in times past, been great search for the treasure.

Mr. Thaxter tells me that the women on the island are very timid as to venturing on the sea,—more so than the women of the mainland,—and that they are easily frightened about their husbands. Very few accidents happen to the boats or men,—none, I think, since Mr. Thaxter has been here. They are not an enterprising set of people, never liking to make long voyages. Sometimes one of them will ship on a voyage to the West Indies, but generally only on coast-wise trips, or fishing or mackerel voyages. They have a very strong local attachment, and return to die. They are now generally temperate, formerly very much the contrary.

September 5th.—A large part of the guests took their departure after an early breakfast this morning, including Mr. Titcomb, Mr. Weiss, the two Yankees, and Mr. Thaxter,—who, however, went as skipper or supercargo, and will return with the boat. I have been fishing for dinners off the rocks, but with intolerably poor success. There is nothing so dispiriting as poor fishing, and I spend most of the time with my head on my hands, looking at the sea breaking against the rocks, shagged around the bases with sea-weed. It is a sunny forenoon, with a cool breeze from the southwest. The mackerel craft are in the offing. Mr. Laighton says that the Spy (the boat which went to the mainland this morning) is now on her return with all her colors set; and he thinks that Pierce is on board, he having sent Mr. Thaxter to invite him to come in this boat.

Pierce arrived before dinner in the Spy, accompanied by Judge Upham and his brother and their wives, his own wife, Mr. Furness, and three young ladies. After dinner some of the gentlemen crossed over to Gosport, where we visited the old graveyard, in which were monuments to Rev. Mr. Tucke (died 1773, after forty years' settlement) and to another and later minister of the island. They were of red freestone, lying horizontally on piles of the granite fragments, such as are scattered all about. There were other graves, marked by the rudest shapes of stones at head and foot. And so many stones protruded from the ground, that it was wonderful how space and depth enough was found between them to cover the dead. We went to the house of the town clerk of Gosport (a drunken fisherman, Joe Caswell by name), and there found the town records, commencing in 1732, in a beautiful style of penmanship. They are imperfect, the township having been broken up, probably at the time of the Revolution. Caswell, being very drunk, immediately put in a petition to Pierce to build a sea-mole for the protection of the navigation of the island when he should be President. He was dressed in the ordinary fisherman's style,—red-baize shirt, trousers tucked into large boots, which, as he had just come ashore, were wet with salt water.

He led us down to the shore of the island, towards the east, and showed us Betty Moody's Hole. This Betty Moody was a woman of the island in old times. The Indians came off on a depredating excursion, and she fled from them with a child, and hid herself in this hole, which is formed by several great rocks being lodged so as to cover one of the fissures which are common along these shores. I crept into the hole, which is somewhat difficult of access, long, low, and narrow, and might well enough be a hiding-place. The child, or children, began to cry; and Betty, fearful of discovery, murdered them to save herself. Joe Caswell did not tell the latter part of the story, but Mr. Thaxter did.

Not far from the spot there is a point of rocks extending out farther into the ocean than the rest of the island. Some four or five years ago there was a young woman residing at Gosport in the capacity of schoolteacher. She was of a romantic turn, and used to go and sit on this point of rock to view the waves. One day, when the wind was high, and the surf raging against the rocks, a great wave struck her, as she sat on the edge, and seemed to deprive her of sense; another wave, or the reflex of the same one, carried her off into the sea, and she was seen no more. This happened, I think, in 1846.

Passing a rock near the centre of the island, which rose from the soil about breast-high, and appeared to have been split asunder, with an incalculably aged and moss-grown fissure, the surfaces of which, however, precisely suited each other, Mr. Hatch mentioned that there was an idea among the people, with regard to rocks thus split, that they were rent asunder at the time of the Crucifixion. Judge Upham observed that this superstition was common in all parts of the country.

Mr. Hatch said that he was professionally consulted the other day, by a man who had been digging for buried treasure at Dover Point, up the Piscataqua River; and, while he and his companions were thus engaged, the owner of the land came upon them, and compelled Hatch's client to give him a note for a sum of money. The object was to inquire whether this note was obligatory. Hatch says that there are a hundred people now resident in Portsmouth, who, at one time or another, have dug for treasure. The process is, in the first place, to find out the site of the treasure by the divining-rod. A circle is then described with the steel rod about the spot, and a man walks around within its verge, reading the Bible, to keep off the evil spirit while his companions dig. If a word is spoken, the whole business is a failure. Once, the person who told him the story reached the lid of the chest, so that the spades plainly scraped upon it, when one of the men spoke, and the chest immediately moved sideways into the earth. Another time, when he was reading the Bible within the circle, a creature like a white horse, but immoderately large, came from a distance towards the circle, looked at him, and then began to graze about the spot. He saw the motion of the jaws, but heard no sound of champing. His companions saw the gigantic horse precisely as he did, only to them it appeared bay instead of white.

The islanders stared with great curiosity at Pierce. One pretty young woman appeared inclined to engross him entirely to herself.

There is a bowling-alley on the island, at which some of the young fishermen were rolling.

September 7th.—...I have made no exploration to-day, except a walk with the guests in the morning, but have lounged about the piazza and veranda. It has been a calm, warm, sunny day, the sea slumbering against the shores, and now and then breaking into white foam.

The surface of the island is plentifully overgrown with whortleberry and bayberry bushes. The sheep cut down the former, so that few berries are produced; the latter gives a pleasant fragrance when pressed in the hand.' The island is one great ledge of rock, four hundred acres in extent, with a little soil thrown scantily over it; but the bare rock everywhere emerging, not only in points, but still more in flat surfaces. The only trees, I think, are two that Mr. Laighton has been trying to raise in front of the hotel, the taller of which looks scarcely so much as ten feet high. It is now about sunset, and the Fanny, with the mail, is just arrived at the moorings.

So still is it, that the sounds on board (as of throwing oars into a small boat) are distinctly heard, though a quarter of a mile off. She has the Stars and Stripes flying at the mainmast. There appear to be no passengers.

The only reptile on the island is a very vivid and beautiful green snake, which is exceedingly abundant. Yesterday, while catching grasshoppers for fish-bait, I nearly griped one in my hand; indeed, I rather think I did gripe it. The snake was as much startled as myself, and, in its fright, stood an instant on its tail, before it recovered presence of mind to glide away. These snakes are quite harmless.

September 8th.—Last evening we could hear the roaring of the beaches at Hampton and Rye, nine miles off. The surf likewise swelled against the rocky shores of the island, though there was little or no wind, and, except for the swell, the surface was smooth. The sheep bleated loudly; and all these tokens, according to Mr. Laighton, foreboded a storm to windward. This morning, nevertheless, there were no further signs of it; it is sunny and calm, or only the slightest breeze from the westward; a haze sleeping along the shore, betokening a warm day; the surface of the sea streaked with smoothness, and gentle ruffles of wind. It has been the hottest day that I have known here, and probably one of the hottest of the season ashore; and the land is now imperceptible in the haze.

Smith's monument is about seven feet high, and probably ten or twelve in diameter at its base. It is a cairn, or mere heap of stones, thrown together as they came to hand, though with some selection of large and flat ones towards the base, and with smaller ones thrown in. At the foundation, there are large rocks, naturally imbedded in the earth. I see no reason to disbelieve that a part of this monument may have been erected by Captain Smith, although subsequent visitors may have added to it. Laighton says it is known to have stood upwards of a hundred years. It is a work of considerable labor, and would more likely have been erected by one who supposed himself the first discoverer of the island than by anybody afterwards for mere amusement. I observed in some places, towards the base, that the lichens had grown from one stone to another; and there is nothing in the appearance of the monument that controverts the supposition of its antiquity. It is an irregular circle, somewhat decreasing towards the top. Few of the stones, except at the base, are bigger than a man could easily lift,—many of them are not more than a foot across. It stands towards the southern part of the island; and all the other islands are visible from it,—Smutty Nose, Star Island, and White Island,—on which is the lighthouse,—much of Laighton's island (the proper name of which is Hog, though latterly called Appledore), and Duck Island, which looks like a mere reef of rocks, and about a mile farther into the ocean, easterly of Hog Island.

Laighton's Hotel, together with the house in which his son-in-law resides, which was likewise built by Laighton, and stands about fifty yards from the hotel, occupies the middle of a shallow valley, which passes through the island from east to west. Looking from the veranda, you have the ocean opening towards the east, and the bay towards Rye Beach and Portsmouth on the west. In the same storm that overthrew Minot's Light, a year or two ago, a great wave passed entirely through this valley; and Laighton describes it, when it came in from the sea, as toppling over to the height of the cupola of his hotel. It roared and whitened through, from sea to sea, twenty feet abreast, rolling along huge rocks in its passage. It passed beneath his veranda, which stands on posts,.and probably filled the valley completely. Would I had been here to see!

The day has been exceedingly hot. Since dinner, the Spy has arrived from Portsmouth, with a party of half a dozen or more men and women and children, apparently from the interior of New Hampshire. I am rather sorry to receive these strangers into the quiet life that we are leading here; for we had grown quite to feel ourselves at home, and the two young ladies, Mr. Thaxter, his wife and sister, and myself, met at meal-times like one family. The young ladies gathered shells, arranged them, laughed gently, sang, and did other pretty things in a young-lady-like way. These new-comers are people of uncouth voices and loud laughter, and behave themselves as if they were trying to turn their expedition to as much account as possible in the way of enjoyment, John's boat, the regular passenger-boat, is now coming in, and probably brings the mail.

In the afternoon, while some of the new-comers were fishing off the rocks, west of the hotel, a shark came close in shore. Hearing their outcries, I looked out of my chamber window, and saw the dorsal fin and the fluke of his tail stuck up out of the water, as he moved to and fro. He must have been eight or ten feet long. He had probably followed the small fish into the bay, and got bewildered, and, at one time, he was almost aground,

Oscar, Mr, Laighton's son, ran down with a gun, and fired at the shark, which was then not more than ten yards from the shore. He aimed, according to his father's directions, just below the junction of the dorsal fin with the body; but the gun was loaded only with shot, and seemed to produce no effect. Oscar had another shot at him afterwards; the shark floundered a little in the water, but finally got off and disappeared, probably without very serious damage. He came so near the shore that he might have been touched with a boat-hook.

September 9th.—Mr. Thaxter rowed me this morning, in his dory, to White Island, on which is the light-house. There was scarcely a breath of air, and a perfectly calm sea; an intensely hot sunshine, with a little haze, so that the horizon was indistinct. Here and there sail-boats sleeping on the water, or moving almost imperceptibly over it. The light-house island would be difficult of access in a rough sea, the shore being so rocky. On landing, we found the keeper peeling his harvest of onions, which he had gathered prematurely, because the insects were eating them. His little patch of garden seemed to be a strange kind of soil, as like marine mud as anything; but he had a fair crop of marrow squashes, though injured, as he said, by the last storm; and there were cabbages and a few turnips. I recollect no other garden vegetables. The grass grows pretty luxuriantly, and looked very green where there was any soil; but he kept no cow, nor even a pig nor a hen. His house stands close; by the garden,—a small stone building, with peaked roof, and whitewashed. The light-house stands on a ledge of rock, with a gulley between, and there is a long covered way, triangular in shape, connecting his residence with it. We ascended into the lantern, which is eighty-seven feet high. It is a revolving light, with several great illuminators of copper silvered, and colored lamp-glasses. Looking downward, we had the island displayed as on a chart, with its little bays, its isthmus of shingly beach connecting two parts of the island, and over-flowed at high tide; its sunken rocks about it, indicated by the swell, or slightly breaking surf. The keeper of the light-house was formerly a writing-master. He has a sneaking kind of look, and does not bear a very high character among his neighbors. Since he kept the light, he has lost two wives,—the first a young creature whom he used to leave alone upon this desolate rock, and the gloom and terror of the situation were probably the cause of her death. The second wife, experiencing the same kind of treatment, ran away from him, and returned to her friends. He pretends to be religious, but drinks. About a year ago he attempted to row out alone from Portsmouth. There was a head wind and head tide, and he would have inevitably drifted out to sea, if Mr. Thaxter had not saved him.

While we were standing in his garden-patch, I heard a woman's voice inside the dwelling, but know not whose it was. A light-house nine miles from shore would be a delightful place for a new-married couple to spend their honeymoon, or their whole first year.

On our way back we landed at another island called Londoner's Rock, or some such name. It has but little soil. As we approached it, a large bird flew away. Mr. Thaxter took it to be a gannet; and, while walking over the island, an owl started up from among the rocks near us, and flew away, apparently uncertain of its course. It was a brown owl, but Mr. Thaxter says that there are beautiful white owls, which spend the winter here, and feed upon rats. These are very abundant, and live amidst the rocks,—probably having been brought hither by vessels.

The water to-day was not so transparent as sometimes, but had a slight haze diffused through it, somewhat like that of the atmosphere.

The passengers brought by the Spy, yesterday, still remain with us. They consist of country traders, a country doctor, and such sorts of people, rude, shrewd, and simple, and well-behaved enough; wondering at sharks, and equally at lobsters; sitting down to table with their coats off; helping themselves out of the dish with their own forks; taking pudding on the plates off which they have eaten meat. People at just this stage of manners are more disagreeable than at any other stage. They are aware of some decencies, but not so deeply aware as to make them a matter of conscience. They may be heard talking of the financial affairs of the expedition, reckoning what money each has paid. One offers to pay another three or four cents, which the latter has overpaid. "It's of no consequence, sir," says his friend, with a tone of conscious liberality, "that's near enough." This is a most tremendously hot day.

There is a young lady staying at the hotel, afflicted with what her friends call erysipelas, but which is probably scrofula. She seems unable to walk, or sit up; but every pleasant day, about the middle of the forenoon, she is dragged out beneath the veranda, on a sofa. To-day she has been there until late in the decline of the afternoon. It is a delightful place, where the breezes stir, if any are in motion. The young girls, her sisters or cousins, and Mr. Thaxter's sister, sat round her, babbling cheerfully, and singing; and they were so merry that it did not seem as if there could be an incurably sick one in the midst of them.

The Spy came to-day, with more passengers of no particular character. She still remains off the landing, moored, with her sails in the wind.

The mail arrived to-day, but nothing for me.

Close by the veranda, at the end of the hotel, is drawn up a large boat, of ten or twelve tons, which got injured in some gale, and probably will remain there for years to decay, and be a picturesque and characteristic object.

The Spy has been lying in the broad track of golden light, thrown by the sun, far down towards the horizon, over the rippling water, her sails throwing distinct, dark shadows over the brightness. She has now got under way, and set sail on a northwest course for Portsmouth; carrying off, I believe, all the passengers she brought to-day.

September 10th.—Here is another beautiful morning, with the sun dimpling in the early sunshine. Four sail-boats are in sight, motionless on the sea, with the whiteness of their sails reflected in it. The heat-haze sleeps along the shore, though not so as quite to hide it, and there is the promise of another very warm day. As yet, however, the air is cool and refreshing. Around the island, there is the little ruffle of a breeze; but where the sail-boats are, a mile or more off, the sea is perfectly calm. The crickets sing, and I hear the chirping of birds besides.

At the base of the light-house yesterday, we saw the wings and feathers of a decayed little bird, and Mr. Thaxter said they often flew against the lantern with such force as to kill themselves, and that large quantities of them might be picked up. How came these little birds out of their nests at night? Why should they meet destruction from the radiance that proves the salvation of other beings?

Mr. Thaxter had once a man living: with him who had seen "Old Bab," the ghost. He met him between the hotel and the sea, and describes him as dressed in a sort of frock, and with a very dreadful countenance.

Two or three years ago, the crew of a wrecked vessel, a brigantine, wrecked near Boon Island, landed on Hog Island of a winter night, and found shelter in the hotel. It was from the eastward. There were six or seven men, with the mate and captain. It was midnight when they got ashore. The common sailors, as soon as they were physically comfortable, seemed to be perfectly at ease. The captain walked the floor, bemoaning himself for a silver watch which he had lost; the mate, being the only married man, talked about his Eunice. They all told their dreams of the preceding night, and saw in them prognostics of the misfortune.

There is now a breeze, the blue ruffle of which seems to reach almost across to the mainland, yet with streaks of calm; and, in one place, the glassy surface of a lake of calmness, amidst the surrounding commotion.

The wind, in the early morning, was from the west, and the aspect of the sky seemed to promise a warm and sunny day. But all at once, soon after breakfast, the wind shifted round to the eastward; and great volumes of fog, almost as dense as cannon-smoke, came sweeping from the eastern ocean, through the valley, and past the house. It soon covered the whole sea, and the whole island, beyond a verge of a few hundred yards. The chilliness was not so great as accompanies a change of wind on the mainland. We had been watching a large ship that was slowly making her way between us and the land towards Portsmouth. This was now hidden. The breeze is still very moderate; but the boat, moored near the shore, rides with a considerable motion, as if the sea were getting up.

Mr. Laighton says that the artist who adorned Trinity Church, in New York, with sculpture wanted some real wings from which to imitate the wings of cherubim. Mr. Thaxter carried him the wings of the white owl that winters here at the Shoals, together with those of some other bird; and the artist gave his cherubim the wings of an owl.

This morning there have been two boat-loads of visitors from Rye. They merely made a flying call, and took to their boats again,—a disagreeable and impertinent kind of people.

The Spy arrived before dinner, with several passengers. After dinner, came the Fanny, bringing, among other freight, a large basket of delicious pears to me, together with a note from Mr. B. B. Titcomb. He is certainly a man of excellent taste and admirable behavior. I sent a plateful of pears to the room of each guest now in the hotel, kept a dozen for myself, and gave the balance to Mr. Laighton.

The two Portsmouth young ladies returned in the Spy. I had grown accustomed to their presence, and rather liked them; one of them being gay and rather noisy, and the other quiet and gentle. As to newcomers, I feel rather a distaste to them; and so, I find, does Mr. Laighton,—a rather singular sentiment for a hotel-keeper to entertain towards his guests. However, he treats them very hospitably when once within his doors.

The sky is overcast, and, about the time the Spy and the Fanny sailed, there were a few drops of rain. The wind, at that time, was strong enough to raise white-caps to the eastward of the island, and there was good hope of a storm. Now, however, the wind has subsided, and the weather-seers know not what to forebode.

September 11th.—The wind shifted and veered about, towards the close of yesterday, and later it was almost calm, after blowing gently from the northwest,—notwithstanding which it rained. There being a mistiness in the air, we could see the gleam of the light-house upon the mist above it, although the lighthouse itself was hidden by the highest point of this island, or by our being in a valley. As we sat under the piazza in the evening, we saw the light from on board some vessel move slowly through the distant obscurity,—so slowly that we were only sensible of its progress by forgetting it and looking again. The plash and murmur of the waves around the island were soothingly audible. It was not unpleasantly cold, and Mr. Laighton, Mr. Thaxter, and myself sat under the piazza till long after dark; the former at a little distance, occasionally smoking his pipe, and Mr. Thaxter and I talking about poets, and the stage. The latter is an odd subject to be discussed in this stern and wild scene, which has precisely the same characteristics now as two hundred years ago. The mosquitoes were very abundant last night, and they are certainly a hardier race than their inland brethren.

This morning there is a sullen sky, with scarcely any breeze. The clouds throw shadows of varied darkness upon the sea. I know not which way the wind is; but the aspect of things seems to portend a calm drizzle as much as anything else.

About eleven o'clock, Mr. Thaxter took me over to Smutty Nose in his dory. A sloop from the eastward, laden with laths, bark, and other lumber, and a few barrels of mackerel, filled yesterday, and was left by her skipper and crew. All the morning we have seen boats picking up her deck-load, which was scattered over the sea, and along the shores of the islands. The skipper and his three men got into Smutty Nose in the boat; and the sloop was afterwards boarded by the Smutty Noses and brought into that island. We saw her lying at the pier,—a black, ugly, rotten old thing, with the water half-way over her decks. The wonder was, how she swam so long. The skipper, a man of about thirty-five or forty, in a blue pilot-cloth overcoat, and-a rusty, high-crowned hat jammed down over his brow, looked very forlorn; while the islanders were grouped about, indolently enjoying the matter.

I walked with Mr. Thaxter over the island, and saw first the graves of the Spaniards. They were wrecked on this island a hundred years ago, and lie buried in a range about thirty feet in length, to the number of sixteen, with rough, moss-grown pieces of granite on each side of this common grave. Near this spot, yet somewhat removed, so as not to be confounded with it, are other individual graves, chiefly of the Haley family, who were once possessors of the island. These have slate gravestones. There is also, within a small enclosure of rough pine boards, a white marble gravestone, in memory of a young man named Bekker, son of the person who now keeps the hotel on Smutty Nose. He was buried, Mr. Thaxter says, notwithstanding his marble monument, in a rude pine box, which he himself helped to make.

We walked to the farthest point of the island, and I have never seen a more dismal place than it was on this sunless and east-windy day, being the farthest point out into the melancholy sea which was in no very agreeable mood, and roared sullenly against the wilderness of rocks. One mass of rock, more than twelve feet square, was thrown up out of the sea in a storm, not many years since, and now lies athwart-wise, never to be moved unless another omnipotent wave shall give it another toss. On shore, such a rock would be a landmark for centuries. It is inconceivable how a sufficient mass of water could be brought to bear on this ponderous mass; but, not improbably, all the fragments piled upon one another round these islands have thus been flung to and fro at one time or another.

There is considerable land that would serve tolerably for pasture on Smutty Nose, and here and there a little enclosure of richer grass, built round with a strong stone-wall. The same kind of enclosure is prevalent on Star Island,—each small proprietor fencing off his little bit of tillage or grass. Wild-flowers are abundant and various on these islands; the bay-berry-bush is plentiful on Smutty Nose, and makes the hand that crushes it fragrant.

The hotel is kept by a Prussian, an old soldier, who fought at the Battle of Waterloo. We saw him in the barn,—a gray, heavy, round-skulled old fellow, troubled with deafness. The skipper of the wrecked sloop had, apparently, just been taking a drop of comfort, but still seemed downcast. He took passage in a fishing-vessel, the Wave, of Kittery, for Portsmouth; and I know not why, but there was something that made me smile in his grim and gloomy look, his rusty, jammed hat, his rough and grisly beard, and in his mode of chewing tobacco, with much action of the jaws, getting out the juice as largely as possible, as men always do when disturbed in mind. I looked at him earnestly, and was conscious of something that marked him out from among the careless islanders around him. Being as much discomposed as it was possible for him to be, his feelings individualized the man and magnetized the observer. When he got aboard the fishing-vessel, he seemed not entirely at his ease, being accustomed to command and work amongst his own little crew, and now having nothing to do. Nevertheless, unconsciously perhaps, he lent a hand to whatever was going on, and yet had a kind of strangeness about him. As the Wave set. sail, we were just starting in our dory, and a young fellow, an acquaintance of Mr. Thaxter, proposed to take us in tow; so we were dragged along at her stern very rapidly, and with a whitening wake, until we came off Hog Island. Then the dory was cast loose, and Mr. Thaxter rowed ashore against a head sea.

The day is still overcast, and the wind is from the eastward; but it does not increase, and the sun appears occasionally on the point of shining out. A boat—the Fanny, I suppose, from Portsmouth—has just come to her moorings in front of the hotel. A sail-boat has put off from her, with a passenger in the stern. Pray God she bring me a letter with good news from home; for I begin to feel as. if I had been long enough away.

There is a bowling-alley on Smutty Nose, at which some of the Star-Islanders were playing, when we were there. I saw only two dwelling-houses besides the hotel. Connected with Smutty Nose, by a stonewall there is another little bit of island, called Malaga. Both are the property of Mr. Laighton.

Mr. Laighton says that the Spanish wreck occurred .forty-seven years ago, instead of a hundred. Some of the dead bodies were found on Malaga, others on various parts of the next island. One or two had crept to a stone-wall that traverses Smutty Nose, but were unable to get over it. One was found among the bushes the next summer. Mr. Haley had been buried at his own expense.

The skipper of the wrecked sloop, yesterday, was unwilling to go to Portsmouth until he was shaved,—his beard being of several days' growth. It seems to be the impulse of people under misfortune to put on their best clothes, and attend to the decencies of life.

The Fanny brought a passenger,—a thin, stiff, black-haired young man, who enters his name as Mr. Tufts, from Charlestown. He, and a country trader, his wife, sister, and two children (all of whom have been here several days), are now the only guests besides myself.

September 12th.—The night set in sullen and gloomy, and morning has dawned in pretty much the same way. The wind, however, seems rising somewhat, and grumbles past the angle of the house. Perhaps we shall see a storm yet from the eastward; and, having the whole sweep of the broad Atlantic between here and Ireland, I do not see why it should not be fully equal to a storm at sea.

It has been raining more or less all the forenoon, and now, at twelve o'clock, blows, as Mr. Laighton-says, "half a gale" from the southeast. Through the opening of our shallow valley, towards the east, there is the prospect of a tumbling sea, with hundreds of white-caps chasing one another over it. In front of the hotel, being to leeward, the water near the shore is but slightly ruffled; but farther the sea is agitated, and the surf breaks over Square Rock. All around the horizon, landward as well as seaward, the view is shut in by a mist. Sometimes I have a dim sense of the continent beyond, but no more distinct than the thought of the other world to the unenlightened soul. The sheep bleat in their desolate pasture. The wind shakes the house. A loon, seeking, I suppose, some quieter resting-place than on the troubled waves, was seen swimming just now in the cove not more than a hundred yards from the hotel. Judging by the pother which this "half a gale" makes with the sea, it must have been a terrific time, indeed, when that great wave rushed and roared across the islands.

Since dinner, I have been to the eastern shore to look at the sea. It is a wild spectacle, but still, I suppose, lacks an infinite deal of being a storm. Outside of this island there is a long and low one (or two in a line), looking more like a reef of rocks than an island, and at the distance of a mile or more. There the surf and spray break gallantly,—white-sheeted forms rising up all at once, and hovering a moment in the air. Spots which, in calm times, are not discernible from the rest of the ocean, now are converted into white, foamy breakers. The swell of the waves against our shore makes a snowy depth, tinged with green, for many feet back from the shore. The longer waves swell, overtop, and rush upon the rocks; and, when they return, the waters pour back in a cascade. Against the outer points of Smutty Nose and Star Island, there is a higher surf than here; because, the wind being from the southeast, these islands receive it first, and form a partial barrier in respect to this. While I looked, there was moisture in the air, and occasional spats of rain. The uneven places in the rocks were full of the fallen rain.

It is quite impossible to give an idea of these rocky shores,—how confusedly they are tossed together, lying in all directions; what solid ledges, what great fragments thrown out from the rest. Often the rocks are broken, square and angular, so as to form a kind of staircase; though, for the most part, such as would require a giant stride to ascend them.

Sometimes a black trap-rock runs through the bed of granite; sometimes the sea has eaten this away, leaving a long, irregular fissure. In some places, owing to the same cause perhaps, there is a great hollow place excavated into the ledge, and forming a harbor, into which the sea flows; and, while there is foam and fury at the entrance, it is comparatively calm within. Some parts of the crag are as much as fifty feet of perpendicular height, down which you look over a bare and smooth descent, at the base of which is a shaggy margin of sea-weed. But it is vain to try to express this confusion. As much as anything else, it seems as if some of the massive materials of the world remained superfluous, after the Creator had finished, and were carelessly thrown down here, where the millionth part of them emerge from the sea, and in the course of thousands of years have become partially bestrewn with a little soil.

The wind has changed to southwest, and blows pretty freshly. The sun shone before it set; and the mist, which all day has overhung the land, now takes the aspect of a cloud,—drawing a thin veil between us and the shore, and rising above it. In our own atmosphere there is no fog nor mist.

September 13th.—I spent last evening, as well as part of the evening before, at Mr. Thaxter's. It is certainly a romantic incident to find such a young man on this lonely island; his marriage with the pretty Miranda is true romance. In our talk we have glanced over many matters, and, among the rest, that of the stage, to prepare himself for which was his first motive in coming hither. He appears quite to have given up any dreams of that kind now. What he will do on returning to the world, as his purpose is, I cannot imagine; but, no doubt, through all their remaining life, both he and she will look back to this rocky-ledge, with its handful of soil, as to a Paradise.

Last evening we (Mr., Mrs., and Miss Thaxter) sat and talked of ghosts and kindred subjects; and they told me of the appearance of a little old woman in a striped gown, that had come into that house a few months ago. She was seen by nobody but an Irish nurse, who spoke to her, but received-no answer. The little woman drew her chair up towards the fire, and stretched out her feet to warm them. By and by the nurse, who suspected nothing of her ghostly character, went to get a pail of water; and, when she came back, the little woman was not there. It being known precisely how many and what people were on the island, and that no such little woman was among them, the fact of her being a ghost is incontestable. I taught them how to discover the hidden sentiments of letters by suspending a gold ring over them. Ordinarily, since I have been here, we have spent the evening under the piazza, where Mr. Laighton sits to take the air. He seems to avoid the within-doors whenever he can. So there he sits in the sea-breezes, when inland people are probably drawing their chairs to the fireside; and there I sit with him,—not keeping up a continual flow of talk, but each speaking as any wisdom happens to come into his mind.

The wind, this morning, is from the northwestward, rather brisk, but not very strong. There is a scattering of clouds about the sky; but the atmosphere is singularly clear, and we can see several hills of the interior, the cloud-like White Mountains, and, along the shore, the long white beaches and the dotted dwellings, with great distinctness. Many small vessels spread their wings, and go seaward.

I have been rambling over the southern part of the island, and looking at the traces of habitations there. There are several enclosures,—the largest, perhaps, thirty yards square,—surrounded with a rough stonewall of very mossy antiquity, built originally broad and strong, two or three large stones in width, and piled up breast-high or more, and taking advantage of the extending ledge to make it higher. Within this enclosure there is almost a clear space of soil, which was formerly, no doubt, cultivated as a garden, but is now close cropt by the sheep and cattle, except where it produces thistles, or the poisonous weed called mercury, which seems to love these old walls, and to root itself in or near them. These walls are truly venerable, gray, and mossy; and you see at once that the hands that piled the stones must have been long ago turned to dust. Close by the enclosure is the hollow of an old cellar, with rocks tumbled into it, but the layers of stone at the side still to be traced, and bricks, broken or with rounded edges, scattered about, and perhaps pieces of lime; and weeds and grass growing about the whole. Several such sites of former human homes may be seen there, none of which can possibly be later than the Revolution, and probably they are as old as the settlement of the island. The site has Smutty Nose and Star opposite, with a road (that is, a water-road) between, varying from half a mile to a mile. Duck Island is also seen on the left; and, on the right, the shore of the mainland. Behind, the rising ground intercepts the view.

Smith's monument is visible. I do not see where the inhabitants could have kept their boats, unless in the chasms worn by the sea into the rocks.

One of these chasms has a spring of fresh water in the gravelly base, down to which the sea has worn out. The chasm has perpendicular, though irregular, sides, which the waves have chiselled out very square. Its width varies from ten to twenty feet, widest towards the sea; and on the shelves, up and down the sides, some soil has been here and there accumulated, on which grow grass and wild-flowers,—such as golden-rod, now in bloom, and raspberry-bushes, the fruit of which I found ripe,—the whole making large parts of the sides of the chasm green, its verdure overhanging the strip of sea that dashes and foams into the hollow. Sea-weed, besides what grows upon and shags the submerged rocks, is tossed into the harbor, together with stray pieces of wood, chips, barrel-staves, or (as to-day) an entire barrel, or whatever else the sea happens to have on hand. The water rakes to and fro over the pebbles at the bottom of the chasm, drawing back, and leaving much of it bare, then rushing up, with more or less of foam and fury, according to the force and direction of the wind; though, owing to the protection of the adjacent islands, it can never have a gale blowing right into its mouth. The spring is situated so far down the chasm, that, at half or two thirds tide, it is covered by the sea. Twenty minutes after the retiring of the tide suffices to restore to it its wonted freshness.

In another chasm, very much like the one here described, I saw a niche in the rock, about tall enough for a person of moderate stature to stand upright. It had a triangular floor and a top, and was just the place to hold the rudest statue that ever a savage made.

Many of the ledges on the island have yellow moss or lichens spread on them in large patches. The moss of those stone walls does really look very old.

"Old Bab," the ghost, has a ring round his neck, and is supposed either to have been hung or to have had his throat cut, but he steadfastly declines telling the mode of his death. There is a luminous appearance about him as he walks, and his face is pale and very dreadful.

The Fanny arrived this forenoon, and sailed again before dinner. She brought, as passenger, a Mr. Balch, brother to the country trader,who has been spending a few days here. On her return, she has swept the islands of all the non-residents except myself. The wind being ahead, and pretty strong, she will have to beat up, and the voyage will be anything but agreeable. The spray flew before her bows, and doubtless gave the passengers all a thorough wetting within the first half-hour.

The view of Star Island or Gosport from the north is picturesque,—the village, or group of houses, being gathered pretty closely together in the centre of the island, with some green about them; and above all the other edifices, wholly displayed, stands the little stone church, with its tower and belfry. On the right is White Island, with the light-house; to the right of that, and a little to the northward,

Londoner's Rock, where, perhaps, of old, some London ship was wrecked. To the left of Star Island, and nearer Hog, or Appledore, is Smutty Nose. Pour the blue sea about these islets, and let the surf whiten and steal up from their points, and from the reefs about them (which latter whiten for an instant, and then are lost in the whelming and eddying depths), the northwest-wind the while raising thousands of white-caps, and the evening sun shining solemnly over the expanse,—and it is a stern and lovely scene.

The valleys that intersect, or partially intersect, the island are a remarkable feature. They appear to be of the same formation as the fissures in the rocks, but, as they extend farther from the sea, they accumulate a little soil along the irregular sides, and so become green and shagged with bushes, though with the rock everywhere thrusting itself through. The old people of the isles say that their fathers could remember when the sea, at high tide, flowed quite through the valley in which the hotel stands, and that boats used to pass. Afterwards it was a standing pond; then a morass, with cat-tail flags growing in it. It has filled up, so far as it is filled, by the soil being washed down from the higher ground on each side. The storms, meanwhile, have tossed up the shingle and paving-stones at each end of the valley, so as to form a barrier against the passage of any but such mighty waves as that which thundered through a year or two ago.

The old inhabitants lived in the centre or towards the south of the island, and avoided the north and east because the latter were so much bleaker in winter. They could moor their boats in the road, between Smutty Nose and Hog, but could not draw them up. Mr. Laighton found traces of old dwellings in the vicinity of the hotel, and it is supposed that the principal part of the population was on this island. I spent the evening at Mr. Thaxter's, and we drank a glass of his 1820 Scheidam. The northwest-wind was high at ten o'clock, when I came home, the tide full, and the murmur of the waves broad and deep.

September 14th.—Another of the brightest of sunny mornings. The wind is not nearly so high as last night, but it is apparently still from the north west, and serves to make the sea look very blue and cold. The atmosphere is so transparent that objects seem perfectly distinct along the mainland. To-day I must be in Portsmouth; to-morrow, at home. A brisk west or northwest-wind, making the sea so blue, gives a very distinct outline in its junction with the sky.

September 16th.—On Tuesday, the 14th, there was no opportunity to get to the mainland. Yesterday morning opened with a southeast rain, which continued all day. The Fanny arrived in the forenoon, with some coal for Mr. Laighton, and sailed again before dinner, taking two of the maids of the house; but as it rained pouring, and as I could not, at any rate, have got home to-night, there would have been no sense in my going. It began to clear up in the decline of the day; the sun shot forth some golden arrows a little before his setting; and the sky was perfectly clear when I went to bed, after spending the evening at Mr. Thaxter's. This morning is clear and bright; but the wind is northwest, making the sea look blue and cold, with little breaks of white foam. It is unfavorable for a trip to the mainland; but doubtless I shall find an opportunity of getting ashore before night.

The highest part of Appledore is about eighty feet above the sea. Mr. Laighton has seen whales off the island,—both on the eastern side and between it and the mainland; once a great crowd of them, as many as fifty. They were drawn in by pursuing their food,—a small fish called herring-bait, which came ashore in such abundance that Mr. Laighton dipped up basketfuls of them. No attempt was made to take the whales.

There are vague traditions of trees on these islands. One of them, Cedar Island, is said to have been named from the trees that grew on it. The matter appears improbable, though, Mr. Thaxter says, large quantities of soil are annually washed into the sea; so that the islands may have been better clad with earth and its productions than now.

Mrs. Thaxter tells me that there are several burial-places on this island; but nobody has been buried here since the Revolution. Her own marriage was the first one since that epoch, and her little Karl, now three months old, the first-born child in all those eighty years.

[*Then follow Extracts from the Church Records of Gosport.*]

This book of the church records of Gosport is a small folio, well bound in dark calf, and about an inch thick; the paper very stout, with a water-mark of an armed man in a sitting posture, holding a spear...over a lion, who brandishes a sword; on alternate pages the Crown, and beneath it the letters G. R. The motto of the former device Pro Patria. The book is written in a very legible hand, probably by the Rev. Mr. Tncke. The ink is not much faded.

Concord, March 9, 1853.—Finished, this day, the last story of "Tanglewood Tales." They were written in the following order:—

"The Pomegranate Seeds."

"The Minotaur."

"The Golden Fleece."

"The Dragon's Teeth."

"Circe's Palace."

"The Pygmies."

The Introduction is yet to be written. Wrote it 13th March. I went to Washington (my first visit) on 14th April.

Caresses, expressions of one sort or another, are necessary to the life of the affections, as leaves are to the life of a tree. If they are wholly restrained, love will die at the roots.

June 9th.—Cleaning the attic to-day, here at the Wayside, the woman found an immense snake, flat and outrageously fierce, thrusting out its tongue. Ellen, the cook, killed it. She called it an adder, but it appears to have been a striped snake. It seems a fiend, haunting the house. On further inquiry, the snake is described as plaided with brown and black.

Cupid in these latter times has probably laid aside his bow and arrows, and uses fire-arms,—a pistol,—perhaps a revolver.

I burned great heaps of old letters, and other papers, a little while ago, preparatory to going to England. Among them were hundreds of —'s letters. The world has no more such, and now they are all dust and ashes. What a trustful guardian of secret matters is fire! What should we do without fire and death?

i. This is a word made by Mr. Hawthorne, but one that was needed.—S. H.

ii. A word meaning in Worcester, I find, "to spring out with speed and suddenness."—S. H.